Praise for Alexis Morgan
and Her Novels

"A bit of mystery, lots of action, plenty of passion, and a story line that will grab your attention from the get-go."
—Romance Reviews Today

"Suspicions, lust, loyalty, and love create a heavy mix of emotions." —*Romantic Times*

"Magically adventurous and fervently romantic."
—Single Titles

"Whew! A unique paranormal story line that sizzles with every page." —Fresh Fiction

"This book sucked me in, and I didn't want to stop reading." —Queue My Review

"Morgan delivers a great read that sparks with humor, action, and . . . great storytelling."
—Night Owl Reviews (5 stars, top pick)

"Will keep readers entranced."
—Nocturne Romance Reads

"This action-packed paranormal romance has a little bit of everything—especially if you love interesting immortal warriors who are sexy as all get-out—and enough action and suspense to keep you riveted until the last page."
—Black Lagoon Reviews

"The spellbinding combination of passionate desires, fateful consequences, and the supernatural . . . [is] totally captivating throughout every enthralling scene."
—Ecataromance

Also by Alexis Morgan

WARRIORS OF THE MIST
My Lady Mage

Her Knight's Quest

A WARRIORS OF THE MIST NOVEL

Alexis Morgan

FIC
MORGAN
08/13

A SIGNET ECLIPSE BOOK

SIGNET ECLIPSE
Published by New American Library, a division of
Penguin Group (USA) Inc., 375 Hudson Street,
New York, New York 10014, USA
Penguin Group (Canada), 90 Eglinton Avenue East, Suite 700, Toronto,
Ontario M4P 2Y3, Canada (a division of Pearson Penguin Canada Inc.)
Penguin Books Ltd., 80 Strand, London WC2R 0RL, England
Penguin Ireland, 25 St. Stephen's Green, Dublin 2,
Ireland (a division of Penguin Books Ltd.)
Penguin Group (Australia), 707 Collins Street, Melbourne, Victoria 3008,
Australia (a division of Pearson Australia Group Pty. Ltd.)
Penguin Books India Pvt. Ltd., 11 Community Centre, Panchsheel Park,
New Delhi - 110 017, India
Penguin Group (NZ), 67 Apollo Drive, Rosedale, Auckland 0632,
New Zealand (a division of Pearson New Zealand Ltd.)
Penguin Books, Rosebank Office Park, 181 Jan Smuts Avenue,
Parktown North 2193, South Africa
Penguin China, B7 Jaiming Center, 27 East Third Ring Road North,
Chaoyang District, Beijing 100020, China

Penguin Books Ltd., Registered Offices:
80 Strand, London WC2R 0RL, England

First published by Signet Eclipse, an imprint of New American Library,
a division of Penguin Group (USA) Inc.

First Printing, March 2013
10 9 8 7 6 5 4 3 2 1

PUBLISHER'S NOTE
This is a work of fiction. Names, characters, places, and incidents either are the
product of the author's imagination or are used fictitiously, and any resemblance
to actual persons, living or dead, business establishments, events, or locales is
entirely coincidental.
    The publisher does not have any control over and does not assume any respon-
sibility for author or third-party Web sites or their content.

To Walter, the best grandpuppy in the world.

You and your folks are such a gift in my life.

Acknowledgments

To the talented women who do such amazing design work for me: Josephine, Laron, Mandy, and Delilah. You help bring my worlds to life, and for that I thank you.

River of the Damned

The Warriors of the Mist are a legend, their origins lost in the shadows of the past. In dark times, it is whispered, the warriors can be summoned from beneath the roiling currents when a champion is needed and if the cause is just.

However, the cost will be high and the risks are great, for if the battle is won, the champion faces judgment by the same gods who had once condemned him to the cold chill of the mountain river. If his performance is found worthy and valiant, at long last the warrior will make the final journey to the great hall where the noble knights of the past dwell for all eternity. However, if the champion is found lacking still, he returns with his brothers to the river.

If the battle is lost, regardless of fault, both the champion and the supplicant will be condemned to the netherworld. Together they will wander without hope and without light, lost in cold darkness until the ages have passed and all that exists ceases to be. Only the powerless and the desperate dare approach the Warriors of the Mist to plead for their cause.

Many years have passed since last a worthy supplicant journeyed to the river's edge, but times are dark and desperation has once again come to the people of Agathia. There is a disturbance in the mists, and the waters grow restless. Someone comes, bringing either disaster or redemption.

The Warriors of the Mist ready their weapons and prepare to meet the enemy.

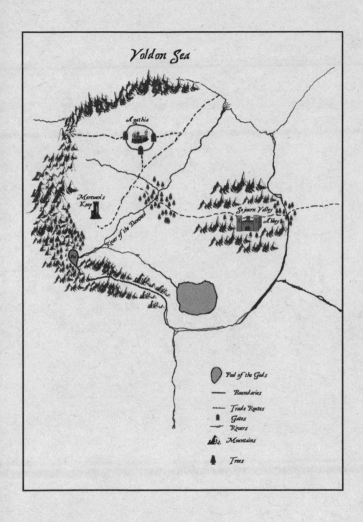

Chapter 1

*T*he mirror-smooth surface shattered, sending a surge of cold water gushing over the side of the bowl to soak Lavinia's skirts. Despite her best efforts to impose her will over the unruly liquid, it continued to ripple and refused to come back into focus—a clear reflection of Lavinia's own agitation.

When her third attempt at scrying failed, she snatched up the bowl and tossed its contents toward the roses in her private garden. Maybe the water would do more good for the plants than it had for her. The simple truth was that she would learn nothing until she controlled her emotions, especially her fear.

"Shall I fetch a fresh pitcher of water?"

Lavinia forced a more pleasant expression onto her face before turning to greet Sarra, who hovered a short distance away. The young girl practically vibrated with the need to be of service.

Lord and Lady, had she ever been that earnest and innocent herself? All things considered, it didn't seem likely.

Injecting a soothing note into her voice, Lavinia shook her head. "No, my child. I will do so myself. The walk will help clear my head."

Then her smile became more genuine. "Besides, Sarra, I do believe it's time for your music lesson. Sister Joetta will be waiting for you."

Sarra's face lit up as she bolted toward the door that led back inside the abbey. Halfway there, she froze and slowly turned back, her eyes wide with chagrin. "I'm sorry, my lady. I forgot."

Then she dropped into a low curtsy with her eyes trained on the floor. "May I be excused?"

Lavinia crossed to where the girl remained frozen in position. She gently raised Sarra's face and then smiled at her with a wink. "All these rules take a while to master, don't they? Go seek out Sister Joetta. Tell her you don't need to report back to me until this afternoon."

Sarra immediately straightened up and surprised Lavinia with a quick hug before continuing on her headlong charge toward the door. "Don't worry, my lady; I'll do my best for Sister Joetta."

"I know you will, little one."

Alone finally, Lavinia sank down on the bench and rested her eyes. She'd been up since before dawn, searching for answers among the forbidden texts. All that her efforts had garnered her were a headache and more questions with no answers.

She'd hoped scrying would prove more useful, but it had failed her as well. Perhaps that walk she'd mentioned to young Sarra would actually help. As much as Lavinia loved the sanctuary of her private garden, sometimes the high walls closed in on her.

She glanced up at the narrow slice of blue sky overhead. How long had it been since she'd last ventured beyond the abbey's thick walls and out into the real world?

It didn't bear thinking about. Even without the responsibilities that kept her firmly anchored where she was, the world outside was far too dangerous a place for her right now. Not all predators that prowled Agathia walked on four legs.

As tempting as it was just to soak up the warmth of the sun, she couldn't. Too much was at stake to pretend everything was all right. She picked up the pitcher and walked back inside, through her office to the hallway that ran through the heart of the abbey. The thick rugs muffled her footsteps as she made her way to the court-yard that surrounded the well.

After filling her pitcher, she savored a ladleful of the cool, sweet water before returning to her garden. This time, she moved slowly as she sought to quiet her spirit. She carefully filled the scrying bowl again and set the pitcher aside. Lacing her fingers together, she closed her eyes and concentrated on her breathing.

Slowly Lavinia centered herself, consciously shutting out the distractions of the world beyond the abbey walls. Next, she shut out the muted sounds of the other sisters going about their daily lives and duties. Finally, she shut out her own fearful thoughts and worries. That was the hardest part.

When she opened her eyes, the water in her bowl was mirror smooth and still. At last! She shuffled a half step closer and stared down into the shallow depths of the water. At first, she saw nothing but the rich green of the glass, but then, piece by piece, a narrow strip of road came into focus.

It was impossible to gauge its exact location, but judging from the terrain, it had to be the trade route that led caravans through the Sojourn Valley and past the abbey. Oddly, though, there was no line of wagons anywhere in sight. Why would the gods show her a stretch of empty road? She started to step back, when a small movement at the edge of the water caught her attention.

Ah, so the road wasn't empty after all. A solitary horse and rider trotted into sight, heading in the direction of the abbey. The image was too small for her to pick out any detail, so she closed her eyes again and concentrated on gathering more information.

When she looked again, the image had changed. This

time the horse was grazing, and the rider was sitting cross-legged next to a small campfire. She leaned closer to the water to get a better look at the man, hoping to pick out enough details so that she'd recognize him if she were to meet him in person—in truth, not *if* but *when* she met him. He would not appear in her vision if there wasn't a connection to be forged between them.

The vision warned that the traveler would soon find his way to the abbey. That wasn't unusual in itself. There weren't many places to stop along the route between Agathia and the lands beyond. Most travelers visited the abbey to partake of the sisters' hospitality.

The real oddity was that few were either brave enough or reckless enough to travel alone. Times were too dangerous, yet this man didn't seem concerned. A prudent traveler also didn't leave a campfire burning out in the open where the light might draw unwanted company.

As she watched, the picture abruptly plunged down like a hawk diving after prey. Her stomach lurched with the sudden change in focus. The man jumped to his feet, his sword appearing in his hand as if by magic. His head spun in all directions, as if he were ready to defend himself from an imminent attack.

Finally, he looked straight up, his strangely pale eyes staring right into Lavinia's. The power of the connection shattered her hard-won calm. She stumbled back from the bowl. What had just happened? Had he truly seen her?

Her heart pounded in her chest, and the air in the garden had grown too thin to breathe. Never in all of her years of scrying had such a thing happened. Her mentor, the prior abbess, had never mentioned the possibility of the window of the water working in both directions.

Rather than risk another look, Lavinia averted her eyes as she carefully covered the bowl with a black cloth. After whispering a short prayer of thanks to the gods for the gift of the vision and asking for the wisdom to understand it, she left the garden.

The gong sounded, summoning everyone to the dining hall. Right now, she was too unsettled to eat, but rituals and routines were important. If nothing else, they provided a sense of order in a world that had long since become dark and dangerous. Yet her earliest memories were happy ones, and she could return to them for comfort. She let her mind drift back to one sunny afternoon when her father had joined her and her mother for a private picnic outside of the capital city. While Lavinia had splashed along the edge of the stream, her parents had held hands and talked softly, their love for each other shining as brightly as the sun.

Her father had been a good man and a kind one. He'd always made Lavinia feel special and loved. It wasn't his fault that his heart had given out on him or that her mother was too weak to continue on without him to protect her from his other family—his real family. She'd long since forgiven them, but the pain of losing so much at such a young age had made her cautious. Here, within the walls of the abbey, she'd found a safe refuge from the outside world. She suspected that peace was about to end.

Maybe later she would let herself think more about the mysterious stranger who was wending his way toward the abbey. Until he actually arrived, there was no way to know if his purpose was for good or for ill.

With that unsettling thought, she fell into line with the other sisters and let their loving presence comfort her.

Duncan thanked the goddess that his friends weren't there to witness him jumping at shadows. Certainly Murdoch would never have let him forget it. After one last look around, Duncan sat back down by the fire. He fed another log to the flames and watched the sparks fly up into the night sky.

That had been the second time he'd experienced the strangest feeling that he was being watched. The first time happened as he had been riding along the trail, his thoughts drifting with the breeze. Between one breath and the next, his mare had snorted and sidestepped, almost unseating him.

He'd looked everywhere, trying to determine what had startled the horse. When nothing obvious presented itself, they'd continued on. Even so, he'd found himself looking back over his shoulder afterward for some distance.

This time, he'd been staring into the fire and waiting for Kiva to finish his nightly hunt. At first he'd thought it was the owl swooping back to their makeshift camp that had disturbed him, but then that same powerful sensation had washed over him.

He'd reacted instinctively to ward off an attack, one that never came. The night was silent; nothing stirred, the only threat the uncanny feeling that someone was out there watching Duncan's every move.

After checking in all directions, he'd started to relax, when he happened to look up. For the briefest instant, the image of a woman, one with worried eyes and a lush mouth set in a deep frown, had superimposed itself over the gibbous moon. Her face had appeared and then disappeared so quickly, he had to have been imagining things.

Even so, he could still see her in his mind with disturbing clarity. She'd been lovely, with the kind of beauty that would haunt a man's dreams. Duncan shifted uncomfortably, his body reacting in a way it hadn't in a long time.

Time to seek his pallet. At first light, he would resume his trek to the abbey. Lady Merewen, the woman whose cause he served, had provided him with a rough map of the area, but there was no telling how accurate it was. At best, it had given him the general direction and a few landmarks to watch for. As far as he could tell, it would take at least one, maybe two more days of hard riding to reach his destination.

Until then, it was just him, the horse, and Kiva. As he thought about his companion, the huge owl swooped down out of the sky with a brace of rabbits clutched in his talons. He carefully dropped them right next to the fire before flying back up to roost on a low branch of a nearby tree.

"Thank you, my friend."

Duncan's breakfast and midday meal for tomorrow were taken care of thanks to the owl's efforts. He made quick work of dressing the two rabbits and putting them on the fire to roast. It wouldn't take long, and it would put him that much farther ahead in the morning. Cold meat and tea would suffice to break his fast at first light. The gods knew there'd been times in his long life he'd subsisted on far less.

As the meat sizzled over the flames, Duncan glanced up at Kiva. "Do you want to sleep in the tree for the night or in the shield?" The bird fluffed his feathers and settled in right where he was. Duncan smiled. "I don't blame you. Did you have a good hunt?"

He reached out with his thoughts to touch those of the great owl. His mind filled with dizzying views of the surrounding land. The connection the two of them shared was so close that Duncan enjoyed the cool slide of the wind through Kiva's feathers. He saw the world through the stark clarity of a raptor's vision and savored the rush of excitement when the bird dove toward his prey.

Duncan didn't need to experience firsthand what happened next. Kiva's table manners were questionable, not that Duncan wasn't grateful for his hunting skills. He also appreciated knowing the bird would stand guard while Duncan slept.

After the meat cooled a bit, Duncan wrapped it in a

cloth and tucked it in his pack to keep it safe from scavengers. His chores finished, he let the fire die down.

"Sleep well, Kiva."

Anyone outside of his narrow circle of friends would think him mad for talking to a bird. But Kiva wasn't a normal owl any more than Duncan was a normal man. He was one of the Damned, an avatar of the gods along with three other warriors and their leader, Captain Gideon. The five of them were closer than brothers.

He missed them. How many centuries had it been since he'd last spent so much time alone and away from his four friends? Well, other than when they all slept under the river, separated from the mortal world. Even then he was still aware of their presence like a soft hum in the back of his mind. At this distance, however, he couldn't sense them at all.

Rather than dwell on it, he closed his eyes and forced himself to relax. He'd picked up one more thing from Kiva's thoughts. There was a caravan of traders making its way toward the abbey. From what he'd been able to see, their camp was at least a day's ride behind him.

If he stayed where he was, they'd catch up with him. As long as he acted the part of a scholar looking for work as a scribe, they might allow him to join them for the remaining distance to the abbey. He'd prefer to arrive as part of a group.

He weighed his options. Lost in a crowd, he'd be better able to assess the situation and then decide how best to approach the abbess. Requesting full access to the abbey's collection of books and manuscripts would be tricky. He wasn't sure what he'd do if the sisters tried to turn him away.

And they very well might. A lot would depend on which gods the sisters worshipped. It was almost too much to hope for that they followed the teachings of the

Lord and Lady of the River, the deities Duncan served. What would the sisters think of his pale-as-death eyes? Again, since he would be arriving as one of many, perhaps it wouldn't be as much of a problem.

On the other hand, time—a commodity that he and his friends had precious little of—was passing. The Damned were given only so many days to accomplish the task the gods had set before them. He couldn't afford to waste two days waiting for the caravan and even more time traveling at the slow pace of the heavily laden wagons.

His mind whirled with possibilities; too many thoughts without direction. For some reason, that made him think of his father. The bastard had wanted a son who was the mirror image of himself, one who lived to drink, fight, and bed lusty wenches.

Instead, Duncan had inherited a heavy measure of his mother's love of knowledge and the gentler arts. While Duncan had a talent with weapons, at the end of the day he'd been happier in his mother's solar, poring over some ancient text, than banging swords or drinking with his father's men.

When his mother died in childbirth, his father had burned her books to wean Duncan from what his father saw as his weakling scholarly ways. The plan had had the opposite effect. Duncan had taken the few texts he'd been able to salvage from the fire and ridden away without looking back.

He'd met Gideon a short time later. Rather than berating Duncan for always carrying a load of heavy tomes with them on their campaigns, Gideon had valued Duncan's gift for tactics and knowledge of military history. The friendship had served them both well.

He rolled onto his side to stare at the fading dance of the flames. None of the Damned had aged a day since they'd first marched into the river to sleep, but on nights like this one, Duncan felt every year of his centuries-long life.

Once again the image of the mysterious woman filled his thoughts. Her beauty was a far better companion as sleep claimed him than his memories. A shame she wasn't real. But then, a man could always dream, even one who wasn't truly human at all.

Chapter 2

*L*avinia had finished her daily rounds through the abbey, stopping to visit with each of the sisters she encountered. It was her way of showing them all that she valued their individual contributions to the abbey. Now it was time to make her way back to her office.

She'd put off another attempt at scrying long enough. Perhaps this time the gods would send a message with a clearer meaning, one that wouldn't keep her awake during the long hours of the night thinking about a man.

She could only hope so.

In the garden, rather than immediately approach the deep green bowl, Lavinia paused to look up to the sky, holding her hands out to the side.

"My lords and ladies, grant me the wisdom to understand what I am about to see."

With trembling fingers, she gently removed the black cloth she'd used to cover the bowl two days before. She intended to change the water, to offer the gods a clean slate upon which to send her a message. But as soon as her hands touched the cool glass, the water swirled and settled into a smooth surface. A series of images appeared and then disappeared, each remaining visible a few seconds after the next one was superimposed over the last.

Some she recognized. Others were unfamiliar.

The first one was Trader Musar and his wife, Ava, sitting on the front of their colorfully painted wagon, their faces looking pinched and tired. That worried her. The trader was normally an outgoing, cheerful man, one who took joy in driving a hard but fair bargain. His wife, a tiny wisp of a woman, was always quick with a smile and a laugh.

Their faces faded, replaced by the outer wall of a large city, Agathia itself. Despite the bright sunshine, the white stone looked tarnished, as if a miasma of sickness had settled over the city. Lavinia's heart ached for those who lived in the shadow of Duke Keirthan. It had been a long time since she'd left the city behind, but she missed it still.

Next a large bird swooped and soared through the sky. Too big for a hawk and the wrong shape for an eagle, it had to be an owl, then, but one far bigger than those that inhabited the valley surrounding the abbey. She leaned down closer to study the image, sensing there was something different about the raptor other than its size. Before she could decide what it was, the image blurred and shifted again.

A group of men on horseback appeared, all heavily armed and watching the horizon for any possible threat. Since they were riding alongside a long line of wagons, each painted more brightly than the next, they had to be the guards who protected Musar's caravan from raiders. If she could see their faces, she might even recognize them by name. Most of Musar's guards had been accompanying him for years.

Aside from the grim look on Musar's face, there was nothing in the vision that was worrisome.

Lavinia was about to offer her prayer of thanks when once again the image changed abruptly. She'd caught only a glimpse of him twice before, but it was definitely the same man who'd been sitting at the campfire two days earlier.

His surroundings were familiar to her this time. In a matter of hours, he would enter the valley below. She had no doubt the abbey was his destination. The gods wouldn't have warned of his coming if he were merely passing through.

While she watched, he pulled back on the reins, slowing his horse to a stop as he looked around. Lavinia started to back away from the image in the water in case he looked up as he had two days ago. But then curiosity mixed with a healthy dose of stubbornness had her holding her ground.

She stared down at the small image, wondering about the odd connection she felt with a total stranger. As with the owl, there was something more to this man. Soon he would arrive at the door of the abbey. Rather than greet him herself, she would wait and watch. Eventually the gods would reveal his purpose to her, and her path would be clear.

She prayed it would be so.

The final approach to the abbey proved to be a switchback trail that led up the steep side of a narrow valley. If Duncan hadn't been looking for the passage, he might have ridden right past it. The abbey had been constructed out of the native stone, making it difficult to pick out much detail about the structure from the road that wandered along the valley floor below.

Before starting up, he stopped at a small stream to let his mare drink her fill. He was tempted to bathe and change clothes in order to make a good impression upon the sisters, but reconsidered. Several days of trail dust and dirt would help his story of needing both a job and a hot meal sound more convincing.

He took time to enjoy a cold drink of water and to finish off the last bit of roasted meat he had in his pack. After picking the bones clean, he tossed them as far as he could throw them. It was time to cease delaying, although it was hard not to worry about what the next hour would bring. What if the sisters did turn him away? Surely the gods guiding his steps wouldn't let that happen.

He had just mounted up when he caught the sound of a rider approaching at speed. Duncan checked the slide of his sword in its scabbard and waited to see if the newcomer came in peace. To Duncan's surprise, the man looked relieved when he spotted Duncan and reined in his horse.

Both man and beast had worked up a sweat, a testament to a long, hard day of riding. The first words out of the stranger's mouth came as a complete shock.

"There you are. I thought I would never find you in time."

Duncan checked to see who else the man could be speaking to, but they were alone on the road. "You were looking for me? Why? Who sent you?"

It wouldn't have been Gideon. He'd have sent his gyrfalcon, Scim, if he'd wanted to get a message to Duncan, or even one of Averel's misfit dogs. Certainly he wouldn't have sent a stranger.

The man dismounted. "I apologize. I should have explained first. My name is Rubar, and I am the captain of the guards for a caravan headed this way. The master trader is named Musar, and his wife is called Ava."

The weary man paused to catch his breath. He was wrong if he thought the introduction cleared up the confusion. Duncan tightened his grip on the sword.

"Their names mean nothing to me."

Rubar shrugged. "No reason they should. You haven't met them yet, but you will. One of the wagons broke a wheel, so the caravan had to stop for repairs."

Duncan wished he'd get to the point. "Which still has nothing to do with me."

The man dismounted and led his horse over to the stream. "Well, yes, it does. Ava is a seer. Do you believe in such gifts from the gods?"

More so than Rubar would ever know. Duncan jerked his head in a quick nod.

"She had a vision about you three . . . no, four nights ago. She said I'd recognize you by the odd color of your eyes and the owl on your shield."

A shiver of dread snaked through Duncan's chest. If the man was to be believed, the woman had the vision right before Duncan had left Merewen's keep. What had her gods told her?

He asked Rubar that question.

"She said the sisters would likely turn you away from your quest unless someone vouched for you. If the wagon hadn't broken down, we would've met you along the way and gotten to know you before arriving at the abbey."

He stared up at the stone building perched on the ridge above. "She said that the honor of our clan rests in your hands."

Then Rubar smiled and held up a hand. "And before you ask what she meant by that, I don't know. I'm not sure she did."

His grin broadened. "Sometimes the gods are pretty vague with their warnings. Not sure if that's a blessing or a curse."

He wasn't telling Duncan anything he didn't already know. "So do we wait for the caravan?"

Duncan knew he could ill afford to waste time sitting down here in the valley when what he needed was housed in the stone building at the top of the ridge. Besides, he had no idea if the trader's woman really had the gift of sight. Yet, if she didn't, how would she have known where to send her man to find him? Circles within circles and none of it making much sense.

"No need to wait, but I'd like to rest my gelding a bit before tackling the trail up to the abbey."

Duncan nodded and dismounted again. While his mare grazed on the side of the road, he studied the guard, liking what he saw. The man's clothing was in good condition, obviously designed for the rough life on the road. He looked comfortable with the knives he wore strapped to his waist, and while Rubar might act relaxed, he also kept a careful eye on their surroundings.

A man didn't survive long as a guard by being careless. When both rider and horse had cooled down, Rubar spoke again. "You seem to be taking it well, especially when I don't even know your name. I was afraid you'd think I was moon touched and have nothing to do with me."

Duncan laughed. "The name is Duncan. I'm here because the abbey is one of the few places that might offer me a post as a scribe. If you can ease my way past the front door, I'm willing to give you the benefit of the doubt."

"A scribe?" Rubar's smile faded a bit as his eyes took in Duncan's own array of weapons and the shield tied on his saddle. "Well, a man sometimes works at many jobs."

"True enough." Scribe, scholar, warrior, avatar of the gods.

"Shall we ride?"

"Yes." Rubar was already reaching for the reins. "And the gods are with us, because we're arriving in plenty of time for dinner. I've been looking forward to Sister Margaret's cooking for weeks."

A short time later, Duncan sat back in the saddle and stared at the building looming up ahead, his destination finally in sight. As his mare picked her way up the last stretch of the steep trail, he wondered what the traders' gods had in mind for him, and how his own would react if it was at cross-purposes to their plans.

Rubar dropped back to ride even with Duncan. He pointed toward the back of the abbey. "That building in the back has guest quarters. The traders prefer to stay in their wagons, but my men and I appreciate the chance to sleep in a real bed when we're not on duty. The sisters don't charge for the rooms, but they do accept donations, or you can do chores for them if you have no coin to offer."

"Good to know. A comfortable bed will be a welcome change."

Anything was better than the rocky ground, although gods knew he wasn't picky after sleeping under several feet of cold water for years at a time.

The trail widened out at the top of the slope. They dismounted and unsaddled their horses. Duncan gave his mare a quick brushing and checked her feet before turning her loose in the pasture. Rubar showed him where to stow his saddle and tack in the stable.

Tired and hungry, Duncan gathered up his packs and followed the guard around to the side door of a low building that jutted out from the main structure of the abbey. Rubar rapped his knuckles on the heavy wooden door and stepped back as it swung open almost immediately. An older woman wearing robes and a bright smile stepped into sight.

Rubar nodded in respect. "Sister Joetta, we are hoping that you have room for us in the guest quarters."

"I always have room for favorite visitors. I didn't know Musar's caravan had arrived. Please come in."

Rubar filed in past the sister. The warm smile she'd offered the guard faded when it came Duncan's time to enter the guest quarters.

She stepped in front of him. "I don't believe we have met before."

He dropped his gaze in an attempt to look nonthreatening. "This is my first visit to the abbey, Sister. My name is Duncan."

"Have you been with Trader Musar long?"

Perhaps the woman was just being friendly, but Duncan's acute hearing picked up the thrum of tension in her voice. Was she always suspicious of strangers, or was it a reaction to him specifically?

Rubar interceded on his behalf. "The caravan had to stop for repairs, Sister Joetta, but it should be here in a matter of hours. Duncan has yet to meet Musar and Ava, but they sent me ahead to help him get settled here. Ava asked that he be allowed to stay until she arrives. Duncan should prove useful around here, though. He tells me he is seeking work as a scribe."

That clearly surprised her. She glanced at Duncan's shield and sword, her suspicion clear now. Scholars didn't often carry such weapons. After a brief hesitation and despite her obvious misgivings, she finally let him pass. "I will relay Ava's message to the abbess. Whether you are allowed to remain will be her decision, but for now, welcome to the abbey. Our evening meal is several hours away. If you're hungry, I'm sure Sister Margaret can provide something to hold you until dinner. Otherwise, Rubar will show you where everything is."

She then barred the door behind him, preventing anyone else from entering the guest quarters without knocking first. For an abbey with a reputation for its hospitality, her caution seemed extreme. He was willing to bet that they were reacting to the effects of Duke Keirthan's brutal rule of Agathia. No one felt safe, not when people were disappearing with no explanation.

First things first. The two of them picked a room at random and stowed their gear before availing themselves of the opportunity to clean up. Duncan sighed with pleasure as he sank down into the shallow hot spring pool set aside for male visitors to use. The heat soaked into his weary body, easing his aches and pains.

Rubar joined him. He leaned his head back against the wall and closed his eyes. For the moment, both men were content to enjoy the soothing waters in silence.

As tempting as it was to linger, Duncan finally reached for the soap and a rag to scrub his skin clean. Soon he would have to present his request to make use of the abbey library in exchange for his labor as a scribe, and he'd like a chance to look around.

Then he'd approach the abbess and hope for the best.

Lavinia finished the abbey's accounts and wrote a summary for the head of their order, who lived on the other side of the mountains. Musar would see that the letter was delivered. As she sealed it, Lavinia smiled. She'd been looking forward to his arrival all afternoon. Both Sister Joetta and Sister Margaret had been to see her about the stranger in their midst, who had arrived earlier in the afternoon with one of Musar's men acting as escort. All she knew was that his name was Duncan, he was seeking a position as a scribe, and he'd spent hours chopping wood for the kitchen. He'd made a good impression so far, but she wouldn't let him have free run of the abbey until she learned more about him.

Although it was true the abbey existed in part to serve travelers, the real reason the abbey had been built was to provide a repository for books and manuscripts of all kinds, a collection they were sworn to protect. As abbess, she alone determined who was allowed access to the library and its contents. She wouldn't risk letting a stranger near the collection until she knew he could be trusted.

After all, the duke could have spies anywhere. On the other hand, if Duncan worked for Keirthan, wouldn't the gods have been more specific in their warning?

A knock at the door interrupted her dark thoughts. She set her correspondence aside and called, "Come in."

Musar let himself in. "Lady Lavinia, it is a pleasure to see you."

He crossed the room to set a small sack on the desk as he sat down. "I received your message that Sister Margaret was hoping to obtain more of this spice."

She reached for her coin purse. "How much do I owe you?"

"This one is free of charge, Lady Lavinia. Consider it a gift in exchange for the abbey's hospitality for my family and my men." He winked at her. "Besides, Ava would have my skin if she thought I wasn't being fair to you."

"You are most generous." She rounded the desk to walk out with him. "Shall we adjourn to the dining hall? Perhaps over dinner you can share any news you've picked up during your travels. Visitors have been few this season, and it's been some time since we've received word from the outside world."

Her friend's smile faded completely as he offered her his arm. "I'm not sure if such news will make for good dinner conversation, but I'll answer what questions I can."

"Good news or not, Musar, I would rather know the truth of how things are. We may be isolated, but matters of the world outside still concern us."

Especially her.

When they reached the entrance to the abbey, Musar took his leave. "I will fetch Ava and then join you for dinner."

"I look forward to it."

He headed out the front door while she made her way to the dining hall. She stopped just short of the entrance, listening to the mix of voices inside. It wasn't often they had guests in such large numbers. The deep rumble of male voices sounded odd among the higher-pitched sound of the sisters talking.

Lavinia straightened her robes and assumed a calm demeanor before crossing the threshold. A quick glance reassured her that all was flowing smoothly. She made her way to her usual seat at the head table. Places had been reserved for Musar, his wife, and several other members of his family.

She caught the eye of one of the servers. "Hold the meal until our guests join us. They should be along soon."

"Yes, Sister. I'll watch for them."

Chapter 3

*L*avinia had just taken her seat when a movement in the far corner caught her attention. Two men filed in from the guest quarters. The first one through the door was Rubar, who had been traveling through the area with caravans for years.

But it was the man who walked in behind Rubar who had Lavinia clutching the edge of the table with a white-knuckled grip. She would've recognized him anywhere. Right now he was laughing at something Rubar had said. But as she watched, his smile faltered and then faded away completely, to be replaced by a slight frown.

Moving deliberately as he had in her visions, he slowly checked out his surroundings, a warrior on alert. When he spotted her sitting across the room, his eyes widened, and his fisted hands dropped back down to his side.

If she hadn't known better, she would've thought he looked straight at her and said, "You!"

What could his reaction mean? Had he somehow recognized Lavinia or merely realized that she was the one who had been staring at him just now?

He took a half step in her direction, but Rubar caught his arm and tugged him in the direction of one of the back tables. Lavinia took a long slow breath to calm her badly rattled nerves. So she'd been right. The vision had been a warning that their paths would cross. Right now it was impossible to know if his arrival was a harbinger of good or evil.

It was tempting to confront him immediately, but Lavinia forced herself to remain seated. She'd learn more from seeing how he approached her. It was interesting that he was with Rubar, the captain of Musar's personal guard. She didn't know what to make of it all.

When the trader and his family came through the door, Lavinia rose to her feet to welcome them. After the meal was served, she'd find some way to broach the subject of Duncan and see what Musar knew of him.

Sister Margaret waited until Musar and his family were seated before she rang the gong to get everyone's attention. As soon as the room was silent, Lavinia offered the prayer of thanksgiving. As she spoke the familiar words, the grace of the gods soothed her spirit and comforted her heart.

When the first course had come and gone, she finally brought up the question. "Musar, I recognize most of the men that you have riding guard on your caravan, but that man sitting with Rubar is new to me. He doesn't seem like your typical guard."

Although she'd addressed her comment to the trader, it was his wife who answered. "You speak of the one who claims to be a scribe in need of work."

Musar frowned. "This Duncan fellow is a puzzle to me. I've met a few scribes in my time. Most are skinny and sit hunched over from too many hours of plying their trade. They have calluses on their fingers, and their skin is permanently stained with ink."

He jerked his head in Duncan's direction. "I spoke to that one at length this afternoon when he helped to unharness our draft horses. He speaks like an educated man, which lends credence to his claim of being a scribe. True, his hands are callused, but from holding a weapon, not a pen. Rubar reported that Duncan carries a warrior's shield, and his sword would cost a year's profits. A good year's profits at that."

Then he shuddered. "And then he has such strange eyes."

Musar dropped his hand down to his side and made one of the common signs to ward off evil. "They are the color of death."

Lavinia felt that was going too far, but then the trader clans were superstitious. She kept her reaction carefully hidden, not wanting to offend her friend. Especially when she needed more answers because Musar's doubts about Duncan echoed her own.

"If you had doubts about his story, why did you have Rubar introduce him to the abbey?"

Ava, who was seated on the far side of her husband, leaned forward to look at Lavinia. "The gods spoke to me about him."

Lavinia knew better than to question Ava's visions. The woman was famous among the trading clans for her ability to foresee the future. Many had benefited from her predictions of foul weather and which goods would sell well in a given year.

"What did the gods say about him?"

Ava and Musar looked at each other, communicating without words in the way couples who counted their time together in decades often did. Finally, Musar nodded.

"Here is what they told me." Ava paused briefly as if preparing herself. When she spoke again, her voice sounded different—deeper, solemn, and with a heavy touch of power. "The scholar comes to seek the truth. Deny him and the price will be paid in blood and the honor of the clan will be destroyed."

The last few words hung in the air, as Ava's shoulders

sagged, the effort to speak for the gods clearly having cost her. Lavinia fought to remain calm, but Ava's pronouncement had left her badly shaken.

What did all of that mean? What truth did Duncan seek? Or whose truth? She appreciated that the gods were sometimes willing to intervene in the lives of their people, but she wished they would speak more clearly.

"Did he say why he came here to the abbey?"

"Nothing other than he was seeking employment."

That made some sense, although it didn't tell her much. Normally if a manuscript needed to be copied, one of the sisters would take on that task. However, it wasn't unheard of for the abbey to decide to take on extra help if the workload exceeded the ability of the sisters to keep up.

She had much to think on. For now, she let her guests turn their attention to Sister Margaret's excellent cooking.

Duncan bowed his head briefly but finally gave in to the need to study the woman standing at the head table with Musar and his wife. It was definitely her image that had been reflected on the moon two nights ago. From her position at the head table, he had to guess she was the abbess herself. He murmured the closing of the prayer along with everyone else. The trappings of religion were one of the few things that remained relatively unchanged from one calling to the next no matter how long the Damned had been gone from the world.

As soon as the abbess quit speaking, young girls began weaving in and out of the tables with large trays of bread and cheese. They were followed by older women carrying large tureens of something that smelled delicious.

Rubar immediately reached for the ladle to fill his plate. "Sister Margaret is a most talented cook. On our last trip through, I tried to talk her into teaching me the secret of her venison stew. She shooed me out of her kitchen, flapping her apron at me as if I were a gaggle of geese."

Then the guard grinned. "If she didn't wield her cleaver like a weapon, I might have tried to force the issue. I'm hoping to bribe her with a new spice I picked up this year."

One taste of the savory meat and vegetables, and Duncan could see why Rubar would risk breaching the walls of Sister Margaret's kitchen. He couldn't remember the last time he'd eaten something so delicious.

As one of the Damned, most of the time Duncan marched out of the river straight into battle. Meals were eaten on the run; cold meat, cheese, a bit of hot tea or cheap wine were their usual fare. He sometimes forgot that food could be something to savor.

Life's greatest pleasures had been missing from their lives for centuries, but that seemed to be changing. It was unsettling for them all. Captain Gideon had found love with the woman they'd been ordered to champion by their gods. Even Murdoch, the most serious of the five warriors, seemed enamored with Lady Alina, Merewen's young widowed aunt.

Duncan's gaze strayed to the head table and the woman sitting there. She was quite striking. He could see she was engaged in a discussion with the trader and his wife. What were they telling her about him? When she happened to glance in his direction, her smile faltered. Rather than give her cause for concern, he immediately averted his eyes and concentrated on finishing his meal.

Odd, but the stew no longer had much flavor.

But even when he wasn't looking at the abbess, he couldn't quit thinking about her. Had she chosen to serve the gods, or had they chosen her? The woman looked awfully young to bear the burden of running an abbey of this size. But then, he hadn't been much older when he'd made his own vow to serve the Lord and Lady, a pledge he couldn't walk away from even if he'd wanted to.

With that cheery thought, he finished his wine and then reached for more.

Chapter 4

Once again a movement in the far corner of the room had drawn Lavinia's eye. Rubar and several of Musar's drivers and guards were preparing to leave. Rather than filing out through the door toward the guest quarters, Rubar and another man broke off from the others and walked straight toward the head table.

Duncan said something, but Rubar didn't respond. She frowned. There was something strange about the way Rubar and the other guard moved; they appeared stiff and awkward, yet purposeful. They split up, each taking a different route between the tables but clearly heading toward Lavinia and her guests.

As she watched, Rubar stumbled into one of the young novices as if he hadn't seen her standing right there in front of him. Normally, he would've said something, at least a quick apology, but instead he shoved past the girl without saying a word.

Did he need to speak to his employer? She started to say something to Musar, but he was caught up in a conversation with his eldest son. She'd wait until he was finished to point out that his men might be in need of his attention.

Duncan followed in Rubar's footsteps, his face set in a grim expression as he stalked after the guard. By the time Rubar had reached the front of the room, the second guard had moved up beside him. Both men stared at Lavinia with the oddest expression on their faces as they came around the end of the table to where she was seated.

Feeling at a decided disadvantage, Lavinia rose to her feet. "Rubar, is there something you needed?"

Their sole response was to draw their swords—and lunge toward her with deadly intent. The tip of Rubar's sword came within inches of her throat. Instantly she jumped back out of range but tangled up with the others at her table, all trying to scatter in the face of the determined attack.

Musar bellowed at his senior guard to stand down as he tried to get his wife and family out of danger. "Both of you, stop! What are you doing?"

He might as well have been spouting nonsense for all the attention the two guards paid to him. No one at the head table had worn weapons to dinner, leaving them all defenseless.

Then a third man entered the fray. Rather than trying to get past the two guards, Duncan upturned the table to form a temporary barrier between the guards and where Lavinia and her guests stood. Food and dishes hit the ground with a crash, making the footing slippery. He then jumped the table to face off against her attackers. His first attempts to force the other two men to retreat met with only limited success.

When Duncan blocked a blow from the second guard, his sword cut deeply into his opponent's shoulder. The man paid no heed to his injury or the blood pouring down his sword arm. Meanwhile, Rubar kept trying to get around to where Lavinia and the others were huddled behind the table. When Rubar couldn't break through, he turned his full attention to Duncan.

Both men were skilled with a blade, but it was clear that Rubar was no match for his opponent. Inch by inch, Duncan forced him to retreat.

Time slowed, heightening each detail, each sound, leaving Lavinia strangely aware of everything in the room. At the far end of the room, Sisters Margaret and Joetta were shepherding everyone they could out of the room through the kitchen. Musar's other guards had drawn their weapons but seemed unsure whom they should be fighting as they formed up a line surrounding the trader and his people.

The only noise in the room was the clanging of swords and Duncan's deep voice ordering his two opponents to stand down. Rubar and his partner remained strangely silent, as if they existed only to swing their weapons.

When Rubar slashed Duncan's leg with a hard hit, Lavinia screamed. For his part, the scribe continued to fight, not giving an inch despite his obvious pain. Finally, when one of his opponents almost slipped past him, his attack turned lethal. In a flurry of motion too quick for the eye to follow, he charged forward.

When he stopped moving, the floor was awash with blood. The nameless guard was clearly dead, but Rubar still breathed. Duncan dropped his sword and fell to his knees. He lifted the wounded man's head onto his lap, brushing Rubar's hair back off his face with a gentle touch.

There was real grief in Duncan's expression as he tried to comfort the dying man.

Rubar struggled to speak. Blood dribbled out of the corner of his mouth as he whispered, "I couldn't control my own hand. This I swear."

Duncan gripped the other man's bloody hand in his. "You were not the one behind the attack, Rubar. Someone else wielded your sword. Your honor remains your own."

Lavinia knelt beside the two men, murmuring the prayers for the dead and dying. Rubar reached out to clasp her arm, soaking the sleeve of her robe with the crimson of his blood.

"I am sorry, my lady. Forgive me. I didn't mean . . ."

"I know, Rubar; I believe you. There is nothing to be forgiven." She could barely choke the words out around the lump in her throat. She had seen his expression change, from battle-ready to one of horror, when Duncan's sword had struck its mark in his flesh.

Duncan stared down at the man, his strange eyes gleaming with the sheen of tears. "Rest in peace, my friend. May the gods welcome you into their arms."

The guard shuddered one last time and then lay still, his eyes open and staring into the afterlife.

For a brief moment, Lavinia let herself grieve for the two men. After one last prayer for their souls, she pushed herself back up to her feet, doing her best to ignore the trembling in her hands and legs. How dare these men bring violence into a place of peace like the abbey! Right now, she had an injured man to see to, one who had saved her life and that of her guests.

Once Duncan's wounds were treated, it would be time to demand some answers. If not from him, then from her gods.

For now, she needed to restore order. "Musar, is anyone else hurt?"

The trader looked ashen, clearly devastated by the events. He had Ava tucked next to him, his arm around her shoulders. At the moment, it was impossible to tell if he was comforting his wife or if she supported him.

"Musar," Lavinia repeated more forcefully, "are any of your people hurt?"

"No, we are unharmed." He slowly raised his eyes up to meet hers. "My lady, I don't know what to say. Rubar was my most trusted man."

Duncan was back up on his feet to join the conversation. "They were not responsible for the attack even if they held the swords."

Lavinia wasn't sure why, but she believed him. For his sake and Musar's, as well as for the souls of the two men, she made a decision. "They shall be laid to rest with full honors here at the abbey."

She caught Sister Joetta's attention. "Please see that these two men are prepared for burial. I'm sure Ava will want to assist with that so that we follow the proper customs for their individual beliefs. Musar, please see to your people and assure them that all is well."

Then she drew a deep breath and added, "However, for now I think it best that your guards be confined to the guest quarters until we determine what really happened here."

Finally, she turned her attention back to the grimly silent man standing beside her who had just saved her life. "Sir Duncan, can you walk to our infirmary, or shall I ask two of Musar's other guards to carry you?"

His deathly pale eyes glittered with determination. "I will walk."

"Then we should go."

She led the way through the throng of traders and the sisters who had returned when the commotion died down. It was imperative that she act as if everything was back under control. At least her robes hid the way her legs trembled, and she curled her hands into fists to control their shaking.

Out in the hallway, she turned in the direction of the infirmary. Every step of the way, she was acutely aware of the man marching along beside her in stoic silence. He'd grabbed a piece of cloth from somewhere and held it over the jagged gash on his leg to control the bleeding. It had to be painful, but other than the deep lines bracketing his mouth, he gave no sign of it.

"In here."

She entered the room first and motioned for him to have a seat on the bench by the door. "I'll fetch Sister Berta. She's our herbalist, but she also has a talent for dealing with wounds."

"My leg will be fine."

It was time for some answers. "And as a scribe, you have a lot of experience with such wounds?"

He didn't bother to respond. They both knew his actions in the dining hall had proven he was far more than a simple scribe. She left him sitting there while she went outside in search of the herbalist. As soon as Sister Berta had Duncan's wound cleaned, the warrior would have to answer to Lavinia.

One way or another, she would have the truth from him. Evil had found its way into the abbey, and more than just her own life depended on regaining control and stopping the spread of the darkness before it grew worse.

Chapter 5

*H*e hurt, the pain burning through his mind, making clear thought all but impossible. When his attempt to open his eyes failed, he used his other senses to try to make out his current situation.

A few things were obvious. He was lying down. The surface beneath him was thickly padded and redolent of lavender and roses. The fabric was smooth and soft. Hardly the kind of bed a soldier enjoyed when on a campaign.

Obviously he considered himself a soldier, another useful bit of information. He served . . . Who was it he served? Why couldn't he remember where he was? As he struggled to remember, the pain in his chest worsened. He moaned, wishing the agony would subside.

A soft, feminine voice entered his thoughts. "Rest easy. You are safe."

He believed her. Surely no one with such a gentle voice would lie to him.

"Sip this."

Her small hand lifted his head and held a cup to his lips. A slow trickle of a sweet liquid made it into his mouth, washing away the desert-dry roughness in his throat as he swallowed.

"We'll see how that settles and then try some broth."

He wished he could speak or at least nod to express his gratitude, but already the darkness was lapping at the edges of his thoughts. When a cool cloth settled on his forehead, he sighed with relief as it chased away the throbbing pain.

"That's good. Rest easy, and I'll check on you again soon."

She walked away, leaving him trapped in this darkness, this void, all alone and confused. Scared. He hated it. The need to connect, to reach out to her, whoever she was, gave him the strength to open his eyes and speak.

"Help."

The single word said it all and said too much. It spoke of fear and his terror of being lost like this forever. Shame colored his thoughts. His honor and pride demanded he should be braver than that. He used to be. He knew that much even if he didn't know anything else, including where he was.

Or even who he was.

His efforts were rewarded. Someone was coming his way. But even through the blur of his unfocused eyes, he knew it wasn't the gentle woman. The shape and size were all wrong. No, this was a man, a warrior, judging by his build.

"You are awake."

There was no relief, only resignation in that simple statement, as if the man found that disappointing. Probably not a friend, then.

He searched for something to say, something safe to ask. "How long?"

"The battle was four days ago."

The words were spoken grudgingly, as if the man hated revealing even that much information. He tried to make sense of the man's attitude. At the very least, it reaffirmed they weren't friends. Did they know each other? Were they possibly enemies? And yet, in his experience, prisoners didn't sleep on fine linens and soft beds.

He studied the man who prowled around the edge of

his vision. His first impression had been right. The man was clearly a warrior. It was written in the way he moved and how he wore his weapons.

He searched his memory. Did he know this warrior by name or even by reputation? Nothing came to mind. Should he ask when he had no information to offer in exchange? Eventually he would need answers if he was to find himself again. Perhaps a different question would garner him some answers.

"Where am I?"

The warrior spun back to face the bed, his face stone hard and angry.

"In Lady Merewen's keep."

Her name niggled at the back of his thoughts, but that was all. He braced himself and asked another question.

"Am I a guest or a prisoner?"

The warrior stepped closer, providing a clearer look at his smile, one that had nothing at all to do with good cheer. "That depends."

"On what?" he asked, only because the warrior expected it.

"On why you stopped Lord Fagan, the man you were sworn to aid, from killing his wife and Lady Merewen."

The words were spoken in little better than a growl. Only dim images came to mind. The harder he thought, the worse his head hurt. How could he account for his actions when he had no idea who he was or why he'd done anything at all?

He settled for the truth. "I don't know."

The warrior leaned forward, clearly furious. "I have waited days to hear your explanation. Playing the fool will not work with me."

"Captain Gideon!"

The warrior jerked back. "Lady Alina."

The woman had returned. This time he could see her clearly. She was lovely, with silvery blond hair and soft gray eyes. Right now those eyes were glaring at the man she called Captain Gideon as she set down the tray she'd been carrying.

"What do you think you're doing?"

The captain softened his voice, but just barely. "He asked if he was a guest or a prisoner. I said that depended on why he defended you and Lady Merewen."

She stood with her hands on her hips. "His actions also saved Sir Murdoch's life."

Gideon stared past her toward the room beyond. "I am well aware of that. It is the purpose behind those actions that I question."

"He's barely awakened, Captain. Your questions should wait until he is stronger."

Before Gideon could argue, she added, "Murdoch is asking for you. Maybe you can get him to sip more of the broth. He needs it if he's going to recover his strength."

There was an odd note in her voice. Clearly she and Captain Gideon were both worried about this Murdoch fellow. Far more worried than either of them was about him, so perhaps his status was indeed closer to prisoner than guest.

"I'll see what I can do. He always was a lousy patient." Gideon glanced back at her. "I'll be next door. Call me if you need me to deal with any problems from him."

The captain gripped his sword, making it clear just how he'd prefer to deal with those problems. The tension in the room faded as soon as the warrior disappeared through the doorway.

His eyes burned, and he could feel sleep creeping up to claim his mind again. He fought against it; he'd been caught in the darkness for too long already. Now it felt as if Lady Alina brought the light with her.

She moved the tray closer to his bed. "Are you ready to try some broth?"

For her, he would try anything. "Please."

Lady Alina propped him up on several pillows before pulling a chair next to the bed so she could help him with the broth. He hated feeling this helpless, but just like Gideon's friend Murdoch, he needed sustenance to regain his strength.

Spoonful by spoonful, he managed to consume almost the entire bowl of savory broth. When she offered him another mouthful, he shook his head.

"I've had enough. It tasted good. Thank you."

"You're welcome." She set the bowl aside and then removed the extra pillows so he could lie down. "Now you should rest. If you need anything at all, either I or Lady Merewen will be close by."

Already his eyes were closing. Before sleep claimed him, she asked one question.

"I'm sorry, but I don't know what to call you. We never heard your name."

He gave her his truth as he slid into the darkness. "I am no one."

Gideon stared down at Murdoch, fighting against the urge to storm back into the other room to gut the prisoner. That was his temper talking, though. For now, the duke's man might prove to be more valuable alive than dead.

His real concern was for Lady Alina's other patient. The gods had gifted the Damned with the ability to heal from almost any injury. Even the most severe wounds were little better than fading scars within a night, two at the most. The battle was four days past; yet Murdoch was still weak as a newborn foal, his color the same gray as the stone walls of Merewen's keep.

"You look as if you swallowed something sour."

The big warrior's whispered words had Gideon struggling to school his expression, hoping to hide his very real concern for his friend.

"You're worrying Lady Alina. She thinks you're not

trying hard enough to drink the broth Ellie the cook sent up for you."

Gideon pulled a stool over next to Murdoch's bed and reached for the bowl. "If you don't finish this, Ellie will be up here to pour it down your throat herself."

Murdoch laughed, wincing at the pain it cost him. "Fine. If you insist on playing nursemaid, I'll try to eat some."

Gideon would've done far more than play nursemaid as long as Murdoch recovered. He'd already seen his friend perish from wounds such as these on the day they were Damned by their gods. Despite all the centuries that had passed, the memory of seeing his dying friends scattered on the shore of the river had yet to fade.

He didn't need this reminder. None of them did. Was the gods' magic fading? Had they somehow broken faith with the Lord and Lady of the River? He didn't think so, but why else would Murdoch continue to suffer? The gods' gifts should have hastened his recovery.

"Your thoughts are dark, Captain."

Murdoch's comment dragged Gideon's attention back to the man in front of him. He realized that he'd been lost in the past and quit feeding his friend. He held out another spoonful of the broth.

After swallowing a few more bites, Murdoch spoke again. "This is not your fault. You are not the one who stabbed me in the gut. The one responsible is dead and buried. So is the man he served."

"I know."

Even so, the guilt still rode him hard. "I am thinking about calling on the gods at the river's edge. Maybe they'll have answers."

Murdoch was already shaking his head. "No, Gideon. At least not yet. I'll be back to normal soon."

Not if Murdoch continued to heal at this rate, and they both knew it. He was improving, but much too slowly. Gideon needed Murdoch at full strength and soon. Reports continued to trickle in about families disappearing with no warning, livestock dead from no apparent cause, and the duke's men hunting for anyone with a touch of magic in his blood. The Damned had only so many days to serve as Lady Merewen's champions and secure the safety of the kingdom. If they failed—

He cut that thought off immediately, although it was never far from his mind. Duncan had ridden out the day before and should be well on his way to the abbey, which meant Gideon's forces were already reduced in number. Soon both Kane and Averel would leave for the city of Agathia to infiltrate Duke Keirthan's stronghold.

Divided forces meant divided strength and twice the worry. He set the empty bowl aside. Murdoch was already dozing off. Gideon waited until his friend was sleeping soundly before standing up. He closed his eyes and offered up a prayer to the Lady to watch over his friends.

"Is he resting easily?"

Gideon had already sensed Lady Merewen's soothing presence in the doorway. She joined him at the side of the bed, her dark eyes worried for his friend.

He nodded as he took her hand in his, twining their fingers together. "He finished the broth even though it wore him out."

"Still, that's a good sign. When he awakens again, I'll send for some more."

"Let me know if you need help feeding him."

Merewen briefly rested her head against his shoulder and then walked away from Murdoch's bed, dragging Gideon with her. They continued in silence until they reached her room, a short distance down the hallway. She didn't stop until they stood on the small balcony that overlooked the bailey below.

He drew in a breath of fresh air, purging his lungs of

the stench of sickness and old blood. The sunshine warmed his skin just as the woman standing next to him warmed his soul. She was bracing herself to speak, probably about something she knew he wouldn't like.

"I hear our guest finally woke up."

"He did."

Gideon let some of his disappointment show in his voice. The man was a complication that Gideon couldn't afford right now, even though he owed the man a debt of honor. The soldier had inexplicably taken the blow that Fagan, Merewen's uncle, had intended for Murdoch after Alina had thrown herself across Murdoch's body to protect him from her husband's murderous wrath.

"I know what he did, but he was one of Duke Keirthan's men, and a high-ranking officer by the cut of his uniform. I have to wonder if he was acting on his own or if his actions serve some other purpose."

Merewen looked puzzled. "How so? He had no way to know that he'd survive Fagan's attack. Duke Keirthan has grown powerful, but it is doubtful even he would have known that my uncle would try to murder his wife. Fagan even admitted he had promised both Lady Alina and me to Keirthan to use for his own dark ends."

The memory of how close Gideon had come to losing Merewen chilled him as if a storm cloud had passed before the sun. He wrapped his arms around her.

"It would appear the act was impulsive on his part. Until we know more about the man, all I can do is keep a close watch on him."

His lady gave him one of those smiles that rivaled the sun for heat. "Truly, my captain, is that all you can do?"

Merewen was trying to distract him. It was working, especially when her hands did a bit of wandering. He pressed a kiss to her forehead before answering her.

"No, that is not all I can do, you minx. I've recently been told that I have many amazing talents."

She slipped out of his embrace to retreat toward the quarters they now shared. "Really? And who would've filled your head with such ideas?"

He loved it when she teased him and loved her for treating him as if he were an ordinary man. Most people feared the Damned, but Merewen had accepted Gideon and his four warriors with such amazing ease.

He prowled after her. "You did, my lady. But if you've forgotten, I stand ready to remind you."

Her eyes immediately dropped lower, checking out the visible proof of that statement. Her smile widened as she backed toward the bed.

"I think you shall have to work hard to remind me."

He unfastened his sword belt and set it aside. "I will endeavor to refresh your memory most thoroughly."

Before Gideon could make good on his promise, Merewen abruptly turned pale and screamed. She fell to her knees and covered her ears with her hands, rocking as if in great pain.

Gideon charged across the room to catch her in his arms. "What's wrong?"

The screams faded to a mournful keening as she shuddered against his chest. There was only one thing that could do this to her. Something had happened to one of her horses, crippling her with the pain she felt through her mental link to the herds.

"What can I do to help?"

Someone pounded at the door, no doubt wanting to know what had the lady of the keep screaming as if she were under attack.

"Come in!"

Kane charged in with Averel right behind him, both with swords drawn and ready to fight. They stood down as soon as they saw Gideon kneeling on the floor and holding Merewen as she sobbed against his chest.

Kane stalked over to the balcony to look around, no doubt hoping to find a target for his weapons. "What happened?"

"I don't know yet. One minute we were—"

He stopped right there and tried again. "I was trying to get Merewen to rest for a while. She was up all night treating the wounded. One second she was fine, and then she was screaming and holding her head."

He held her close, wishing he could do more. "Merewen, you need to tell us what happened."

"It's the horses." Her answer came out in short gulps, the tears still pouring down her face. "They screamed in pain. I don't know how many, but they're dead. All dead."

Gideon's stomach plummeted, his fears confirmed. "Can you tell me where? We need to see what has happened."

"I'll go with you."

When she tried to stand up, he supported her until she regained her balance. He wanted her to stay right where she was, safe within the walls of the keep, but he knew better than to try to stop her from going. The horses were her life's work, the wealth of her clan.

"Kane, saddle our horses. We'll join you shortly. I'll want you to come with us. Averel, you stay here. Post extra guards. I'll send Scim aloft to scout ahead for us. This could be a distraction to draw us out before another attack."

The young warrior took off at a run. Kane lingered long enough to pat Merewen on the shoulder, offering his own bit of rough comfort.

When Gideon was sure Merewen could stand on her own, he strapped on his sword. Then he offered her his arm for support as they hurried down the steps to the great hall below. He caught the attention of one of the servants.

"Tell Lady Alina that Lady Merewen, Lord Kane, and I have business to attend to out on the plains. I'm not sure when we'll return. After you speak to her, tell the cook that we'll be gone and not to hold the evening meal."

"Yes, Captain."

Good to his word, Kane was waiting out near the gate with the horses saddled and ready. After giving Merewen a boost up onto her mare, Gideon mounted Kestrel. Kane led the way out of the gate on Rogue, who was Gideon's stallion's rival for the mares that ran free on the grasslands.

Once they were clear of the keep, the three horses needed no urging to break into a full gallop, nor did they require direction. Merewen's gods had gifted her with a magical connection with the horses under her care.

Right now, with her face so pale with pain and grief, Gideon thought it more of a curse than a gift. Someone would pay for hurting Merewen this badly. Maybe not today, but soon Gideon would hunt down the proper target for his fury.

And when he did, blood would run.

Chapter 6

Duncan gritted his teeth as the elderly herbalist tended his wound. He suspected her real talent was for torture rather than healing, but at least she was thorough. She'd scrubbed the wound clean and then poured some foul potion over it that scalded his skin.

And all of it was for naught. By tomorrow, the wound should heal on its own. In two days, the scar would have faded enough to look years old, but he said nothing. Lady Lavinia already doubted his story about being a scribe in need of work. He couldn't risk finding out what she'd do if she learned he was something more than human.

At least he didn't have to feign how much it hurt. Lady Lavinia kept her gaze averted unless she thought he wouldn't notice. Didn't she have more important things to do than watch him getting his leg stitched up? He was at enough of a disadvantage sitting there with his pants down without having an audience, especially when that onlooker was an attractive woman.

At long last, Sister Berta snipped the thread. "Now, young man, you'll need to keep that wound dry and clean for at least two days to give it a chance to heal."

Young man, indeed. He was older than Berta by centuries, but that was his secret to keep. He watched as she tottered across the room to the shelves full of jars and bundles of dried herbs. After picking up and then discarding several, she found the jar she'd been looking for and added it to a stack of clean cloths she'd set out earlier.

"Leave it open to the air when you can. Then use this twice a day when you replace the bandage."

"I will, Sister Berta. Thank you for your kindness."

She patted him on the cheek. "You were a good patient."

He bit back a grin and set the bundle of supplies she had handed him down on the bench beside him while he righted his clothing. Lavinia immediately looked away while Berta watched his every move, probably to make sure he didn't need assistance.

Finally, he braced himself for a new onslaught of pain and pushed himself up to his feet. It was nothing he hadn't experienced dozens of times before, but that didn't mean he relished the experience.

Lavinia joined him at the door. "I would speak to you about what happened in the hall. My office is close by if you are up to walking that far."

There was no way to avoid the conversation, but what he really wanted was an opportunity to check through Rubar's possessions. He waited until they'd left the infirmary behind.

"I will walk that far."

If it killed him. Right now the pain made that seem likely. Odd. Normally, no matter how horrific the wound, the pain always faded quickly. It was one of the few positives about being one of the Damned, allowing them to fight on when other men would've been screaming in the dirt. This time, though, his leg was on fire, the burning bone-deep all the way from his hip to his ankle.

He did his best to ignore it as he hobbled down the passageway, trying to keep up with his companion. Right now he needed to ask her a question—a favor, really. Aiming for his best guess as to how a humble scribe might approach the problem, he kept his voice low and soft. "My lady, might I make a suggestion?"

She shot him a dark look. "Humble doesn't suit you at all, Sir Duncan. Besides, the scribes I am acquainted with don't wield a weapon with such skill, and most knights I've met are barely literate."

He should've known she wouldn't have achieved the rank of abbess at such a young age without being a good judge of people, not to mention possessing a fierce intellect. Still, he was mildly insulted by her assessment of his abilities.

At this point it would serve no purpose to deny that he'd won his spurs, so he didn't bother to try. "I assure you, my lady, that I am both literate and capable of performing all the usual duties of a scribe."

She stopped to give him a considering look. "Perhaps later you'll explain to me why a swordsman of your skill would want to seek employment with a pen rather than your blade. If you're in need of money, a warrior would earn far more than a scribe."

The number of men who had died upon his sword didn't bear thinking about. "Perhaps the reason is as simple as a preference for spilling ink rather than spilling blood."

That truth cut a little too close to the bone for comfort. Rather than linger there, he started walking again, leaving Lavinia to follow as she would.

When she caught up with him, she laid her hand on his arm. "Your suggestion. What is it?"

It was the lightest of touches, but its impact on him was fierce. Suddenly, his leg wasn't the only part of his body that was making it difficult to walk. He stared down into her face. The plain gray robes did nothing to disguise her beauty. Now wasn't the time for such thoughts, especially about her. He tried to concentrate on the real problem at hand.

"Could you ask that all of Rubar's possessions and

those of the other guard be brought somewhere they can be examined? The clothing they were wearing as well."

She looked at him with a great deal of suspicion. "I can, but what do you hope to find?"

He gave her the only answer he could. "I'll tell you as soon as I know."

Within minutes Duncan was settled in Lavinia's office, staring through the window at a truly amazing garden. What it lacked in size, it certainly made up for in a riot of color and variety. He would've been quite content to find a book and sit out there, reading for hours on end.

It was unlikely Lady Lavinia would invite a man, especially one she held in such obvious distrust, to share her private garden. With all of her responsibilities, she probably hoarded the hours of peace that could be found there. It was what he would have done.

Interesting. He moved closer to the window. The metal stand in the center of the garden held a bowl, perhaps one meant to lure birds with a drink of water. If so, why was it covered with a black cloth?

A noise caught his attention. Duncan cocked his head to the side to listen. Footsteps were headed in this direction. He stepped back from the window and returned to the chair the abbess had offered him. He wouldn't want her to think he'd abused her trust by snooping around in her office.

When the door opened, he was leaning back, his eyes closed as if he were enjoying a few minutes of rest.

"Sir Duncan, are you awake?"

Once again he fought against the urge to smile. She was testing him, hoping to catch him in a moment of weakness.

He opened his eyes and offered her a small smile. "Just plain Duncan will do, Lady Lavinia."

"Fine then, Just Plain Duncan. I have arranged to

have all of Rubar's possessions and weapons brought to one of our workrooms."

She stalked around the end of her desk to sit down. "I don't know what you expect to find, but I hope it is worth offending the trader clans. I have asked Musar and his wife to join us so they can assure their people that we mean no disrespect."

If the situation had not been so dire, Duncan would've enjoyed sparring with the lady. As it was, he needed to reassure her that his intentions were to clear the names of the two guards.

"Although I didn't know the second guard, I had nothing but respect for Rubar."

He sat up straighter in the chair and stretched his leg out, trying without success to find a comfortable position. "He went out of his way to befriend me. He was also one of the few who did not feel the need to ward off evil every time I walked by."

At least Lavinia didn't wince or avoid looking at his paler-than-death eyes as so many others did. "Back in the dining hall you made it clear that you believe Rubar wasn't in control of his own actions."

Duncan met her doubt head-on. "Someone used both men as weapons aimed directly at you. We need to learn how that was done and by whom."

"How do you know they weren't trying to get to Musar and Ava? They were seated right beside me."

He didn't blame her for asking the question, but he'd already considered that option and rejected it.

"If Rubar wanted to kill Musar, he would've had plenty of opportunity while they were on the road. Staging an accident could be arranged easily enough or even slipping poison into the trader's food."

He wished he could offer her a less frightening answer. "I've gone over what happened in my head. Both men were hunting for you. If they'd been after the trader or his wife, logically they would've approached them from the other end of the table."

She wanted to argue; he could see it in her eyes. Then she shook her head. "Before we jump to hasty conclusions, we'll go through their belongings."

Her tone made it clear that she didn't hold out much hope that they'd find any answers by rooting through Rubar's clothing and possessions. He was as reluctant as she was, but for different reasons. It was yet another foul violation of the friendship that Rubar offered Duncan from the instant they'd met.

And how had he repaid the man? With a sword through his gut. The guard's face would be added to the long list of those that haunted Duncan's dreams. And when a man slept for decades at a stretch, he spent a lot of time with his regrets.

The sound of someone knocking dragged Duncan back to the moment at hand. Lavinia opened the door to reveal Musar.

He gave an awkward bow. "We have brought everything to the workroom as you asked. Sister Berta will prepare the two men for burial, but she thought you might want to examine their bodies before she proceeds."

Lavinia glanced at Duncan. He nodded, although he wasn't sure what could be learned when the cause of death was already known.

"Very well." Musar sighed. "I will stand in for the dead men's families to ensure our customs are honored."

"I would appreciate that, Musar. We'll do that first so that you can reassure your people that their friends will receive the honor and care due them."

She stepped past him and led the way back to the infirmary. Duncan hadn't actually been invited, but he followed them anyway.

The two men had both been stripped of their bloody clothes and covered with muslin. Lavinia slowed to a stop and bowed her head as if praying. Duncan suspected it was also her way of postponing what needed to be done.

He allowed her a few seconds to collect herself and then stepped over to where Rubar lay on the same bench where Berta had stitched up Duncan's wound. He pulled down the sheet as far as Rubar's waist. The fatal wound was jagged and ugly. He swallowed hard and continued his examination.

It didn't take long. There were no unexpected marks on either man. He gently pulled the sheets back up to cover the bodies, aware the whole time of Musar and Lavinia watching his every move.

Lavinia stepped closer to him. "Did you find anything?"

Duncan shook his head. "No, but I didn't expect to. If there'd been some physical reason for Rubar to attack, he could've done so at any time over the past few days, but Rubar acted completely normal right up until dinner."

"Very well, then. Shall we move on to the workroom?"

The trader nodded. "I will be just a few minutes. I will let my wife know we've finished."

Musar walked out of the infirmary far faster than he'd walked in. Duncan didn't blame him. "Shall we go to the workroom?"

"I should also tell Sister Berta that we're finished in here."

She left Duncan alone with the two men he'd killed. He closed his own eyes and murmured a prayer to the Lord and Lady of the River, asking them to wash the two souls clean of the darkness that had caused their deaths.

"Amen."

Lavinia's softly spoken word startled him. He hadn't realized he'd said the prayer aloud. He schooled his features to reveal nothing of the churning emotions he was feeling at the moment.

Even so, she looked at him as if she were seeing far more than what was on the surface. "You follow the Lord and Lady, then."

It wasn't actually a question, but he nodded anyway. "Yes, I serve them. Is that a problem?"

"Not at all. I find their teachings interesting, but perhaps we should save this discussion for another time. The workroom is just across the hallway."

Ava and the other traders' wives were waiting outside the door. Ava met his gaze, but the others looked away as their fingers moved in the familiar gesture against evil. He was sorry they felt that way about him, but there wasn't much he could do to change their opinions of him.

Besides, Duncan had just killed two of their people. The two men had been the ones in the wrong, but Duncan was the outsider. It was no surprise they'd closed ranks against him.

Inside the workroom, Musar stood on the far side of the table, leaving Lavinia and Duncan free to search through everything the two men had owned. Duncan started with their saddles and tack. He ran his hands over every inch of the well-worn leather and found nothing. No hidden pockets where something might have been stashed.

From there Duncan moved on to the weapons. The swords were good quality, but plain, as were the knives. Functional rather than fancy, meaning Rubar had spent his money on the steel, where it counted.

Next, he went through the small chests that held their extra clothing and a few personal possessions. Still he found nothing that would account for their behavior.

He reached for the pack that Rubar had carried into the abbey's guest quarters. It held the usual kind of items a man who lived on the road would have: a change of clothing, a comb, a bit of soap, and a few other odds and ends. The second man's pack was much the same.

That left only the clothing they'd been wearing at the time of their deaths. The shirts were slashed and bloody, but otherwise unremarkable. The same was true of the pants. Both sets of boots were worn but serviceable. Duncan neatly folded what he could and set it all aside.

When he picked up a coin purse, a shiver of dread cold washed straight up Duncan's arm. He dropped the small leather bag and stepped back.

Lavinia had been standing off to the side, watching his every move but making no effort to assist him. "Duncan, what's wrong?"

"I'm not sure."

He pointed to the bag. "Musar, which man did that belong to?"

The trader squinted to stare at it, still not approaching the table. "It belonged to Teo. That's his mark on the side."

"So you're sure the other one belonged to Rubar?"

Musar studied it in turn. "Yes. Again, that's his mark. You'll find it on almost everything they own. It helps people who live in close quarters like the caravan wagons keep their belongings straight."

Duncan braced himself and picked up the second purse. He immediately felt the same shiver of revulsion. This time, rather than tossing the bag down, he tugged the strings open and dumped the contents out on the table. He did the same with Teo's, keeping the contents in separate piles.

Whatever it was he was feeling, he had no desire to touch it with his bare fingers. He used his knife to sort through the coins in each group. It didn't take long to figure out which token was giving off the dread darkness.

He carefully sorted through Teo's, quickly finding an identical coin. Would the other two people in the room sense the same power in the coins as he did? Perhaps a test was in order. Using the tip of his knife, he arranged five coins from each purse in a row, including the one that he knew to be the source of the problem.

"Lady Lavinia, would you please come closer? You, too, Musar."

When they were flanking him, he said, "Don't touch any of the coins. Simply hold your hand over them and tell me what you sense."

As soon as Lavinia had her hand in position, her face turned pale. She jerked her arm back down to her side, wiping her palm on her robes as if it felt unclean. Musar was a little slower to react, but in the end he pointed at the right coin. He looked a bit stunned.

"What is that?"

"Those two coins have been ensorcelled. I suspect it was Teo who brought them into the abbey."

He glanced at Musar. "I mean no disrespect. Someone gave him those coins deliberately, but the spell wasn't triggered until he entered the abbey. He wouldn't have sensed anything until then."

Lavinia was noticeably quiet. What was she thinking?

Something niggled at the back of his mind, something about a coin. Finally, it came to him. "Earlier this evening, Rubar and Teo were joking about a bet they'd made. Nothing huge, just the kind of wager men who are friends will make with each other. Something silly, like who can hit the center of a target with his knife. Rubar had won the bet and was nagging Teo to pay him."

He stared down at the two gold coins, identical to the others scattered on the table except for the cold, slippery feel of evil they gave off. "I am thinking that Teo paid off the wager with one of these coins. I don't know how he came by them, but it was only by chance that it was Rubar who ended up with the coin."

It was ever more clear that Rubar had been the true innocent in all of this. Grief tasted bitter on Duncan's tongue. Then he noticed Musar's hand reaching out to snatch the coin. Duncan grabbed his arm and pushed the trader back against the wall, putting himself directly between him and the table.

The man struggled against the hold Duncan had on him. He was no match for the strength of one of the Damned, but he was no weakling, either. If Musar managed to grab the coin, there was no telling what he would do. If he attacked Lavinia, Duncan would defend her, and the last thing he wanted to do was kill another man today. He already bore the burden of two innocent souls.

Lavinia caught Musar's arm with both hands and kept him from reaching past Duncan.

"Musar, stop! You risk the same fate as your men if you touch those coins!"

By then, the trader's eyes were wild, making it unlikely that mere words would get past the craving that had taken control of him. Duncan did the only thing he could. He stepped back far enough to give himself room to maneuver and slugged the trader with every bit of strength he had in him.

Musar stumbled back against the wall as his eyes rolled up in his head. Then he sank to the floor in an ungraceful heap. At least for the moment he was safe from the trap of the coins.

Duncan flexed his hand and stared down at the unconscious trader. "We need to get him out of here. We also need to search the rest of the caravan to make sure no one else has one of these coins. Do you agree?"

"Yes, I do."

Lavinia stared at Duncan, her eyes narrowed in suspicion as she backed away from him. "You know a great deal about magic for a man who claims to be a lowly scribe. Why is the magic not affecting you? You can sense it, but it doesn't call to you as it did to Musar."

He had no time for such games and followed her step for step. "I wasn't the target of the attack. You were. If I hadn't been there tonight, we wouldn't be having this discussion at all. You'd be dead."

"We still have no proof that this was anything other than a random attack."

He wanted to shake her, to make her realize the danger she was in. "Lie to yourself if you will, but don't bother lying to me."

She flinched as he continued to batter her with his words. "This kind of magic doesn't come cheaply. Someone spilled innocent blood to create the spell in those coins. I might have my own secrets, but I'm guessing you do as well."

Before she could respond, Musar moaned. They needed to get him out of the room before the coins asserted their influence on him again.

Duncan backed away from the abbess, mad at himself for having lost his temper and madder at her for refusing to admit the truth that was right before her eyes.

"Let's get Musar out of here, and then decide how best to destroy those coins."

Lavinia nodded, slowly regaining her normal air of authority. "We'll take him to my office."

The two of them hefted Musar up off the floor and muscled him back out of the workroom. Once they had him settled in the chair in Lavinia's office, Duncan started for the door.

"Where do you think you are going?" Lavinia's words cracked like a whip.

He looked back at her. "I was going to fetch his wife to see to him. When he's feeling better, we'll need to search the caravan."

"Fine, but you and I will do the searching. I don't want to place anyone else at risk."

She poured Musar a glass of water as she spoke. "And when we're done, you and I have a lot to talk about."

He bowed his head slightly. "Indeed we do."

Chapter 7

Merewen didn't need the carrion birds circling high overhead to know where to look for the dead horses. Their familiar presence was gone, leaving nothing but a cold blank space where their life force used to be. Her mare refused to take another step closer to the grassy knoll up ahead. Even Gideon and Kane struggled to control their mounts.

Finally, the three humans dismounted and left the horses behind. Merewen wished she could remain with them, but that was the coward's way out. She owed it to the horses, both living and dead, to investigate what had happened.

From where they stood, they had clear visibility for a mile in all directions, and it appeared they were alone. Gideon and Kane positioned themselves on either side of her, swords drawn. She understood their need to find a target for their anger, something solid to fight.

The pain in her head had faded enough that she could concentrate. She started up the final rise to where she could already see the first horse sprawled in the grass. There would be more; how many, she couldn't tell. When the attack had come, she'd sensed ten, maybe fifteen horses in full panic, all in pain and stampeding out of control.

She could only pray that they hadn't lost the entire

band of mares. Bracing herself for the worst, she walked up the steep slope. Gideon wrapped his free arm around her shoulders, offering his support.

The sight in front of her was a horror to behold, stealing her breath and robbing her limbs of strength. When she cried out, Gideon spun her around so that she wasn't looking at the bodies that littered the hilltop.

It helped that she could sense Gideon's own outrage at the atrocity. Gradually, she regained control, suppressing the emotions that would not serve her well at the moment. Grief would have to wait until later.

She forced herself to turn back, to count the dead. One, two, three, four, with three more a short distance away twisted in a tangle of bodies and legs. Starting with the closest corpse, she did a quick examination, trying to determine the cause of death. While she worked, Gideon and Kane split up to circle the hilltop, each studying the ground on his side.

Gideon reached the far end first. "Kane, did you find anything?"

The other warrior had knelt down to get a closer look at something in the grass, but he shook his head. "Nothing useful. All the tracks likely belong to these horses. No sign of any human footprints. No blood. Nothing that would explain their deaths."

When the warrior stood up, he scrubbed at the mage mark on his face. "We're too exposed up here. We shouldn't linger."

Gideon started back toward her. "Merewen, what can you tell us?"

Reluctantly, she touched each of the first three horses in turn, hating that their bodies were still warm, that they looked as if they would eventually wake up and return to their grazing. But no, they were dead, murdered by some terrible means that left no mark. She'd sensed this magic once before after a bolt of lightning had struck Gideon's falcon avatar, sending Scim plummeting from the sky. The black chilling residue of the spell left her stomach queasy.

"It has the same feel as the magic that almost killed Scim. It's blood magic and meant to destroy whatever it touches. Kane, do you agree?"

The dark warrior joined her, standing over the closest mare. He slowly bent down to run his fingers along the horse's chest and then up the neck. When he touched the forehead, he jerked his hand back and wiped it on his tunic with a look of disgust.

"It's the same, only far stronger. If this much power had hit Scim, he would've died instantly."

She had more horses to check. When she got close enough to get a look at the last carcass, she gasped. "Gideon, this is the mare that delivered a colt the day my uncle attacked our keep."

Fear for the foal had her spinning in all directions, looking for some sign the young animal had survived the attack. "Do you see him anywhere?"

The two men circled the area, but with no success. Where could he have gone? Had he been taken? No, that made no sense. Humans would've left their mark on the hilltop.

She closed her eyes and reached out to Kestrel and then Rogue, sending pictures of the foal and asking for their help with images rather than words. The two stallions snorted and stamped their feet before separating to do their own hunt. It didn't take long.

Rogue whinnied loud enough to draw his rider's attention. "Down there." Kane pointed toward a small stand of bushes at the base of the hill.

Merewen half ran, half skipped down the steep slope. At the bottom, she slowed to a walk, unable to force herself to move faster, reluctant to find out the colt had suffered the same fate as his dam. On the other hand, if the colt was alive, she didn't want to startle him into bolting.

Gideon yelled, "Wait for us."

She ignored him. If there was danger, the horses would let her know. Both Kane and Gideon quickly joined her, each with his back to her as they scanned the area for any threats. Kestrel hung back, but then stallions didn't take care of their young. They protected the band as a whole.

It was Rogue who was acting out of character. He stood close by, watching her every move with obvious suspicion. When one of the bushes shook, she jumped. Both of her self-appointed guards turned, ready to fight.

"Sorry, the movement startled me."

She waited until they relaxed slightly before continuing forward. To her surprise, Rogue joined her at the last minute, poking his big head over the top of the bushes as the colt stepped into sight. Ignoring her, he lifted up his nose to sniff at Rogue.

The big stallion snorted but stood rock still, letting the young animal get used to his presence. Finally, the colt limped forward to stand near Rogue, trembling as he stared at the three humans. Merewen's heart leapt in surprised joy at the unexpected sight of the scarred stallion standing guard over the small colt.

Smiling and pitching her voice low and calm, she crooned, "I need to see how badly you've been injured, little one."

The colt shivered and tried to retreat, but Rogue blocked his way. Merewen knelt down and checked the colt from nose to tail. He was fine except for being hungry and having a slightly strained foreleg.

"No broken bones." She backed away to consider the options. "We need to get him back to the stable master so Jarod can take care of him."

She considered the distance back to the keep. With his leg hurt, it was unlikely the foal would be able to walk that far.

Kane's deep voice gave her the answer. "I'll carry him on Rogue."

An hour earlier she would've denied that was possible, but the stallion had obviously decided the young animal was his to protect.

"Gideon, can you help me lift the colt?"

He nodded and sheathed his sword. She held the colt to prevent the small animal from trying to run off while Kane mounted Rogue. Then the two of them lifted the foal high enough to settle him across Kane's lap. The little fellow was clearly not happy, but quickly calmed down when Kane wrapped his arms around him and held him close.

Rogue started back toward the keep, keeping his pace slow and easy. It would take far longer to return home, but she wouldn't begrudge one minute of the time. Saving one small life didn't make up for losing the others, but it was a start.

And when she found out who had killed those beautiful, innocent animals, there would be a reckoning in Agathia.

Murdoch stood out on the small balcony that overlooked the bailey below. Definite progress had been made on rebuilding the stable in the past few days. He wished he had the strength to be down there helping. There was something good and clean about swinging a hammer, pounding a nail in to hold two pieces of wood together. It was a simple act of pure creation that could stand for decades beyond the lifetime of the men who built it.

"Should you be out of bed?"

He didn't bother to look back over his shoulder. "I can stand." Which didn't really answer the question. "And I won't get stronger flat on my back in bed."

"At least sit down."

The worry in Alina's voice hurt him more than the wound in his gut, and possibly did more damage. It was Murdoch's duty, his calling, to protect her. Instead, when he'd crawled out of his sickbed, he stumbled more than walked this far, his muscles weak and shaky.

Alina had saved him in the attack; she'd thrown herself between Murdoch and her husband's blade to offer up her life for his. If one of the enemy fighters hadn't jumped forward to take the blow himself, Alina would've died, pinned to Murdoch's body with her husband's sword.

The nightmare images played out in his mind whether he was asleep or awake. Right now, she crept closer, unsure of her welcome. He stood his ground, averting his eyes despite how much he craved the sight of her.

"Gideon and Kane rode out with Lady Merewen. Do you know what was wrong?"

Alina finally joined him out on the balcony, clinging to the far side of the small space. "From what Averel told me, Merewen and Gideon were in their quarters when she suddenly started screaming."

Alina glanced toward Murdoch. "Someone attacked the horses out on the grasslands. That's all we know at this point."

The news didn't surprise him. It was just one more thing he couldn't do anything about. "Would you send for Averel and ask him to see me?"

She studied him for a long second, her gray eyes seeing far more than he liked. "Why?"

If he confessed the real reason, she'd likely refuse. On the other hand, he hated the idea of lying to her about anything. She'd been mistreated enough by a man who should've cherished her. He spit out the truth before he could stop himself.

"I need to walk for a while to build up my strength, but I don't know how far my legs will carry me. Averel can make himself useful for once and catch me if I fall. Of course if that happens, he'll never let me forget it."

Instead of protesting, Alina actually smiled at him. Nothing he'd said was amusing. "What?"

She closed the distance between them to give him a careful hug. "That is the first time you've sounded like yourself since you were hurt. I'll relay your request to Sir Averel. I'm sure he'll be happy to escort you for a few laps up and down the hall."

She gave him a narrow-eyed look. "Before that, though, you should eat something. I'll have a meal brought up."

Then she was gone.

Women. Did they ever make sense? One minute she was questioning whether he should be out of bed at all, and the next she was almost dancing because of something he said. Rather than ponder a mystery he'd likely never solve, he walked back inside.

He made it as far as the door, which opened out into another room. It held a single bed for the other patient Alina had been tending. From where Murdoch stood, the man appeared to be asleep, but his breathing pattern gave him away. He was alert and well aware of Murdoch's approach.

"Give it up, man. I know you're awake."

Slowly, the duke's man turned his head in Murdoch's direction, his eyes cold with a predator's gaze. "What do you want?"

Under other circumstances, Murdoch would've wanted him dead. But regardless of what the man had done in the service of his master, Duke Keirthan, he had saved Alina's life and quite possibly Murdoch's as well. For that he owed the bastard.

"I want to know why."

The trooper gave him a blank look. "Why what?"

Murdoch curled his hands into fists, wishing he had a

suitable target for his frustration. Well, he did, but he wouldn't hit a man who couldn't even sit up, much less stand on his own two feet. Murdoch yanked a chair over beside the bed and slowly lowered himself down. When he was seated, he tried again.

He enlarged upon his question, spitting out each word slowly and clearly. "Why did you betray your liege lord? The man is a bastard and not worthy of a warrior's loyalty, but yet you served him."

The trooper closed his eyes and turned away. Murdoch thought he was going to refuse to answer. Finally, the man turned back, the expression in his eyes bleak.

"I'll tell you the same thing I told your captain: I don't know."

Murdoch could imagine how well that answer would have settled with Gideon. "You don't know why you not only betrayed Duke Keirthan but also Lord Fagan, the man the duke sent you to defend?"

The man flinched as Murdoch's words lashed at him, his pale skin flushed as if feverish. He clutched the top of his blanket, his knuckles white with the effort.

"And you know for certain that I served these men?"

Murdoch nodded. "You were seen leading the duke's forces, and you wore his symbol on a chain around your neck."

"So I'm a traitor, a man without honor."

On one level, Murdoch agreed with his assessment, but something about the man's reaction rang wrong somehow. He needed more information.

"I would hear your version of the events of the other night."

The trooper stirred restlessly, trying to push himself up. Murdoch leaned forward and helped stuff another pillow under his head. He understood the need to not appear helpless. He hated that they had even that much in common.

When he was settled again, the trooper said, "I will tell you what I know. It's not much."

Leaning back in his chair, Murdoch crossed his arms over his chest. "I'm listening."

"I'm a soldier. I know this to be true because of the calluses I have on my hands." He showed Murdoch his palms. "These tell me that I am a trained swordsman, but not if I'm any good."

Murdoch conceded that much. "I myself didn't see you fight, but they tell me you wore the uniform of an officer. I doubt that means you were incompetent."

The trooper took that much in and nodded before he continued. "If you and your captain are to be believed, I served a man named Duke Keirthan, and through him, Lord Fagan, although I don't know why."

He was making no sense. "How could you not know something as simple as who it is you serve?"

Again, another long pause. "Believe me or not, but the memory of my life began when I awoke in this bed. I cannot recall anything about my life prior to that minute."

He stared up at the ceiling as if hoping to find answers there. "I remember nothing of the battle that brought me here or what I've done that would make me your enemy. However, I understand that I am your prisoner and will face judgment for my acts."

This time when he looked at Murdoch, his expression appeared unnaturally calm. "But if you want explanations, I have none to offer. I remember nothing of my life, nothing of *me*. Not even my own name."

Murdoch wasn't sure he believed the man. In fact, he didn't want to, but the glint of fear in the trooper's eyes gave the weight of truth to his outrageous claim. It didn't change the fact that the man had served the duke and had no doubt killed good men as part of that service.

Maybe he deserved to die for his crimes, but not if he

didn't know what he'd done or why. In the past, Murdoch had known other soldiers who suffered temporary confusion after a blow to the head. The trooper showed no sign of a head wound, but that didn't matter; the results were the same.

Murdoch didn't have it in him to see the man executed for crimes he didn't remember committing. Once his memory returned—if it returned—there would be time enough to decide the trooper's fate.

"I believe you, although I'm not sure why I should." He considered the possibilities. "I will ask Captain Gideon to withhold judgment until such time as your memory returns."

"And if it doesn't?"

"Then we will let the gods decide your fate." Murdoch pushed himself back up to his feet, ignoring the tugging pain of his stomach wound.

He paused before leaving. "Until then, what would you like to be called?"

The trooper gave it some thought. When he answered, it was with the first spark of humor Murdoch had seen in his expression. "Call me Sigil. Since we don't know my real name, it seems proper for me to be known simply by the duke's symbol that I wore."

Murdoch offered his own hint of a smile in return. "Sigil it is then. We will speak again."

As he walked away, Sigil murmured, "I'm sure we will."

Then in a louder voice, he called out, "Can I know your name as well? And who it is that you and Captain Gideon serve?"

"I am called Murdoch. We are the Damned, avatars of the gods." With that happy thought, he returned to his room to await his dinner.

Chapter 8

$\mathcal{A}$ll Duncan wanted was to seek out his bed in the guest quarters and lie down. Blood still oozed through the stitches in his leg, and the surrounding flesh was swollen and raw. Maybe the ointment the herbalist had given him would help, but he hadn't had time to apply it since she'd closed the wound.

Spending several hours searching through the caravan hadn't helped either his injury or his mood. Granted, he didn't particularly care what the trader and his people thought of him. He'd killed two of their own and didn't expect to be welcomed with open arms.

However, considering he'd prevented the assassination of Lady Lavinia, the least they could do was wait until he was out of sight to start warding off evil. But no, as he approached each wagon, the owner went through all the motions, only to repeat them again as soon as Duncan walked away.

Maybe it wouldn't have made him so angry if Lavinia hadn't been there to witness their behavior. He needed her to trust him enough to allow him access to the abbey's library. Otherwise he would have failed Gideon and his friends. How likely was he to succeed on his mission when everyone around him thought he was the spawn of darkness?

Night had fallen several hours ago, but Musar had insisted that the search be finished so the caravan could leave at first light. The trader wanted them to ensure that his clan wouldn't carry the evil with them when they returned to their winter homes. While Duncan and Lavinia searched the wagons, Rubar and the other guard were quietly buried in the small cemetery in the valley below. Later, after the traders were gone, Duncan would pay his respects to the two men.

When they'd finally finished with the last wagon, the abbess had asked him to wait in her office, although she didn't say why. Perhaps it was because they still needed to determine what to do with the tainted coins. Earlier, they'd locked them away in a heavy steel box, where they should stay for now, for safety. It was far too dangerous to deal with magical artifacts of such power at night. According to the memories his friend Kane had shared with the Damned, blood magery was born of darkness and was at its peak strength during the night. No, it would be better to take action in the bright light of day.

So there he sat, unsure of what else needed to be said tonight, although he had his suspicions. It was unlikely that Musar's remaining guards would appreciate sharing quarters with the man who killed two of their own.

The only question was if Lavinia would offer Duncan another room or if she'd order him to ride out immediately. He still needed to persuade her to let him look through the library before she turned him away from the abbey. He settled back in the chair and let his eyes close. These few minutes might be the only rest he'd get for hours to come.

"Sir Duncan, wake up."

A hand on his shoulder giving him a bit of a shake jerked him back to consciousness. He blinked several times and looked around to remind himself of where he was—in Lavinia's office. The candles on the wall had burned down a good inch since he'd drifted off.

Lavinia waited until he sat up straighter to speak. "I'm sorry I kept you waiting so long. I'm sure you're exhausted."

"It has been a long day for you as well."

The dark circles under her eyes were proof of that. She'd managed to get through everything without breaking down, but the whole affair had taken its toll on her. He was used to people wanting to kill him. He doubted she was.

The thought had Duncan wanting to put his arms around her to keep her safe from all threats. Although he hardly knew the abbess, something in her quiet dignity spoke to him. Yet he doubted the gesture would be appreciated. He settled for asking, "Are you all right?"

Her smile didn't last long. "I will be, especially after a good night's sleep."

He understood the sentiment. "About that. Do you think Sister Berta would mind if I slept in the infirmary tonight? I would rather not force my presence on Musar's men if I can help it. I'm sure Musar has forbidden them to come after me, but I would rather not provoke them unnecessarily. They've been through enough."

"Actually, I've already given the matter some thought." Lavinia bit her lower lip. "If it's all right with you, I'd rather you not sleep in the infirmary. That would be the next logical place for them to look."

She picked up a lantern off her desk. "If you'll follow me, I'll take you to a room that I doubt any of Musar's clan knows about. I had Sister Joetta move your belongings while Musar and the others were at the funeral."

"I appreciate your forethought."

He stood up, doing his best to ignore the fresh stab of pain when he put his full weight on his injured leg. Lavinia started toward him, but he waved her off.

"I'm fine." Or he would be when he could lie down.

She didn't appear to believe him, but she allowed him his pride. "We don't have far to go."

She led him outside through her private garden where the night air was heavy with the perfume of roses and night-blooming lilies. He drew a deep breath. The rich scents reminded him of his mother in a way. She'd loved flowers of all kinds, something else about her that his father had never understood. To him, a plant was worthless unless it provided feed for animals or humans. He'd thought it foolish to value something simply for its beauty.

Duncan started forward again. Now was certainly not the time to get lost in his past. Those events were centuries old and the people involved had long since turned to dust. For the Damned, the present was all that mattered. They had been called here for a purpose, and their faithful service might at last provide them respite from their damnation.

Lavinia stopped at a narrow doorway hidden behind a trellis covered in a thick vine. She pressed her palm against the smooth wood. "Put your hand beside mine."

When he did as she asked, she adjusted the position of his hand slightly, the warmth of her touch against his skin far more distracting than it should've been. As she murmured a few words, a gentle tingle started in his fingertips and spread up his arm.

Magic! His first instinct was to jerk his hand back, although it was already too late. She'd already invoked the spell, but as with Lady Merewen's gift with horses, Lavinia's incantation didn't bear the stench of dark magic. In fact, the sensation was almost pleasant.

When she finished speaking, there was a soft click as the door swung open, and he could again move his hand. Lavinia lifted the lantern higher to illuminate the room beyond. He half expected the air to be stale and the walls covered in cobwebs, but instead everything was fresh and clean.

For a few seconds, they both remained in the doorway as Duncan studied the room before them. There was a narrow bed along one wall beside some shelves, and his belongings had been left in the corner on the floor. On the other side were a table and chair. Judging from the stack of blank paper, a jar of pens and brushes, as well as various bottles of ink, the room was intended to be used by a scribe.

Perfect.

Lavinia walked ahead of him to set the lantern down on the table. "Will this do for tonight?"

"It is far nicer than I expected."

"Tomorrow we will decide what to do about the coins. Afterward, we can talk about your duties here at the abbey."

"So you've decided that I can stay."

"For now. You may change your mind after I explain what I have in mind for you."

She looked around one last time, the light bathing her beauty in a soft glow. It was only with great effort that he could turn his gaze back to the room itself.

"For now, is there anything else you need?"

Her. The kindness of such a beautiful woman toward him offered temptation almost beyond his control. Duncan slammed the door on that line of thinking. He had no right to be thinking of her that way, even if he'd give anything to know if that lush mouth tasted as sweet as it looked.

"I'll be fine."

"Then I shall see you in the morning. The door and that window are both warded against anyone but me and you."

Interesting to discover the magic she wielded did have an edge to it. But surely the Lord and Lady of the River, the gods he served, would've warned him if her gift was tainted by evil. He felt no misgivings in her presence. Quite the contrary, in fact.

"I will go now. My personal quarters are on the other

side of the courtyard." She pointed to the door on the far wall.

"Thank you, my lady. You've been more than generous."

"You are welcome."

She stepped back out into the courtyard but paused to look back at him. "It is just an indication of how tired I am that I cannot remember if I thanked you for saving my life. If not, please accept my gratitude. It was a miracle of the gods that you were here when I most needed a champion."

That had him smiling. Little did she know.

"Sleep well, Lavinia."

She smiled. "You as well, Just Plain Duncan."

Then she was gone, leaving him standing there grinning after her. He made quick work of getting ready for bed. Before blowing out the lantern, he applied a thick layer of the salve to his leg, hissing when it stung. But then a soothing, warm heat spread through his skin and down deep into the muscles, leaving a blessed numbness in its wake.

He stretched out on the bed, happy to be without pain for the first time in hours. As he gave himself over to sleep, his last thought was of the beautiful woman courageous enough to tease one of the Damned.

Lavinia paced the length of her office. Despite the late hour when she'd finally sought her bed, she'd been up at first light to watch Musar and his clan set off. She hated the new tension between them and prayed that time would heal the wound. She didn't fault the trader or his clan for the attack. She didn't even blame the two men who'd actually come at her with swords.

However, she wasn't so sure that in some manner Musar didn't blame her, and perhaps he'd be right about that. She no longer doubted the attack had been aimed at her. If his men hadn't come into contact with her, they might have lived long lives with their honor unquestioned.

She had her suspicions about the source of the dark magic, but that was her secret. Soon, with Duncan's assistance, she would see what she could do to destroy the coins.

Not that she completely trusted Duncan. There was far more to the man than he wanted her to know. Part of what she felt was a straightforward reaction to a handsome man, but it went beyond that. He carried with him an energy unlike anything she'd ever before experienced, and yet he lacked the feel of any mage she'd encountered.

No, he was more like a conduit for magic, the tool of a more powerful hand.

She shuddered. If that were true, was he controlled by the same mage who had sent the coins out into the land to seek her? Her instincts said no, and she'd told Duncan the truth last night. The wards she'd placed on his quarters were intended to keep anyone other than herself and him out. What she hadn't told him was that she'd also set the ward to keep him in. If he'd tried to leave the room, he would've been rendered unconscious until she arrived to release him.

But he'd slept through the night. She'd removed that half of the wards when she first awoke. For now, she couldn't afford to treat him as a prisoner. When she learned more of his true purpose in coming to the abbey, she'd decide how to proceed.

The door to her office opened just far enough to let her novice peek in. "Lady Lavinia? Was I supposed to meet you here instead of in the library?"

Lavinia wanted to bang her head for forgetting, but she carefully schooled her expression. "No, Sarra, the mistake is mine. I should've sent word to Sister Joetta that I would need to cancel our class this morning."

Sarra's hopeful look faded. "I understand."

Lavinia motioned for her to come in. "I'm sorry. I would far rather spend the time with you."

Duncan's deep voice joined the discussion, startling both females. "Instead, she has to put up with me. I apologize for usurping your time with the abbess."

Sarra, who had little reason to trust men, scooted closer to Lavinia. Duncan kept his distance and did his best to look harmless. Lavinia thought it likely that he recognized Sarra's reaction for what it meant and appreciated his attempt to reassure the girl.

The little girl stared at him with something akin to fear in her eyes. "You're the man who killed those two bad men last night. The ones who wanted to hurt Lady Lavinia. Are you glad they died? I am."

He flinched but nodded. Then he stepped closer and knelt down so that he didn't tower over Sarra.

"We haven't been introduced. My name is Duncan."

"My new name is Sarra. It used to be Elizabeth."

When the little girl realized what she'd said, her eyes grew round. "Sorry. I wasn't supposed to say that. My name is Sarra. My old name is a secret, so can you forget I said it? It's important."

To give Duncan credit, he took the little girl seriously. "I'm very good at keeping secrets, Sarra. You honor me by trusting me with yours."

Sarra looked to Lavinia for reassurance. What could she do but nod?

Duncan went on talking, his expression grave. "Sarra, those were not bad men. Someone else tricked them. I stopped them the only way I could, but their deaths make me sad, not happy. I wish there had been some other way to keep them from hurting Lady Lavinia. I know that's hard to understand, but I hope you believe me."

Sarra's small body thrummed with tension. "But bad men killed my father and stole my mother. I hate them."

There was such sadness in Duncan's pale eyes. He reached out to touch Sarra's cheek. "That's understandable, little one."

To Lavinia's amazement, Sarra responded by giving Duncan a hug. Since coming to the abbey, she had avoided any contact with the few men who passed through. Clearly Duncan had passed some test for Sarra to respond to him in such a way. It was something to think about. For now, Lavinia had pressing business with the man.

"Sarra, I promise to spend time with you when I can, but right now Sir Duncan and I have work to do. Why don't you go see if Sister Joetta has time to work on your music?"

The little girl immediately dropped into a low curtsy. "May I be excused?"

"Yes, you may."

Sarra skipped toward the door, her good mood obviously restored. At the last second, she stopped abruptly to return to Duncan. She frowned, her small mouth a straight line.

Her voice shimmered with power when she spoke, sounding far more adult than it should have. In fact, it was deep and male. "We are sorry you were hurt, Sir Duncan, but trust that you'll find your way back soon and find yourself at peace at long last."

Once the words were spoken, both Sarra's smile and little-girl voice returned. "They wanted you to know that."

Then she skipped away, leaving the two adults staring after her.

Duncan didn't know what to say. For the moment, he delayed responding at all while he rose back up to his feet. His leg wasn't happy with him for putting it through the effort, but the pain helped disguise his shock.

That was three times he'd encountered magic since arriving at the abbey. The little girl's magic didn't feel corrupted as the coins did, but it left him a bit shaken and seriously concerned for Sarra.

"Tell me about her." He glared at Lavinia, making sure she knew it was an order, not a suggestion.

"She came to us a few weeks ago. A passing tinker had found her half starved and alone with her father's corpse. She refused to say a single word for days after being left here at the abbey."

Before continuing, Lavinia walked out into her garden. Duncan followed her and took a seat on the closest bench. The warmth of the sun did little about the chill in Lavinia's words. "From what we've been able to piece together, Duke Keirthan's men came for her mother and killed Sarra's father for defending his wife. It was a good thing he'd hidden Sarra, because I fear they would have taken her as well since strong gifts for magic often run in a family. From what Sarra says, there are voices that tell her things sometimes. It would be easy to doubt the truth of that, but you've heard the proof for yourself."

"Her gift is for telling riddles?"

He massaged his thigh, telling himself that the bite in his words stemmed from the pain from his wound. In truth, Sarra's words left him confused and hurting. He didn't need a reminder that his time was limited. Soon he'd sleep in the river again, which was anything but peaceful.

She shot him a chiding look. "To be truthful, I've never encountered a talent like Sarra's before. Sometimes she simply finds lost objects, saying a voice told her where to look. Other times, she makes a pronouncement like she did for you. I've cautioned her about using great care around others, but most especially in front of strangers. If the voices want her to say something, I've asked that she say it to me first so that I can be the one to relay the message without involving her. This is the first time that she has spoken directly to someone else."

Lavinia had been circling the garden, stopping to touch a flower here and there. "We gave her a new name in hopes of protecting her identity. Nothing will keep her safe for long if it gets out that she speaks for the gods."

Lavinia was right about that. They already knew that Keirthan had been after Lady Merewen because of her rare gift. Even as his power increased, the duke's hunger for more magic and the swath of violence he left across the kingdom grew by the day.

"Sarra's secret is safe with me, but you have good reason to be concerned. I haven't been in Agathia for long, but I do know that her mother is only one of many who have disappeared."

Lavinia spun back to face him. "And what brought you to Agathia, and more specifically, what brought you here to the abbey?"

He'd wondered how long it would take her to get back to that question. Before he laid his truth on the table, though, they had other matters to deal with. He conceded a little ground.

He stood up, crossing to stand right before her. He liked that she failed to be intimidated by his superior height and size. "I have need of your library."

"To what purpose?"

"Research."

"Before I grant you even that much, I want your help in deciding what to do with the coins."

Before he could accept, she added, "It is obvious that even a house of worship isn't safe from attack, and Sarra is not the only one who has sought sanctuary here. Earlier this morning, I gave Musar money to hire some guards for the abbey. Many spend the winter in the town near his winter quarters with nothing to occupy their time until the caravans start up again in the spring. He'll send men he can vouch for, but I want someone I trust to take charge of them."

He certainly hadn't expected that. It was also interesting that she looked away briefly when she said that Sarra wasn't the only one who'd taken refuge from the duke inside the abbey walls. Did that mean Lavinia was one of the others?

For now, he asked, "You trust me?"

This time her eyes locked on to his. "As much as I trust anyone right now."

He wasn't going to lie to her. "I can't promise how long I can remain here. At best, only until my research is complete. But before I leave, I will make sure the men he sends are well trained and trustworthy."

"Then we have a deal, Sir Duncan. Now we should study those coins."

As he followed her out of the garden, she added, "Just know that any time you spend in the library, I will be right there beside you. We don't allow anyone in there unsupervised."

The idea of spending hours upon hours in her company pleased him far more than it should have.

Again, he gave her his truth. "I wouldn't have it any other way."

Chapter 9

The hallway of the abbey had never been this long before. Lavinia was sure of it. Somehow overnight the building had grown in length or else it was the burden of the steel box containing the two coins that made it seem that way. She'd ordered the passageway cleared, reducing the possibility that someone else might be ensorcelled by the curse they carried.

As she and Duncan made their way to the far end of the building, she sensed the other members of the community hovering behind closed doors. More than once she heard someone chanting a prayer of the light as they passed by. She would've preferred to keep the details of the attack secret, but it had happened right in front of everyone. Even so, she would protect the others as best she could.

"How much farther?"

She glanced at her grim-faced companion. He'd insisted on carrying the box, but the effort was taking its toll on him. She thought about offering to take a turn carrying the heavy burden but decided against it. Knowing male pride, she suspected he would refuse. She paused to light a lantern and picked it up. "Not far now."

The passage led deep into the hillside, so there were no windows to let in the sunlight. Normally, it didn't bother her, but today it was as if the weight of the hill pressed down on her shoulders. Did Duncan feel it, too?

At the far end, she pulled out her ring of keys and sorted through them for the correct one. After several tries to turn the key, there was a loud click that echoed up and down the hallway.

The door swung open on well-oiled hinges. She stepped through first, chanting a small spell to ignite the mage lights inside the heavily warded workshop. They flickered to life, the soft blue-white glow chasing the shadows back into the farthest edges of the large room. Next she set the lantern back out in the hallway outside the door. It was never smart to bring flames into the room when there were spells to be invoked.

The dome-shaped ceiling soared a good distance overhead, making the room seem even bigger. In the center stood a round table fashioned out of a single piece of granite. Despite all of the magic that had been wrought upon the stone, its surface still gleamed mirror smooth.

She pointed toward the table. "Set the box there."

Duncan did as she asked, obviously glad to relinquish his burden. He stood beside her, looking around with a worried look. "What is this place?"

"It is circles within circles."

Her answer failed to satisfy him. Clearly he didn't understand the significance of a series of concentric circles. That reassured her. No serious practitioner of magic would've failed to recognize the design and function of the room.

"The hill that surrounds us is the first circle. Next come these curved walls that surround us."

She pointed to a pair of rings made of light green stones set into the darker green floor. "Those form the circles that surround the table, which in turn is a circle itself. According to the oldest chronicles of our order, this room was the reason the abbey was built in this spot. They wanted a safe place to practice magic."

If anything, her answer made him even more unhappy. He stepped closer to the center of the room, his odd eyes taking in everything. He stared at the mage lights for a long time, his mouth set in a grim line. She noted that his hand rested on the grip of his sword as if ready to ward off an attack.

He finally turned to look at her. "And what kind of magic do you practice here? What is its source?"

No answer was far better than a lie. They had business to attend to, business that could not be delayed for the length of time it would take for her to explain who and what she was.

"Duncan, this room will protect us from an attack by whoever created the spell on those coins. It will also contain any backlash we set off by trying to destroy them."

His eyebrows snapped down. "Lady Lavinia, one of these days I hope you will answer my questions directly."

It would be such a relief to be able to truly unburden herself, to share the heavy load that sat squarely on her shoulders, but she couldn't. Far more than just her own life depended on her ability to hold her secrets safe.

"I think we both have reasons to keep our true purposes to ourselves, Sir Duncan. Perhaps it would be best if we did what we came here for."

"Fine. We will get started."

Duncan immediately approached the steel box and held his hand out for the key. She hesitated briefly before letting him take charge but then handed it to him. He'd already proven his ability to resist the pull of the dark magic that had been infused into the coins. She'd yet to touch them directly, but even passing her hand over them had left her skin feeling unclean.

"Before you open that, I need to invoke the wards."

"If you must." His hands were clenched in fists, his knuckles white with the effort. "What do you need me to do?"

Yesterday he'd seemed far more relaxed around the

coins. Why was he so tense now? She kept her own voice calm, her words slow and easy. Magic was unpredictable enough without the clumsiness that stress could bring with it.

"First, remove your weapons and leave them outside in the hall. Keep your smallest knife with you, though. You will want to use it to avoid touching the coins for as long as possible. When you're done, stand next to the table, because the wards are not keyed to you. I will bring up each successive one and then join you in the innermost circle."

Duncan quickly stripped off an alarming number of weapons and piled them out in the hallway. When he was ready, he stood in grim silence as she set to work. She pressed her hands against the wall at the far side of the room. Reaching for the natural power of the dirt and stone and life upon the hillside, she drew its strength into her and then set it free to flow through the structure of the walls that surrounded them. She didn't know if Duncan could feel the pure beauty of all the living force that made up the world, but it washed her spirit clean.

She moved one quarter around the room and knelt to touch the first circle in the floor. The stones flashed brightly before once again fading to their normal color with only a faint sparkle to hint at the power of the ward.

Another quarter turn brought her to the innermost circle. This one flashed even more brightly at her touch. By now, her skin tingled almost to the point of pain from the various layers of magic that held them barricaded inside the circles of power.

Finally she approached the table and placed her hand on its center. She repeated the last invocation twice before the stone's surface shimmered brightly with a flash of fire. When the last bit of energy sank deeply into the stone, she nodded to Duncan.

"Now you may begin."

He studied her for several long seconds. A myriad of questions flashed in his eyes but remained unspoken. Eventually he would give voice to them, and she dreaded that moment. At least he realized that now wasn't the time. He looked away from her with some effort and turned his attention to the table.

His hands steady, Duncan opened the lock and lifted the lid of the box. He inserted the tip of his knife into the loop of the leather thong that held the coin purse closed and lifted it out onto the table. He then closed the box and set it back down on the floor and under the table. Smart man. There was no telling what the magic in those coins could use as a weapon.

Already she could feel the throbbing beat of the dark magic. She closed her eyes and drew more of her own power to counter it. Duncan tugged at the leather thong to untie the bag. She hated the thought of those coins touching this place that had always been used to invoke the natural power of the earth, but she could think of no place better for dealing with them.

The two coins spilled out onto the granite with a dull thunk, sounding far too heavy for their small size. Duncan drew a small pair of tongs from the leather pouch he wore on his belt. She admired his forethought as he carefully lifted the first coin with the tongs rather than using his fingers.

He held it up to the light and carefully studied first one side and then the other. "This looks no different than any of the other gold coins I have seen. What do you think?"

As she stepped closer, she concentrated on keeping her breathing slow and even, knowing any agitation on her part would affect her control over the power she'd poured into the wards.

"You are right. On the surface, there is nothing that

distinguishes them from other coins from Agathia. The likeness is of the current Duke Keirthan."

Duncan cocked his head to the side and looked from her to the coin and back.

"Do you know of any reason the duke might want to kill you in particular?"

Lavinia lifted her gaze to meet Duncan's head-on and did the only thing she could possibly do. She lied.

"No, I don't."

When Gideon returned from dealing with the loss of Merewen's horses, he looked like hell. At least his countenance brightened upon seeing Murdoch marching along the hall with Averel's assistance.

Gideon crossed his arms over his chest. "About time you left that bed."

Murdoch kept trudging toward him. "Yes, well, somebody had to give young Averel here something to occupy his time besides playing with those flea-bitten dogs of his."

"Hey, now. It's one thing to insult me, but leave my dogs out of it." Despite his protest, the young knight shot Gideon a quick grin.

"Averel, I'll stay with Murdoch while you go check in with Kane. We brought back a foal that might need your touch with young animals."

Averel's smile faded. "How bad was it? How does Lady Merewen fare?"

Gideon clenched his fists at the memory. "Bad enough. Seven horses were killed by the same foul means as the attack on Scim. She's taking it all pretty hard, but having the foal to fuss over is helping. Right now she's out in her workshop brewing a special mix to feed him until they can find a mare to nurse him."

As they passed by a window, Gideon paused to look out, probably trying to give Murdoch time to catch his breath before continuing on without being obvious about it.

"Tomorrow, she's going to send Kestrel out to move the herds closer to the mountains. There's no way to know how far that magic can reach, but we're hoping the hills and valleys will provide some protection against the attacks. I don't know what else we can do. We must find the source of this evil, and soon."

"Duncan should reach the abbey any day now. He'll find answers for us."

Averel sounded far more convinced of that than Murdoch was, but then the young knight always was the most positive of their group.

"I hope so for all our sakes." Gideon's own doubts showed in the deep lines bracketing his mouth as he moved on down the hall. Murdoch started walking again.

The three of them reached the far end of the hall and wheeled around to start back. Gideon continued. "Kane is in the stable with Jarod, trying to keep the foal calm and warm."

Unexpectedly, he smiled. "Even Rogue has taken an interest in the foal, refusing to leave his side. Not sure what to make of that."

"I'll go check on them." Averel clapped Murdoch on the back. "Don't wear yourself out completely. You promised me a game of chess later."

Murdoch nodded. "I'll be waiting."

Gideon waited until Averel was gone to ask, "So how are you really feeling?"

Murdoch gave up trying to put on a brave front and let his shoulders sag with weariness. "As if I don't make it back to my bed soon, I won't make it at all."

"Want some help?"

"No, but stay with me that far." He stopped about halfway down the hallway and leaned against the wall for support. "I had an interesting conversation with Sigil, my fellow patient."

Gideon's eyebrows shot up. "Sigil? So we finally have his name. That's something."

Murdoch gave Gideon a weary smile. "Not exactly. His memories only go back to the moment he awoke in that bed. He cannot recall how he came to be there, much less his own name. He picked Sigil because I told him we'd recognized him as the duke's man by the symbol he'd been wearing when he took the blow intended for me."

"And you believe him?"

Murdoch stared past Gideon toward the trooper's room. "He certainly has every reason to lie about it. He knows he will stand judgment for the crimes he has committed in the duke's name."

The trembling in his knees worsened. It was time to get back to his room while he could still make it that far on his own. "However, I think Sigil is telling the truth as he knows it."

Gideon looked disgusted. They both knew he didn't need any more complications, and the duke's man was definitely that. "Whether or not he's telling the truth, keep a close watch on him. The man didn't become an officer without a willingness to kill in the duke's name."

Murdoch slowed again, finally stopping to lean against the wall once more. "Yes, but it's also true that he saved Alina from Fagan, and me as well. I hate that I owe him a debt of honor, but that doesn't change the fact that I do."

Gideon shared his frustration. "What would you have me do? We cannot allow him to wander freely in the keep. One act of mercy cannot absolve him of everything that went before."

And if anyone understood that, it was the Damned. After Murdoch and the others had failed in their duty centuries ago, the gods had allowed them to redeem their honor by serving as their avatars. The price they'd paid for such a boon was the knowledge that someday they would face final judgment, either finding peace in the halls of their forefathers or eternal damnation. There was no middle ground. With that in mind, Murdoch considered their two options regarding Sigil: keep him or kill him.

A tough choice. Killing a nameless enemy in battle was hard enough, but the more time they spent with Sigil, the harder it would be to order his death. Murdoch also suspected Alina, with her tender heart, would be devastated if it came to that. She saw the man as heroic for saving their lives. She wouldn't appreciate nursing the man back to health just so the Damned could execute him soon thereafter.

"For now, let's give him a day or two more to see what happens. If his memories come back, we'll deal with him the same way we would have any of Keirthan's other men. If they don't, we'll keep an eye on him and see if we can put him to use against his former master."

Gideon didn't look any happier about the situation than Murdoch was.

"Let's get you back to your bed."

Murdoch pushed himself off the wall and shuffled forward. He knew his friend would lend him support if he needed it, but a man had his pride. He'd make it back to his bed on his own if it killed him.

And right now, it felt as if it just might.

Sigil shifted in his narrow bed, trying to find a more comfortable position. He'd been lying there too long, his body stiff and sore from inactivity. There was also the stress that came from trying to look calm while two warriors stood out in the hall and discussed whether or not to kill him.

Perhaps they thought they were far enough away that he couldn't hear them, but he doubted it. He might not know who he was, but he was certain about a few things. One was that he was used to trusting his instincts when it came to judging the nature of a man's character.

There was something different about Gideon and Murdoch, and even that younger one who was clearly part of their inner circle. It was more than the easy camaraderie of men who served together. He'd been too caught up in his own predicament at first to notice that all three of them had the same freakishly pale eyes.

Given their very different physical appearances and builds, it was doubtful that it came from a shared bloodline, which left only one explanation. They'd been marked by magic, but what kind he couldn't say.

They were headed in his direction. If he could believe their conversation out in the hall, he'd live to see another day. Finc. He supposed he should be relieved about their decision.

But this not knowing was killing him.

He braced himself and pushed himself upright. When the pain didn't knock him right back down, he kicked his legs free of the quilt and swung his feet down to the ground. He took sitting up for the victory it was, a step back toward normal.

Just as Murdoch shuffled across the threshold, Sigil stiffened his spine and pretended he wasn't about to fall right back down on the mattress. Captain Gideon followed his friend into the room, making sure to keep himself between Murdoch and Sigil.

Did he really think Sigil could offer any kind of threat right now? At the moment, a stiff breeze would knock him flat. It was more likely Gideon's habit to scan any room he entered for possible danger.

Murdoch's reaction to seeing Sigil sitting up was slightly friendlier. Gideon's pale eyes remained ice-cold, but there was a small degree of warmth in the wounded warrior's gaze and maybe a hint of guilt because of the conversation he'd had with his captain a few minutes earlier.

Sigil didn't hold it against him. After all, until the night of the battle, they'd fought for opposing sides. And if Duke Keirthan was anywhere as bad as he'd been told, what kind of man would serve him? No one Sigil wanted to be, or at least he'd like to think so.

Murdoch paused at the foot of the bed. "Good to see you sitting upright. Maybe the next time I decide to prowl the hall, you'll be up to walking with me."

Even if Gideon wasn't particularly friendly, Murdoch's invitation seemed sincere. However, right now the big man was weaving from side to side. Sigil struggled to stand up to catch him. When that failed, he settled for a verbal warning.

"Watch it, Murdoch!"

Gideon had been too busy staring at Sigil to notice. He belatedly grabbed Murdoch's arm in time to keep him from toppling over. After wrapping it around his own shoulder, he braced himself to support his friend's considerable weight.

"Damn it, Murdoch; get back to bed before Lady Alina comes in and finds you sprawled on the floor. If you get hurt again, she'll come after me with a dull blade."

Murdoch laughed even as he let Gideon support him. "It might be worth a few extra bruises to see that."

The doorway was too narrow for the two of them to clear standing side by side, so Gideon angled his position to go through first. Murdoch looked back at Sigil one last time.

"Do you play chess?"

"Yes, I do." Something else he knew for certain, another small step forward in regaining his identity. "I think I'm pretty good at it."

Murdoch nodded as he disappeared into his room. "Guess we'll both find out tomorrow which of us is the better man."

Sigil's brief surge of victory faded as quickly as it had come. He already knew the answer to that particular challenge, and it wasn't him.

Chapter 10

There'd been an odd note in Lavinia's voice that had Duncan thinking she'd just looked him straight in the eye and lied. The question was why?

Now wasn't the time to confront her, not with all that dark magic pulsing in the coins. He smiled at her in response, making sure his expression reflected less acceptance and more accusation. Her fair skin paled, but she didn't recant. Fine. They had a more pressing problem right now.

"How do you suggest we destroy the coins?"

She stared at the bright, shiny gold, biting down hard on her lower lip while she thought. He was hit with the impulse to soothe that small hurt by kissing away the pain and her worry. The strength of that urge shocked him. The Damned weren't given to impulsive behavior, especially not him.

It was far more in character for him to study a problem from all angles, to research, to ponder. He didn't know if it was the swirling currents of magic that surrounded them or the presence of Lavinia herself that had his blood running hot. He tamped the impulse down as best he could, not liking the threat to his control when they could least afford it.

"Well?" he prompted.

Lavinia continued to stare at the coin. "I would learn more if I were to touch it directly."

He remembered her reaction to just holding her hand above it yesterday in the workroom. "If you're sure."

"I'm not sure of anything, but I need to know the true nature of the spell before I can best discern how to counter it." She drew a shuddering breath and held out her hand.

He held the coin over her upturned palm and released it. As soon as it touched her skin, she hissed as if it burned, but her hand held steady. She closed her eyes and slowly curled her fingers around the coin. After a time, she gently laid the coin back down on the table and picked up the second one. "It has been infused with the duke's personal power."

She glanced at him briefly. "I have encountered his work before, but never anything this intense. His gift has grown in strength."

The second coin dropped back down on the granite surface with a dull thud. It was as if the magic embedded in the metal had increased the coin's weight a hundredfold. Lavinia immediately wiped her hand on her skirt.

"It was created with blood magic, not simply drawn off his own personal source of power." Her dark eyes were sorrowful when she stepped back. "Someone bled to fuel these weapons."

Duncan stared at the coins, repulsed by the depths of the duke's perfidy. "Bled unto death?"

"There's no way to know for sure. But from what I know of the duke, he is not a trusting man, and his hold over Agathia is tenuous. He can't risk having many witnesses to the kind of magic he is practicing for fear his subjects will rise up against him. As long as there are only whispers of his villainy, he can continue to build his strength."

Once again, she stared at the coins. "The blood may have been a willing donation by one of his followers, but more likely it came from a victim. Someone with a touch of power of his own."

Duncan thought of the young girl who'd spoken to him in Lavinia's office. "Like Sarra's mother?"

Lavinia nodded. "Magic begets magic. Even blood that carries only a weak gift can be used to enhance the power of a spell, especially at the hands of a powerful mage."

"And Duke Keirthan is such a mage?"

She nodded, her eyes looking in every direction but Duncan's. "He is now, although he didn't used to be. His family line has produced some fine mages over the centuries, good men and women who have served Agathia well."

"But Keirthan himself isn't one of them."

Her expression was bleak. "No, he's not. He's a jealous, spiteful man who will steal what he doesn't rightly own or deserve, no matter the cost to others. He does not deserve to rule Agathia."

In a sudden burst of motion and power, she screamed out a plea to the gods of the earth and sky, her words spoken in an old tongue as she slammed her hand down on top of the two coins. The air around them crackled with a flash of heat and light that sent them both stumbling back. If Duncan hadn't caught Lavinia when he did, she would've fallen across the circle of stone in the floor, breaking the wards that surrounded them.

His ears hurt from the clap of thunder created by the clash of Lavinia's spell with the blood magic. Power bounced around them, trapped inside the wards, buffeting them both as if they were caught within a maelstrom. When it finally burned itself out, all that was left of the coins was a small pile of dust.

Duncan had no idea precisely what Lavinia had been thinking about right before she destroyed the coins, but there was no mistaking the grief in her voice or the trickle of tears down her cheeks. This time he didn't resist the impulse to offer comfort. He gathered Lavinia in his arms, keeping his touch gentle.

To his surprise, her arms snaked around his waist and held him in a death grip. He wasn't sure how to react, but he hoped his embrace conveyed the simple concern of a friend for a friend.

In truth, however, the sweet press of her body against his had him thinking along entirely different lines. Having gone centuries without the pleasure of a woman in his arms, much less his bed, was no excuse for taking advantage of a woman who was clearly in pain. Shame had him easing a little more room between them.

He sensed Lavinia pulling herself back together, her hold on him loosening. Finally, she breathed deeply and lifted her face to look up at him.

"I apologize for losing control. At the very least I should've warned you before I attempted to destroy the blood magic. Were you hurt in the backlash?"

He used the pads of his thumbs to wipe the last few tears from her soft skin. Then he forced a smile. "My ears may never be the same, but otherwise I'm fine."

At first she looked horrified but then realized he was teasing. "Next time I'll remind you to stuff cotton in your ears."

This time his grin was genuine. "I think I'll remember on my own."

He should back away now and let her go, but he couldn't bring himself to take that first step. Not with Lavinia staring up at him with a sunshine-bright smile. "We did it!"

For the first time she looked truly happy. "That we did!"

On impulse, Duncan picked Lavinia up and swung her around in a circle, the two of them laughing in relief. The coins no longer called out to them with a terrible power; their first obstacle had been vanquished. Holding her high enough that she was looking down at him, he stared at her lush mouth. In a moment of weakness, he gave in to the impulse to end their brief celebration with a simple kiss; except there was nothing simple about it, not with the jolt of heat and hunger that rolled through him as soon as his lips brushed across hers. He immediately broke off the kiss, lowered her back to the ground, and stepped away, breathing hard and fighting the urge to pick up where they'd left off.

When he could speak, he said, "I apologize if this is forbidden, Lavinia. I would not tarnish your honor."

"Or your own."

"Or my own," he agreed.

Her mouth softened into a smile. "It is not forbidden, but neither is it wise. I serve the gods, but not as a sister who has taken vows."

Still, she made no move to step back. Her indecision only fueled his own. They both had obligations, duties, people who depended on them, roles to play. But those things existed only beyond the confines of this room, their existence for the moment held at bay by the wards that Lavinia had invoked.

Inside those layers of power, there were only the two of them sharing this one moment, the weight of their burden lightened by the comfort of each other's touch. Wise? Perhaps not, but damned if he was going to regret this opportunity to remember what it was like to be wholly human and a man.

Her expression turned serious. "This cannot happen again, Sir Duncan. We can't . . . I can't."

When she struggled to find the words, he hushed her with a finger across her lips. "I know. We both have responsibilities and vows to fulfill."

Lavinia stepped back, putting far more distance between them than a few inches of space.

"We should go."

"Yes, we should."

He bent down to retrieve the empty steel box while

she released the wards that had them penned in. As he followed her to the door, he had one more thing to say, something that needed to be spoken before they returned to the world on the other side.

"Lavinia, there's one more thing."

"Yes?"

"I have no regrets and would hope that you feel the same way."

Her smile was infinitely sad. "If you have no regrets in your life, Duncan, then you are indeed blessed. I have many, but kissing you will not be one of them."

When Lavinia stepped through the door, she was once again the abbess, her slender shoulders bearing all the weight of that office. He stopped to retrieve his weapons, but she kept going. She never stopped to look back, not even once.

Chapter 11

"**Y**our wine, Sire."

Ifre Keirthan, Duke of Agathia, didn't bother looking up from the manuscript he was studying. "Just set it down and go. Tell everyone else that I am to remain undisturbed until the evening meal."

When he finally raised his eyes to stare across the desk at the servant, he spoke in a grave tone he knew would not be misunderstood. "If anyone does cross that threshold, I will be most displeased."

The servant swallowed hard, his face already covered with a sheen of nervous sweat. "Y-yes, Sire. I will ensure that your wishes are carried out."

"Good. Now go."

Keirthan watched the man bolt for the door and smiled. Striking fear in his underlings was such a pleasure. He turned his attention back to the passage he'd been trying to translate. He'd never been the scholarly one in the family, but now he wished he'd paid more attention to his brother's efforts to teach him the old tongues.

Too late now. Ifre glanced at his brother's portrait on the wall and smiled. There'd been that unfortunate accident that ended up with Armel dead, followed by Ifre Keirthan regretfully assuming his brother's duties as ruler of Agathia. The official period of mourning was almost over, but he'd kept his brother's portrait where he could look at it and gloat.

He set down his pen to savor the moment. Armel had possessed a vast potential as a mage. Magic had come easily to him, and so had the gift for tongues that so many of the old texts were written in—especially the forbidden ones.

Everyone knew Armel had been blessed, but potential magic was worthless when a man was burdened with a conscience and an overabundance of honor. No, it only had value when a man had the courage to exploit that potential and to let it take him down the darker roads where true power could be found.

A man like Ifre.

"Armel, you would be amazed at what I've accomplished." He lifted his glass in a mocking toast to his much-detested older brother. "And horrified, which is even better."

Time to get back to work. He'd managed to strengthen the spell he'd been working on for weeks, enough that he'd succeeded in sending several bolts of death soaring across the grasslands. He wasn't sure what the bolts had killed, but he'd savored the pain and terror right up until the energy had burned itself out.

The effort had left him exhausted, but the sweet taste of death more than made up for the temporary discomfort. What he really needed was to find a way to repeat the spell, but this time aim the backlash at someone else. He'd drained the woman whose blood had fueled the spell. Maybe he should've kept her alive long enough to bear the brunt of the pain. He jotted that thought down in his notes to consider later.

There had to be a way to do that, which led him back to the text he'd been working his way through one word at a time. He'd make faster progress if he hired someone to translate the archaic language for him. The drawback would be having to trust the scribe to keep his mouth shut about the nature of Ifre's studies. For now, he'd continue to struggle along on his own.

Ifre sounded out the next word and considered its meaning. Light? Sun? Fire? It could be any one of the three, depending on the context. He slammed the pen down again and soothed his frustrations with another glass of wine. He'd sent men ranging far and wide to hunt for his old tutor as well as to search out the hiding place of another of the man's most favored students.

The tutor was dead—another unfortunate accident, but not one of Ifre's making. The other student had disappeared after sending word that death was preferable to spending one minute of time in Ifre's service.

He smiled again up at his brother's likeness. "I will find her. When I do, her death will be her last gift from me."

As he took one last sip of wine, he choked, spewing the wine out onto the text and his notes. His throat contracted hard, as if a fist had him in its grasp, making it impossible to swallow or breathe. Pain exploded like acid in his veins, sending him pitching headfirst to the floor.

The thick rug did little to cushion his fall as his whole body shivered and shook. His feet drummed on the floor, and his arms flopped and flailed like a trout tossed out onto the grass drowning in the air.

Was he dying?

He tried to call for help but couldn't shove enough air past the blockage in his throat to form the words. The noises he made were little better than the croaking of a frog, and a pitifully small one at that.

Even if he had managed a clear call for assistance, it was doubtful anyone would respond. Not after his demand to be left undisturbed. All he could do was ride through the pain and pray it would pass. For an eternity, his body jerked and twitched as his head pounded and thumped against the carpet. His teeth bit deeply into his tongue, and the coppery tang of his own blood clogged his throat.

Slowly, so slowly, control of his muscles returned. As the last few shudders faded away, all he could do was lie there on the floor, covered in sweat and too weak to lift even his hand. His first full breath finally convinced him that he would survive this attack.

For that was what it was. Someone somewhere had countered one of his spells, perverting Ifre's own power and turning it into a weapon to be used against him. It had to be one of the coins, or maybe several of them, considering the strength of the attack. If his unknown foe had destroyed even one more of the ensorcelled gold pieces, Ifre had no doubt that Agathia would've been looking for a new duke to assume the throne by nightfall.

He pushed himself up to rest on his elbows briefly before gathering enough strength to sit upright. When he managed to hold that position for a few minutes, he scooted closer to the desk, needing its support to crawl back up into his chair.

Gradually, his eyes could focus again. At least he'd survived the experience without anyone knowing that he'd been susceptible to attack. Since the death of his more popular brother, he'd imposed his rule over Agathia with a brutal hand. The people were cowed by his power, which was how it should be. That he could be killed from a safe distance didn't bear thinking about.

He needed to get to his secret chambers down below and see what he could learn about how the backlash had been triggered. If he could trace it back to its source, he would learn the whereabouts of another mage, one with a powerful gift in his or her blood.

The coins had been keyed to engender a killing rage in their bearer if he were to come in contact with dear, sweet Lavinia. Her refusal to serve his cause had shown more common sense on her part than he'd ever given her credit for.

No doubt she'd guessed he wanted her for more than her ability to decipher the old texts. With luck, soon he would know her location. He'd send another troop of his royal guard to search for her. Too bad Terrick wouldn't be there to lead the expedition.

He spared a brief thought of regret at the loss of the captain of his guard. He had no doubt Terrick was dead, murdered by Fagan's niece and her band of hired thugs. When on a mission, all of Ifre's guards wore a pendant that tied their minds and souls to him. They also allowed him to drain their life force to fuel his magic. He'd felt the loss of nearly all the men he'd sent with Lord Fagan.

That bastard had failed to regain control of his family home from his niece, Lady Merewen, and no doubt died in the process. That had cost Ifre not only access to Fagan's gold, but also the use of the fool's niece. Looking back, he should've insisted on Fagan bringing Merewen to the city as soon as he'd realized her potential. It had been a calculated risk to trust Fagan to keep her pure and safe. However, if she'd spent time at court, she would've been missed once Ifre claimed her for his studies. Nobles tended to notice when their own kind disappeared.

Eventually, he would still sacrifice her on his altar. Granted, if she were no longer a virgin, the strength of the blood sacrifice would be greatly weakened when he slit her throat to feed the ever-greedy flames of his magic.

When he was sure he could trust his legs to support him, Ifre walked to the door and called for Lady Theda, his brother's widow who now served as Ifre's chatelaine. He'd order her to bring him food, taking pleasure in using her as a superior servant. Once he'd replenished his strength, the hunt for Lavinia would begin again.

Lavinia maintained her composure all the way to her office. She returned the steel box to its usual place on the shelf behind her desk. Taking comfort in the familiar surroundings, she found the quiet at the center of her being and savored a moment of peace.

It wouldn't last long. Too many thoughts and emotions were at war inside her head, all vying for control. They started with the memory of Duncan's kiss. She was no innocent; she'd left the outside world for reasons other than to serve the gods. Even so, her limited experience had left her unprepared for the overwhelming impact of this one man.

Who was he really? Certainly not the simple scribe he claimed to be. It was plain to see he'd spent far more of his life with a sword in his hand than he had holding a pen. She didn't doubt his word that he could perform the duties of a scribe, but why would he want to?

Despite the powerful magic she sensed whenever she was in his presence, he was clearly uncomfortable when confronted with even a simple warding spell. A man of contradictions, that was Duncan.

She considered the matter of the coins she'd destroyed. Her wards had held strong, preventing the explosion of power from harming those within the abbey walls. It was unlikely that any except the most sensitive of the sisters had felt even a whisper of its power.

That didn't mean the duke himself had remained unaffected by the destruction of the coins. He'd used someone else's blood to tie the death magic to the gold, but he'd also poured some of his own essence into the spell. It would be nice to think that his fortress in the capital city was too far away and too well warded against outside attack for him to have felt even a ripple of energy.

Comforting, yes, but only a fool would cling to comfort instead of facing reality. The most she could truly hope for was that he sensed the destruction of the coins and that was all. Even that was nothing she could count on, not with other lives depending on her leadership to keep them safe.

She'd also sworn to protect the library at any cost from men like Ifre Keirthan. To be honest, she was surprised that he hadn't already sent his men to attempt to steal the collection to add it to his own. If he was aware of its contents, he would crave the knowledge it would afford him. Selfish bastard that he was, he'd want it all for himself. Ifre was well aware that knowledge was power, especially when it came to all things magic. If he was the only one with the ability to wield it, then his position as duke was safe.

The position he'd stolen in the first place.

Someone had to break the people of Agathia free from the yoke of his tyranny. Fear tasted sour, but so familiar. She'd lived with it as her constant companion for far too long. Destroying Keirthan's coins was the first direct action she'd taken, and even that was to save herself, no one else.

She turned to face her garden and the deep green bowl that awaited her attention. Should she risk scrying? No doubt Duncan would make his way back to her office soon. If she started now, perhaps with luck, the gods would gift her with answers before he came knocking.

Outside, the warm breath of the sun teased her skin and the soft breeze was perfumed with the sweet scent of flowers. Both combined to soothe her agitation, increasing the likelihood of success when she uncovered the bowl. Feeling cleansed by the simple beauty of the day, she lifted a pitcher of water high over the bowl.

With a smile, she slowly tipped it until the water poured out in a silvery stream that sparkled in the bright light of the sun. When the bowl was full, she set the pitcher aside and sought out the calm that had eluded her for most of the morning.

It was there, hovering just out of reach. She closed her eyes and let the worries of the day slip away, leaving only the good things, the ones that reminded her that life was worth living. The beauty of the flowers that surrounded her; the friendship she shared with the other sisters here within the strength of the abbey walls.

Then another image pushed all the others right out of her head: Duncan. Being held in his arms, the kiss they'd shared, and remembering what it felt like to be a woman with a woman's desires and dreams.

Perhaps not the best imagery to focus on when approaching the gods, but then they were the ones who'd warned her that his presence in her life would be significant. The thought made her smile as she stepped closer to grasp the edges of the bowl and willed the water to show her what it would.

Ripples upon ripples offering her no clarity. She let her hands drop back down to her side. The disturbance wasn't coming from her this time, but from the intruder in the garden. Lavinia didn't bother to look. She knew who it was.

"If you plan to stay, at least come closer so that you can see what the water reveals."

"You scry?"

Duncan's deep voice came from over her shoulder, as if he were leery of approaching the bowl directly.

"Sometimes," she answered honestly. "More often than not, I get frustrated by my efforts and toss the water at the roses."

He chuckled. "That explains how lush this garden is."

His wry comment had her wanting to join in with his laughter. "Duncan," she chided, "this is serious business, not something to be taken lightly.

"Believe me, I have good reason to never take speaking with the gods lightly, Lady Lavinia."

She glanced back over her shoulder at him, wondering at the sudden change in his tone. His eyes, so pale in color, stared at her with such pain and a wisdom that was far older than he should've possessed at his age.

Then he blinked, breaking the connection. "Would you prefer that I leave you alone?"

"No, I want you to stay."

Which was true, and preferably for far longer than a simple scrying.

Duncan decided it was cowardly to stand behind Lavinia rather than at her side. He should've realized that the bowl was not intended for birds to bathe in. Even now, the glass hummed softly with the magical vestiges of Lavinia's prior scryings. How had he missed that earlier? Perhaps he was more aware of it now because he was so aware of her.

"What should I do?"

"Stand still and stay quiet. If you lean closer, you should be able to see whatever the gods choose to show me."

He nodded and watched Lavinia prepare herself for another attempt to query her gods. It should bother him. None of the Damned trusted magic. But just as Gideon had accepted Lady Merewen's gift as something pure and clean, Duncan had come to the same conclusion about Lavinia's.

He could only hope that he was thinking with his brain and not letting his personal desires overrule his common sense.

As she softly chanted, her always lovely face took on an otherworldly glow, peaceful and stunning to behold. She took his hand in hers and grasped the edge of the bowl with her other one. She gave him a pointed look and then turned her gaze to the opposite side of the bowl. Following her unspoken directions, he twined his fingers with hers and then gingerly clasped the edge of the glass.

The quiet hum he'd been hearing increased in volume enough to give him gooseflesh on his arms. Determined to see this through, he ignored the slightly unpleasant sensation as he waited to see what came next.

The water splashed over the edge onto his fingers. He realized he was holding the glass with too much force. As he eased up on his grip, Lavinia arched an eyebrow and smiled at him, he hoped in approval. If calm was what was needed, that was what he would give her.

Abruptly, the water stilled, its dark surface resembling a miniature of the deep pool where the Damned slept as they waited until the gods needed them to defend their people again. He fought the urge to back away, hating the reminder. Days were steadily passing, one by one, ever shortening the time he had left before the water would once again steal away years of his life.

When next he awoke, Lavinia's life would be only a dim memory, a woman long gone from the world. Rather than think about her death, he concentrated on this moment, taking comfort in the warmth of her fingers touching his.

Lavinia finished whispering her words of power, leaving the garden silent except for the beating of their hearts and the ebb and flow of air in their lungs. The tension continued to build as they waited to see if the gods would speak.

A small ripple at the center of the bowl slowly spread, leaving in its wake a picture of a room, one filled to the brim with books, manuscripts, and scrolls. It was as if he were seeing the room through the eyes of another, slowly turning to reveal more detail. A man was seated at the table beside the window, holding up a page to the sunlight streaming in through the rippled glass as if trying to get a clearer look at the writing on the page.

It wasn't hard to recognize himself, even if he wasn't used to seeing himself through another's gaze. He was speaking, although the water didn't share the sound of the words with Duncan and Lavinia. She stepped into sight, joining him at the table to look at the passage that held his attention. When her hand came to rest on his shoulder as they studied the page, Duncan could've sworn he felt the phantom weight of her palm as they stood there in the garden.

The picture dissolved, flashing to another scene, this one more familiar to him. Murdoch was walking in a hall that Duncan recognized from Lady Merewen's keep. His friend was moving slowly, as if in great pain. Duncan frowned. By now, Murdoch's injuries from the battle should've been long healed. Did the gods show a jumble of the future, the past, and the present?

It was a question to ask Lavinia when this was over.

Once again the water stirred. This time the chamber was unfamiliar to him, although it bore some superficial resemblance to the one where he and Lavinia had destroyed the coins that morning. He had no doubt he was looking into a mage's lair. But whose?

After a few seconds, a man strode into sight. He stepped up to what had to be an altar, but one adorned with shackles. That alone was enough to send a shiver of cold dread racing up Duncan's spine. Judging by the death grip she now had on his hand, Lavinia was no happier with this image.

She stared down at the water as if her worst nightmare were playing out before her. The man held a knife up, and his lips moved as he chanted a spell. Despite the silence of the scrying bowl, Duncan felt the darkness and evil intent in the mage's words.

Without warning, the man slashed open the palm of his hand and then laid the blade of his knife across the gaping wound. Instead of the blood dripping down onto the altar, the bright silver of the steel turned crimson and pulsed with a heartbeat of its own.

Lavinia whimpered, her face now a frozen mask of horror.

Abruptly, the mage in the water jerked his head up to stare at the ceiling in his room—or possibly at Lavinia. Acting on instinct, Duncan yanked his hand free and used his arm to drag Lavinia back from the scrying bowl. Shoving her behind him, he grabbed the bowl and heaved its contents at the flowers.

Then they both stood in horrified silence while the water sizzled and steamed. As they watched, it blackened all of the plants it had touched, leaving a path of destruction in its wake as it dripped down onto the ground.

Chapter 12

"**D**rink this."

Duncan shoved a full goblet of wine at Lavinia and then poured a second one for himself. Right now, he wasn't sure there was enough wine in all of Agathia to numb the memory of what they'd just witnessed.

Lavinia sat on the bench in the garden, staring warily at her scrying bowl as if it would leap out and attack her at any second. At least the wine had put some color back in her cheeks. For a while there, Duncan had been afraid she was going to faint on him.

Granted, swooping in to catch her in his arms held a certain appeal, but he never wanted to see that look of utter terror in her eyes again. She hadn't said a single word since they'd both watched the water smolder and burn its way down the wall, killing everything in its path. The terror of the experience had silenced her.

Duncan hated that his efforts to break the connection to the mage had left a mark in her garden, a visible reminder of the evil they had witnessed. He tried not to hover, but he wouldn't leave her alone until he was sure that she was all right.

Later, he'd write a summary of all that had happened for Gideon. He hesitated to send Kiva so far from his side, but it was imperative for the captain to know what was going on. The separation would weaken Duncan's ability to fight, but Kiva would be gone only two days, three at the most. It was a risk worth taking.

"How did you know?"

Duncan had been staring down into his wine as if the Lady of the River would reveal her truth to him. He'd settle for a brief glance of her purpose for placing him in Lavinia's path. Drinking down the rest of the wine, he set the empty goblet aside. "How did I know what?"

Although he understood exactly what she was asking.

Lavinia shot him a look that made it clear she found his attempt at subterfuge disappointing. She clarified her question anyway. "How did you know to break the connection? That he could see us?"

"Because I saw you."

He meandered closer to where she sat, pausing to admire a rose. He'd only seen such color before in the heart of a fire, yellow fading to orange and then to a deep red.

"When I was on the road coming here," he continued as he sat down beside her. "The first time I sensed your scrutiny I was riding along lost in thought when my horse acted startled. Although I couldn't see anything threatening, I had the uncanny feeling that someone was watching me. It passed, so we continued on."

He couldn't help glancing toward the blackened plants. "That night, I was sitting at my fire when the feeling came back, but stronger this time."

Lavinia drew his attention back to her. "You jumped to your feet and pulled your sword."

"That I did." He offered her a small smile. "I probably looked a proper fool, but the feeling was so real."

She smiled back. "Not at all. I thought you looked very manly, ready to do battle."

"Jumping at shadows is not manly," he countered, but her remark pleased him anyway.

"When I didn't see anything near me, I happened to look up at the moon and saw your face reflected there.

Well, I didn't know it was your face, just that I saw a beautiful woman looking down at me. It was but a glimpse, one so fleeting that I wasn't sure I'd actually seen it at all."

He suspected the flush of color in her cheeks was due to his compliment rather than the wine. She nodded as if something he'd said had just solved a puzzle for her.

"That was why you recognized me at dinner the first night you were here."

"Yes. It was quite a relief, actually. I thought perhaps my mind was addled. Perhaps it is, but at least I know the lady in the moon was real."

It was time to ask harder questions. "Who was the man we just saw?"

"Duke Keirthan himself." She shuddered. "It was clear from the power in those coins that he has grown in strength since we last crossed paths. That blood-eating knife is definitely something new. I've never heard of such a weapon. Have you?"

"No, and I'm guessing it's not a good thing. Have you ever had such a connection with someone through scrying other than with me and Keirthan?"

"No, and I've never read anything that would even hint that such a thing was possible. I should go research the matter right now."

Duncan caught her arm before she could stand. "No, you've done enough for one morning. Your hands are trembling, either from weakness or from fear. Either way, you need to rest for a while and then eat a hearty midday meal before you take on anything else."

She tugged her arm free of his grasp. "Knight, scribe, and now nursemaid. Do you have any other talents I should know about?"

Good, the tartness in her comment meant that her spirit was on the mend. He wondered what her response would be if he mentioned a few other skills he'd like to demonstrate for her. Another kiss would be a good start, and his imagination provided some heated images of where it could lead to. He gave the only answer he could, his words truthful but full of regret.

"Nothing we should explore right now."

She bit her lip again in the way she did when she was thinking hard about something. "That is too bad, but no doubt you're right."

This time when she tried to stand up, he didn't interfere. "I think I will do as you suggest and lie down for a short time. After we eat, perhaps you would care to join me in the library. I can show you around and then you *will* tell me what exactly you hope to find."

He nodded, acknowledging her demand. He would tell her everything he could and hope that it would be enough to convince her to help him.

"I will be honored to join you, my lady."

He put a little more room between them. "I should return to my own quarters until then."

She walked away. Unlike earlier, this time she looked back and smiled. "Thank you for saving me again, Duncan. It's becoming a habit of yours."

"It was my honor."

He offered her a quick bow, falling back on the safety of formal manners. As much as he appreciated the invitation to join her in the library, he would've liked being invited into her personal quarters even more. He trusted that was an unworthy thought, but he couldn't find it in himself to regret it.

For now, he'd take advantage of her absence to tear out the dead plants. She didn't need the reminder haunting her garden just as the memory haunted her eyes. He pulled them out by the roots just as the Damned would soon destroy the last trace of Duke Keirthan, or die trying. If it took the last breath in his body, the last drop of blood in his veins, he would make this world safe for Lavinia.

* * *

Murdoch woke up feeling . . . better? Not good, exactly, but definitely a vast improvement over the past few days. He moved slowly, just in case he was mistaken. No, his body did what he asked of it without complaint and without pain.

Excitement won out over caution as he stood up and took several strides back and forth across the confines of his room. The patter of his feet on the cool stone of the floor sounded strong to him, no longer the weak, old man shuffle he'd been limited to since the night of the battle.

What should he do next? Get dressed and then maybe he'd walk down to the great hall below. He was tired of his own company, and the man in the next room wasn't the jolliest of companions.

First off, though, a bath was high on his list, provided his wound had finally closed completely. He pulled up the long shirt that had been his sole attire since he'd been wounded.

Facing the window to catch the morning light, he stared down at the jagged scar that stretched across his stomach. Next he poked and prodded at it. Tender but not painful. All good. Yes, a bath could be on the list.

"Oh my goodness, I'm so sorry."

The mumbled words were followed by the sound of retreating footsteps. Running footsteps, actually. A woman's steps.

Damnation! Murdoch yanked his bed shirt back down to cover his nether regions. He prayed it had been one of the servants who'd walked in when he was checking out his injuries, leaving more than just his scar open to view.

His luck had obviously run out. More footsteps were coming his way, this set much heavier. Murdoch turned to face his latest guest.

Gideon stepped through the door, a puzzled look on his face. "What happened to send Lady Alina bolting back to her quarters? Did Sigil do something to upset her?"

Murdoch wasn't about to explain. "Maybe she forgot something."

Gideon shrugged and ventured farther into the room. "You're looking less like death and more like someone who needs to get back to work."

His grin widened. "You know how I feel about my men getting regular weapons practice. I figure you owe me almost a week's worth of opportunities to bruise you up for worrying us so much."

Murdoch appreciated the rough sentiment. "Order me up a hot bath and some clean clothes. Once I'm presentable, I'll follow you down to the bailey and watch you bang blades with Averel or, better yet, Kane. Maybe I'll even give you some pointers, so that when I'm in the mood to pick up my sword again, you'll be ready for me."

For the first time in days he was actually looking forward to the hot sweaty work of weapons practice.

Gideon gave Murdoch a long look. "Truly, how do you feel today?"

Murdoch allowed a small smile to peek through. "Right now even guard duty sounds like fun. Anything is better than being stuck here in bed all day."

The other man looked both relieved and happy. "That's good news, my friend. Very good news. I'll go let the servants know to bring you a bath."

Then Gideon dropped his voice, "How about Sigil? Any progress there?"

Murdoch thought back to the chess game the two had played the night before. "Physically he is well on his way to full strength. His memory has yet to return. It's odd the things he does remember: how to play chess, how to read—those sorts of things. I'm guessing if you put a sword in his hand, he would know how to fight. It is only the bits and pieces of who he really is and how he came to serve Keirthan that he cannot recall."

"How convenient. Mayhap he simply doesn't want to remember those things."

That was what Murdoch thought, too, but then who could blame the poor bastard? If he did remember and revealed his true loyalties, then chances were he'd be executed for his crimes. If he didn't remember, he still had to live with the knowledge that he'd served a master who dealt in death and blood magic.

Sigil was no doubt as sick of the same four walls as Murdoch was. "I'll bring him down with me. It will do the both of us good to breathe some fresh air."

"Fine, but keep him close. Not everyone will be happy that we've let him live."

Murdoch made shooing motions toward his friend. "I will. Now run along like a good servant and order a bath and clean clothes for me and our guest next door."

"Servant, is it?" Gideon flashed him a dark look. "You might want to remember that we *will* cross swords again."

He headed for the door, still grumbling. "This is the last day I will play your servant, Murdoch. I have better things to do with my time, and a long list of people to worry about."

Then he stopped in the doorway. "I'm glad you're off that list."

Murdoch nodded. "Me, too."

He waited until Gideon was gone before checking on their prisoner. Sigil was out of bed, staring out the small window. It was doubtful he could see much through the thick glass, but Murdoch understood his need to see something—anything—beyond the confines of the room. The walls were closing in on them both.

Without looking away from the window, Sigil spoke.

"Are you sure you really want to stand close to me if we venture outside? I wouldn't want you to be hit by a blow aimed for me."

"I'm willing to risk it."

Sigil finally turned to face him. "And why would you do something so foolish? You're just now recovering from the kind of wound that would've killed most men outright."

"True, but then I am not most men."

Sigil considered Murdoch's words and then nodded. "And I would guess that neither are your three companions—Captain Gideon, Averel, and Kane."

"Actually, all told there are five of us. You were unconscious when Duncan left the keep."

Sigil wanted to ask more questions, his curiosity plain in his dark eyes; yet he remained silent. That was all right. Murdoch wasn't any more eager to share his truth than Sigil was to regain his own memories.

Before their conversation could continue, the first servants arrived, carrying a pair of tubs and buckets of water.

"Sigil, once we're presentable, I'll escort you outside. The sunshine will do us both good."

"Mayhap something out there will bring back more of my memory."

"Mayhap," Murdoch agreed, although he wasn't convinced that would be a good thing. But such things were better left to the gods to decide.

Rather than worry about it, he headed back into his own room. He had his own problems, such as how to apologize to Alina.

Chapter 13

*L*avinia stood back and watched the flow of expressions across Duncan's handsome face: wonder, excitement, and something akin to awe. He wandered from one shelf in the library to the next, his fingers trailing over the old leather and parchment with total reverence.

She knew exactly what he was feeling. She'd experienced the same overwhelming excitement the first time she'd walked into the abbey's library. She'd been but a child, but the love of learning knew no age limits. A dozen lifetimes wouldn't be long enough to absorb all the knowledge contained within its walls, but she'd love the freedom to try.

They both had work to do, but nothing would be accomplished until Duncan finished his explorations. She knew better than to get between a scholar and his books. Far better to let him wander at will until that first burst of excitement had time to run its course.

But then he turned abruptly and headed in the wrong direction. She moved to intercept him, but he stopped on his own. After a quick glance back at her, he frowned and held his hand out at arm's length. He moved his palm in a horizontal line as if tracing a solid wall rather than a powerful, but invisible ward against intruders.

He backed away but still stared at what he shouldn't have been able to see. "Is this the same thing you created with the circles in the workroom? What would happen if I charged right into it?"

How much to tell him? Some secrets were meant to be kept even from people close to her. But then she thought about how he'd quietly removed the blackened plants so that she wouldn't have to see them again. His thoughtfulness had touched her deeply. Perhaps it was time she trusted someone, because she couldn't do this all on her own anymore.

Not after Keirthan had managed to attack her within the abbey walls. Once he traced the destruction of his blood magic coins, he'd try it again. If he couldn't control her, he'd kill her. It was that simple.

Lavinia joined Duncan. "No, they're not the same, although the spells are similar in construct and intent. The ones I invoked this morning are meant to keep the magic confined inside them."

She infused a little more power into the spell so that it flared brightly. "This one is an avoidance ward. The way it's supposed to work is by making anyone who approaches simply turn back. Most people never realize it's even there. They just lose interest in whatever they wanted to look at in that part of the library."

"But I can see it."

It was difficult to tell from his inflection whether he was stating a fact or asking a question. She did the same thing in reply.

"Only someone with a strong affinity for magic would be able to do that."

Duncan turned his back on the ward, the pale silver of his eyes glittering with anger. "I have no affinity for magic."

Could he really not know? "I meant no offense. Perhaps you are an exception, but I know of no other reason that you would've sensed the spell."

He let out his breath in a frustrated puff. "No offense taken. Over my lifetime I have learned to mistrust magic in any form. I obey the Lord and Lady of the River, and they have no tolerance for their followers practicing the dark arts."

She wanted to argue more, to point out the steady hum of magic she felt whenever she was close to him and that not all magic was dark in nature. For now, however, she needed his cooperation more than she needed his temper.

"Again, I apologize, Duncan. I'm not sure why you are sensitive to the wards."

It was time to take charge. "Let's be seated over there."

She pointed toward a large table a safe distance from where they now stood. Until she better understood Duncan's true purpose in coming to the abbey, she didn't want him anywhere near the books and grimoires protected by the barrier.

He paused to study the ward and the books on the far side before following her over to the table. His expression said he knew exactly what he was looking at and that she was deliberately keeping him from exploring them. She sat down in the chair with her back to the wall and motioned him toward the chair on the opposite side.

She'd ordered a pot of tea and some of Sister Margaret's pastries to be delivered to the library for the two of them to share. Hopefully, a civilized discussion over tea and sweets would garner her more information than an inquisition.

Duncan accepted the offer of tea and stirred in a large dollop of honey. He wrapped his hands around the mug and breathed deeply of the steam. She was about to ask her first question when he started talking.

Rather than meet her gaze, he continued to stare down into his tea. "I was sent here by Captain Gideon, my liege, because we need answers, and the abbey is reputed to have a collection of . . ."

His voice trailed off as his attention once again strayed in the direction of the warded section of the library. "Shall we say, rare resources?"

She sipped her tea. "Not that I am admitting that any such books exist, but I find I am most curious. Why would two warriors need to study such books, especially when you say the gods you serve forbid the use of magic?"

Now she had his full attention. Whether that was a good thing or not, she'd yet to decide.

"Let us not play games, Lady Lavinia. We share a common enemy, one who grows more powerful every day. I may not like magic, but I cannot fight against something I don't understand. The Lady of the River has decreed that Captain Gideon and the men who fight at his side must protect Lady Merewen and her people in Agathia from attack at all costs. We have already accomplished part of that goal by wresting control of her family lands from her uncle, Lord Fagan."

Lavinia fought down a wave of revulsion. "I met Lord Fagan once and pity anyone who was at his mercy. The man attempts to hide his cruelty beneath a thin coat of charm, but his true nature shows in his eyes and his smile."

At the moment, Duncan's own smile was anything but charming. "Be assured the man will no longer be a threat to anyone, especially his niece."

So Fagan was dead. Keirthan would not be pleased. "I'm surprised that the duke did not come to Fagan's assistance."

Another one of those smiles, his eyes focused inward. Whatever images Duncan's mind held were not pleasant ones. "He did, in fact. Their efforts to regain control of the keep and its lands were not successful."

All right, then. She'd been right all along about Duncan's prowess with a sword. His friends must be equally fearsome in battle. "So if Lady Merewen is safe from her uncle now, I repeat my question. Why would you and your liege have need of the forbidden resources you refer to?"

Duncan began pacing in the confined space surrounding the table. "Because from the first day that we were charged to protect Lady Merewen, we've known that Lord Fagan was but a symptom of the disease infecting this land. We suspect that Duke Keirthan himself is the source of the contagion. We also believe that his twisted magic is behind the unexplained disappearances of people, not to mention recent attacks on animals."

He did an abrupt turn to stare down at her. "We are right about that, aren't we? You know for certain that Keirthan is responsible."

There was no use in lying now, especially to a possible ally. She jerked her head in a quick nod. "He is."

"Do you understand the nature of the evil he is unleashing?"

"Not completely."

How much should she tell him? Nothing? Everything? She had no desire to oppose Keirthan alone, especially if he was now strong enough to corrupt even her ability to scry. At this rate, his magic would soon grow beyond her ability to counter it at all.

Duncan splayed his hands on the table and leaned across its expanse to glare down at her. "I have no time for guessing games, Lavinia. With every minute we delay, more people suffer and die at the hands of that bastard."

Her own temper rose up to meet Duncan's, her hands slapping down on the smooth surface of the table in counterpoint to his. "Then sit down and listen. I am no servant wench to be bullied by the likes of you."

The brief flare of anger burned itself out. "Please, Duncan."

He straightened up, his own expression softening. "My apologies, my lady. You are not the proper target for my frustrations."

Then his mouth softened into a small smile. "Indeed, I cannot ever remember kissing an enemy or even wanting to."

The air around them crackled with a new energy, a vibration that had nothing to do with the protective wards. After living so long with worry and fear, it was tempting to circle around to the other side of the table and lose herself in Duncan's strong arms.

But then the moment passed. He winked at her and dropped back down in his chair. She should be relieved. Her life was complicated enough without indulging herself in a bit of lust, which was all it could be. Instead, she was disappointed, almost bereft.

"Back to the matter at hand, then. You and your captain are right. The newest Duke of Agathia is behind the darkness you sense and the attacks on the people of that area."

Duncan looked confused. "The newest? Has he not held that throne for long?"

"No, Ifre Keirthan assumed the title after Armel, his elder brother, died."

Duncan sat slouched in his chair, but not for an instant did she think he was taking anything she said lightly. "Was the previous duke anything like this one?"

"Not at all. Like his father before him, Armel Keirthan was a strong ruler, one capable of protecting his land and people from attack. He was known to be both wise and fair. His only weakness was trusting those close to him, and so he did not recognize the viper within his own court."

She truly did not want to continue. It hurt too much, but she would see it through to the finish.

"Armel was magically gifted far beyond his brother, Ifre. In truth, he had more inborn talent than anyone in his family for several generations running. But Armel was cautious with its use, saying that the stronger the magic, the harder it was to control. Far too often it would turn on the mage and control him."

"What happened?"

"His younger brother had no such caution when it came to magic, especially because his was the weaker gift. Ifre grew jealous of Armel. Power was his goddess, and he could not understand why his brother did not worship her as he did.

"In the end, Armel died in what was reported to be an accident. His son caused the death, and it is said that it destroyed his mind. Ifre assumed the throne that same day. He went through the motions of a state funeral for Armel, but there was no real grief in him. Outsiders might have been fooled, but those who knew him well were convinced otherwise."

"You knew him well, then, this Ifre. I would guess that means you lived at court."

She'd revealed more than she'd meant to, but she couldn't find it in herself to regret telling him the truth. Besides, if they were to work together efficiently, it would be best if she didn't have to guard every word she spoke.

"At one time, I knew both Armel and Ifre well, although I left life in the court when I was still quite young. When I was summoned to return for the state funeral, I knew something was amiss. Ifre was entirely too smug when he thought no one was looking, and he was careful to ensure that no one was allowed to speak with Armel's son or even see him."

"Did you know the son well?"

"We played together as children, but I have not seen him since I was first sent away to be educated and trained."

Duncan refilled her tea and then his. "Did you miss your brothers while you were gone?"

She should've known Duncan was smart enough to fill in the gaps in her story. "They were my half brothers. But, yes, I did. I still do."

The past whirled through her mind, reminding her of the good times that were now but dim memories. Lavinia nodded at Duncan's questioning look, and continued on, although this part of the story was hard for her. "Their mother was the duchess and married to my father, Cambrell. My mother held his heart but not his name. My half brothers were more than a decade my seniors."

Duncan didn't press for more answers, but she offered them anyway. "As long as my father was the duke, no one could force him to send my mother away. Theirs was a love match, and his wife tolerated his mistress's presence only because he would have it no other way."

For a moment, she was caught up in the past, remembering the precious moments that her father set aside from his duties as duke to spend with her and her mother. Those had been far better days than what came afterward.

"Shortly after my father died, Armel gave in to his mother's demands that both my mother and I be sent away. I think he would've allowed me to stay, but my mother was nothing but an embarrassment to the royal family."

"Where is your mother now?"

"She died within months of my father. His death broke her heart, and she wasn't strong enough to stand up to those who shunned us. That was when I was sent here to study. The sisters have been good to me."

"You've spent much of your life here, then?"

"No, I've only recently returned to this abbey. I have spent time in several others to continue my education."

She braced herself. Duncan had made his low opinion of magic and its practitioners all too clear. He already knew that she had some ability with it. How could he not? He'd witnessed firsthand her ability to scry and to work with wards. Both those were considered lesser gifts. She'd often wished that was as far as her abilities had developed.

Duncan set his mug aside and leaned forward, elbows on the table and his expression painfully blank. "The gift for magic bred true in all of your father's children."

"Yes, it did. Armel and Ifre inherited their magic from him. My mother had her own abilities, so my gifts are a mix of the two. Ultimately, I was banished from Armel's court when I used my powers to strike at anyone who had hurt my mother."

Evidently Duncan had finally run out of questions, because there was nothing but silence between them now.

Duncan studied the woman sitting across from him. Right now, she looked braced for a blow, obviously expecting him to strike out at her for her earlier lie. "How old were you?"

She blinked twice before answering. "How old?"

"When you attacked the people who hurt your mother?"

"Twelve."

He looked disgusted. "What did they expect? One minute you were the beloved child of the duke. The next, your father was dead, and, through no fault of your own, you and your mother were ostracized. Of course you fought back. Any child would."

Lavinia sat up straighter. "You sound as if you've had your own experience with something similar."

If she was going to show him the scars of her past, the least he could do was share his. "My mother was a well-bred gentlewoman entangled in a political match. Instead of wedding her to someone who would appreciate her love of art and music and literature, she was handed over to my father, a brute of a man. Weapons, drinking, and wenching were all that he valued."

He didn't mean to say more, but one last bit slipped out. "I took after my mother. He hated me for that."

If there was sympathy or, worse yet, pity in Lavinia's expression, he didn't want to see it. Instead, he dragged her attention back to the restricted area of the library.

"We must learn how to counter the magic Duke Keirthan is practicing. Lady Merewen's late father accumulated an extensive library, but nothing that held the answers to our questions. In his journal, he described this library, saying that the abbess would let him peruse only a portion of the collection."

Lavinia accepted the change of subjects without comment. "I'm not surprised. Many of the manuscripts housed here are unique. Most are written in languages no longer spoken or understood."

He finished for her. "And some cover subjects far too dangerous to be trusted in the hands of just anyone."

Once again, he leaned forward, letting her see his determination. "I'm not just anyone, Lavinia. Now, we've wasted enough time, time I don't have. Do we work together on this or not?"

"You will still train the guards for us when they arrive?"

"I will."

Her expression grew harder. "You promise on your honor that you will not attempt to remove any of the books from the abbey?"

He wanted to refuse outright. What if he needed the actual grimoires with him in order to counter the duke's magic? There might be multiple spells that they would need to access.

Perhaps she would accept a compromise. "I promise not to do so without your knowledge." He didn't make her permission part of the requirement.

She was already shaking her head. "No, Duncan, I will have your word on this. The sisters have labored long and hard to gather and preserve this library. Many of the volumes are quite rare."

Duncan didn't care. "Not to mention many that are forbidden. I have heard that a prior duke, most likely your father, ordered certain books destroyed. I'm guessing that many of those exact ones are sitting on those shelves behind me."

"They were forbidden for good reasons."

This was getting them nowhere. "Perhaps so, but then it is obvious that someone else besides the sisters has held on to copies. Perhaps your father's intentions weren't to protect the world from the dark magic, but to make sure that only his bloodline would have access to the knowledge."

"How dare you! My father ordered those destroyed because of the dangerous knowledge they contained. He was trying to protect his people from those who would twist the magic to their own purpose."

"Just as your brother is now doing."

She flinched as if his words had landed an actual blow. "I am not responsible for his actions."

An ugly thought formed in Duncan's mind. "A man with a more suspicious nature might wonder about that, Lavinia. After all, it was your father who ordered the books destroyed; yet they still exist. It is also your brother who has invoked spells from the forbidden grimoires. And you, the daughter and sister of the past three dukes, are the one charged with limiting access to the only collection of books that might hold the answers to countering Ifre Keirthan's dark magic."

Lavinia had been about to sip her tea. Instead, the cup slipped from her fingers as she stared at him in obvious shock. Her mouth worked, but at first no words came out. When they did, they cut like razors.

"You dare to question my honor! If I were my brother's partner in this business, why would he use his blood magic to try to assassinate me?"

He studied her reactions and decided her outrage was sincere. To make sure, he prodded her one last time. "Why indeed? A deal that turned out badly for him, perhaps? What did he offer you?"

Her color paled. "He offered me a position of honor in his court if I would assist him with his studies. I refused."

That much made sense. "And he wouldn't tolerate such an insult. If you won't stand with him, then he won't let you live long enough to stand against him."

Before she could respond, he kept talking. "I apologize for doubting you, my lady, but it still remains imperative that I begin hunting for answers. The longer we delay, the more likely your brother will succeed in his next attack on you or on those I am sworn to protect."

Lavinia was busy sopping up the spilled tea, perhaps buying herself time to gather her thoughts.

When she was finished, she clasped her hands in her lap as she spoke. "While we are questioning motives, I have a few suspicions of my own. There were no attacks aimed at the abbey or at me until you arrived. It is only your claim that Musar's guard brought the coins into the abbey. You also killed the only two men who could've given witness to the truth of that story."

Damn, he'd hoped she wouldn't put those facts together in quite that way. Again she was showing what an astute mind she possessed. Before he could counter her accusation, she held her hand up to keep him quiet.

"Then, for a man who claims to not like magic, you reek of it. You say you and your captain are bound to protect Lady Merewen. But then again, I have only your word for that."

"I do not reek of anything, much less magic!"

Her smug smile was most irritating. "Then explain your eyes, Sir Duncan. You think I don't recognize a man who has been marked by the gods when I see one? Yesterday you could hardly walk because of the wound on your leg. Yet today your limp barely shows. Who are you really? Or better yet, what are you?"

Duncan rose to his feet, the power of the Lady of the River running hot through his veins. He suspected his eyes glowed as he stared down at her.

"I am one of the Damned, Lady Lavinia. Captain Gideon and the four of us who serve with him are also known as the Warriors of the Mist, and we serve the Lady of the River as her avatars. She sends us into the world when there's a cause she deems just, to do her bidding."

He had no idea how she would react to his announcement, but she surprised him by immediately leaving the table and heading right into the forbidden section of the library. He trailed after her, hoping she was finally going to allow him access, but the ward snapped closed behind her. He could see but a dim outline of her moving around in the farthest corner of the room.

She wasn't gone long. She returned carrying a thin volume in her hands. As soon as they returned to the table, she already had it open, flipping through the pages. When she found the passage she was looking for, she stopped to read it. It took a while. Her lips moved as she silently sounded out the words, obviously having to translate the meaning from the original language.

There were various accounts of how he and the others had become the Damned, but they all told the same basic facts. He could've read it for her, but at this point he doubted she would've trusted him to translate it accurately for her.

Finally, she looked up, her eyes wide with wonder. "The owl is your avatar."

How did she know that? "Yes, his name is Kiva. Right now he sleeps in my shield in my quarters, but he has been my willing companion even before my service to the Lady."

"I should've recognized your name as soon as you mentioned your captain. There are stories going back for centuries about a band of warriors who appear in times most dire to champion the people the gods have deemed worthy."

She flipped through several more pages and then turned the book so that Duncan could see it. There was a painting of five warriors, all carrying shields and brandishing swords. All in all, the likenesses weren't bad, although Gideon would not be pleased to learn such artwork existed.

"That's my captain on the right. From there stand Kane, Murdoch, me, and our youngest member, Averel."

Lavinia pulled the book back, studying the picture and then looking at him. "This book is at least five hundred years old. That would mean you and your friends . . ."

When she couldn't come up with a number herself, he supplied one. "As near as we can figure, we have not aged a day since we first marched into the river to sleep nearly two millennia ago."

Obviously she was having a great deal of trouble making her mind believe what was right in front of her. "But, Duncan, you look no more than thirty years of age."

Good guess. "Physically, I'm but eight and twenty. The world changes. The Damned do not."

She pulled the book back to her side of the table and continued to read for several minutes. He settled back in his chair, stretching out his legs and leaning his head back to stare at the ceiling—anything to avoid watching Lavinia dive into his personal history, even though it would be a relief to have it out in the open between them.

How would she feel about having kissed a man who'd been born before the language she was reading had ever been spoken? In his time, young women were often wedded to older husbands because it took time for men to establish themselves enough to support a family. A woman would overlook a decade or two in age difference; the same could not be said for a thousand years or more.

That was depressing even though he had no right to even be thinking along those lines. He had taken a vow to serve the goddess. There was no room in his life for a mortal woman.

Lavinia closed the book and stood up. "If you'll follow me, I'll adjust the wards to allow you to pass. I understand that you are reluctant to invoke magic of any kind, but I would also like to teach you how to restore the wards yourself."

His first instinct was to refuse, but there was a note in her voice that had him needing to know more. "Why, Lavinia?"

She blinked hard, trying to hide the thin sheen of tears in her eyes. "It's only a matter of time before Ifre figures out where I have taken refuge. He's my brother and knows me well. He could use that knowledge against me and any magic I have used to protect the abbey and the library. He wouldn't be able to break through your wards, at least not easily."

Had she not listened to what he'd said? "I have no gift

for magic, and you already know that I cannot remain at the abbey once I find what I am looking for."

He ignored the small stab of pain in his chest, forcing himself to continue. "For the time I am here, if there is a way I can support your wards by creating my own, I will do so."

Rather than accept his vow with solemnity, she giggled.

"You find this amusing?"

She stopped laughing, but the grin remained. "I'm sorry, but from the expression on your face, those words tasted as if they were lemon sour."

He reluctantly gave in and smiled in return. "You know how I feel about magic."

"Yes, I do. For now, though, why don't I allow you through the wards so you can begin your search. If I can be of assistance in translating anything written in the dead languages, let me know."

This time his grin was more genuine. "Those languages were alive and well when I was born, but I appreciate the offer."

She cocked her head to the side and studied him. "Truly? I still have trouble believing you are old enough to be one of the legendary Damned."

He winced a bit at her description. But to prove his point, he picked up the book she'd set aside and read it aloud, first in the old tongue and then in translation.

Lavinia leaned closer to study the text. "So that's how you pronounce those last two words. I had them wrong. Perhaps if we have time, you can help me master the language as it should be spoken."

Time was the one thing he couldn't promise her. "I would love to."

Which was nothing less than the truth.

Chapter 14

*A*lina stepped out on her balcony to watch the men at weapons practice in the bailey below. Since her niece had brought the captain and his men into their lives, it seemed as if all she ever heard outside her window was the clang of sword against sword.

Most of the time she ignored the noise, but not when Murdoch was among those out there training. She winced as he barely avoided a hard blow. At the same time, she admired his skill. For such a big man, he moved with uncanny grace and speed.

Especially when he was trying to avoid her, which he'd been doing since that morning she'd walked into his room unannounced when he had his bed shirt rucked up to his chest. Did he think she hadn't already seen all of his manly attributes? It wasn't as if she had treated his wounds and seen to his bodily needs with her eyes closed during those first perilous hours after he'd almost been killed.

Of course, at the time she'd been too worried about him to notice much more than how his wound was healing and when his fever had broken. Standing there in his room in the early-morning light, he'd looked strong, powerful, virile. Even now, after three days, the image remained burned in her mind in stark detail.

If only she'd had the courage to stand her ground rather than retreating. From the way he'd mumbled an apology from outside her door a short time later, Murdoch had assumed she'd been offended. Nothing could have been farther from the truth. All that muscle and masculine strength had left her feeling unsettled, overheated, and hungry.

Even if she could find the courage to explain that to him, it would do her no good. If she walked into a room, he walked out. If she strolled in the garden, he kept to the ramparts above. If she had dinner in the hall, he snatched some meat and cheese and bolted for the door.

It would be funny if it weren't so frustrating. Even if he had no interest in her as a woman, she thought they had at least been friends. She thought back to the day he'd introduced her to Shadow, the huge mountain cat who served as his avatar and companion, and then walked with her in the garden. It had been one of the best moments of her life.

The sound of Murdoch yowling with pain snapped her attention back down to the scene below. He was rubbing his ribs and glaring at his opponent. She wanted to charge down there and tear into whoever had just landed such a painful hit, but Murdoch would not thank her for interfering.

Did the man have no sense? It had been only a few days since he'd been too weak to sit up on his own. Now he was out there facing off against the man they called Sigil. She wanted to rail at the pair of them, but she wasn't in the habit of pursuing lost causes.

Perhaps they had the right of it. They all knew it was but a matter of time before Duke Keirthan attacked again. He was not the sort of man to accept defeat with grace. They had already survived two assaults on the keep, the first being when Murdoch and his friends had wrested control from her late husband's men; the second when Fagan had tried to reclaim his hold on the family lands— and her.

She shivered in the bright sun. By custom, she should have been wearing dark gray, the appropriate color for a recent widow. To do so would imply that she grieved over Fagan's death, but that would be a lie. At best, what she felt was regret Fagan hadn't been the man he could've been.

Murdoch and Sigil had resumed their practice. They were certainly a contrast in styles and movement. Sigil's build was lean, while Murdoch was easily the largest man in the keep. The fiendish grins on their faces as first one and then the other gained the upper hand in their match were the only real similarity between them.

Once again, Sigil landed a telling blow that had Murdoch cursing as he jumped back out of range.

Clearly frustrated, he glared at his opponent. "That's the third time you've managed that trick. Show me how it's done."

This time they lined up side by side as Sigil went through the motion slowly, repeating it again and again, faster each time. Soon Murdoch had the maneuver mastered, and they faced off again.

As she watched the two of them in a dazzling display of skill, she realized she was no longer alone on the balcony. Shadow bumped into her, demanding to be petted. Alina leaned down to give the big cat a thorough scratching.

"Your master shouldn't be out there this long, but we both know he wouldn't appreciate my fussing over him."

She wished the cat could advise her on how best to approach the animal's skittish master. Shadow simply yawned and proceeded to go to sleep. So much for getting any help from that corner.

Alina was about to return to her embroidery, when a shouting match broke out down below. Several of the men-at-arms stood facing Murdoch and Sigil with their weapons drawn. There was no mistaking the anger in their expressions.

She strained to hear what was going on as Murdoch planted himself directly between the armed men and Sigil. He brandished his own sword, forcing them to retreat a few steps.

His deep voice vibrated with fury as he shouted at them. "Stand down, the lot of you."

She held her breath and prayed they'd listen. Right now Murdoch and Sigil were badly outnumbered, and it was getting worse.

Standing there and doing nothing wasn't an option. Alina bolted back inside to search for Captain Gideon, hoping she would find him in time.

Damn, Murdoch had been afraid of this. The last thing he wanted was to hurt one of Merewen's men while protecting Sigil.

"I said to stand down. Put away your weapons, and we'll talk."

"We don't want to talk. We want him dead," the bravest of his opponents shouted back.

"What's your name?"

The man didn't bother to glance in Murdoch's direction. "Don't know what my name has to do with anything, but it's Ewan."

"Ewan, lower your blade so we can discuss this calmly."

"There's no need for talking other than to find out why he has a sword."

Murdoch took a step forward, forcing the man to retreat yet again, hoping to divert Ewan's attention from Sigil to him. "Because I gave it to him."

Several more men arranged themselves beside their outspoken friend, a clear indication of whose side they were on.

Ewan continued shouting. "My brother died fighting against that bastard Fagan and his men. Why are we letting this murderer live?"

Sigil moved up next to Murdoch. The maneuver didn't do a thing to calm the situation, but at least he had his sword tip down in the dirt.

"Get back."

The stubborn fool shook his head and stayed right where he was. "I'm the one they want. I won't hide."

Murdoch wanted to kick Sigil's backside for him, but then he would've done the same if their positions were reversed. He liked that about him, even if it only served to escalate the situation.

Murdoch moved to put more distance between them. They'd need ample room to maneuver if things went out of control. "This man is my prisoner. I will not allow him to be harmed."

"He doesn't look like a prisoner with a weapon in his hand." Ewan brought up his own sword. "He should've been executed immediately. If you don't have the courage, then stand back and let us take care of it."

That did it. No one got by with calling Murdoch a coward. No one. If words didn't get his point across, his sword would.

Using the strength and speed granted to him by the goddess herself, he charged forward and knocked Ewan's sword out of his hand before the man could muster any kind of defense.

Then Murdoch grabbed him by the collar and lifted him off the ground, choking off the guard's ability to breathe. "Do you really want to question my honor, Ewan? Because I'm telling you right now that men have died for far less."

Ewan managed to sputter, "N-no."

Murdoch looked around at the remaining guards, meeting each one's gaze head-on. "Now, stand down and put away your weapons."

As he waited, he sensed more men approaching, but these were friends. Averel's dogs arrived just ahead of their master, with the captain and Kane right behind them. They aligned themselves on either side of Murdoch and Sigil.

The last one to show up was Shadow. She planted herself in front of several of Ewan's companions and yawned, showing off her fangs. From the way several backed away, her point was made.

Gideon's voice was remarkably calm. "Murdoch, I'm sorry I'm late. I was looking forward to facing off against Sigil here myself."

Murdoch slowly lowered Ewan back to his feet and loosened his hold enough to let the man draw a full breath. "You're not too late. Ewan and his friends here were just asking why we would give Sigil a sword."

"Did you tell them that I thought your suggestion that we might learn more from him about how the duke's men fight had merit?"

Murdoch had said no such thing, but he wasn't about to mention that at the moment. "Sigil already taught me how to counter a move that he used to slip past my guard three times. I would be glad to teach my friend Ewan here how to do it myself."

Gideon stared at the guard for several seconds. "What do you think, Ewan? Not many can best my friend Murdoch with a sword, so you'd learn a lot from him. Wouldn't you like that?"

Clearly the man wanted to refuse. But as he looked from Gideon to Murdoch and back, he knew he was trapped. Finally, his head bobbed up and down in agreement.

Gideon clapped his hands and then rubbed them together as if the bout were something he'd looked forward to all day. "The rest of you partner up. Kane and I will work with each of you one-on-one in turn while Sigil assists Murdoch in teaching Ewan his lesson. Averel, get them started, and I'll be with you in a minute."

The rest of the men drifted away to do as Gideon had

ordered. Ewan stood back and waited, his anger still evident in his posture. He clearly hadn't appreciated Murdoch's rough treatment, but he was smart enough to realize that he was lucky to be alive.

Murdoch motioned for Ewan to join him. "I'm sorry about your brother, Ewan. Now let me show you how Sigil here would've killed me three times over. Then I'll let him show you how to counter the move. Your mother's already lost one son."

He then leaned in close, letting Ewan see the vestiges of anger in his eyes. "It would be a shame for her to lose another one because he insulted the wrong man or was too stupid to learn the skills it takes to stay alive."

Ewan swallowed hard, but he gamely faced off against Murdoch with Sigil calling out suggestions to them both. As tempting as it was to beat the guard bloody, Murdoch's vow to protect Merewen and her people took precedence.

With that in mind, he set about making the man a better swordsman, but the bastard was going to pay for the lesson with a lot of sweat and pain.

"But, Sire, I would be remiss if I didn't advise against taking two doses of this potion so close together."

Did the healer think Ifre was a total fool? The man might be the best healer in the city of Agathia, but Keirthan knew a fair amount about herbal concoctions himself.

The problem wasn't the body's intolerance of multiple doses, but the likelihood the patient would learn to crave the potion. Ifre's will was stronger than that. Even if it wasn't, right now he needed the drug more than he needed a lecture. Twice in one day he'd been struck with the backlash from magic spells. The pain was beyond bearing.

"Give me the potion now and leave more in case I need it later. Then you may go."

He injected enough authority in the order to have the healer scrambling to prepare the dosages. Ifre braced himself against the noise the man made as he measured and stirred, the glassware clinking and clanking loud enough to raise the dead.

"Here you are, Sire. Do you need my assistance in drinking it?"

Ifre pried his eyes open to glare at the obsequious fool. As if he'd show any more weakness than he already had. "No, thank you. I will be fine."

He forced himself to flatter the healer, knowing he might require the man's services again sometime.

"I do appreciate your coming on such short notice. Theda will see you out now." Ifre glared at his sister-in-law. "Pay the man, and tell everyone that I'm not to be disturbed."

The healer accepted the small purseful of coins from her, his smile becoming more genuine when he felt the weight of the silver. "Please don't hesitate to send for me if the headaches don't improve soon. I am at your service."

After he bowed and followed Theda out of the room, Ifre picked up the flagon of medicine and gulped it down, grateful for the honey and cloves that masked the herb's bitter flavor. Now it was only a matter of time before the pain faded. He could only hope by tomorrow morning he would be back at full strength.

If he wanted to track down Lavinia's location, he'd need to be at his best. It shouldn't be hard, especially if the destruction of his blood magic coins had come from the same area as her feeble attempt to spy on him. But the longer he delayed, the worse his chances were of following the trail back to her.

He staggered across the room to lie down on his bed. Even with his eyes closed, the room continued to pitch and roll. He tangled his fingers in the blankets and held on as he waited for the medicine to take effect.

Finally, a pleasant fog nibbled at the jagged edges of his pain, diminishing its strength enough so that sleep could overtake him. As he eased into a deep slumber, he hoped he would dream of dragging his traitorous half sibling back to the capital city in chains.

Picturing Lavinia broken and bloody left him smiling. As he continued to float betwixt sleep and wakefulness, he thought about her image. Any details he could recall might help track her down. He'd only caught the briefest glimpse of her before he'd been slammed back against the wall by the power she'd unleashed.

Her hair was the same. That sharp gaze of hers still reflected her powerful intelligence. He'd sensed there was someone else with her. He hadn't seen enough to know if her companion had been male or female, so that bit of information was no help.

There'd been something about Lavinia's clothing. Something different. Thanks to the powerful potion and the lingering pain, he couldn't bring the image into focus. Tomorrow, though, he'd figure it out. Once he did, he'd set about making his dreams about Lavinia in chains come true. She would pay for defying his command.

Chapter 15

"No, the 'g' makes a softer sound."

Lavinia tried again, most of her attempts to copy Duncan's pronunciation meeting with only limited success. At least he was patient with her, praising her successes without laughing at her failures.

"Nageth."

When he nodded, she repeated the word twice more to lock it in her memory.

Duncan pointed toward the next page. "Now read the next passage all the way through, and then translate it for me."

She faltered over fewer words this time. When she reached the end, she picked up her pen and began the laborious process of changing the old tongue into the modern one. She envied the ease with which Duncan read the ancient languages. So far she'd listened to him read from texts written in four different languages, and suspected he was fluent in several others.

Had she been a jealous person, she might have hated him for it. Instead, she found the combination of his scholarly and warrior natures compelling. Her elder brother had also had a scholarly bent, but Armel had never been the kind to pick up a sword and lead his men into battle himself. Ifre was a coward who killed from a distance.

She suspected Duncan would've been content to spend his life lost in his studies, but his duty came first.

His inborn sense of honor demanded that he stand strong for those who could not defend themselves.

He glanced up and caught her staring. "Did you need help with a word?"

Her cheeks flushed hot as she pushed the parchment toward him. "No, I'm finished."

He held the paper up to the light, his pale eyes skimming the page in quick order. She walked over to the closest shelves and studied the titles while she waited.

The scrape of his chair warned her that Duncan had finished reading. He joined her at the bookshelf, his expression still somber as he handed the paper back to her. She braced herself to receive his verdict.

Then he grinned at her. "I couldn't have done better myself. You got all the tenses right and even caught the subtle nuances of the idiom the author used in the second paragraph."

"Truly?"

"Truly. You obviously have a gift for languages."

His approval warmed her straight through. She'd met few men in her life who appreciated women who were their equal or superior in education. Even most of the other sisters protected the library out of duty, not out of love for the knowledge contained within its walls.

This connection with Duncan was special, a gift to cherish. She smiled back at him, two scholars enjoying the moment.

"You remind me so much of my mother."

All right, that wasn't quite the connection she was feeling. The woman had obviously meant a lot to Duncan, but rather than feeling complimented by the comparison, Lavinia felt mildly insulted. "Your mother?"

His smile softened and his striking eyes twinkled. "You're the first person I've met since her death who understands the simple pleasure to be had in acquiring knowledge for its own sake."

Then the focus of his eyes dropped down to her mouth and back up again. "But to make myself clear, what I feel for you is something entirely different."

"And what do you feel for me?"

"Something I shouldn't." He leaned closer. "This."

His mouth settled over hers, a soft brush of lips and then another. In no mood to be teased, she dropped the paper and captured his face with both hands. He immediately deepened the kiss, his tongue sweeping across hers, hot and demanding.

This time neither of them held back. Now that she had Duncan's full attention, she pressed against the hard planes of his chest and dug her fingertips into his shoulders. He responded by wrapping one arm around her waist while he spread his other hand on the curve of her hips, lifting her up to her tiptoes.

Her conscience told her they should stop, that this behavior was out of bounds for an abbess, even one who hadn't sworn to give her life over to the service of the gods. But right at that moment, she wanted nothing else as much as she wanted to savor this small bit of pleasure.

They both knew their mutual attraction was a momentary thing, two like-minded souls reaching out to each other. It was about proximity, not permanency. And wasn't that a sad, sad thought?

"Ahem."

Lavinia wanted to curse. As tempting as it was to try to ignore Sister Joetta, duty came before pleasure. Duncan knew it, too. He immediately backed away, but there was no mistaking the regret in his expression. That gave her the courage to face her friend.

"Yes, Sister Joetta?"

"I'm sorry to interrupt your, um"—she paused to look from Lavinia toward Duncan and back—"studies. However, there are armed riders approaching from the direction of Trader Musar's winter quarters."

"Thank you, Joetta. Sir Duncan and I will join you shortly."

She returned to the table where they'd been working and gathered up the books they'd used. "We should return these to the shelves first."

Joetta nodded and withdrew. Duncan hung back, giving Lavinia some much-needed time to gather her scattered thoughts.

The abbey had always welcomed visitors of all kinds with open doors, offering hearty food and clean beds to anyone who journeyed through the valley below. Lavinia hated changing that policy, but right now she had no other choice.

If Lavinia were an ordinary sister, she wouldn't have considered changing the open-door rules. But in her case, her brother Ifre hunted her for far more sinister reasons. He either wanted her magical gifts to feed his need for power, or he wanted her dead. There would be no compromise, no love lost between the two siblings.

The blood magic coins had been only the beginning. Ifre wouldn't stop. The memory of him staring up at her through her own scrying bowl still gave her a deep sense of terror when she thought about it.

Duncan's hands slipped around her waist again, this time holding her gently within the safe harbor of his arms. "I'll make sure the guards are well trained, Lavinia. If they are as good as Musar promised, they'll be able to defend the abbey against attack, even from a much larger force."

"I don't want anyone to die defending us."

"It may not come to that, not if our search provides the answers we're looking for. We've already made good progress today. Once I get the men settled in their quarters, I'll continue the search later this evening."

She rested her head against his shoulder. "What will you do when you find the answers?"

What a foolish question, when she already knew his response. He'd leave.

"My friends and I will use the information to put a stop to Duke Keirthan's evil."

"And if you can't stop him?"

He didn't answer at first. Finally, he said, "The Damned have never failed to protect those we've been sent to champion, Lavinia."

She tried to take comfort in that, but had they ever faced someone like her brother?

"Shall we go meet the guards?"

Duncan pressed a soft kiss to the top of her head. "Yes, before it gets any later. They'll be tired from riding all day, but I want to evaluate their skills as soon as possible."

"We need to restore the wards before we go. Do you want to try?"

A new layer of tension rippled through Duncan before he released her. He stepped away and faced the back corner of the room. Bringing up his hands, palms out, he repeated the words she'd drilled him on earlier. As he spoke them, the words seemed to hang in the air, shimmering with power.

Then the wards snapped back into place with a loud crackle. They wavered a bit and then settled down. Duncan stared at the display of power with something akin to horror in his expression.

"Well done."

He glanced down at her, his mouth set in a grim frown. "I was truly hoping that it wouldn't work. I'm not sure how the Lady of the River will feel about one of her warriors learning to invoke magic."

"What will happen if she disapproves?"

He shrugged. "It is impossible to know. Each time we return to the water's edge, we face her judgment not as individuals but as a group. What one does affects us all."

"That hardly seems fair."

His laugh was bitter. "The gods don't concern themselves with being fair. We made a bargain with the Lady, my friends and I, and we will honor that agreement."

"And if she doesn't approve of your efforts?"

"Let's worry about today's problems," Duncan said as he started toward the door.

Even though Duncan avoided responding to her question directly, she could guess at the answer. He and his friends weren't called the Damned for no reason. If they failed to meet the goddess's expectations, they would pay dearly for that failure.

It wasn't fair. Yet as Duncan said, the gods didn't worry about such things. As she followed Duncan out the door, she prayed this time would be different for him.

Duncan studied the twelve men lined up in front of him. They varied in size, coloring, and manner of dress but were identical in the ways that really mattered. When he'd asked them to lay out all of their weapons for inspection, the results had been impressive in both quantity and quality.

How many of them had known Rubar or the other guard? He didn't bother to ask, figuring Musar would've explained the situation to them. If they'd had a problem with Duncan, they could've turned down the job. Or else, one or more could be waiting for an opportune moment to seek revenge. Not being a mind reader, all he could do was proceed as if he trusted them and keep a wary eye out for an ambush.

He stepped back from the table. "Pick up your weapons, and then partner up for some sword practice."

As he waited, he overheard one of the men grumble about having been in the saddle all day. Duncan had been expecting to hear something of the kind. In fact, he'd been hoping for it.

He scanned the group, acting as if he didn't know who was responsible for the complaint.

"I'm sorry. I didn't realize in this part of the world that bandits only attack caravans when they know the guards are rested and at their sharpest."

Josup, who appeared to be the unofficial leader of the group, shot one of his companions a disgusted look. "The only well-rested guards I know are either out of work or dead."

He turned his attention back to Duncan. "You be wanting to see if we can earn our keep protecting the sisters. I might be wondering the same thing about you."

Duncan grinned at him and drew his own sword. "Fair enough. Shall we?"

The two faced off while the others stood back to watch from a safe distance. It didn't take long for everyone to know that Duncan was the better swordsman, but only just. Josup had nothing to be embarrassed about. Against most anyone else, he would've had little trouble either disarming or dismembering his opponent.

Duncan sheathed his sword and held out his hand to his opponent. Josup grinned as he clasped Duncan's hand in a firm grip. "It's been a while since I've faced someone of your talent, Sir Duncan. I wouldn't want to face you in a battle for real."

"I'll take that for the compliment it is and say the same about you." He turned back to the others. "Well, the two of us know what we can do. Let's see how the rest of you measure up."

This time there was no hesitation or grumbling. Josup joined in to keep the numbers even while Duncan circled around, making suggestions as he did. Overall, he was impressed. Musar had chosen well. Granted, these men were used to fighting from horseback while guarding the caravans, but their footwork was far from shoddy.

He didn't know about them, but he'd had enough for

one evening. After all, he still had hours of work ahead of him in the library.

"Halt!"

The men formed up in front of him, breathing hard but still at attention. "We need to stand guard over the abbey. Four six-hour shifts of three men each. You can partner up as you see fit. If no one volunteers to take the first shift, we can draw straws or throw dice."

It didn't surprise him that Josup already had his two partners picked out. "We'll take the first shift."

"Good. I'll ask Sister Margaret to send out food and drink for you. The rest of you eat and then get some rest. You're going to need it. I'll be working with each group of you for an hour before you go on duty. Any questions?"

Several of the men looked to Josup and then down to the ground. He gave them all a disgusted look as he stepped forward. "Trader Musar told us about what happened with Rubar and Teo. He said that you killed both men in defense of Lady Lavinia."

"That's true. I did."

Josup looked a bit surprised. Did he think that Duncan would've lied about it? Or that he'd offer excuses? His honor would've demanded he speak the truth even if there hadn't been an entire room full of witnesses to the fight.

Duncan stood tall and met Josup's hard expression directly. "I didn't know Teo, but Rubar was a good man, one who was kind to me. I regret his death more than you can imagine, but know that I had no choice."

Another of the men spoke up. "Musar said that as well. If he hadn't vouched for you, we wouldn't be here."

A third joined the conversation. "You're likely to be wondering if any of us bears a grudge and if you need to be careful of turning your back on us."

Duncan crossed his arms over his chest, not sure where this was headed. "The thought did cross my mind."

Josup took a step forward. "In battle, your life depends on the man standing next to you. If you can't trust him, then you're fighting enemies on two fronts. Musar and his wife both testified that it was blood magic that caused the death of our friends, not you. Their word is good enough for us."

"Fair enough. If any of you have questions, I prefer you come to me directly. If you have suggestions on how to make the abbey safer from attack, let me know."

Before anyone else could speak, the dinner bell rang. Perfect timing. "After dinner, I have work to do in the library. If you have need of me, have the sisters send for me."

Then in a show of faith, he turned his back on them and walked away.

Upon entering the dining hall, he joined the men at the corner table, the same one Rubar and the other guards had used. As he sat down, he spotted Lavinia at her usual spot at the head table. There was an empty seat next to her. Had it been for him? Possibly, considering the odd expression on her face when she noticed him back in the corner.

He hadn't wanted to presume that she'd want him there. He also thought it best to distance himself from her, especially in front of the other sisters and the new guards. Her reputation could suffer, something a woman in her position could scarce afford.

He let himself be drawn into the conversation among the guards. From what he could gather, they'd all served together at various times over the years. Musar had done a good job in selecting the men, a debt Duncan would likely never get the chance to repay.

He would make sure Lavinia knew, though. She'd sleep better knowing the men who patrolled the abbey knew what they were doing. As the various courses were brought to the table, he watched as she carried on an animated conversation with Sister Joetta and Sarra, the young novice.

As if sensing his gaze, the young girl turned in his direction and smiled. He nodded back to her. She'd lost so much in her young life, yet she'd retained much of her innocence. It infuriated Duncan to know that as long as Ifre Keirthan ruled Agathia, she'd never be safe. The bastard had much to answer for.

And if it took every last breath Duncan had, he would see to it the man faced a reckoning. All of which made him wonder how his friends were faring. He wasn't used to being isolated from them like this.

Tonight, after he finished in the library, he would send Kiva flying back to Gideon. The captain would want to know what progress Duncan had made. At the same time, Duncan needed even that tenuous connection with his friends. Watching the easy camaraderie among the guards had reminded him of how lonely he was without the other Damned.

Once again, he found himself watching Lavinia. If Gideon were here, he could talk to him about this jumble of feelings he had for her. Surely Gideon would understand, what with his own powerful connection to Lady Merewen. Come to think of it, Duncan also owed Murdoch an apology.

Averel wasn't the only one who'd teased the big man about Lady Alina. But then none of them expected to encounter such women in their lives. It was just another reminder of how much they'd all lost when they'd offered their souls and their service to the Lady.

Feeling the weight of his past, he sipped his wine and stared at the one woman he'd ever met who could have laid claim to his heart.

Chapter 16

"My dear sister, it is past time for you to return to the family home...."

Ifre Keirthan stood warming himself beside the circle of fire in his underground chambers and considered his options. His efforts to trace his sister's scrying had netted him nothing—how dare she go to such lengths to hide from him?

Now he would have to resort to tracking the coins instead. It was definitely a more complicated spell, but one that should produce more reliable results. He returned to the altar and began his preparations. First, he hung a fresh map of Agathia and the surrounding lands on the wall.

He'd spent a great deal of money to obtain the most accurate map in existence, one drawn by a master cartographer from the trading clans. Some of the routes through the mountains were known only to the clans, and it was information they didn't share with anyone. Ever. But with enough money coupled with the right threats on the table, it was possible to pervert the loyalty of anyone, even a mapmaker.

A movement behind him drew Ifre's attention back to the altar. He smiled as he turned to face the woman who was chained to the four pillars that formed the cornerstones of the altar.

"Ah, yes, you are awake now."

He drank in the luscious sound of her whimpers, soaking in the extra spice of fear and dread in the woman's voice. She must know what was coming. She should. This was her third time to offer her up her blood to fuel his spells. Each time, the magic she provided was weaker, which meant he'd have to burn more of his own reserves. He'd have to replace her soon.

He drew his dagger, the blade once again a dull silver. When he finished feeding the steel from the woman and then his own vein, it would be pulsing crimson and ready to invoke the tracking spell he'd built into the coins. Once he learned the direction of their paths, he would send the troops out to fetch his sister.

He couldn't wait. The magic in Lavinia's veins would garner him enough strength to bring the entire country to heel. Once he had all of Agathia firmly within his grasp, it would be time to seize power beyond his own borders. After all, power begat power—magic even more so.

Already he'd unleashed far more magic than his late brother had in all the years he'd served as duke. Once Ifre had perfected control of his weapon, he would strike at will. No one would dare stand against him.

Tomorrow, after he'd rested from the effort it took to search for Lavinia, he'd attack within the kingdom again. The last burst had hit somewhere close to Lord Fagan's estate. Soon he would aim at the keep itself. Blasting Lady Merewen's home out of existence would serve as a good example to any other potential traitors.

His plans made, it was time to get to work. He opened the book to the right page. He'd memorized the words but preferred to read the actual text to avoid any mistakes. Carelessness would prove deadly to him, not just his victim.

Right before Armel's death, Ifre had found several of the banned grimoires in a locked chest that had been handed down to his brother. Their existence had been a bit of a shock, considering his father had ordered all such books to be gathered up and destroyed.

Obviously, he'd secretly retained copies for himself and his heirs. Ifre had been impressed by the sneakiness of it, although he suspected his father had not done so out of greed for power. More likely, he'd done it in case someone else had held back a few of the grimoires for some fell purpose.

Ifre lifted his knife high in the air and began to chant, ignoring the mewling pleas from his unwilling donor. When the last echo of the words faded away, he slashed downward, opening her thigh to the bone. The knife was greedy today, soaking up her blood as fast as it poured out of her veins.

When the flow slowed to a mere trickle, he sealed the wound, not that he much cared if she survived the loss of blood. Her magic was all but gone now anyway.

He next cut his own palm, wincing at the pain. Ashamed of his own show of weakness, he added a second cut, this one deeper, allowing the knife to drink its fill. After cauterizing his palm, which added another layer of pain, he marched over to the map and stabbed the blade into the symbol for his home and shouted the last few words of the spell at the top of his lungs.

With a crack of thunder, a tiny flame started at the tip of the knife and traced a spiderweb of black lines across the surface of the map. Wisps of smoke followed the trail, smelling of burned parchment and blood.

Ifre waved his hand back and forth to clear away the last of the smoke to study what truths the spell had revealed. He'd sent out twenty of the coins. A quick count of the trails showed that eighteen were still on the move, seeking their target. Several of those trails led beyond the boundaries of Agathia and therefore were unlikely to produce any results. It was always possible Lavinia

had taken refuge in a neighboring land, but his gut instinct said she'd stick with the familiar.

The familiar. Something niggled at the back of his
mind, the same feeling he'd had yesterday when his
headache had prevented him from pursuing the thought.
Forcing the memory wouldn't work. He ignored it and
studied the remaining two trails.

They'd started off here in the capital city just as the
others had. From there, they'd traveled together; their
path meandered all over the area. Why? Who'd been carrying them? He traced the line singed into the parchment, slowly making sense of what he was seeing.

It was a trader's route, which accounted for the twists
and turns. Caravans stopped anywhere there were enough
people who might need their wares. The trail continued
until it disappeared in a small valley between two mountain ranges. At that point, there was nothing left of them
except a black smudge on the paper.

The two coins had been destroyed right there on the
eastern border of Agathia. Nothing showed on the map,
so there was no settlement of any size. That didn't mean
there weren't permanent residents in the area.

He left the map hanging where it was and stepped off
the dais long enough to retrieve an atlas from his private
collection. Needing a place to spread it out, he summoned his servants.

When the first two arrived, Ifre pointed toward the
altar. "Take her. If she lives, cleanse her wound and then
feed her. If not, you know what to do."

Ifre waited impatiently for them to follow his orders.
They knew not to dawdle. Experience had taught them
that his need for fresh blood required a steady flow of
prisoners. It was only one short misstep from servant to
sacrifice.

When they were gone, he opened the book to a de-
tailed map of the Sojourn Valley. Ah, yes, there was a

reason for a caravan to stop in such a remote area. He'd forgotten about the abbey at the entrance of the valley. All things considered, Ifre had little doubt someone in that distant abbey had recognized the blood coins for what they were and destroyed them.

Since the coins were keyed to react only to someone of his bloodline, that had to mean that the traders had come into contact with Lavinia. After all, their family had dwindled down to just the two of them.

And now he knew what memory had been floating at the edge of his thoughts. In the brief glimpse he'd had of Lavinia through her scrying, she'd been wearing robes. Yes, the style was right for one of the sisters or, more likely, an abbess to wear. Somehow he doubted his little half sibling would settle for being an ordinary sister.

Since his coins had been destroyed, he had to think Lavinia had survived the incident. He smiled. She wouldn't live long beyond their next encounter. He'd send out enough troops to tear that abbey apart stone by stone if that was what it took to drag her back to his side.

He'd prepare another of his talismans especially for her. Once the soldiers had her subdued, all they had to do was slip the necklace around her neck to render her docile. From that point, she would follow them back to the capital city without question. The bonus was that as soon as she wore his talisman, he would be able to draw from the deep well of her magic to supplement his own.

It should take a troop of the royal guard three days of hard riding to reach the abbey. He rubbed some warmth into his hands, ignoring the still-tender scar on his palm.

"Yes, dear Lavinia, soon you and I will be reunited. Then nothing and no one will stop me."

At that, he went in search of the latest captain of his personal guard to give the man his marching orders. The sooner Lavinia was captured, the sooner he could turn his attention to shoring up his control of the nobles and the riches in their holdings across all of Agathia.

Gideon should've known Kane would follow him up to the ramparts. He'd come up here to clear his head and think things through. So much for a few minutes' solitude. With his eyes on the rolling grasslands beyond the palisade, he asked, "What now?"

"I need to leave soon, Gideon, if I'm going to be of any help." Kane shifted from foot to foot in an uncharacteristic show of nerves. "It will take time to insinuate myself into the duke's household guard."

"So you keep telling me."

Kane was right. That didn't mean Gideon wanted to hear it. His friend's plan to infiltrate Duke Keirthan's personal guard made sense. Having a spy on the inside would greatly increase their chances of overcoming the duke's efforts to subjugate his people.

Having Averel follow Kane into the capital city, passing himself off as a troubadour, was the only thing that made the idea palatable. Gideon trusted Kane with his life, but the mage-marked warrior would be riding into the source of the blood magic that was casting its deadly shadow over the countryside.

If all of the Damned were together, there was no way the taint of the magic could overcome Kane's inborn sense of duty and honor. Alone, though, with the pulsing heart of Keirthan's twisted magic so close at hand, there was no telling how the warrior would be affected.

Centuries ago, Kane had turned his back on the teachings of his grandfather, a dark mage of incredible power. Yet the mark on Kane's cheek proved the connection was still there, written not just on his skin but in his blood and bones.

"Well? Am I going or not?" Kane practically spit the words out between clenched teeth.

They both knew Gideon had no choice. "Tell Averel to get ready. The two of you will ride out in the morning."

"But—"

Gideon cut off the other man's protest. "I know you prefer to travel at night, but we still haven't heard from Duncan. If he's going to send word, it will be after dark when Kiva arrives."

The other warrior stared out at the horizon. "He's fine, Gideon. Duncan knows how to take care of himself."

"We all do." Gideon slammed his fist against the rough-hewn wooden wall. "But we almost lost Murdoch, didn't we? It took *days* for him to heal. That's never happened before, not since the goddess claimed us as her own. Duncan's been gone for days with no word, and now you and Averel are leaving. I don't like it. We've always fought our battles together. Now we're scattered like leaves on the wind."

He clapped his friend on the shoulder. "I know you'll do fine, and the knowledge you will gain will make it easier to defeat the enemy. Yet I hate the whole idea. Besides, who will keep my sword skills sharp if you're not around?"

He softened the last bit with a smile.

"That would be me."

They both turned to face Murdoch, his deep voice finally sounding at full strength.

The big man rolled his shoulders and stretched. "We both know Kane always goes too easy on you, Gideon. He thinks embarrassing you in practice makes us all look bad. Personally, I relish those moments."

Gideon made sure his answering smile showed a lot of teeth and a hint of meanness. "We'll see about that bright and early in the morning. Maybe a small wager would be in order."

Murdoch gave him a dubious look. "What do you have in mind?"

Gideon didn't blame him for being suspicious. It wasn't as if the Damned ever had much use for money. "Jarod needs extra help cleaning the stables. Whoever loses the bout has to spend the rest of the day shoveling out stalls."

"Fair enough." Murdoch glanced back over his shoulder. "In fact, tell you what. We'll include Sigil, here, in the deal. We'll all three fight. The two losers haul cartloads of manure."

Gideon looked past his friend toward the duke's man, who had become Murdoch's silent shadow since they'd both left their sickbeds. "Are you all right with helping the stable master?"

Sigil shrugged. "I'd rather feel useful."

Then with a sly smile, he added, "But then who says I'll be the loser? I find the idea of sitting in the shade watching the two of you sweat most appealing."

It was the first time he'd acted more like an ally of the Damned than like their prisoner. Obviously Sigil was feeling more comfortable around them, not necessarily a good thing. Could he be biding his time, waiting for them to get careless around him, so that he could escape?

Regardless, Gideon didn't relish the thought of having to execute a man he'd come to like.

"Big words, Sigil. I'll look forward to bringing the two of you a cool drink of water after you've been at it for a few hours."

The prisoner merely nodded, but Gideon suspected the man was actually pleased to be included in their antics. At least someone around there was happy. There was also a limit to how much Gideon was willing to trust him.

"Sigil, if you'll excuse us, I need to talk to these two."

Murdoch interceded. "Why don't you wait for me over by the gate to the pasture? I told Jarod the two of us would give him a hand with the horses. I'll be along shortly."

Sigil nodded a second time. "If you'll excuse me, Captain. Kane."

Gideon waited until he was well out of hearing range before speaking again. "Kane, whether we hear from Duncan or not, you and Averel leave at dawn. It should be safe for the two of you to ride together for a while, but closer to the city, you'll need to separate. No one should see the two of you together."

Kane gave him a long, hard look. "We'll be fine, Gideon. *I'll* be fine."

He should've known Kane would sense Gideon's real worry. "I know that, but I'd feel better if one of the birds was going to be with you. Averel's dogs run fast, but it will still take them longer to bring back messages."

"Scim can find us if need be. He's done it before."

True, but the gyrfalcon had already been attacked by the duke's magic. Gideon hated to put him at risk again. He loved his feathered companion, but he loved Lady Merewen even more. Besides, it was her safety that the Damned were sent to ensure. Any and all of them were expendable when it came to carrying out their mission.

Suddenly, he needed to see Merewen, to hold her while he could. "Let me know if you need any help getting ready, Kane. Murdoch, you'd better catch up with Sigil. The men seem to have accepted him since he's started helping with the training, but let's not tempt fate."

Kane waited until Murdoch was gone to speak again. "If you don't hear from Duncan soon, send Scim after us. The route to the capital closely parallels the one Duncan was following to the abbey for the first two days at least. It would be easy enough for us to change directions to check on him."

"True, but it would also delay your arrival in the city.

As you said, it will take time for you to find a way to join the duke's guard."

Then Kane asked, "When are the other landholders coming to meet with you?"

"In two days' time. It would be nice to find some allies in this fight, but I don't hold out much hope. Most will be reluctant to lend me their best fighters because that will weaken the defense of their homes. If I can't convince them that the only way they'll rid Agathia of the duke's predations is to band together, then I fear for the success of our mission."

And that would cost not only the Damned but Merewen herself dearly.

"You'll convince them."

Gideon wished he had Kane's confidence. The one positive was that after he spoke to the leaders, he would know one way or the other if the Damned would be facing Keirthan with an army at their back or on their own. And from there they could plan their attack.

Kane had started to walk away but turned back one last time. "Gideon, trust in the Lady and in us as we all trust you. We've never failed before, and we won't this time. Have faith. Doubt only weakens us all."

Once again Kane was right. In battle, doubt and fear could kill as many warriors as the enemy did. He watched Kane round up Averel to start packing while Murdoch caught up with Sigil to help with the horses. It was definitely time to find Merewen and steal a few minutes from planning and plotting to be with the woman who held his heart in her hands.

Chapter 17

*L*avinia quietly stepped into the library. Duncan was right where she expected him to be, hard at work, his fingers stained with ink as he took notes. When Duncan finally reached the end of a page, she spoke. "I thought I'd find you in here."

Duncan looked up at her, obviously surprised to see her standing there. His pale eyes blinked rapidly against the brightness of the mage lantern she carried with her. "I didn't get started as early as I'd meant to. It took a while to get the new guards settled in."

"What are your first impressions? Are they what you expected?"

She knew he wouldn't be sequestered here in the library if he was at all concerned about the men Musar had sent to her. Yet it provided an excuse to talk with Duncan.

"They are fine." Then he smiled. "Actually, better than fine. I couldn't have done a better job picking them myself. Over the years, I've known their kind before and recognize the type. They take their duties seriously but don't have anything to prove."

The burden of worry she'd been carrying lightened at the news. "I am most glad to hear that."

Duncan continued. "After I leave, Josup will make a fine captain for your guard. The other men listen when he speaks and respect his opinion."

She focused on what Duncan was telling her, trying her best to ignore the stab of pain that came from knowing he would soon disappear from her life.

"I'll be sure to thank Musar. Having him handpick the men was a definite gift from the gods."

She wandered closer to the table. "Have you found a new thread of information to follow?"

"I think so. I've found a few references to a blast of power that can kill at a distance." Duncan frowned and shuffled through his notes. "I'm sure I wrote down which book to read next. It's here somewhere. Once I track down that spell, I am hoping it will also indicate how to counter it."

When he reached for another book, she stopped him by capturing his hand in hers. "You've done enough for one night, Duncan. You've had a long, busy day. So have I, and I cannot seek my own bed knowing you are still in here working."

All right, that was a bit of a stretch of the truth, but he wouldn't stop unless she made him. That much was clear.

She gave his hand a tug. "Tomorrow will be here soon enough, and you'll think better after some sleep and a good breakfast."

He stared down at their joined hands and then slowly raised his gaze to hers. There was a flash of heat in those pale eyes that hadn't been there a second before. She really should let go and step back. It would be smarter than standing there wishing the table would simply disappear, leaving nothing standing between them.

Telling herself that he needed to straighten his notes and return the books to their shelf, she released his hand. As soon as she did, she missed that small connection.

Duncan didn't say anything as he stowed the books and papers where they'd be protected, saving back one page covered with his neat script. He folded it until it fit in a small pouch he then tucked into his belt. How odd. When at last he was finished, she started to restore the wards, but he stopped her.

"Let me."

Surprised by his request, she lowered her hands and let him take over, even though he was clearly uncomfortable using magic, even such a simple spell. This time the wards popped back into place smoothly. Despite his obvious misgivings, he had a knack for it. Deciding that particular opinion wouldn't please him, she kept it to herself.

"I wanted to make sure that I have that spell memorized."

Duncan sounded a bit gruff, maybe even a bit embarrassed.

She blew out the candles and picked up the mage lantern to light the way for them. He picked up his shield as they walked out. He eyed the light with a frown.

"How does that work?"

"It's another small spell. I like it because it doesn't carry the same danger as open flames do around books and papers. Touch it if you'd like."

When she held it higher to give Duncan a closer look, he cautiously tested the glass with his fingertips.

"Warm but not hot." He tipped his head to the side to better study the lantern. "If they're safer, why don't you use them throughout the abbey?"

She shrugged. "Not many can command the spell, and not everyone is comfortable around magic. I use it only when I'm alone or in my private quarters."

As they started walking again, she added, "The spell is similar in nature to the one you've mastered for the wards. I can teach it to you if you would find it useful."

She could see that he was clearly tempted by her offer, but finally he shook his head. "Let me think about that. I certainly can understand the value of such a spell when working around rare and fragile manuscripts and books."

They'd reached the door to her private garden. "If you decide you'd like me to show you the spell, let me know."

When she started outside, he remained where he was. Was something wrong? "Duncan, aren't you coming?"

"I'm sorry, Lavinia. I think I should move back to the guest quarters with the other men. I'll gather up my things and go now. If you don't mind, there's one thing I need to do here in the garden first."

Rather than merely nodding, she asked, "Were these quarters unsatisfactory?"

He stared down at her before looking past her toward the door on the far side of the garden—hers, not his. "Not at all. I worry what the men, as well as the sisters, will think if I continue to share your private quarters, even if I am sleeping in a separate room. I would not want to call your reputation into question."

"But I trust you." She sounded needy to her own ears.

Those oddly pale eyes flashed hot again. "Mayhap it is myself I don't trust, Lavinia."

How was she supposed to respond to that? No doubt a wiser woman would thank him for his concern and then stand back out of the way while he gathered his things. He was right. Having him move back to the guest quarters would be the best thing for both their sakes.

But right now, she didn't want what was best for her. Not if it meant seeing Duncan only from across the dining hall at meal times or the odd moment they could share in the library.

Before she could say anything, Duncan brought his shield out of his room over to the bench and propped it against the wall. Turning toward her, he said, "You might want to cover your eyes."

"What are you going to do?"

He gestured toward the shield. "That's not simply a painting of an owl. It truly is Kiva, my companion and avatar."

Before she could think of a coherent thing to say, Duncan murmured a series of words in the old tongue. She'd wielded enough magic herself to recognize the power in each word he uttered. After he said the last word, there was a heavy silence followed by a flash of light that nearly blinded her.

She threw her arm up to shield her eyes, but it was too late. When her vision cleared, Duncan was standing there with an enormous owl sitting on his arm. Where had that bird come from? But a glance at the shield, empty now except for the black outline of an owl, answered that question.

"Duncan, what kind of magic is this?"

"A gift from the gods." He smiled as he stroked the bird's chest feathers with his free hand. "I found him when he was but a young fledgling and barely able to fly. When the Lady of the River took me into her service, she allowed him to come with me."

Despite the evidence right there in front of her, Lavinia struggled to believe what her eyes were telling her. "I saw him in the scrying bowl. He's real."

Duncan chuckled. "Very. Come pet him. Kiva has always liked the ladies."

She did as he suggested, enjoying the soft tickle of Kiva's feathers against her fingers. The bird's huge amber eyes stared at her with an unsettling amount of intelligence, as if he could read her thoughts.

"He's handsome." Like his owner.

"He certainly thinks so. I swear, he spends half the night preening." Duncan carried Kiva over to the bench and waited for the bird to hop down. When he reached for the small pouch containing the note, its purpose became clear.

"You use him to carry messages." Amazing.

"Yes. I'm already late in sending a report to my captain. Kiva will get it to him faster than the fastest courier could."

When the pouch was securely tied to Kiva's leg, Duncan once again offered the bird his arm. He stroked the bird's head one last time before flinging him upward. With a quick series of powerful strokes, Kiva caught the night air under his wings and soared up into the darkening sky. He circled overhead several times before winging his way westward. She thought she heard him call out right before he disappeared from sight, as if saying farewell.

"That was amazing."

Duncan continued to watch the sky for several seconds. "I know. Even after all this time, I feel blessed to have him in my life. It will take Kiva at least two nights to reach Gideon and return. That's the longest we'll have been apart in centuries."

Then he looked a bit embarrassed, as if he'd revealed too much. "I should get my things now. The hour grows late."

"You don't have to be alone, Duncan. Stay here tonight." Then, to make sure he understood what she was really offering, she walked over and bolted the door to her office, ensuring no one else could enter her private garden. Then she added, "Stay here with me."

He'd already started for the small room where he'd slept the past couple of nights. "Are you sure?"

"Yes. Maybe." Then she admitted the truth. "But I'm scared of what I feel for you."

To make sure he understood that didn't mean she'd changed her mind, she once again took his hand and tugged him farther out into the garden. With a shy smile, she whispered the words to dim the lantern.

Then it was just the two of them, alone in the shadows, the only illumination coming from the moon overhead. The spicy, sweet scent of the flowers and the silvered light gave the whole garden its own magic, a small world to be shared by only two.

If Duncan was willing. He'd yet to do more than stand there, the sharp edges of his handsome face stark in the pale light. She turned away, on the verge of retreating to the safety of her room when he finally spoke.

"You weave a powerful spell, my lady, with nothing more than a smile."

Duncan eased close to stand behind her. "I dreamt of your beauty that first night after I saw your face in the moon overhead. You have haunted my dreams ever since."

His hands began to gently unbraid her hair, letting it tumble down her back. Odd that such a simple thing could feel so intimate, more so than even a kiss. Then she felt the tickle of his breath against her skin as he nuzzled the side of her neck.

"Your beauty is something to be savored slowly."

Her scholar possessed the words of a poet. She leaned back against the hard strength of his warrior's body and arched her head to the side in encouragement. He murmured his approval as his fingertips trailed down her shoulders to settle at her waist.

"How far do you want this to go, Lavinia? Although I would be grateful for even this much, I want so much more."

If it hadn't been for the deep huskiness in his voice, she might have doubted the truth of that. What would it take to rattle his incredible control?

She turned to kiss the side of his jaw and was rewarded by a small tremor that rolled through his big body. "I want it all, Duncan, everything you have to offer."

"I can't offer you everything, Lavinia. My life and soul

belong to the goddess. However, I promise to give you every minute that I can."

She understood being bound by the chains of obligations and promises. "Then that will be enough, Duncan."

For the first time, she faced him directly. As he watched, she unfastened the belt of her robes and loosened the ties to let it slide down off her shoulders to pool at her ankles. Duncan offered her his hand as she stepped out of her slippers.

Wearing nothing more than a chemise left her feeling a bit chilled in the evening air, her nipples pebbling up, the soft cloth abrading her most sensitive skin. Yet she found herself reluctant to immediately retire to her bedroom.

Duncan stepped back to remove his belt and sword. His own tunic quickly followed; yet he hesitated before removing anything else.

She tested the smooth strength of his shoulder with the palm of her hand. "Kiss me."

"Anything you desire, my lady."

Duncan caught her up in his arms, holding her tight against the heated flesh of his chest, yet making her feel so fragile and feminine in his embrace. His mouth found hers and then all ability to speak or even think disappeared completely.

Duncan swept past the barrier of Lavinia's lips with his tongue, plunging deep, savoring the sweet flavors to be found there. As he tasted and explored her mouth, his hands learned the lush curves of her body. The robes had done little to disguise how perfectly she was built, but exploring all that soft, womanly flesh with nothing more than a whisper of linen between them had him aching for more.

She deserved a gentle wooing, not a mad rush to have

her on her back. He lifted her up without breaking off the kiss and retreated to the bench that ran along the wall behind them.

When the back of his legs hit the cool stone, he sat down and settled Lavinia astride his lap. When the position brought the juncture of her legs in direct contact with his shaft, he thrust upward, groaning at the sweet connection between them. Lavinia responded by rocking hard against him, the surge of heat startling a moan from each of them.

He splayed his hands across the curve of her hips to still her motion. "My lady, you're weaving a spell of amazing power tonight."

Her mouth curved up in a seductive smile. "I am certain that it takes two to create this kind of magic, Duncan."

"I do believe you have the right of it."

The crush of her breasts against his chest was sweet, but it wasn't enough. He lifted her higher, enough so that he could brush his tongue over the dusky tip of one breast and then the other. The delicate fabric of her chemise was no barrier at all.

"Duncan!"

Lavinia dug her fingers into his shoulders as he suckled one breast, working it with both his lips and the barest hint of teeth. At the same time, he eased one hand between them, seeking the damp center of her need. She rested her forehead against his as he pressed harder, her breath coming in quick bursts.

The situation was quickly reeling out of control. If they didn't seek the comfort of Lavinia's bed soon, he'd end up taking her on this cold stone bench. She deserved better.

He slowed his touch, carefully banking the fires of their passion. "We should take this inside."

Her eyes heavy lidded, she smiled down at him. "Yes, let's."

Before she could stand up, he kissed her again as he muscled them both up off the bench. She broke away from him long enough to drop the wards that protected her door. He was glad she was thinking clearly enough to take care of it. His own mind could focus on only one thing: stripping them both down to the skin. The time for any kind of barrier between them was gone.

Inside, he set Lavinia back down on her feet. She immediately brought the mage lights in the room up to a soft glow and turned back the covers on her bed. That done, she faced him as she slowly removed her chemise. At that moment, Duncan wasn't sure he could talk, much less manage the coordination it would take to remove the rest of his own clothing.

The lady, though, would have none of it. "Duncan, if you think you're going to wear those boots in my bed, you are sadly mistaken."

Her teasing comment broke the hold the sight of all the silken skin had on him. Had he always been this inept with women? He didn't know because he couldn't remember the last time he'd actually been with one. Most likely it had been that night when he and all four of his friends had slipped away from their duties guarding a caravan just before they were claimed by the Lady of the River.

Now wasn't the time to get lost in the mistakes of his past. Hopping on one foot and then the other, he yanked off his boots and tossed them aside. His trews followed, leaving him standing there, the evidence of his hunger for Lavinia at full attention.

Lavinia made no attempt to disguise her approval. "Duncan, you are certainly . . . impressive."

He was very afraid he blushed, but the approval in her voice only fueled his need for her. He sauntered forward, giving her plenty of time to watch him if it brought her such pleasure.

This time, when they embraced, he was aware of the many contrasts between them. Her feminine build made him feel oversized and awkward. Lavinia's hands were soft to the touch, unlike his, callused as they were from years of holding a weapon. His body was all hard edges, whereas she was a delight of soft curves, the perfect fit for a man's hands. His hands.

He wanted her. Now, with all the rush of a callow youth caught up in the throes of his first love. That wasn't so far off the mark. He'd never given his heart to a woman, and he was in no position to do so now.

But he could give her body the worship it deserved. He caught her up in his arms and gently laid her down in the center of her bed. Bless her, she immediately held her arms out to him.

"The night passes too quickly, Duncan. We've dawdled enough."

"You should be courted."

She shook her head. "We both deserve better than we've had, Duncan. Now may be the only chance we have together. Let's not waste a single minute."

So he took her at her word and stretched out beside her, drinking in the scent of her hair as he caressed every part of her. Lavinia was not a shy lover, a trait he found delightful.

She wrapped her fingers around his shaft and gently slid her hand up and down its length as she pressed a series of nibbling kisses across the line of his jaw and then downward along his neck to his chest.

He tangled his fingers in her hair, loving the feel of it sliding across his skin. His control was slipping. Soon he would have to stop her or lose it all together. It was time to turn the tables on her.

He caught her hands in his and gently pressed her over onto her back. She started to protest, but he stopped her with a kiss.

"I promise to go slower next time."

His words came out as little better than a growl, but his lady didn't seem to mind. He rose over her, kneeling between her feet. Running his hands up the inside of her legs, he spread them wide. Lavinia's head kicked back when he reached the apex to stroke her gently, making sure her body was ready for what he planned next.

She raised her hips, showing her pleasure as he tested her passage. "Duncan, now, please!"

Who was he to deny a lady? Mindful of the difference in their sizes, he moved over her, careful to support his weight with his arms. Once again she clasped his shaft firmly, guiding him right to where they both wanted him to be. With a series of quick thrusts, he settled his cock deep inside her slick heat.

He held himself back, waiting for her to catch her breath. Lavinia smiled up at him and wrapped her legs around his hips, driving him deeper still.

"Are you sure?" He prayed she was ready for him because he wasn't confident how long he could hold back.

Her eyes were huge as she nodded. "This feels so good, so perfect. I want more."

He withdrew and thrust forward again, this time hard and deep in one stroke. Her hips rose up to meet him, her hands reaching up to hold on to his shoulders, her fingernails digging hard into his skin. The sharp pain snapped the last of his control.

He gave Lavinia everything he had to give—hard, fast, and nearly desperate. Yet his lady demanded more, so he called on the strength and endurance the goddess had given all of her avatars. At last Lavinia keened in release, the first ripples taking him with her. He shuddered deep within her as he found his own satisfaction.

And as the two of them lay there, twined in each other's arms, waiting for their hearts to slow back to normal, the moment was so perfect, he wondered if anything would ever be the same again.

Chapter 18

*W*hat was happening? The sound of running feet down the hallway brought Lady Alina to her door to peer out. If she had to guess, the first set of footsteps had belonged to Captain Gideon. Then the door opened a second time, and Merewen followed him downstairs.

Alina quickly dressed. She'd been awake anyway, dark dreams having left her unable to sleep. Curiosity had her following after them. If there'd been any danger, the captain would've made sure Merewen stayed in her room with the door barred. As Alina picked up a candle to light her way down the stairs, a brief taste of jealousy over Merewen's happiness with the captain made Alina feel ashamed. She should be glad that her niece had found a man who made her feel cherished, protected.

Captain Gideon was as different from her late husband as a man could be: honorable, fierce in battle, and gentle in bed. She'd asked Merewen about that, even knowing it was an improper question. After all, a man had the right to use his wife's body as he saw fit, not that Gideon and Merewen were actually married. She wasn't even sure what she would have done if Merewen's answer had been anything other than yes.

No, that wasn't true. She could have turned to Sir Murdoch for help. He and Gideon might be friends, but he would have defended Merewen if it had been necessary.

"Lady Alina, what are you doing about this hour of the night?"

The man himself had caught her unawares. At least this time she didn't humiliate herself by throwing her arms up to defend herself as he loomed up out of the shadows.

"I heard Lady Merewen and the captain run past my room and down the stairs. I wanted to see if something was amiss."

The huge warrior kept his distance, telling her that he'd noted her reaction to his sudden appearance despite her best efforts to hide it.

"Duncan's owl has returned. They are outside waiting for Kiva to come to perch. I came in to get some food for the bird. He's bound to be exhausted."

To show that she wasn't afraid of Murdoch and hadn't been from the first time they'd met, she stepped forward to place her hand on his arm. "Shall we go to the kitchen and see what we can find? Then we'll hear what news he has brought from your friend."

He stared down to where her fingers rested on his sleeve. A ripple of tension flowed through his muscle, but then he nodded. "I would appreciate your help. The cook would come after me with one of her knives were I to invade her territory uninvited. Ellie will forgive you more readily."

As if he'd be afraid of anything, although Murdoch had been as skittish as a young kitten around her since she'd walked in on him when he'd been all but naked. She was at a loss as to how to deal with it.

He'd apologized even though he'd done nothing wrong. She was the one who'd been caught staring at him. And how many times had she recalled the image of his powerful body in the days since? Especially when she stared at the night sky and wondered what it would be like to have Murdoch lying in her bed.

"May I borrow your candle?"

"Of course."

He stepped away from her, leaving her in the edge of the darkness as he used the flame to light several others to drive back the shadows. She remained motionless, taking advantage of the moment to drink in the sight of Murdoch as he walked around the kitchen, peering into pots and checking the shelves for something suitable for the owl to eat. He even picked up a loaf of bread and sniffed it.

That made her smile. Murdoch happened to glance in her direction as the first giggle escaped. "What?"

She tried to stop, but the moment was a bit too ridiculous. "There you are, creeping around in silence because you're afraid of Ellie, hoping to find something for an owl to eat. I doubt he'd want the bread that she set aside for the morning meal."

Murdoch's stern expression softened just enough to let her know he wasn't angry with her for teasing him. Finally, he relented, and grinned back at her as he returned to her side.

"Do you have a better idea?" His deep voice echoed off the walls as he looked down at her, his light-colored eyes glittering in the candlelight.

She nodded. "An owl might be happier with one of the mice that Ellie is always complaining about."

Murdoch responded by putting his finger across her lips and tilting his head to the side. She couldn't discern what he was listening to, not when he surrounded her with his size and strength. But rather than feeling crowded by him, she felt . . . cocooned. Safe.

She liked it. Liked him. Wanted him.

That startling realization confused her even more. After her wedding night in Fagan's bed, she'd never for one moment wanted a man in that way. There'd been too much pain, humiliation, and brutality. But after meeting Murdoch, she wondered if things could be different with another man. No, not just another man. *Him*.

He eased away slightly, moving toward the table behind them. With that little bit of space between them, her mind cleared enough for her to think of something else. Finally, she heard it, too—the sound of tiny feet skittering across the counter behind them. With a move that was too fast for her to follow, Murdoch lunged toward the table, his big hand coming down on the wooden surface with a hard slap.

"Missed!"

But Murdoch kept at it, finally managing to capture the rodent with a bowl he'd snatched off a nearby shelf. When he removed his hand from the upended bowl, it continued to scoot across the tabletop, heading right for the edge.

Alina was not overly fond of vermin of any kind, but she couldn't help but pity the wee beast. Murdoch stopped the crockery from going over the edge and lifted the edge far enough to grab the mouse by its tail. Then he gave her a perplexed glance as if unsure what to do next.

"Shall we take Kiva his meal?"

Murdoch held the mouse out at arm's length, clearly unhappy with the situation. "I suppose so."

"On the other hand, it would hardly be our fault if that mouse made a daring escape."

Murdoch immediately carried the mouse over to the other side of the kitchen. He pushed the door open just far enough to let the mouse go. No doubt it would soon find its way back inside, but for now it was gone

Murdoch wiped his hands on a rag and then returned to Alina's side. "I won't tell if you won't. They'd never let me live it down. We both know I could've killed it if I'd wanted to."

He was so handsome standing there, genuinely worried that he would seem less than manly for sparing the life of a mouse. Instead, it only proved to her once again that he was at heart a gentle man, one who treated those within his care with tenderness.

"You honor me with your trust."

Alina spoke with great solemnity, as if she were swearing a vow of great import, not one intended to save him a small bit of embarrassment. He'd also noted that she showed no sign of renewed skittishness around him. He'd been worried about that ever since she'd walked in on him the other day.

Her pretty eyes were so serious as she stared up at him. Her silvery blond hair was down about her shoulders, reminding him that this was the middle of the night. No doubt it was highly improper for the two of them to be alone, but he couldn't make his big feet take one step away from her.

Instead, they moved forward, closing the small distance between them. He made sure she had every opportunity to back away, but she held her ground.

"Alina, I very much want to kiss you." He spoke the words gently, hoping not to frighten her. "I know I have no right to ask such a boon, but it would be a gift I would cherish forever."

She worried at her lower lip briefly before answering. "I would like that very much, Murdoch, but I fear that I will only disappoint you."

Damn Fagan to hell and back. Even though the bastard was dead and buried, he still continued to haunt his lady wife. Now was not the time for anger. Murdoch gently clasped Alina's shoulders, letting her grow accustomed to his touch before pulling her closer.

"There is nothing you could do that would disappoint me, Alina. I'll go as slowly as you need me to. If you want me to stop, you need but to say so."

She stepped into his embrace. "I'll be fine. After all, it is just a kiss."

Just a kiss? It was and it wasn't. They both knew this would change their relationship forever. There was no going back, not after this. If she could muster up the courage to trust him with a small part of her heart, then he could do the same.

He enfolded her in his arms as if she were made of the finest glass, but she felt solid and so very real. Her mouth curved in a tentative smile as she rose up on her toes. He made sure to meet her halfway, knowing instantly he'd never forget the moment their breath first mingled, the second their lips first touched.

It was perfect.

Alina leaned into him, clasping her hands around his neck for support. The sign of trust tugged at his heart. He kissed her slowly, but thoroughly, keeping his hands anchored firmly at her waist. It nearly killed him not to explore farther, to follow the feminine curves downward to the flare of her hips or up to test the fit of her breasts in the palms of his hands.

A kiss was all he had asked for. It was all he would take unless she offered more.

With a soft sigh, her lips parted and stayed that way. A man could only resist temptation for so long. His tongue darted forward briefly before retreating. To his delight, hers followed suit. The sweet sweep of her tongue across his lips, to delve into his mouth, however briefly, left him burning.

"Alina, are you wanting more? Because if you're not, we need to stop now." For the sake of his sanity.

"Maybe a little more?"

It might kill him if they stopped, but he would. "As much or as little as you want. Touch me any way you want to, anywhere you want to."

She looked over her shoulder, reminding him they were hardly someplace private. Ellie or any of her workers could walk in at any time.

"Kiss me again, but then we should stop." Then she smiled up at him, her eyes alight with temptation. "For now."

For now? Did she mean? Rather than pursue that line of thought, he did as the lady asked and kissed her with everything he had.

Where had Murdoch gotten off to? It shouldn't take this long to fetch some raw meat for a hungry owl. Gideon settled Kiva on one of the railings in front of the stable. After the big bird ruffled his feathers and settled in, Gideon untied the pouch from Kiva's leg and waited for someone to bring a light so he could read the enclosed message.

Even with his enhanced eyesight, he couldn't make sense of Duncan's long missive in full darkness. Merewen had returned to the hall to fetch a torch, but that was after Murdoch had gone looking for something to feed Kiva. After the owl had a small meal and a chance to rest, he could do his own hunting if he needed something more.

But Duncan's avatar would be anxious to return to his master. Dawn was but a short time away, leaving Gideon just the coming daylight hours to read the note and decide how to proceed. Then he'd compose an answer to send back to Duncan.

All of that coupled with Kane and Averel riding out at first light had him gritting his teeth. He hated sending his men on a mission without him, and prayed for the gods to watch over his friends. Kiva stirred restlessly and drummed his wings, probably picking up some of Gideon's own tension.

"Everything's fine, Kiva. You'll get a good meal, sleep the day away in the rafters, and head back to Duncan at dusk."

Gideon crooned the words, hoping the same tone that soothed his own avatar would work on the owl as well. While he spoke, he watched the door to the keep, waiting for Merewen to return. She'd quickly become his anchor in this world. With her at his side, he could face anything, even the departure of the friends who'd never been far from his side for centuries.

At last she appeared with Murdoch right behind her. Gideon leaned forward, trying to see who was walking at his side. The light from the torch Merewen carried reflected off the other woman's silver blond hair.

What was Alina doing up at this hour?

Her presence most likely explained why it had taken Murdoch so long to return. The way those two danced around each other would be entertaining if Murdoch had unlimited time with which to woo his lady. Alina deserved a man who would treat her well, which included being able to stay by her side through life. But all things considered, Gideon had no right to judge.

Which drew his eye right back to Merewen. He took such comfort and strength from her simple acceptance of him and his men. She had no idea what it meant to them to be treated as friends, not just warriors sent by the gods to fight her battles.

At least Murdoch had a bowl in his hand. Even in the dim light of the torch, it was obvious that Murdoch and Lady Alina had done more than simply find a meal for Kiva.

The big man gave Gideon a sheepish look. "Sorry to be gone so long, but we were ... I was ... that is, I hesitated to raid the kitchen without asking Ellie. You know how she is about people invading her domain."

Alina joined in the explanation. "We looked around but couldn't find anything suitable. It was fortunate that one of Ellie's assistants arrived to stoke the fire for the morning meal. He was able to show us where we could carve up some meat for Kiva."

All of that poured out in one breath with Alina and Murdoch studiously avoiding even glancing at each other. Merewen gave her aunt a speculative look. Gideon wasn't the only one wondering what else the two had been doing besides raiding Ellie's larder.

Now wasn't the time, though. He held up the paper to the light. As Murdoch began to feed bits of meat to Kiva, Gideon read the message aloud. He didn't keep secrets from Merewen, and Lady Alina had a right to know what was going on as well. He read it through and then a second time to make sure he hadn't missed anything. When he was done, he folded the paper up and returned it to the pouch.

He counted off the important points. "Duncan is at the abbey and has been given a temporary position there. He saved the abbess's life from an attack caused by another bout of blood magic. She's hired him as a guard rather than a scribe, but she's allowing him to search the library for an explanation of the blood magic and how to counter it."

He paused to review it all in his mind. "He'll return when he has the answers. Did I miss anything?"

Merewen frowned. "He doesn't say if the attack was aimed at the abbess specifically or if she happened to be in the way. Do you think it was something like what killed my horses?"

"It doesn't sound like it. From what we saw when Scim was hurt, there was nothing anyone could've done to prevent it. If she hired Duncan as a guard, she must have thought a swordsman could keep her safe."

Murdoch had finished feeding the owl. "I hate him being so far from us, especially alone. He has few equals with a blade, but there's only so much one man can do."

Gideon nodded. "Let us hope the goddess guides his quest for knowledge so he can return to us without delay."

He glanced at the sky. "It grows light. Kane and Averel will be stirring soon. Murdoch, I know you'll want to see them off. After they're gone, seek out your bed for a few hours since you were on guard duty most of the night."

This time there was no missing the way Murdoch's eyes immediately sought out Alina or that she blushed before quickly looking away. Again Gideon said nothing. After all, the goddess had given Gideon permission to deepen his relationship with Merewen, telling him that his feelings for her strengthened his commitment to their mission.

He could only assume that Murdoch's obviously strong feelings for Alina would have the same effect. Furthermore, he had the lingering fear that they were going to need all their strength to turn back the tide of darkness Duke Keirthan had unleashed upon this land.

Only yesterday afternoon they'd received reports of another deserted crofter's cottage, but with the family's personal belongings still scattered about the place. Several farmers had complained of finding a cow or a goat dead without a mark on them. How long would it be before the magic killed humans as easily as it did their livestock?

He turned back to Kiva, hoping to hide his worry and fear for the people of Agathia. He knew the taste of failure; after all, that was how he and the others had become

Damned by their gods in the first place. He'd lived with that burden of guilt for centuries, and the people who had died on their watch had been little better than strangers to him.

How would he ever forgive himself if he couldn't save Merewen and her people from Keirthan's evil? That answer was actually simple: He never would.

Chapter 19

Keirthan clutched the talisman that tied him magically to the captain of his guard, infusing it with more of his own magic. Another few drops of blood would seal the link between them. While out in the field, all of his men wore a similar device, each one keyed specifically to its bearer. Through the charms, he had total control over their will.

The talismans ensured the men would remain loyal when away from the capital and would obey any order given to them by Ifre or the captain of his guard. They were incapable of thinking for themselves beyond their basic bodily needs and the ability to fight.

Creating the talisman for his captain was more complicated. The man needed his ability to think for himself in order to command the others. That meant finding a delicate balance that satisfied Ifre's need for control but left the man enough free will to provide effective leadership.

It really was a damned shame that Ifre's prior captain, Terrick, had perished in the failed attempt to regain control of Lord Fagan's keep. He'd had a powerful gift for magic, one that Ifre had kept in a weakened condition by siphoning it off through the connection of the talismans. Having to replace Terrick had been an irritation. Well-trained fighters with a hefty dose of magic in their blood were not easy to find.

This time he'd had to settle for one with no gift for magic but a good head for tactics and a decided lack of morals. As a result, Ifre had to constantly monitor the connection between them to avoid weakening the captain to the point he would be useless in battle.

Still, a man had to work with the tools he'd been given.

Now, if he could bring dear Lavinia back to the capital, he'd have a powerful source of magic to augment his own. It would be tricky, but the potential gains far outweighed the possible risks.

To that end, he finished reinforcing the last talisman with another quick burst of magic. He'd already ordered the captain to prepare to ride to the abbey. As far as the men knew, they were being sent to arrest a woman who was a threat to their leader. That much was true, even if she had yet to make any overt moves against his rule.

But she would. His every instinct told him that much. Lavinia had good reason to hate the rest of her family. They'd stripped her whore of a mother of all the wealth and influence their father had given the woman. Not that Ifre felt sorry for his own mother. Too weak to protect her station in life, she'd deserved to be usurped.

The men would depart by midday. No sooner than the thought crossed his mind, Lady Theda rapped on the door and opened it just far enough to make herself heard.

"The men are ready for your inspection."

"I will be right there."

Ifre straightened his robes and checked his appearance in the mirror. He looked regal. Handsome, even. His older brother had always been considered to be both better looking and smarter. And yet those two qualities hadn't kept Armel alive.

In contrast, Ifre would soon control enough land that he could give himself a promotion. King Keirthan the First had quite a nice sound to it.

He picked up the basket of talismans already on their chains and carried them outside himself. The one time he'd had a servant carry the necklaces for him, the man's mind had been little more than an empty shell by the time Ifre had finished inspecting the troops. Ifre could always find another servant, but explaining what had happened had been problematic.

Outside, lined up in neat rows, the troops waited for him. At Ifre's appearance, their captain barked an order, bringing them all to attention.

Ifre called out, "I honor you and your service to the people of Agathia."

Then, with appropriate solemnity, Ifre made his way down the line, bestowing a talisman on each man, which wouldn't be at full power until after they left the city. It wouldn't do for the nobles or other influential people to see the guards lose every bit of their free will. While they might not care about common soldiers, they were smart enough to realize that what Ifre could do to the guards, he could also do to them.

He saved the captain's talisman for the last. Ifre had already given him the one he'd prepared specially for dear Lavinia. As he shook the man's hand, applause rang out from the crowd that had gathered to watch the troop's departure.

Ifre retreated to the highest step as the men mounted up. They moved out in formation, the horses' hooves clattering on the stone road, and the pennant bearing the Duke of Agathia's family sigil waving in the air.

All very dramatic. All very satisfying.

And when they succeeded in dragging Lavinia back to the capital, Ifre's real play for power would begin.

Leaving his lover's bed to return to his own was one of the hardest things Duncan had ever done. Lavinia's quarters were warded against intrusion, but one of the sisters might come knocking at any time. The last thing he wanted to do was embarrass her.

Right now, all they could wonder was why he hadn't moved in with the rest of the guards. If anyone were to see him leaving her room in the early hours of the morning, it would remove all doubt about the new turn in their relationship.

He paused to stretch his muscles in the pale light of early dawn. The sun had barely crested the horizon, leaving the garden still heavily shadowed, the night not quite ready to relinquish its hold on the world. He breathed deeply and smiled. The air was sweetened by the fragrance of the pale moonflowers, their blossoms already closing with the first kiss of the morning light.

The flowers slowly folding in on themselves reminded him that time was quickly passing. The guards would be changing shifts soon, and he wanted to check in with the men before they sought out their own pallets. If there'd been any problems, they would've sent word, but he still liked to know if their patrol had passed quietly.

Before he reached the door of his room, he paused. Someone was spying on him. He sensed the irritating weight of their gaze targeted right between his shoulder blades but couldn't figure out where they were hiding. The only vantage point that made sense was the window that looked out into the garden from Lavinia's office. Moving slowly, as if still studying the flowers in the garden, Duncan made his way around to where he could casually look in that direction.

No enemy could've made it that far without the alarm being raised, so it had to be one of the sisters. The only question was how long had she been watching before he'd noticed?

Had she seen him slipping out of Lavinia's room?

When he finally saw the spy, his tension drained away.

What was Sarra doing in Lavinia's office at this hour? He forced a smile on his face and headed toward the door.

"Hey, little one, you're awake early. Did you need Lady Lavinia for something?"

When Sarra didn't immediately respond, he knelt down to her eye level. Still, she stared through him, as if completely unaware of his presence. She had that same odd look in her eyes he'd seen before when the spirits had spoken through her.

He touched her face, hoping that bit of contact might bring her back out of the trance she was trapped in. Her skin was cold to the touch, and her lips were tinged with blue. Fear for the little girl had him up and running back outside to Lavinia's door and already calling her name.

He found her sitting up, the blankets pooled around her waist. Ordinarily he would have paused to drink in the sight of all that creamy skin gleaming in the soft yellow glow of the mage light. Not this time, however, with little Sarra in trouble.

"It's Sarra. She's standing in your office. She wouldn't speak, and her skin is ice-cold."

"I'll be right there," Lavinia said as she left her bed. "Take my blanket to wrap her in. This isn't the first time we've found her wandering about the abbey awake and yet sleeping."

Sarra didn't appear to be asleep to him, but perhaps Lavinia had the right of it. He hoped so. Grabbing the blanket, still warm from Lavinia's body, he hurried back to Sarra. She stood in the exact same spot, staring at the garden with glassy eyes. He wrapped her in the blanket.

"Lady Lavinia is on her way, Sarra. When she gets here, tell us what is wrong."

There. Finally, a small flicker of awareness flashed across her face, but then it was gone again. Still, it gave him hope. He pulled her into his arms and carried her outside to the bench to sit in the first bright beams of sunlight, hoping their warmth would get through to her.

Lavinia, her hair tousled from the night's activity, hurried out of her room, still fastening the belt of her robes. The sight stole his breath, but he forced his attention back to Sarra.

Lavinia joined them on the bench, slipping her arm around her young friend's thin shoulders. "Sarra, what's wrong? Can you talk to me?"

No response. Seeing the little girl caught up in a sticky web of magic made Duncan want to strike out, but his sword was useless against an invisible enemy. Sarra was so cold. Mayhap he could do something about that.

"You stay with her while I run to the kitchen and fetch some hot tea for her. For all of us."

Duncan had gone but two steps when Sarra abruptly spoke. Or someone spoke through her.

"Duncan, Warrior of the Mist, Damned by the gods and yet their avatar."

He spun back to face the girl, unsure how to react. Finally, he whispered, "I am here."

Sarra tipped her face up as if to look at him even though her eyes remained unblinking. "You will find the answers you seek, but you must hurry. Men ride this way, seeking, hunting. If they find you . . ."

She paused to glance in Lavinia's direction. "Or if they find your lady or me, all will be lost. Everything you and the Damned have done will be for naught."

He forced himself to speak calmly. "What men are coming, Sarra?"

"The men with no will, their souls and hearts devoured by the evil one whose mark they bear. He has set them upon the trail of the coins. That path will lead them straight here."

Lavinia joined the conversation. "Sarra, when will these men get here? And whose mark do they bear?"

The little girl tilted her head to the side and frowned, her posture far too adult for one of her few years. "Soon. Days, not weeks. They come in number."

Tears streaked down Sarra's face. "He has used all her magic, and now she lies dying. It's what will happen to all of us."

"Who, Sarra? Who is dying?"

For the first time, she answered with a child's voice and a child's grief. "My mother. The bad man has used her all up."

When she started sobbing, Duncan's heart broke.

"Is she resting quietly?"

It was the third time since Sarra had cried herself to sleep that Duncan had poked his head into Lavinia's office to check on the little girl. They'd coaxed her into eating a few bites of honeyed porridge and then drinking some tea. Berta had laced it with a mild herb to help Sarra sleep.

Lavinia looked over toward the pallet they'd made for Sarra on the floor. The child hadn't moved since she'd lain down.

"She seems to be at peace. Berta said the herb would wear off in four or five hours, so Sarra should awaken soon."

Duncan came farther into the room. "I hope when she does, that she is back to herself. But even if the voices have relinquished control over her, she'll still carry the memory of her mother's suffering and the threat against all of us."

"We all hurt for her."

In truth, Lavinia hurt for them all. "Have you made any progress this morning?"

He shook his head. "No, I've been working with the guards to prepare for an attack. I discussed strategy with Josup. Given how narrow the switchback trail is, there's no way for an armed force to approach the abbey except in a column of two horses walking side by side."

He walked over to the window to stare out into the garden. "Even with the limited number of guards we have, they will be able to defend the abbey."

She cringed over the thought of those men offering up their lives for her and the other sisters. That anyone would actually consider laying siege to an abbey was horrifying. Images of the sisters huddled inside while men died outside filled her head. Worse yet, what would happen to them all if Ifre's men actually breached the walls?

Her eyes were drawn back to Sarra. The little girl had suffered so many losses already.

"When you go, you must take Sarra with you. She trusts you, and she'll be safer that way. I'm going to send some of the younger sisters across the pass to another abbey, and Ifre will logically assume that she went with them. The head of the order will see to it that they are safe there, and my brother won't dare attack because he'd start a war."

Duncan's pale eyes were the color of a sword blade when he looked at her. "And what about you? Your half brother hunts for you. If Sarra is right, the real reason he's sending his men here is to find you."

The sleeping girl whimpered, stirring restlessly. It was impossible to know if she was having a nightmare or if she was reacting to the escalating tension between Lavinia and Duncan.

"We'll discuss this later. Joetta promised to come sit with Sarra soon. When she does, I'll join you in the library."

He started to protest, but Sarra cried out in her sleep again. Lavinia ignored Duncan to go sit down on the floor to rub Sarra's back, crooning to her in a soft voice to lull her back to a sound sleep.

A few seconds later, she heard the door close. He'd gone. Good. She didn't want him to see her tears. Did he really think she wanted to watch him ride away with Sarra? She knew full well that once he was gone, she'd never see him again.

Gods above, that thought hurt. She had no regrets about inviting Duncan to share her bed, nor would she turn him away now. The memories they'd created together would last her a lifetime. They'd have to. Would he remember her?

Her father's death had taught her there was nothing to be gained by dwelling on that which could not be changed. It was true then; it was true now. That didn't make it any easier to accept.

Her door opened again. Had Duncan returned? She used the edge of her sleeve to wipe a stray tear off her cheek before turning to face him. To her relief, it was Sister Joetta.

"I'm sorry it took me so long, Lavinia. Lessons ran late." Joetta kept her words to a whisper as the two of them stared down at Sarra. "How is our little one?"

"She had a rough time earlier, but she's been resting peacefully for a while now. I'd expect her to awaken within the hour."

Lavinia stepped back, not wanting to disturb the girl's sleep while they talked. "Are you able to sit with her? I need to continue my studies in the library."

Joetta held up a basket. "I brought my sewing to work on. I've already told Sister Margaret that I cannot help serve the midday meal."

"That's good. I appreciate everyone's help."

Joetta touched Lavinia's hand. "You never have to bear a burden by yourself, Lady Lavinia. After all, the goddess teaches us that a burden shared is a burden no more. We know that the attack the other night was no accident. It was aimed at you."

She smiled, the deep wrinkles on her face showing her age. "I know of your connection to the ruling family."

The prior abbess, now the head of the order, had suggested Lavinia keep that secret. She'd never spoken of it to anyone in the order, not even to her closest friends. "How long have you known?"

"From the time you first walked through the door." This time her smile was sad. "I knew your mother. She was a lovely woman, and you look very much like her."

"But you've never said anything."

Joetta set her basket down. "It was obvious that you felt it necessary to protect your identity. I'm guessing that your family connection has come back to haunt you."

Before Lavinia could respond, the older woman continued. "Margaret and I both think young Duncan is here because of the increasing darkness spreading out from the capital city. The traders and others who pass through here whisper of it when they think no one is listening."

Lavinia hid a smile at her friend's referring to Duncan as a young man. Joetta would be shocked to find out exactly how old he was. "Sir Duncan says there have been attacks that strike from out of the sky with no warning. There are also reports of families disappearing from their homes yet leaving all their possessions behind and food still on the table."

She nodded in Sarra's direction. "Then there was the attack on her family."

As Lavinia gathered up the few things she needed to take with her to the library, Joetta slipped in one more question.

"And what role does Sir Duncan play in all of this?"

The older woman gave Lavinia a considering look before continuing. "According to old superstitions, the odd color of his eyes marks his service to the gods. If so, it is my guess that his arrival here in time to save you was no accident."

It was a relief to have someone to talk to. Lavinia stared out into the garden. "He has four friends, all of whom are sworn to protect a landholder to the west of us named Lady Merewen. The duke hunts her as well. Duncan is here to search the forbidden books for a way to counter my half brother's blood magic. He's waiting for me in the library now."

Joetta looked shocked. "You've allowed Duncan access to those books, alone and unsupervised? That's forbidden."

The sister's tone was not accusatory, but she was clearly worried. What could Lavinia say?

"I trust him, and not simply because he saved my life. Sir Duncan has provided me with good advice on how to make the abbey safe from attack. Also, Sarra likes and trusts him. You know how few people she allows to get close, especially men. I think that speaks well of his character."

She shivered as she glanced at the spot where the scrying water had burned the plants. The incident had left her reluctant to contact the gods again. "I fear there may be an armed force heading in our direction. If so, time is running short to find the answers we need."

"But those forbidden books are supposed to be hidden from outsiders and with good reason."

She didn't need to be second-guessed. "True, Joetta, and I have been working with him as time allows. Duncan speaks the old tongues as if he grew up speaking them."

Which he had, although she kept that part to herself. "With the two of us searching through the old texts together, we will accomplish more than if I struggle through on my own."

Joetta nodded slowly. "I trust your judgment and accept the necessity of breaking the rules in this instance. What would you have us to do to prepare in case we come under attack?"

Lavinia didn't want to have to think about such a possibility, but avoidance would be foolish and shortsighted. "Tell Sister Margaret we'll need food and water should we have to take refuge in the warded workroom. Ask Sister Berta to ensure we have enough of her ointments and herbal remedies to treat a number of wounded. Bandages, too. Perhaps some old sheets can be bleached clean and cut up for that."

The urgency she felt to join Duncan in the library was growing stronger, so she started for the door. At the last second, she stopped and looked back.

"There's one more thing you can do, Joetta: pray. Pray for all of us."

Chapter 20

Duncan skimmed passage after passage, rapidly turning the pages with minimal regard for their delicate condition. His mind was divided between the words in front of him and the awareness of each minute that passed. Time stopped for no one, least of all for the Damned. Minute by minute, hour by hour, the days passed with no way to slow their pace. The longer it took to find the spell to counter Duke Keirthan's blood magic, the less time they'd have to invoke it.

Well-planned strategies couldn't be simply thrown together. The moment two armies clashed was preceded by hours, days, or even weeks of planning. Soldiers didn't reach the battlefield by accident or in solitude.

He ran his finger down the next paragraph. When he reached the bottom, he started to turn the page but hesitated. Had he missed something? Backing up to the top, he began again, reading it aloud and translating from his native tongue as he went.

By the time he'd finished half the page, he knew he'd finally stumbled across something useful. Before he could continue reading, Lavinia walked into the library. He marked his place and walked around the table to meet her.

"How is Sarra?"

Lavinia set her mage light down on a nearby shelf. "Still sleeping. Sister Joetta is with her."

Some of the weight of worry eased in his chest. He brushed a lock of Lavinia's hair back from her face. "That's good to hear. How about you?"

She shrugged and rubbed her arms. "I'll be fine. Seeing Sarra like that is always distressing, but this episode was the worst I've seen."

Most likely because the dire predictions in Sarra's pronouncement were aimed squarely at the three of them. It probably didn't help that Lavinia had gotten very little sleep during the night thanks to him. He hoped she didn't have regrets—far better to focus on what he'd been reading when she'd come in.

He let a little of his excitement show. "I've found something. I was reading it over a second time when you came in."

A few of the shadows in her eyes were replaced with hope. "Really?"

He returned to the table and spun the book around so that they could both see the page. He read it to her in translation. When he was finished, he turned to the next page, only to discover the next pages were on a different subject altogether. On closer inspection, he realized that several pages had been torn out, taking the rest of the passage with them.

Frustrated, he stepped back, his hands clenched at his sides in anger. "Why is nothing ever easy? If I didn't know for a fact that the Lady of the River wants the Damned to succeed, I would swear the gods were conspiring against us."

"What's wrong?"

When he pointed at the barely noticeable ragged edges of the torn pages, she sighed. "I'm sorry. Many of these books were rescued at the last moment, and some were already partially burned. We've mended what we could."

Lavinia picked up the book and turned back to the

page he'd been studying. She read it silently even though her lips moved, forming each word as she sounded it out. Fine. Maybe she could make more sense of it than he had.

When she finished, she set the book down and studied the shelves. "I'm sure I've encountered that same reference before. The question is where."

She walked up and down the shelves, stopping occasionally to trail her finger over the titles on the spines of the books. Under other circumstances, he would've been content to watch her make her way down the row of books. She so clearly shared his love of knowledge for its own sake.

The way she touched the worn leather bindings was sensuous in nature, her pleasure obvious. It reminded him of how she'd used those same hands on him during the night. She breathed deeply, savoring the musty scent of old leather and parchment. Had the gods ever created another such woman? Not that he'd seen in his long life.

Frowning now, Lavinia picked up one volume but returned it after a brief glance at the pages inside. She tried a second and then a third. Finally, on the fourth try, she did a skipping step as if celebrating before returning to the table.

Opening the two books side by side, she pushed the new one toward Duncan. "Read that passage aloud while I follow along. If I'm right, yours contains the missing pages."

For a second time, Duncan read the words as written and then repeated them in translation. While the book Lavinia had was missing the rest of the article, his continued on for several pages. What a relief that the new book had the passage intact. He stopped to reread a few paragraphs.

"I find this section confusing. It talks about balance in

the world, one thing being the opposite but equal of the other."

He stopped to point at the words on the page. "Then it goes on to say the blood of the body holds power over the one who spills it with ill purpose. Something about the master becoming the slave."

Then Duncan moved forward a few paragraphs. "Here it mentions another kind of power, one that surrounds the body and fills the world. To wield the power in blood, it must be spilled. It weakens the donor and empowers the mage, yet the spirits of both are devoured."

He looked toward Lavinia. "That sounds like what Duke Keirthan is doing. However, this other magic is definitely different. The source of its power is taken in and then shared without damaging the spirit or soul as long as the one who wields the magic remains strong and pure of purpose. If not, it will burn out of control and destroy everyone."

So how was it different if it could still consume the mage? He went back to the text again. "It loosely translates as 'both the same and different.' I'm also not familiar with the word that describes the second magic, though. It's similar to the word for dirt, but that's not quite right. When confronted with the blood magic, this dirt magic will prevail if the mages are of equal strength. At least, I think that's what it means."

He ran his fingers through his hair in frustration. "Maybe it will come to me later when I've had more time to think about it. The rest of the book talks about what the dirt mage needs to do to fight against the blood magic."

He expected Lavinia to comment, even if she disagreed with his translation. When he finally looked up, she was staring down at the page, her dark eyes stark with pain just as Sarra's had been earlier.

A chill washed through him. "Lavinia? What's wrong?"

She pointed at the word he didn't know. "It doesn't mean dirt. It means earth."

He read the sentence again, inserting the new word in the place of dirt. It read the same to him. "There's a difference?"

"Yes. Earth has two meanings, only one of which is the dirt beneath our feet. It also refers to the world itself and everything in it. Ifre has become a blood mage, an abomination in the eyes of the gods. An earth mage draws power from the natural life energy of the world that surrounds us all."

That made more sense than his original translation. "So what kind of spells would an earth mage perform?"

"Mostly little things. Mage lights, for example." She finally looked him in the eye. "Or scrying. Sometimes, if she's very lucky and good at what she does, she can destroy a blood mage's coins."

Everything shifted. For the longest time, all he could do was stare at the woman in front of him, the same woman he'd spent the night worshipping with his hands, his mouth, his entire body. The very one who had managed to wedge herself inside his heart was an earth mage. And he would guess she possessed considerable abilities, the kind of mage he needed to send into battle against her own brother. Her half brother, really, but that didn't change anything.

Lavinia looked poised to run. He didn't blame her, but then where could she go that she wouldn't be hunted down? Now that the pieces had all come together, he understood why Ifre Kcirthan was so determined to find her. She was very likely the one person alive who could counter all of the blood power the man had accrued. He either needed to take her captive or kill her.

Nothing else would do.

He looked around the library, allowing himself to

soak in the sight because it would be the last time he saw it. Once again it was time to put away the scholar and let the warrior take over.

"Pack your things, including this book, Lavinia. Kiva will return soon with word from Gideon. Once we know what he has to say, we'll leave. Riding hard, we'll reach Lady Merewen's keep within a few days."

But Lavinia was already shaking her head. "No, I cannot simply abandon the abbey. My duty lies here. I don't want you to leave, but I understand that you have to go. I'll order the younger sisters to pack quickly so two of the guards can escort them to our order's headquarters. The rest of us can take refuge in the warded workroom if necessary."

Duncan's temper flared hot. "That's your answer? To hide here behind these thick walls while the people of Agathia die at the hands of your brother?"

Lavinia flinched as if he'd hit her with his fists rather than words. He hated hurting her, but how could he return to Gideon leaving their most potent weapon behind? He stepped back to let his temper cool. If anger wouldn't work, maybe logic would.

"You want Sarra to be safe. You want to protect the other sisters as well. The best way to do that is to put an end to your brother's predations on all of his people. These walls can't protect you. Ifre already got through them once using the coins. This time he's sending men with swords. Who will protect Sarra if he succeeds?"

"I've already said that she should go with you."

Her words were spoken in a monotone, as if she had no emotional connection to either him or the girl. He recognized that for the lie it was. She cared deeply, especially about Sarra, probably because the two of them had so much in common. Both had lost their parents at an early age and possessed a powerful, magical gift, one not comfortable to live with.

She cared just as deeply about him. What she hadn't said with words, she'd conveyed with the gift of her body. A woman in her position wouldn't have lightly invited a man into her bed. Their bodies had joined together in a song of joy that had burned bright and hot. Duncan would remind her of that fact. Right now. No more arguments, no more words.

He set the book down with far more care than he'd picked it up. Silently, he gathered up his papers and set them and the ink bottle aside.

"Duncan?"

She sounded nervous. Good.

He waited until everything was all neat and tidy before turning to face her. One look at his face had her backing away, which only served to inflame his already precarious mood.

"You're not going anywhere, Lavinia. Not until we've finished this discussion."

He emphasized that last word, letting his eyes travel from her head to her toes, lingering along the way.

She froze, but then straightened her shoulders and put her hands on her hips. "Do not think that one night gives you the right to make demands on me, Duncan."

He prowled closer. She stood her ground, but she wasn't as calm as she wanted him to believe. Her pupils were dilated, and the pulse point at her throat belied her calm. He crowded her even more, stopping only when there was not even an arm's distance between them.

Last night had been the first time in centuries that he'd bedded a woman, and the experience only left him craving more of the same. Not more of just any woman; more of Lavinia. And he meant to have her. But as determined as he was, he wouldn't take that final step forward until she gave him permission. But unless she refused him, he was going take her right there in the library. On the table, against the wall, on the floor. He didn't care where as long as he claimed her as his own.

"I want you, Lavinia. Right now. Right here," he added, just to make himself clear.

She swallowed hard, her eyes dropping down just far enough to verify the truth of that statement. The length of his tunic hid the most visible evidence, but she sensed the truth of his statement. A woman always knew when a man craved her touch the way that Duncan wanted hers.

"You're being scandalous. I do not like it."

He smiled, infusing it with a little heat and a lot of hunger. "Scandalous? Not yet, but I plan to be."

"What if someone were to walk in?"

She hadn't said no. Satisfaction only heightened his craving for her. "Shove a table against the door or throw up one of your wards. Use that earth magic for something even if you won't use it to save your homeland."

That probably wasn't the wisest thing he could've said, but he wouldn't apologize.

"How dare you!"

She turned her back to him. Had he succeeded in driving her away? No, thank the Lady, she was chanting. He recognized the words as a variation on the spell she'd taught him. When she finished, the air crackled and snapped, leaving the two of them encased within a wall of pulsing light.

"Can anyone else see that?"

"No, and you shouldn't be able to, either. If someone starts in this direction, he'll change his mind and walk away."

He held his hand close to the barrier, enjoying the tickle of its power on his skin. "So why does this ward look different than the other one you showed me?"

"Because this one also ensures no one can hear us. If we're going to argue about your dragging me back to your captain, I don't want to alarm the other sisters."

Argue? Is that what she thought he had in mind? Anger slipped through his veins, ripping away the tenuous control he had on his need to have her.

This time he left no room between them. Glaring down at her, he made his position clear. "I will not argue with you, Lavinia. You've already made up your mind to stay. Now that I have my answers, I will leave whether you ride with me or not. I'll take Sarra with me since you asked it of me, but no place will be safe for her as long as Ifre Keirthan lives. But if these are to be our last hours together, I don't plan to spend them arguing. I want you to think of this moment when I ride out of your life."

As he spoke, he touched the racing pulse at the base of Lavinia's throat. Her emotions were running high, a match for his. He ran his finger down and down, between her breasts, across the soft curve of her belly, stopping short of where he really wanted to be.

Then he pushed her against the nearest wall and kissed her as if there would be no tomorrow. It wasn't much of an exaggeration. The moment he rode down the switchback trail, their time together would be at an end. Not just for now, but forever.

And that truth cut a jagged hole in his heart that would never heal.

Lavinia should fight. She should push him away, tear down the wards, and run, leaving Duncan and the library behind. But somehow instead of shoving Duncan away, she dragged him even closer. Evidently that was the sign he was waiting for.

He grabbed her by the waist and lifted her up, holding her against the wall, pressing his battle-hardened warrior's body against hers. He continued to kiss her, reminding her how it had been to be the focus of his passion during the night. She could feel his hand between them as he jerked at the lacings of his trews.

Then he yanked the heavy fabric of her skirt up to her waist. With her legs free of its encumbrance, she wrapped them around his hips, bringing her core right against the rigid length of his manhood. Duncan's hand slipped between her legs where the thin fabric of her undergarments offered little resistance to his strength. Once he'd dispensed with that last barrier, he grasped her by the back of her thighs and drove himself in deep and hard.

She screamed his name at the abrupt invasion. Last night he'd been all consideration and patience. Not this time. As soon as he'd buried the thick length of his shaft inside her, he withdrew and did it again—and yet again, each time panting her name.

"Take more of me, Lavinia. Take it all."

She nodded and brought her legs up higher, this time around his waist. The move changed the angle of penetration, allowing him to drive in just that much deeper, that much harder.

"Duncan, don't stop; please don't stop."

As his hips were thrusting hard, he buried his face in her shoulder, working the tender skin there with his lips and teeth. The sensation shaded toward pain, almost more than she could bear. She loved it. Tension coiled deep within her, building, tightening, throbbing hot as he continued to flex his hips. The world quickly narrowed down to the cold hard wall at her back and the burning heat of the man who held her prisoner in his arms.

This wasn't a seduction, but a claiming. They both knew that Duncan might leave her behind, but he'd also leave his mark on her skin and in her soul. Duncan drove them both on and on until her body broke free of the world's tethers and everything around her shattered.

Including her heart.

Chapter 21

"Tell me something, Captain Gideon. Why should I take your word for anything when I know nothing about you?"

Gideon stared across the table at the man who laid claim to the lands a day's ride east of Lady Merewen's estate. He was well aware that he made the man nervous. It was true for all the men who'd answered Merewen's summons.

Eventually, if they spent enough time with him, they might learn to ignore the strangeness of Gideon's eyes. They'd get used to Scim staring at them from the perch behind Gideon's shoulder and the way Shadow liked to prowl under the table, looking for food scraps and mice. Maybe then he'd get past the urge to drag them out to the bailey and use his sword to teach them exactly who was in charge and why.

Gideon remained impassive, letting none of his temper show. Leaving these men bruised and battered might improve his mood, but it wouldn't move him any closer to his goal of forging an army, one capable of taking on the duke himself.

"I understand your reluctance, Sir Gilford. If I were in your place, I would feel the same way."

Gideon paused to take a drink of wine and then leaned forward to rest his elbows on the table. He looked at each man in turn, trapping their gaze with his.

"If we had an unlimited amount of time, we'd go hunting and swap tall tales over flagons of ale to get to know each other better. However, time is the one thing I do not have to waste, so I'll settle for being blunt."

Gilford mirrored Gideon's action, leaning forward and glaring at him from across the expanse of the table. "By all means be blunt, Captain Gideon. You've already dragged all of us here for no obvious reason. Why fall back on good manners now?"

That did it.

"By a show of hands, how many of you have led an army into battle? I'm not talking about a skirmish with bandits. I'm talking war."

He stared at Gilford, waiting for his response, although Gideon already knew the answer. Up and down the table, not a single hand moved. He had no doubt that most of the men were trained with weapons and had men-at-arms who were as well. He told them that much.

"None of you have ever had to defend anything larger than a single caravan or perhaps your own home, so you have a decision to make and very little time to make it. I'm sure your first choice would be to return to your homes, bar the gates, and hope that Duke Keirthan's move against the people of Agathia somehow passes you by."

He forced himself to lean back in his chair, wanting them to listen to his words more than he wanted to make them feel threatened. "If I were one of you, I might make that same choice myself. I'm telling you right now that it would be the wrong one."

"And what makes it wrong? None of our keeps has been attacked. Lady Merewen's problems with Lord Fagan were a family dispute, nothing more."

Gideon didn't bother trying to figure out who posed the question. It didn't matter. Someone had been bound to ask it.

"True, we did take back Lady Merewen's home from her late uncle and his men, but it was far more than a family dispute. Lord Fagan had promised Lady Merewen to the duke to use for his own foul purpose. His lady wife, as well."

He paused to let that sink in. "Several of you have reported that people have gone missing from their homes, never to be heard from again. What do you think is happening to them?"

The same voice spoke again. "We don't know that Keirthan took them, and we have only your word that Lady Merewen's cause against her uncle was just."

This time Gideon did look. "Are you questioning my honor, Sir Gable? Because if you are, we can take that discussion outside right now and let our swords decide whose honor is beyond question."

The silence was telling.

Finally, Sir Gable mumbled, "No insult was intended."

Gideon didn't bother saying none was taken and moved on.

"Keirthan is using blood magic to strengthen his hold on Agathia by sacrificing the very people he should be protecting. We think he wanted Lady Merewen because she inherited her father's gift with the horses. Keirthan would use her magic to fuel his own. His strength is growing daily. If he reaches his full power, no one will be able to stand against him."

He slid his fists off the table, his knuckles white with fury. He preferred not to let the others see how strongly the threat to Merewen affected him. Better to let them go on thinking he and his men were a group of mercenaries she hired to regain control of her family's lands.

Eventually they would learn that Gideon shared her bed; he'd deal with that when the time came. For now, he wanted to keep everyone's attention focused on the inevitable confrontation with Keirthan. The duke might not be ready to strike, but the battle was coming. Nothing would stop Keirthan's predations except his death.

Gideon meant to make sure the bastard was rotting in his grave before the Damned were called back to the river, even if he had to dig the hole himself.

Gilford spoke again. "I have lost more than just people. I raise sheep, large numbers of them. This time of year, the shepherds keep the flocks up in the high valleys where the grazing is good."

He cracked his knuckles, the snap of the bones echoing in the brief silence while everyone waited for him to continue.

"One of my men rode all the way back down to the keep to tell me wild stories about finding four or five, even as many as eight of my prime stock dead. Not a mark on them. He said it was as if they'd fallen over right where they stood."

Gideon nodded. "Lady Merewen has lost horses in the same manner. All I can tell you is that the weapon is a bright light, like lightning thrown as one would throw a rock."

Then he pointed toward Scim on the perch behind him. "We didn't see the attack on the horses, but that was what happened when my gyrfalcon was attacked shortly after we arrived."

"Yet your bird lives." Gilford leaned to the side to get a better view of Scim. "Why didn't he die?"

Gideon shuddered at the memory, not caring if the men around him saw it as a weakness. They had no idea about the powerful bond between him and the falcon. "He almost did. All we can think was that Duke Keirthan hadn't yet developed complete control of his weapon, and it wasn't up to full strength."

It was time to press the small advantage this new turn in the conversation gave him. "If Keirthan can kill your livestock from a distance and take your people without your knowing it, how long before he comes after one of you? Or your women and children?"

Sir Gable poured himself another flagon of Merewen's finest wine. "We have only your word that Keirthan wanted to take Lady Merewen. Perhaps she claimed that as an excuse to overturn the duke's order that rightfully gave Lord Fagan control of this estate as the eldest male. We all know that managing a family's fortunes is a man's duty. Women simply don't have the mind for it."

Murdoch's grip tightened on his drink, as if he were fighting the understandable urge to break something over Gable's thick head. Before Gideon could think of a suitable reply—one that didn't involve blood and pain—another voice joined in.

"Why, Sir Gable, I'll remember that next time you're in need of a new mount for your wife. It's obvious that you no longer have faith in my ability to ensure my horses continue to breed strong and true. That's truly a shame."

The chill in her words was enough to shrivel more than a man's pride. Gideon sincerely hoped Merewen never aimed that particular smile in his direction. She took the empty seat next to him as she continued.

"Please give Lady Gable my kind regards and my regrets. I'm sure she'll understand why you couldn't purchase that dappled gray she's been admiring so much."

By that point, Gable looked as if the dappled gray had just stomped all over him. It didn't help that several of the other men started laughing. Sir Gilford actually raised his cup in salute.

"Well played, Lady Merewen, but please consider how reluctant he'll be to return home without the mare. You might have mercy on him."

He smiled in Gable's direction, making it clear there was little love lost between the two men. "For a substantial price."

"I'll take your advice into consideration, Sir Gilford."

Then Merewen took her own measure of the men who had gathered at her request. "None of us wants war, least of all me. I have already lost men, ones who were loyal to both my father and me, in the fight to regain control of the keep. That night, Fagan's captain set fire to the stable when it was full of horses."

There was an audible gasp from around the table. "What kind of fiend would do such a thing?"

"The kind my uncle surrounded himself with."

Her voice was choked thick with the remembered horrors of that night. Gideon picked up where she'd left off.

"Fagan returned a week later with a force of the duke's men riding with him. I have fought more battles than any of you can dream of, but I have never seen the like of those men. They fought in total silence, never talking, not even to scream when stricken with the most dire of wounds."

Murdoch spoke for the first time. "If your ruler doesn't hesitate ensnaring his own men with blood magic, what do you think he would do to an enemy?"

Those words hung over the gathering as if written in the air for all to read. It was time to let the men discuss the matter alone. Either they would join the Damned or they wouldn't. Once Gideon knew which it would be, he'd be able to make plans.

"Gentlemen, we have given you much to consider. Sir Murdoch and I will withdraw now to allow you freedom to discuss the matter without our interference."

He rose to his feet and offered his arm to Merewen. She started to accept, but Gilford stopped her. "My lady, I would appreciate it if you would stay. We may have questions that only you can answer."

As he spoke, he gave her a pointed look before turning his gaze to Gideon and Murdoch. Before answering, Merewen looked to Gideon, her own questions reflected in her dark eyes. She wanted to know how much to share with her neighbors about the nature of the Damned.

"Tell them whatever you deem necessary."

Then he bowed and walked away, Murdoch at his back as usual.

They didn't stop until they reached the walkway above the gate in the palisade. It would give them a place to pace without revealing their nerves to the group. Up there, away from Merewen's people and the visiting nobles, the air felt cleaner, easier to breathe.

"I hate this."

Gideon pretended to misunderstand. "Walking the perimeter? At least up here, we're not having to bite our tongues when we're being insulted by Sir Gable."

Murdoch chuckled. "That posturing fool! From the look on his face when Merewen threatened to keep the mare, I would guess that his wife has taken possession of all of his family jewels."

"He did look a bit pale, didn't he?"

They stopped to stare down the narrow road that led away from the gate and out into the grasslands beyond. Murdoch had nearly died down there only days ago.

"I was talking about us, Gideon. This endless cycle of fighting alternating with sleeping under the chill of the river. Think it will ever end?"

"I don't know. Mayhap I could've negotiated a better bargain with the goddess, but at the time I didn't know how. Besides, we were all too busy dying to think much beyond trying to draw one more breath."

That wasn't much of an exaggeration. If he hadn't called on the goddess to help them, the five of them would've all bled out by that river, their bodies scavenged by animals and their bones left to bleach in the sun. Some days, he was half convinced that would've been the better bargain.

Murdoch's big hand came down on Gideon's shoulder. "I can't bring myself to regret our decision. We've helped a lot of people over the centuries."

"True, but no matter how many times we beat back those who would prey on the innocent, they keep coming back even stronger. Lord Fagan was but a petty tyrant compared to what we're learning about Duke Keirthan."

He started walking again. "At least Duncan should be returning soon. I'd feel better about all of this if the five of us were together."

Gideon looked around again to make sure he wouldn't be overheard. "I didn't say anything to Merewen because I didn't want to worry her, but something happened the day after Kane and Averel rode out. I decided to send Scim after them to make sure they were all right. But when I tried to join with him, I couldn't. Not at first, anyway. When I finally did, I couldn't maintain the connection for more than a minute, maybe two. That's never happened before. I fear the separation is weakening us all."

Murdoch didn't look all that shocked. "I had trouble calling Shadow from my shield as well. I had to repeat the spell four times before she appeared. I've been reluctant to send her back."

"I don't blame you, but I'm sure things will improve when Duncan and the others return." At least he hoped so.

"I never thought I'd admit this, but I actually miss Hob's ugly face prowling around the keep." Murdoch looked a bit sheepish. "Don't tell Kane I said that. He'll think I've gone soft."

A movement down in the bailey caught their attention. Gideon had hoped it was Lady Merewen coming to fetch them back to rejoin the discussion. Instead, it was Lady Alina out strolling with Shadow at her side.

Murdoch stared down at her with a voracious hunger

in his eyes. As if she'd felt his gaze, the lady in question stopped to stare right back up at him, her hand shading her eyes from the sun.

"Have you bedded her yet?"

Gideon already knew the answer to that question, but Murdoch was immune to hints and subtlety. The only way to get through to him was to lay it all out for him in plain words.

The big man jerked as if he'd been hit. "Hold your tongue, Gideon. She's a lady, and I will not allow you to speak of her in such a way."

"You want her."

Murdoch growled, his eyes narrowing. "I do, but that doesn't make it right."

Even knowing he was treading on the edge of a fight, Gideon continued. "She obviously wants you."

Murdoch gave him a shove. "She's a new widow, and her dead husband was a cruel bastard. He treated his horse better than he treated her."

Gideon shoved back, providing his friend with a target for his frustration.

"So teach her it doesn't have to be that way. Alina has seen the difference between you and Fagan. Certainly she would have never looked at him the way she looks at you. And don't tell me the reason the two of you took so long to find food for Kiva was because you didn't know where Ellie keeps the meat."

Murdoch's face flushed red. "Have a care for the lady's reputation."

Softening his voice, Gideon tried to make Murdoch understand what he was trying to tell him. "If you felt nothing for her, I would not have spoken at all. All I ask is that you think about this. The goddess herself says our cause is strengthened because my heart is involved. Why wouldn't that be true for you as well?"

Most of the anger drained out of Murdoch's stance.

When he spoke again, his voice reflected grief, not temper. "I cannot remain here for Lady Alina. What if I left her with a child? It would destroy any chance she might have for finding another man, one who will treat her gently."

Gideon wanted to hit his friend, but that was his own guilt speaking. Did Murdoch not realize that Gideon paced the floors at night and worried about the same things? He gave the only argument he could.

"And what if Lady Alina never finds another man she trusts to teach her that a man can be gentle?"

While Murdoch mulled that over, Gideon stared out at the grasslands. It was a view he'd come to love, the endless flowing waves of green and gold. In the distance, a band of mares stood grazing, their foals capering about with each other. For the moment, all was peaceful.

It wouldn't stay that way.

Eventually, Keirthan would strike again, and the next attack would be worse than the last. Gideon turned back toward the keep. Down below, Lady Merewen stepped into view on the arm of Sir Gilford. The two of them paused to speak briefly as she looked around the bailey, clearly looking for Gideon. He nudged Murdoch, and the two of them started down the stairs.

From the pleased look on Merewen's face, it appeared they might have gained some allies. He hoped so. He really did.

Murdoch knew his strengths; the politics of dealing with powerful men weren't among them. He was more likely to bang heads than argue logic to get his point across. Right now, Gideon was better served having Lady Merewen at his side. And maybe that was only an excuse to veer off and go in search of Lady Alina and Shadow.

He found the pair sitting on a bench in the corner of

the small herb and flower garden. Both of his ladies often enjoyed a bit of quiet in the warmth of the sun. He paused to soak in the picture they made: the dangerous cat and the gentle woman, both holding special places in his heart.

Without looking in his direction, Alina called to him. "There is room for you beside me."

She was talking about the stone bench, but the image that filled his mind was her making room for him in her bed, in her arms, in her body. He silently cursed Gideon for putting such ideas in his head.

He walked toward her, each step taking him that much closer to temptation and perhaps his salvation. When he reached her side, Alina smiled up at him. Her sweet face reflected the heat of the sun above, melting away the damp chill of the river that had soaked into his bones.

She patted the seat next to her. "Sit by me."

He did as she asked, as always feeling the difference in their size. Her beauty simply stole his breath away. When she slipped her hand into his and gave it a squeeze, he stared down at her fingers entwined with his.

"I can't stay."

Alina frowned. "But you just got here."

Once again his lack of talent with words had him stumbling to make his meaning understood. "I'm talking about when the fighting is done. The five of us will leave. We have no choice."

He half expected her to remove her hand. Instead, she scooted closer to him. This time she spoke in whispers. "I suspected as much. My niece has let slip a few things that made that clear. I know she is keeping track of the days until the solstice but has not said why. I would like to hear the story from you directly."

"Are you sure? It is not a happy tale."

"Neither is mine, but that didn't keep you from befriending me. I would be honored if you would trust me with your truth."

Should he? Yes, he wanted no more secrets between them. For once the words came easily. He spoke of his youth, how Gideon had saved him, and how he and the others came to be known as the Damned. When he ran out of words and breath, Alina looked up at him, her pretty eyes sparkling with tears. "Thank you for sharing this with me. It explains so much."

Nothing had changed; yet in the telling, his mood brightened and the burden of his years grew lighter. "Thank you for listening and understanding why I cannot stay."

"I will pray that the goddess will grant all of you peace when you stand at the river's edge."

"That means a great deal to me, Alina."

The quiet of the garden settled over them again. For the moment, he was content to share this peaceful time with Alina.

After a few minutes, she drew a deep breath and sat up straighter, but she made no effort to move away from him. "Murdoch, there is a favor, a boon really, that I would ask of you."

"Anything within my power is yours."

Her eyes dropped to stare down at their hands, a spot of bright color staining her cheek. "Before I tell you what it is, I need to tell you a bit of my story."

She lifted her face up toward the sky and drew a slow breath. "My father was a good man, but a poor one. My mother loved him, and they were happy together. When Lord Fagan approached my parents about courting me, my father was thrilled. He never saw beneath Fagan's slick polish and wealth to the real man beneath. I would've followed my father's wishes regardless, but in truth I was flattered that such a handsome, powerful man would be interested in me."

"Fagan fooled more than your father, Alina. Several of the men in there talking to Gideon and Lady Merewen are having a difficult time believing your late husband's villainy."

She nodded. "All I wanted was a happy marriage like my parents had. But from the day Fagan and I took our vows, I forgot what it was like not to live in constant fear."

Before he could respond, she smiled. "Thanks to you, I've remembered. Such moments should be cherished, because life can change dramatically between one breath and the next."

Murdoch could only agree. "That it can."

"So, about that favor. I understand your duty to the Lady of the River must come first. Having said that, I have strong feelings for you, ones I would like to think you have for me as well. At least it has seemed that way. I have no right to ask this of you, but I would be happy, in fact honored, if you would share your time with me in the way your captain shares his with Lady Merewen."

Had he fallen asleep? Because he had to be dreaming. Was Lady Alina truly offering to . . . asking him to . . . He couldn't even allow himself to think that it might be possible.

As he struggled to accept the gift she had offered him, he realized they were no longer alone. Sigil had approached but stopped a short distance away. He waited until Murdoch looked in his direction to speak.

"Lady Alina, I apologize for disturbing you, but Captain Gideon has sent me to fetch Sir Murdoch."

Of all times. Murdoch considered ignoring the summons, but that would only bring Gideon looking for him himself. Obviously something of importance had happened. Perhaps the visiting landowners had come to their senses and decided to join the Damned in fighting Duke Keirthan's tyranny.

"Thank you, Sigil. Tell him that I'll join him shortly."

He waited until Sigil bowed and retreated out of hearing. "Lady Alina, I regret that I must go."

She nodded, still refusing to look up at him. "Of course, I understand. Please forgive my forward behavior."

He wasn't about to walk away, not when she thought he was using the summons as an excuse to avoid answering her.

"You misunderstand me, my lady. Gideon wouldn't send for me for no reason, else nothing would drag me away from your side. And when we again face judgment before the goddess, leaving you will be the hardest thing I've ever done. If knowing all of that, you still want me, then I am yours."

She rose to her feet, gazing up at him with such wonder in her eyes. "Truly? You will come to me tonight?"

"Truly."

He brushed a soft kiss across the back of her hand. "Until then."

Her smile outshone the sun. "Until then."

Chapter 22

*I*t had been three days since Ifre's men had left. Through his connection to their talismans, he knew they'd yet to encounter their target. Soon, though. They would reach the abbey within the day.

"Then, dear sister, either you will be on your way back to me or you'll be dead."

He allowed himself a small chuckle. "Actually, you'll be dead either way, but it would be such a waste of your gift for you to die on the sword of one of my men. I have such wonderful plans for you here."

Looking around his underground chambers, he realized he was bored. Perhaps it was time to unleash another practice volley of his weapon. The last time had taken far less effort on his part. A simple command, a cup of blood, and then the right words had been enough to send forth several bursts of its power.

"So where shall I send you?" he asked as he gathered the necessary supplies. Then the perfect solution came to him. Perhaps a small greeting to his sister was in order. Before setting the attack in motion, he clasped the talisman that tied him to the captain of his guard. With enough concentration, he could see through the man's eyes and perhaps gauge how close the troop was to the abbey.

How odd. The captain sat staring up at the crest of a tall hill. Why? Ifre didn't pay the man to enjoy the scenery. After blinking several times, the focus improved. Ah, so that was what had captured the captain's attention: the abbey sitting up there on the bluff. Could the timing be any more perfect?

Surely the blessings of the gods were with him. Ifre sent a mental command to the captain to hold the men there on the valley floor. A few blasts from the weapon would surely convince Lavinia to listen to reason. If not, well, then the consequences would be on her head, not his.

He began chanting while slowly pouring the cup of blood into the bowl. Finally, he added the special herbs and spices that unleashed the power and sent the balls of fire soaring across Agathia to batter the walls of the abbey. He watched through the captain's eyes as the explosions echoed down the valley and the stone walls above shook with the impact.

Duncan packed the last of his personal belongings and looked around. The room was stripped bare, with nothing left to show that he'd ever been there. That was the way it should be. He hated it.

The sound of women's voices carried across the garden, reminding him that he wasn't alone. Right now Lady Lavinia was attempting to convince Sarra she wasn't trying to get rid of her, that the decision to send her with Duncan was for her own safety.

Sister Joetta was in there, too. It was difficult to tell whose side she was on in the discussion. Clearly she cared deeply for the little girl and hated to see her leave. She also wanted her to be safe.

Duncan was not looking forward to riding for days with a brokenhearted little girl. Not when she'd lost her second home in only a few months. This would all be so much easier if Lavinia would listen to sense and come with them.

As one of the Damned, he understood duty, and Lavinia believed hers was to stay with the sisters. She'd promised to defend the abbey, its residents, and the library. It was a burden she wouldn't set aside lightly. Perhaps she had the right of it.

His instincts, though, said that her motivations were based more on fear than on a driving need to prevent the books in the library falling into the wrong hands. She possessed the very gift that could counter her brother's evil. If she were to join forces with the Damned, she could do far more to defend not only the abbey but all the people of Agathia.

The women argued still. As Duncan walked in, Lavinia threw her hands up in the air, and Joetta's face was set in a mask of unhappiness. Sarra stood with her arms crossed over her chest, her chin thrust out in a stubborn determination not to give an inch. She shot Duncan a look meant to burn him where he stood. Clearly Lavinia had gained no ground in convincing Sarra to leave with him.

Lavinia turned her frustration in his direction. "You tell them. The only way Sarra will be safe is to go with you. They will not listen to me."

Did she think he had all the answers? Before he could say anything, it occurred to him that two of the people in that room were able to communicate with the gods. While Sarra had no control over her gift, Lavinia most certainly did. As much as he hated magic, there was no avoiding its taint when it was the enemy's most potent weapon.

"Lady Lavinia, why not scry? Perhaps that would provide us all with some answers."

Her first response was to immediately stare out at the bare wall in the garden, a constant reminder of what happened the last time she'd called on the gods for guidance. He understood her hesitation, but if scrying could provide any help, the risk was worth it.

"I'll stand with you."

Finally, she nodded. "Sarra, please draw me a fresh pitcher of water. Hurry."

The little girl looked from Duncan to Lavinia and back again. Sister Joetta gave her a pat on the shoulder. "Please do as you are asked."

"Fine. I will."

She snatched up the pitcher and charged out of the room, leaving the three adults staring at the door in silence. Finally Joetta spoke again. "I hate this for her, for all of us. I will take her with me after she brings the water. The two of us will seek out a quiet spot and practice her music. She'll like that. I will also pray the gods will guide us all."

Lavinia's smile was definitely forced. "Thank you, Sister. Knowing Sarra is with you will make it easier for me to concentrate. The last time I attempted to scry, it did not go well."

Duncan suppressed a shiver at the memory. He dreaded looking down into the depths of that bowl, but he would do it for Lavinia.

Sarra must have run all the way to the well because she was already back, leaving a steady drip of water in her wake. She practically shoved the pitcher at him.

"Thank you, Sarra."

Joetta moved up beside her. "Come, Sarra. We will leave them now. Perhaps you would like to work on that new piece that we've started."

Sarra ignored Joetta to send Lavinia a hard look. "If I leave, how will I know that you are telling me the truth about what you see?"

Joetta gasped in shock. "Sarra, apologize right now! The abbess would not lie to you."

"She already has. She told me I would have a home here as long as I wanted one." She turned her back, her small shoulders hunched and shaking.

"See how long that promise lasted. She can't wait to send me away." Sarra choked the words out between sobs.

Her pain stabbed Duncan's heart. He caught her up in his arms and held her close. She struggled briefly before finally wrapping her arms around his neck as she soaked his shoulder with her tears. He tried to soothe her, patting her back with the palm of his hand.

When the tears finally slowed, he spoke to her again. "Sarra, we understand that you want to stay here with Lady Lavinia. So do I, but sometimes we have to do things we don't want to do because the gods ask it of us. You would be in danger if you remained here. No one expects you to like this, but we are asking that you trust us to do what's best."

She leaned out far enough to look him in the face. "You don't want to leave Lady Lavinia, either?"

He wished he had thought to tell Lavinia that earlier when they were alone. She deserved to hear it privately, but he couldn't lie to Sarra. Not about this. "No. I would stay here forever if I could."

Sarra weighed his words for several seconds before finally nodding. "I'll go with Sister Joetta. I'm not promising to go with you, not until Lady Lavinia sees what the gods have to tell her."

Duncan mustered up a smile for her. "I agree to your terms."

He kissed her forehead before setting her back down. Sister Joetta took her hand, giving him an approving smile. "Shall we see about that music, little one?"

Lavinia waited until the door was closed to face Duncan. He was a man of many gifts: warrior, scholar, and now comforter of young girls. She ignored the packs he'd carried in with him, not needing the reminder that their hours together were all but gone. She had a few aches left from the intensity of their earlier encounter in the library, but they would soon fade. She wished they wouldn't; she wanted to hold on to every reminder of Duncan that she had.

Had he really meant that he wanted to stay here forever? With her or with the library? She couldn't find the words to ask. But when he held his arms out to her, she didn't hesitate, hoping he took as much comfort in their embrace as she did.

"Thank you for helping with Sarra."

She felt a chuckle rumble through his chest. "The little minx drives a hard bargain. Despite her small stature, she's both stubborn and strong."

"That she is."

It was time for Lavinia to be strong as well. The gods would not have given her the gift of scrying if they didn't believe she could bear its burden.

"Shall we go outside?"

Duncan tightened his arms around her briefly before stepping back. She picked up the pitcher of water and led the way out into the garden. Duncan uncovered the bowl and made sure it was sitting level in its holder. When he was done, she stepped forward and slowly filled it with water.

Duncan assumed the position on the opposite side of the bowl as she sought the place of deep calm within her. Immediately the water smoothed to a mirror-bright surface, reflecting only the blue of the sky above. As they waited, she remained painfully aware of Duncan's presence.

If only the gods would find it in their hearts to let him stay in her life. She'd learned early, though, that to wish for impossible things only led to pain and disappointment.

The water rippled as the first images came into focus. She and Duncan both leaned forward enough to watch.

The first picture was of two men riding across the grass-lands together. Duncan immediately frowned.

"What?"

"Those are two of my friends, Kane and Averel. They've already left Lady Merewen's keep. I was hoping to return before they had to go."

The image faded, flashing this time to two men standing together at the top of a wooden palisade. "Those are Gideon and Murdoch."

This time Duncan sounded happier. Seeing his friends and fellow warriors after being separated from them had to please him. As their faces faded away, the water darkened. Her first instinct was to stop, to back away, but she remained right where she was. If the gods had more to reveal, her duty was to watch and learn.

This time there were three horses, all moving at a full gallop. The view was too distant to identify the riders.

As she strained to make out the details, the water rippled again this time. At first, the view was a familiar one. She seemed to be standing at the top of the switchback trail that led up to the abbey from the valley floor. Then, in a stomach-churning dive, she plummeted to the floor of the valley, this time to stare up at the walls of the abbey.

The attack would be difficult, leaving his men exposed the whole way up the hillside. The trail was narrow, barely as wide as a wagon, which would limit how quickly he could get his men to the top. Would an abbey have armed guards? Unlikely, but it couldn't be counted out.

Goddess help her, she wasn't seeing through her own eyes. Trapped in the vision, she lost herself in the mind of a man, a soldier—no, a captain, in the royal guard. The burden of Keirthan's sigil around his neck was oddly heavy, its power a steady burn where it rested against his chest. Through the captain's gaze, Lavinia studied the men who surrounded him, all oddly still as they stared up the hillside.

What were they waiting for? Then she knew. Through the sigil on the captain's chest, she sensed Ifre's distant presence. She drew back, fighting the urge to break free. If she ran now, she wouldn't know what he was up to, what form his next attack would take.

Then it played out in the captain's mind. Ifre was going to unleash his blood magic, aiming it in a first strike directed at the walls of the abbey. She yanked her mind free from the grasp of the vision and backed away from the bowl.

Duncan stared at her, looking puzzled. Had he seen nothing of that?

"Lavinia! What did you see?"

She couldn't find the words, but then she didn't need to. Not when the entire building shook with the first blow from Ifre's attack.

Chapter 23

*W*ould they never leave? Gideon had better things to do with his time than play host to this gaggle of nobles, but he reined in his growing irritation. He needed their help and wouldn't risk offending them.

"Captain Gideon, may I have one last moment of your time?"

Sir Gilford could have more than that if he needed it. The knight's opinions clearly carried a lot of weight with the others, and he'd been the first to promise his aid. "Certainly."

They walked a short distance from the others. "I will send my men as soon as I return home. As much as I'd like to say your assessment of Duke Keirthan and his plans for Agathia is wrong, I cannot. I will also talk to several of the smaller landholders in my area to see what they can do to assist. Most likely they can only send a man or two, but I suspect you will need all the help you can get."

He shot a dark look in Sir Gable's direction. "Despite my neighbor's promises, I wouldn't count on his men arriving at your gate any time soon."

"I thought the same," Gideon admitted. "I'm more worried about him warning the duke."

To his surprise, Gilford laughed. "Not likely. He's too much of a coward. He'll hide inside the stone walls of his keep until the battle has been decided and then sidle up to the winner."

Then he held out his hand. "It has been interesting meeting you, Captain. When this is all over, perhaps we can find time to share a few flagons of that wine you mentioned."

"I would enjoy that, Sir Gilford."

"As would I."

He meant that, but there would be no time, not with the gods' judgment looming on the horizon. He accompanied Gilford back to where the remaining visitors were all mounting up to ride out. Gideon signaled for the guards to open the gate. Once the last one rode out of sight, it felt as if everyone within the keep gave a huge sigh of relief. The meetings had been stressful for Gideon and Merewen, but all those extra mouths to feed and horses to care for had been a burden on all her people.

His lady joined him, her own weariness showing in the slump of her shoulders as she leaned against him. "Think they will fulfill their promises?"

"Gilford pulled me aside to say he will send his men within days. He said we shouldn't count on Sir Gable, but I'd already figured that out for myself."

On the whole, Gideon was pleased with the agreements they'd reached with the rest of the landholders from Agathia. Each of them had sworn to send Gideon a number of their knights, men-at-arms, and bowmen to use as he saw fit.

They'd demanded that if anyone's home came under attack, Gideon would send assistance. He'd agreed, but only if he had the men to spare. That was unlikely to be the case, and the landholders would know it, too, once they thought it through.

The enemy had a small army at his command and could attack on several fronts if he so desired. That meant

Gideon had to avoid scattering his limited resources too thinly, thus rendering them vulnerable and ineffective. They had only one real goal: defeat the duke himself. He'd laid out that cold truth for the landowners. They understood his logic; that hadn't meant they liked it.

Sir Gable argued that Gideon's first duty was to protect all of the landholders, not just Lady Merewen. He might as well have saved his breath, especially considering he'd earlier insulted Gideon's honor and questioned Lady Merewen's right to regain control of her clan's land. Did he really think any of the Damned would ride to his rescue?

The two of them took comfort in each other's company for a short time, but then Merewen stepped away. "Jarod sent word that he would like me to look at one of the mares for him, so I should go."

"After you're done, get some rest. This past day has been hard on all of us."

She smiled at him, her love warming his heart. "That it has."

After she walked away, he climbed to the rampart where Murdoch had been pacing back and forth while the nobles rode out. As Gideon joined him, he said, "That's a much happier look on your face than you had earlier, not that I blame you. I'm glad to see the last of them for a while."

As the two of them fell into step, Gideon couldn't help but agree. "True, but we shouldn't complain too much. We have garnered more help, even more than I'd dared hoped for."

"If they follow through on their promises." Murdoch looked out toward the riders. "Sir Gable isn't smart enough to see that either we band together or we die separately."

Gideon didn't argue the point. The past had taught them to be grateful if someone else joined them in the fight but to only depend on each other. They could only hope that this time would actually be different.

They walked the perimeter of the bailey. Since they had been cooped up inside most of the day, the fresh air felt good. The sun was already fading to the west. Soon Ellie would start serving the evening meal. After that, Gideon had plans that involved only him and Merewen.

"What's that?"

The mild note of concern in Murdoch's voice jerked Gideon back to the moment at hand. He looked all around and saw nothing amiss. Then he realized his friend was looking up. Following his line of sight, Gideon spotted what had snagged Murdoch's attention.

"Looks like Duncan sent Kiva back to us again. Maybe his news couldn't wait until he got here himself."

Gideon led the way back down to the center of the bailey to give the big bird more room to maneuver. "That's what worries me."

Murdoch watched as the bird did a slow-wheeling turn overhead. "Do you want me to fetch something for you to feed Kiva?"

Gideon wasn't so worried that he couldn't take a little time to tease. "The last time the poor bird almost starved by the time you and Lady Alina found him some scraps to eat."

Murdoch flushed red. "We didn't want to touch Ellie's supplies. You know how protective she is about her domain."

Gideon's snort said it all. By then Kiva was already winging his way downward. This time Murdoch offered his arm to the bird, freeing Gideon to untie the message pouch as soon as Kiva landed. He braced himself to support the owl, who was far heavier than most of his kind.

"What did Duncan have to say?"

Nothing good. Gideon's mood grew grim as his eyes

scanned the paper. "Duncan has found some answers. By now, he'll be on his way back, but he won't be coming alone. He has a little girl riding with him, one whom Duke Keirthan is hunting for."

All of the Damned had a soft spot for children. More than anyone, the young suffered most when the adults in their lives couldn't protect them. Or, as in Murdoch's own case, those were the very adults who were the threat.

"If Duncan comes under attack, he might not be able to protect her by himself."

"He'll need help."

Murdoch didn't sound happy about the prospect of several days of hard riding, but they both knew logic dictated that he should be the one to go. As their leader, Gideon needed to remain close to the woman they were all sworn to protect.

He handed Kiva off to Gideon. "Tell Duncan to be on the watch for me. I'll go get packed now."

"Take five of the men with you."

Murdoch immediately rejected Gideon's offer. "If Keirthan attacks the keep again, you'll need every man you have, especially with Kane and Averel gone. I'll make better time and draw less notice traveling alone. Besides, I'll have Shadow with me."

Gideon stroked Kiva's chest to keep the tired bird calm. It didn't work because the owl drummed his wings and dug his claws into his arm, a reflection of Gideon's own agitation.

"I don't want you out there alone."

Before he could say anything else, an offer of help came from an unexpected source. Sigil planted himself in front of them and said, "I could ride with Murdoch."

Neither man said a word; they simply stared at Sigil with those unnaturally pale eyes. They'd be insane to trust him, but he'd grown tired of doing nothing. He might not remember simple things like his own name, but he was a warrior and used to serving a cause.

Murdoch spoke first. "Are you sure you want to do this?"

Sigil nodded but focused his attention on Gideon, knowing the captain would be the one he needed to convince. Murdoch had long since stopped treating Sigil as a prisoner.

"I will not be missed here, and you're clearly not happy about sending Murdoch on his own."

Gideon pointed out the obvious. "You could end up fighting against men you've served with."

"That's true, but if this Duke Keirthan is as bad as you say he is, they've chosen the wrong side in this battle."

Gideon arched an eyebrow in surprise. "As did you."

Sigil shrugged, fighting to remain calm while inside he was anything but. His instincts screamed that this opportunity could be the first real step toward finding himself. "So you tell me, Captain. If I served the wrong master, my honor demands that I make amends regardless of the cost."

Gideon slowly smiled, and the enormous owl settled down. "That attitude is something my men and I have some experience with. Murdoch, I'll leave the final decision up to you."

Murdoch's big hand came down hard on Sigil's shoulder. "We ride within the hour."

Gideon started for the corral. "I'll see to Kiva and ask Jarod to saddle your horses. Then we'll meet at the gate."

"We'll be there. Sigil, let's go."

Murdoch started for the hall, but Sigil remained frozen where he stood. They'd accepted his offer. Amazing. Surely that meant on some level they trusted him—at least a little. It was amazing how much that meant to him.

"Hey, Sigil, are you going stand there all day?"

Feeling better than he had in ages, he took off, running to catch up with Murdoch. Inside the hall, the warrior headed for the kitchen and stuck his head in the door.

"Ellie, I'll be needing supplies for four for six days."

Sigil found it amusing that the man was careful to remain outside of Ellie's domain. Even as a newcomer to the keep, Sigil knew it was risky to interrupt that woman's tightly managed schedule. She looked up from the bird she was dressing. From the look she gave them, he could only be glad she was holding a spoon, not a carving knife. "You'll have to wait until I get this on the spit to roast."

Murdoch probably figured telling her that Gideon wanted them gone within the hour wouldn't carry much weight with Ellie. Instead, Murdoch played on her sympathy.

"I know this is a bad time, Ellie, but we received word that Duncan is riding this way with a small child who is being hunted. He may need our help keeping her safe."

Ellie didn't look any happier, but she handed off the bird to her assistant and wiped her hands. "I'll have your supplies ready shortly. Now get out of my kitchen so I can work."

"Thank you."

"I'm not doing it for you."

They backed away, waiting until their backs were turned before grinning at each other, happy that Murdoch's ploy had worked. The two of them headed upstairs to pack. It wouldn't take Sigil long. All he owned were the clothes on his back, one spare outfit, and the few odds and ends that Lady Alina had given him that had belonged to her late husband.

There was one more thing he needed if he was going to be of any help to Murdoch and Duncan. He'd better ask now before Murdoch disappeared into his quarters.

"Uh, Murdoch?"

Odd. The warrior had been heading toward Lady Alina's quarters rather than his own. Murdoch spun back in Sigil's direction, looking suspiciously guilty for a second before his face quickly became a blank slate.

"What now?"

Sigil's temper flashed hot as he snapped, "Sorry to bother you, but I'll need something other than a practice sword if I'm to be of any use to you."

Murdoch slapped his forehead. "By the goddess, of course you do. Come with me. I have the sword they found near your body. If it's not yours, then we can check the armory for something more to your liking."

Inside Murdoch's quarters, he unwrapped the sword and held it out. Sigil accepted the weapon, smiling as he tested its heft with a few practice swings. It was a quality blade, one that felt familiar to his hand.

He sheathed the sword and fastened the belt around his waist. It was a perfect fit, making it even more likely the weapon had indeed been his, one more piece of his prior life back in place.

"How is the sword, Sigil? Will it do?" Murdoch asked as he gathered his things.

"It's fine. In fact, I'm sure it is mine."

He drew the blade again, running a fingertip down its length. There was one more question to be asked before he returned to his own quarters.

"All things considered, Murdoch, it strikes me as odd that you and Captain Gideon would trust me to fight at your side. If I served Duke Keirthan, aren't you concerned that I would join his forces again if given the chance?"

Murdoch stopped what he was doing, turning to face him, his arms crossed over his chest. "Betray us, and you won't live long enough to serve your former master. However, if you give me your word that you will not betray our cause for the duration of this mission, then you're welcome to come. If it would compromise your honor to do so, then I'll tell Gideon that I would prefer to go alone."

He then picked up his gear and started for the door. "If you decide to come, meet me at the gate. Time grows short."

Sigil caught up with Murdoch a few steps down the hall and planted himself directly in front of him. "I give you my word, for what it's worth, that I will not betray you. I'll be there."

"Good. Go get packed. I'll be down in a few minutes."

As soon as Sigil was out of sight, Murdoch stopped in front of Alina's door and knocked. She answered immediately and stood back to let him in.

"You finished your meeting with Gideon early! I've been counting the minutes until . . ." Her words trailed off as she stared at the packs in his hand. Her smile faded.

"You're leaving."

It wasn't a question, but he nodded anyway. "Duncan sent word with Kiva that he's returning with a child who is being hunted by Keirthan. He might need help protecting her."

"Then of course you must go."

At least she looked as disappointed as he felt.

"I am truly sorry, Alina, but I should only be gone a few days. When I return, we can still"—he paused to look past her toward the four-poster bed in the far corner—"share our time together. That is, if you haven't changed your mind by then."

"I'll be waiting for you."

She stepped forward to wrap her arms around his waist and laid her face against his chest. He held her close, savoring the opportunity to pretend she truly be-

longed to him, that they had a chance at a future together.

But they didn't. By now Sigil and Gideon would be
waiting for him at the front gate. For years, duty was all
he'd had to keep him going. That was no longer enough,
not when he'd had a taste of what it would be like to be
a normal man with a woman who might learn to love
him. He forced himself to step back, to let her go. But
Alina held on, refusing to let him retreat. Stubborn
woman.

"Sir Murdoch, have you not forgotten something?"
Her smile was flirtatious, her stance all feminine temptation.

He looked around the room. What could it be?

She took pity on him and explained. "Were you going
to leave without kissing me? I think that would be most
ungentlemanly of you."

Murdoch liked this bolder version of Alina. He bowed
his head. "My apologies. I will hasten to correct that
oversight."

Then he lost himself in the beauty of the moment.
Despite the difference in their size, they fit together perfectly. Her kiss was an ambrosia unlike anything else
he'd ever tasted. Would that he could feast upon her
sweetness for the rest of his days—and nights.

For these few stolen moments, his duty would simply
have to wait a little longer.

Chapter 24

*D*uncan jumped back from the scrying bowl, already drawing his sword. "We're under attack. Stay here!"

As usual the woman didn't listen. Lavinia was only a few steps behind him as he cut through her office. He wasn't surprised that she ignored him when her friends and the abbey itself were in danger. He gave up and waited for her to catch up. Together the two of them ran toward the front of the abbey. He ignored the shouts and screams as he tried to make sense of the situation.

"Lavinia, what did you see?"

"It's Ifre. His men are gathered at the base of the hillside. I saw through the captain's eyes that they were waiting for something to happen. Through the connection between my brother and his captain, Ifre ordered them to hold back while he unleashed his weapon against the abbey."

She was short of breath, but he couldn't afford to slow down. He'd figure the rest out for himself. Keirthan had obviously traced his coins back to the abbey and sent his men after Lavinia

Keirthan was battering the walls of the abbey with a stronger version of the same weapon he'd used against Scim. The way the entire building shook with each impact left little doubt that he'd found a way to increase its power. How many of the people had been sacrificed to extend the weapon's range this far?

Keirthan probably thought the sisters would surrender meekly rather than see the place destroyed. Well, both the duke and his guard were in for a surprise. It was doubtful that they expected to encounter an armed resistance.

Even if the explosions did weaken the abbey's walls, weak walls didn't change the fact the duke's men could only approach by way of the switchback trail. Armed with bows and arrows, the abbey's guards could pick off attackers at a distance.

If any made it all the way to the courtyard outside the abbey door, then Duncan would be waiting to dispatch them with his sword. But he was getting ahead of himself. He ran to join the abbey's guards where he could assess the situation.

At the end of the hall, he looked back toward Lavinia. She'd hiked the skirts of her robes, enabling her to run faster. She was only a few feet behind him again.

He held up a hand to stop her. "Gather the sisters and take them to the warded workroom. Do it now, Lavinia, while the guards and I deal with the attack."

She wanted to argue. It was clear in the stubborn set of her mouth, but she nodded. Rather than turn back, she ran straight toward him. Instead of arguing, she clasped his face with both hands and tugged him close for a quick kiss.

"Stay safe, Duncan."

Then she was gone, already shouting orders to the sisters. Despite the dire circumstances, he couldn't help but grin. In all of his long life, he'd never once had a woman kiss him before he headed into battle. He found he liked it.

Another crash against the walls snapped him out of the momentary distraction. Time to make sure Keirthan's men didn't make it past the front door of the abbey.

*　　　*　　　*

Duncan found Josup standing in the courtyard tying off a bandage on the arm of one of the other guards. When he was finished, the wounded man picked up his bow and arrows and loped back toward the wall.

Duncan sheathed his weapon for the moment. "What happened to him? Have they breached our defenses?"

"Not yet. He got hit with a piece of falling rock. The wound was more bloody than serious. As far as we can tell, the duke's men are still at the bottom of the hill."

Josup gave Duncan a considering look. "All those drills you insisted on have proven valuable. Everyone knew right where to go and what to watch for."

They both instinctively ducked as the abbey took another blast. Josup looked disgusted. "I was a soldier before I decided I'd live longer as a caravan guard, and I've fought in my fair share of battles. Never saw the like of those bolts of light coming out of nowhere."

"I don't think anyone has. They're coming from Duke Keirthan himself. His blood magic."

When the ground quit shaking, they ran for the ladder that would take them to the best vantage point to see what was happening on the trail below. He prayed Keirthan would soon run out of bolts to lob at the abbey. When that happened, the real fighting would begin.

From above, it was easy to see that the walls had been hit hard, but they were still sound. No gaping holes had opened up that would allow Keirthan's men easy access to the abbey's interior. Duncan silently prayed to the Lady of the River that they would continue to hold.

As he watched, three more flashes of white-hot light came soaring down from above. The first one hit the wall below where he stood. The jolt sent Josup toppling backward over the edge, but Duncan hauled him back up to safety.

The other man grinned at him. "Thank you. That was close."

The second blast flew overhead to land in the middle of Sister Berta's herb garden. The elderly woman wouldn't be happy about the damage it caused, but at least it had missed the well and the guards.

The third volley hit the top of the trail, sending an avalanche of rock and dirt rolling down the hillside. If the damage was bad enough, it might impede the duke's men's ability to reach the abbey. Duncan might be glad about that part, but not if it also damaged the road enough to make it difficult for him and Sarra to ride back down.

For the moment, a blessed silence settled over the hillside. Josup and Duncan both looked up on the bluff overhead where their lookout was perched. The man's hands moved in a flurry of gestures that Josup understood.

"They're coming, riding two by two. There're about twenty of them."

It could have been worse. "Signal the bowmen."

Josup used the same hand signals to tell the others that the enemy was on the move. It would be a few minutes before they got into range.

"I'll check on the sisters. Send a runner if you need me before I get back."

Josup nodded as he nocked an arrow, keeping it aimed at the last turn in the trail below. They'd already discussed strategy. The plan was to wait until the enemy had made the final turn before attacking. They wanted to trap the bastards in a withering fire of arrows, blocking any retreat to safety and at the same time preventing them from reaching the abbey.

Duncan hustled back down the ladder and ducked inside the door near the abbey's kitchen. He checked each room as he passed it to make sure there were no stragglers. Before the real fighting began, he needed to know that all of the women had taken refuge in the workroom. As long as the sisters were safely tucked in behind Lavinia's powerful wards, he and the guards could concentrate on fighting without having to worry about them.

He paused to listen. Silence. The kitchen was empty, pots still simmering over the fire. No movement from the dining hall, no heartbeats within the immediate vicinity. Good. He headed down the hallway toward the workroom and spotted Lavinia standing outside the door.

"Lavinia? Why aren't you inside with the others?"

Her eyes were wide with fear, but her voice was calm. "Because I'm waiting for Joetta to finish counting to make sure we found everyone. Once I'm sure all of the sisters are inside, I'll join them and reset the wards. How are things outside?"

The pressure in his chest eased. "The blasts have stopped for now, but there's no way to know if they'll begin again. Maybe they won't because the duke's men have started up the trail. Once you're inside, promise you won't open the door unless you know it's me or Josup."

She licked her lips, her hands nervously clenching and unclenching. "I promise, and we will all pray for the safety of you and the guards."

"I'll let the men know."

When he started back, she called after him, "They are connected to the duke through the emblem they wear on a chain around their necks. Remove those, and you break the link. Bring the talismans to me, and I'll destroy them."

He nodded but didn't tell her that he had no intention of letting the duke's men get close enough for him to grab them by their necklaces. Even so, it was helpful to know the enemy's weakness.

Outside, the guards remained poised to fire. He rejoined Josup. "The sisters are all safely behind a stout door."

Knowing the guards shared his basic distrust of magic, he didn't mention that it was warded. It was enough for the men to know that for the moment the women were safe.

He did share the information about the duke's emblem. "If you can shoot through those, it will weaken their connection to their master."

Come to think of it, that explained what had happened to the warrior who had nearly sacrificed his own life to save Murdoch and Lady Alina from Fagan. Destroying the two coins had caused enough of an explosion. He could only imagine what that backlash would do to a man's mind.

A movement on the trail caught his attention. The first of the troopers had reached the last turn.

"Hold steady. Wait for my signal."

Josup passed along the order, each man whispering to the next one along the wall. It wouldn't be long now. Duncan silently counted the men as they came into sight. Already two-thirds of the troop were on their final approach to the abbey.

They rode in eerie silence, looking neither to the left nor to the right. Why weren't they watching for an attack? Only their leader appeared to be aware of his surroundings. Duncan's skin crawled at the realization that these men had been ensorcelled by their master, their free will taken from them.

"What is wrong with them?" Josup whispered.

"I've seen this before. The duke has taken possession of them through those necklaces they each wear. They will fight without question until they are dead. They don't talk."

He shuddered at the memory. "They don't even scream when wounded. To a man, they'll bleed out and die without a whimper."

Josup immediately made a gesture meant to ward off

evil. Duncan didn't blame him, but now wasn't the time for superstition. It was time to fight.

"Fire!"

The arrows flew and the dying began.

It didn't take long. With the guards firing from above, it was more of a slaughter than a battle. The horses panicked from the sting of arrows and the smell of blood. Several of the duke's men were unseated and died beneath the hooves of their horses, which were struggling to break free of the attack.

A few riders, through luck or skill, made it to the top unscathed; Duncan, Josup, and several of the other guards waited for them. Normally, fighting from horseback gave the rider the advantage over a man on foot. But in the confined space, the horses had little room to maneuver.

The captain dismounted while ordering his men to do the same. They formed up in a line, swords drawn. There were only six of them, but no one made it into the duke's personal guard without being an accomplished swordsman. They had earned the right to act confident.

But then none of them had ever faced off against one of the Damned before.

Duncan offered the captain a mocking salute, and the fight began in earnest. The man was better than good; he was highly skilled with a real talent for reading Duncan's intentions before he could carry them out. It had been a long time since he'd crossed swords with someone of the captain's caliber. Normally, as an avatar of the gods, Duncan's speed and skill far outstripped those of a mere mortal, but right now he was struggling to hold the man at bay. It niggled at him, but he had to keep his mind in the battle.

His own men were caught up in a vicious battle against the enemy, but he couldn't help them, not yet.

From out of nowhere, Kiva swept past Duncan to attack the duke's men from above. Even with his gods-enhanced strength and speed, the bird must have nearly killed himself to have completed the trip to Gideon that quickly; he had to have flown day and night, not stopping except to deliver Duncan's message. Yet here he was, doing his best to lend his aid to the battle. Duncan sent his gratitude as he dodged another attack himself. If he didn't concentrate on his own opponent, the captain might get past him. The man was capable of slaughtering Josup and his men, leaving Lavinia and the sisters at his mercy.

That was not going to happen—not while Duncan had a breath in his body. He feinted to the right and then back to the left, drawing the captain off balance long enough for Duncan to score a telling hit, drawing first blood. Just as he feared, his opponent ignored the wound, ignored the pain, ignored everything except his desire to kill Duncan.

As the man lunged toward Duncan in another attack, the necklace around his neck swung out from his chest, momentarily drawing Duncan's attention. Mayhap he should consider Lavinia's suggestion and attempt to sever the connection between Ifre Keirthan and his men.

He caught the chain with the tip of his sword and yanked up hard. The maneuver left him open and vulnerable, and his sword slid free of the chain just as the captain's blade connected with Duncan's right side. Unlike his ensorcelled opponent, he had a harder time ignoring the painful blow to his ribs.

He aimed at the chain again. This time it slid down to the thicker portion of his blade. Putting all of his power behind his effort, he yanked up and away from the man's neck once, twice, and again. On the third time, the chain snapped, and the talisman fell to the ground as the captain stumbled backward, trying to regain his balance.

Duncan retreated several steps to see what would happen next.

The captain stumbled to a halt, his eyes blinking slowly as if he'd just awoken from a heavy sleep. Maybe he had, but he woke up angry and ready to fight. One glance at the horror that surrounded them, and he screamed out his fury and charged Duncan.

All finesse was gone, and victory would be a simple matter of stamina and luck. So much for hoping that the man would lose the will to fight when his connection to the duke was severed.

This would be a fight to the death. Duncan forced the man to retreat several steps. Pressing his advantage, he kept the man on the defensive. He stumbled back into one of the horses, which were still penned in by the fighting. When the animal tried to lunge out of his way, the impact sent the captain flying forward right onto Duncan's sword.

His eyes widened in shock as he sank to his knees, staring down at the sword stuck into his chest. He grasped the blade with his hand in an attempt to drag it back out, probably hoping to undo the damage that had been done. Duncan helped him with that, yanking his bloody blade free. Leaving the captain to finish dying, Duncan turned his attention to aiding his own men with the last two of the duke's guards still standing.

For a few seconds, there was silence, broken only by the low moans of the wounded and the dying.

Josup's arm dripped blood where it had been sliced open to the bone. Duncan ripped off a piece of his tunic and used it to bind the wound until Sister Berta could treat it. One of Josup's men had been killed, but the rest were more or less whole.

Duncan took charge. "Some of you, gather the bodies and cover them with blankets. We'll decide what to do with them later. The rest of you, catch the horses and see to them. Store their tack in the stable and turn them loose in the corral."

One of the guards reached for the captain's necklace. Duncan caught his arm and then picked up the chain with the tip of his sword.

He lifted it high. "Do not touch any of these. They're tainted with Duke Keirthan's magic. I'll collect them myself."

The guards backed away. Even if Duncan wasn't immune to the Duke's magic, he wouldn't have risked his men being ensnared by the talismans. When he had all twenty chains hanging on his sword blade, he pounded on the door for the remaining guards to let him in.

Inside, he went into the kitchen to find a rag or sack to put the talismans in. Once he had them safely stowed, he debated whether he should stop to clean up before letting Lavinia know that this wave of attack had been soundly defeated for now. No doubt Duke Keirthan was already aware it had failed.

Vicious tyrants like Lavinia's brother wouldn't give up easily. The bastard had already shown himself to be wildly reckless in his attacks. If he'd had a little more control, those bolts of light could've easily destroyed the abbey and everyone inside. A man willing to kill innocents so indiscriminately had to be stopped. Surely now Lavinia would agree to come with him to Lady Merewen's keep.

Duncan marched through the abbey, heading straight for the workroom. He barely noticed Lavinia's wards as he pushed through them. The door opened just as he raised his fist to pound on it. When Lavinia peeked out at him, his temper flared.

"What are you doing opening the door without asking who is out here? What if it had been the duke's men?"

She frowned at him. "I knew it was you. No one else could've gotten through my wards without setting them off."

That did little to reassure him. "The fighting is done, and Sister Berta is needed."

She stared at his bloody tunic. "Are you injured? And what about our guards?"

He ignored the question about him. "We lost one. Several of the others are wounded. Josup's arm will need to be stitched up."

"And Duke Keirthan's men? Do they need their wounds treated as well?"

When Duncan shook his head, her fair skin paled. "How many?"

"Our lookout counted twenty as they approached. It seems unlikely any escaped."

There was nothing to be said that would make Lavinia feel better or ease the sick knot in his stomach. They both knew those men were as much victims of Keirthan's greed as their own men.

"These are the medallions they wore. I'll leave it up to you what to do with them."

She accepted the bag. "We'll say prayers over the men who wore these."

That was as much as they could do for them, and they could not spare a moment for regrets. It wouldn't take long for Keirthan to regroup and plan his next move. But before he could strike out at Lavinia and the abbey again, Duncan planned on robbing him of his intended targets.

"Once the guards have been seen to, tell the sisters to pack their things."

Lavinia stepped out into the hallway and closed the door behind her. "I've already told the younger sisters they will be moving to the abbey where the mother superior resides. Sarra knows that she will be leaving with you."

All of that was good, but it wasn't enough. "Tell the rest of the sisters they will be leaving as well."

"But—"

It was time to lay it all out for her. "Your brother attacked an abbey full of defenseless women, Lavinia. Soon he will know his men have failed to capture you. Do you really think a second failure will make him any less determined? If those bolts had hit the abbey any harder, we would've been digging your bodies out of the rubble."

He crowded closer. "It's your decision, Lavinia. But I'm telling you right now that if you don't leave here soon, this place will no longer be your abbey; it will be your tomb. Order your friends to ride to safety, or tell them to say their final prayers and make peace with their gods."

There was nothing left to say. Either she'd listen or she wouldn't. If she didn't make the right decision, he'd do what he could to convince the sisters himself, but he couldn't expend much time doing so.

He'd already sent Kiva to tell Gideon he was heading back to the keep with Sarra. Those plans hadn't changed, with one exception. If Lavinia wouldn't come with him of her own accord, he'd tie her across the saddle and drag her back with him that way. He'd rather she came willingly, so he'd give her a chance to make the right decision.

"Tell Berta that her patients will be waiting in the infirmary."

Resisting the urge to kiss her one last time, he walked away.

Chapter 25

*L*avinia stared at Duncan's back, her mind numb with pain. So many dead. She prayed for their souls; she prayed for wisdom; then she prayed that this nightmare would end.

What had she done to make Ifre hate her enough to risk killing so many innocent souls to come after her? Even the men who had chosen to serve him might have done so out of loyalty to Agathia without realizing their ruler had been corrupted by a driving need for power.

She had to clear her head. Important decisions had to be made. Now. She retreated back into the workroom where she was quickly surrounded by the comforting presence of the other sisters. They all had questions. She didn't have many answers.

Raising her hand for silence, she drew a deep breath and told them what she knew. It didn't surprise her that their reaction was a volatile mix of relief, distress, and fear. Berta immediately left to care for the wounded, taking the two sisters who served as her apprentices with her.

Lavinia envied them their clear sense of purpose. Margaret started to follow after them to see what could be salvaged of the food that had been left on the fire.

"Please wait, Sister. I have a couple of announcements to make, ones you should hear."

Once again, the room grew quiet. Lavinia took a few

seconds to study the women assembled in front of her. She knew them all by name; some she'd known since she was a child; others she'd met when she'd returned to the abbey. Each was dear to her.

"The attack is over, but Duke Keirthan will come at us again. At me, really. I'm the one he wants. The reasons aren't important right now, only that you are safe before he tries again."

The women exchanged worried looks. She didn't blame them. "Here's what we're going to do for now. Sister Berta is taking care of the wounded. She will need help dealing with the large number of dead. If your own duties don't require you to be elsewhere, please seek her out to offer your aid."

She moved on to more pleasant subjects. "Sister Margaret and her helpers will put together a meal for all of us. Again, please assist her in any way that you can."

Finally, she turned to her own role in all of this. "I will be returning to my office to seek the guidance of the gods and to make plans for what should come next. Unless it's an emergency, I would appreciate not being disturbed until I join you in the dining hall."

Thank goodness for Sister Margaret's ability to take charge. In seconds, she'd shooed everyone out of the workroom except for Lavinia herself. When they were gone, she set the bag Duncan had given her on the table and stepped back to reset all the protective wards.

Once their soft glow surrounded her, she spilled the talismans out on the granite tabletop. Their pulsing darkness beat at her senses, the blood magic's filth making her feel unclean without even touching them.

How best to destroy them? One by one or all of them at once? She suspected the release of the power her brother had fed into them would cause a backlash, weakening him at least for a short time. Would destroying them all at once cause him irreparable harm?

What kind of person was she that she hoped it would? The answer was easy. She wanted to be the kind of person who would do whatever it took to stop his attacks on the people of Agathia.

Using the cloth bag to protect her hand from having to touch the talismans directly, she quickly laid them out in a circle on the table with the largest in the middle. When they were arranged to her liking, she raised her hands in the air, palms up and fingers spread wide.

"Lords and ladies, guide me with your strength. Let those whose blood was spilled to form these abominations rest in peace."

The air around her thrummed with a pulsing power that shone brightly with a pure light, slowly consuming the darkness carried by the talismans. When all of the darkness was centered over the one in the middle, she clapped her hands as hard as she could and called on the power of the rocks and earth and air, and then invoked the secret name of the goddess.

As the last word rang out, the smallest of Ifre's sigils burst apart, but the black stone in the largest one continued to flash brightly. Lavinia paused to draw a deep breath and then shoved a final pulse of power into the talisman, crushing it into a fine powder. The effort left her feeling as if she'd been running a long-distance foot race.

She waited a few seconds to make sure the talismans no longer had the ability to work their evil. When she was satisfied the danger was past, she lit a small brazier and swept the dust into it, letting the heat of the fire destroy any last connection to Ifre's magic.

The flames burned hot, first blue, then green, and finally a fine healthy red and orange. She waited several minutes before dousing the fire. Exhausted, her work finished, she released the wards and dimmed the mage lights in the workroom. The spells had left her tired, but she still needed to seek the guidance of the gods, and that meant scrying again.

After filling a pitcher with fresh water at the well, she walked down the hallway, soaking in the comforting sounds of life within the abbey walls. She was relieved to see that Sister Margaret had put Sarra to work in the kitchen, keeping her busy and distracted. As Lavinia made her way through the familiar surroundings, it seemed as if she were saying good-bye to her life here at the abbey. She wasn't sure why. Until she attempted to hear from the gods through her scrying, nothing was decided.

When she reached her office, she wasn't surprised to find Duncan waiting for her. Rather than speaking to him right away, she headed straight outside.

He followed her into the garden but stood back out of her way. She emptied the bowl and then refilled it with fresh water. Silently, the two of them assumed their accustomed positions on opposite sides of the green glass as the water churned and swirled.

She stared across into Duncan's pale eyes as if she would find the answers to her questions there rather than in the swirling water. When his grim expression softened slightly, some of her own tension faded.

The surface of the water slowly smoothed out to reveal the first image. The sisters stood grouped around a large funeral pyre, their heads bowed in prayer. She shuddered at the size of the fire; too many had died that day.

The vision of the flames faded away to reveal several of the sisters riding in the farm wagon they used once a year to haul supplies back from the capital city. This time it was leaving the abbey loaded down with baggage and wooden crates. Other sisters rode behind the wagon surrounded by grim-faced men led by Josup.

So the gods agreed she needed to send the sisters out

of Ifre's reach. She recognized Margaret, Joetta, and Berta, but where was she? She leaned closer but didn't find herself in either the heavily laden wagon or on horseback.

She continued her vigil, hoping that the gods would choose her destiny for her. Once again the water swirled, erasing everything that had been reflected there.

"Guide me, please. This I pray."

But instead of the goddess who ruled over the fields and forests, a different form appeared in the water, rising up out of the surface fully formed out of the crystal clear liquid. Despite her diminutive size, there was no mistaking the power the goddess wore as comfortably as she did her clothing.

Even if Lavinia didn't immediately recognize the woman, Duncan obviously did. He dropped to his knees and bowed his head.

"My Lady of the River."

"Sir Duncan, my avatar and warrior."

Lavinia's own knees gave out on her. Never before had she heard of a god appearing in person to speak directly to a mere human. But then Duncan was not an ordinary man. Although he was showing his respect, he did not appear to be particularly afraid. She was.

"How can I best serve you, my lady?"

Rather than answer Duncan immediately, the goddess gestured with her hand, leaving Duncan frozen and staring out of eyes that were no longer pale, but a rich, dark brown. What was happening here? The goddess then turned to study Lavinia. She wanted to look away from the Lady of the River, but the power of the goddess's gaze held her prisoner.

"It appears that Captain Gideon is not the only one of my avatars whose heart has been claimed by someone other than me. My Duncan is a fierce warrior and a brilliant scholar. He's known little of love and gentleness in his life; yet his soul and honor remain unsullied."

The goddess floated closer to Lavinia's side of the bowl. "Rise to your feet and answer me this, Lady Lavinia. Are you worthy of such a man? In truth, I have my doubts. Your fear overrules your wisdom. He deserves better."

The words lashed at Lavinia, leaving their mark on her heart. Only a fool would argue with a goddess, but she felt compelled to defend herself. "I was seeking the wisdom of the gods, my lady."

The goddess snorted in derision, hardly an expression Lavinia would have ever expected from one of the holy ones. The Lady then shook her head.

"My child, it is not up to the gods to direct each step you take in your life. That would steal your free will from you. It should be your own choices, right or wrong, that guide your life. Don't search in the water for your answers. Search within your heart."

Then the goddess tilted her head to the side, once again studying her with an intensity that left Lavinia feeling weak. "You have great potential. Do not waste it. Your people need you."

She turned her attention back to Duncan. "And this man needs your strength of purpose as well. Your indecision weakens him and divides his loyalties. That must cease immediately. Fail to give him what he needs, and it will have disastrous consequences. More than his life is at risk. His soul is as well. Know that it will take all of us—gods, avatars, and the people of Agathia—to defeat what your brother is about to unleash upon this land."

When she gestured again, awareness flowed back into Duncan's expression. He blinked, and his eyes were once again pale, bearing the mark of his service to the Lady.

"Sir Duncan, your captain has need of you. Do not delay returning to his side. Your enemy grows stronger."

He shot a quick look at Lavinia before nodding. "I will ride for the keep before first light."

"Sooner would be better, but I understand that there is much left to do before the good sisters here will be safe. Just remember that the days until we will meet at the river grow shorter with each passing minute. Use your time wisely."

Once again Duncan bowed. "I will endeavor to do my best."

The goddess laughed softly. "That is all I have ever asked."

Then her form blurred and flowed back down into the bowl. The surface of the water remained mirror smooth, but no more images appeared.

Duncan gently picked up the bowl and poured its contents on the ground where the plants had been burned by the water poisoned by Ifre Keirthan's dark magic. This time the few plants that were left swayed and grew several inches in a matter of seconds.

"Amazing."

He returned the bowl to its stand. "Yes, she is. I'm sorry if her presence frightened you."

Frightened was too weak a word for the rush of emotion she'd experienced, but Lavinia kept that to herself. "Does she often appear to you and your friends?"

He frowned. "No, in the past we've seen her only when it was time for the five of us to face her judgment. However, she appeared to Gideon not long after we were called forth by Lady Merewen. I don't know what to make of it except that we've all sensed that this calling is different. We're not sure why."

Lavinia found herself blurting out, "Your eyes were the prettiest shade of brown."

She'd clearly confused him. "What?"

"While the Lady spoke to me, it was as if she'd turned you into living stone. You looked the same as you always do except your eyes were dark brown, not pale like they are now."

Duncan stared down at the empty bowl, his expression sad. "Until I came into the Lady's service, they were brown like my mother's."

He crossed to where Lavinia stood. "The Lady truly spoke directly to you, yet I didn't hear any of it. What did she say?"

When she nodded and stepped toward him, he held out his arms. At his touch, even the kiss of the sun felt warmer on her skin. Together they banished the chill of fear she'd been living with for hours.

Laying her cheek against Duncan's chest, she did her best to explain. "Your Lady said I should search in my heart for answers, not in the water. That the gods cannot make all of our choices for us without stealing that which makes us human."

Then she smiled. "I'm not sure your goddess thinks I'm good enough for you."

She felt the wave of shock roll through Duncan at her announcement. "In truth, she said that?"

Lavinia nodded. "My indecision and fear are weakening your ability to do your duty."

Duncan's arms tightened around her. "I have never failed the goddess in my duty. I will not this time, either."

"I know that, and so does she," Lavinia assured him.

But she had decisions to make, her own honor to protect. It would be far easier for her to think clearly if she were alone with her thoughts. "There is much to be done before morning. I will need to get the sisters organized to leave. After that, I will pack the books that cannot be left here for Ifre to find. I'll also set aside the ones that will be of the most use to you and your captain."

Despite her brave words, her body trembled with all that had happened and her continuing fear about their uncertain future. Duncan gently tipped her chin up, bringing her gaze up to meet his.

"You're not alone in this, Lavinia. We will face the future together, no matter what it brings."

Then he kissed her with such sweetness that it brought tears to her eyes. The Lady of the River had said Duncan was a good man, his honor and soul shining mirror bright. If the goddess had been right about Lavinia claiming Duncan's heart, she would have to work hard to be worthy of such a gift.

She kissed him back, pouring into the embrace everything she felt but couldn't yet give voice to.

Then the dinner bell rang and shattered their brief moment of peace. It was time to rejoin the others and set their plans into motion.

Once again Ifre had taken to his bed. Damn his sister! He'd been laid low as soon as the slaughter of his men had begun. His weakness had been compounded a short time later when the backlash from the destruction of his talismans hit him. The remaining power in the connection had snapped back hard enough to leave him screaming in pain.

His physician's foul concoction had barely begun to work, leaving Ifre queasy and nearly immobilized.

Lavinia would pay for this. That was all that mattered now. He imagined her stretched out on his altar, her arms and legs chained to the posts as he carved her up into tiny pieces. Her agony and her blood would provide the final push, releasing the cloud of blackness he'd worked to create.

Even now, it stirred within him, approving of the direction of his thoughts.

Once he had the darkness firmly within his command, no one would dare stand against him. First of all, he would sacrifice any who dared impede his relentless march toward total power. To distract himself from the pounding in his head, he began to count off the people he would go after first.

He smiled.

All those sisters had conspired to hide Lavinia from him. They moved to the top of his list. There were others who'd done more to thwart him, but knowing her friends died because of her would only increase the power he could harvest from Lavinia's agony.

Next would come the bastards who had slaughtered his men. When had the abbey hired armed guards? Probably right after Lavinia destroyed his coins. It was doubtful that she'd remain cowering in the abbey now, but he'd send another troop of men to find out.

When he could crawl back out of bed, the first thing he would do was cast a tracking spell, using his blood to enable his men to follow Lavinia. Even though she and he had different mothers, their father's blood would've forged a common bond between them. As he thought of her blood and his, he sensed another presence, one that was both new and increasingly familiar. It caressed his mind, polishing the jagged edges of his pain into exquisite sharpness.

Even from his room on the top floor, he sensed the blackness pulsing down below in his private chambers. He reached out with his mind, absorbing its strength. It raced through his body, arousing his bloodlust. Oh yes, this was what he'd been working toward all along.

He slowly sat up on the edge of the bed and considered his options. There was bound to be someone available that no one would miss. One of the servants perhaps. It would take but a touch of his hand right now to capture a woman's mind, making her willing to follow him down below to his chambers.

Once there, he would release his hold over her. What fun would it be if she had no will left with which to resist him?

He straightened his clothes and checked his image in

the mirror. Right now the sweet blackness was running so hot within him, he feared that it would show in his face or at least his eyes. But, no, the image he saw reflected in the mirror was completely normal.

It was time to cull his newest victim from the herd. Then the evening's festivities would begin. He'd feed the darkness and reap the rewards for his efforts. This time when he went after Lavinia, no power in the world would stand against him.

He descended to the great hall. A slow ripple of awareness rolled through the room as his courtiers noticed his arrival. As usual, they all vied for his attention. If they knew his truth, they wouldn't be strutting around the room like so many colorful birds. They'd be running for the door and the fastest way out of town.

He let them think they were safe. For the moment they were, but not for long. As he wended his way through the room, stopping to chat with a few people along the way, he kept his eye out for a likely victim.

A movement on the far side of the room caught his attention—a pair of servant girls. Luscious and sweet, they looked as if they were fresh from the country, their skin tanned from the sun and their limbs strong from physical work.

They would be perfect for his purpose. The only question was which one to choose. Blonde or brunette? But then again, why did he need to choose at all? He approached them, pasting a look of embarrassed concern on his face. As soon as they recognized him, they dropped into a low curtsy.

"I know you are both busy, but I'm afraid that I have need of your services."

The older of the pair immediately got a suspicious look in her eyes although she tried to hide it. "We should let Lady Theda know where we'll be, my lord. She won't be pleased if we abandon our posts."

He chuckled good-naturedly. "I'll make sure she knows that I borrowed you."

As soon as he touched her cheek, her eyes lost their sharp focus. Her younger companion was easier to capture. They trailed along behind him as docile as could be as he led them toward the door that led to the lower level of his home. He'd send them on ahead to wait for him and join them later. They were his to use as he saw fit, but he'd prefer their disappearance not be associated with him for now.

Theda would guess, but she wouldn't say anything. She stood to lose too much if she tried to interfere with his plans.

He locked the door behind the two women and hoped they enjoyed the journey down below. After all, it was the last one they'd ever make. Come midnight, their dying screams would fuel the hunt for his sister.

Three hours later, he led his two guests into his private chambers. The blackness shrieked inside his head, demanding more blood. Ifre put a hand on the wall to steady himself as the ravenous hunger battered against the inside of his skull. With the power behind his magic growing stronger, so did its need for more blood and more pain.

Ifre did his best to placate the shapeless monster, promising the blood would start flowing within minutes. As he and his two companions made their way down the passageway, he found himself staring at the soft sway of the older one's hips. His manhood stirred to life, a different hunger making itself known.

He smiled. Oh yes, he would feed the blackness a fine meal indeed.

The next morning, tired but satisfied with the night's pleasures, Ifre strolled outside with members of his court trailing along behind him. The bright sunshine immediately pierced his eyes with painful shards of light, causing him to stumble. One of his courtiers caught his arm to steady him. Ifre jerked his arm free but forced himself to acknowledge the man's gesture with a quick nod before continuing on.

His growing connection to the darkness coiled and writhed within his chest in reaction to the light. The unsettling sensation slowed his steps and made it difficult to continue forward to where his men awaited their orders. Finally, Ifre took refuge under a nearby tree, its thick foliage providing enough shade to give him some respite.

The darkness demanded he return to the comfort of his secret chambers, away from the light and back to the blood. Ifre fought for control, all the while pretending to inspect the troops in mounted formation in front of him. With a great deal of effort, he subdued the darkness enough to speak to his army.

He stepped forward. "Soldiers of Agathia! I have received word your captain and his men have been slaughtered by the same enemies who killed my friend and loyal subject, Lord Fagan!"

A ripple of shocked anger rolled through the troops, causing their horses to stir restlessly.

"I want you to track down those responsible for the death of your leader and your brothers. I had sent them on a mission to the abbey at the edge of the Sojourn Valley to convey an invitation to Lady Lavinia, my sister. Instead, they were greeted with treachery and death."

Ifre drew himself up to his full height, looking suitably grim and resolute. "Here are your orders: Find those responsible and make them pay for their crimes."

One particularly brave individual called out, "And what of your sister? Has she been taken prisoner?"

Was it time to announce her betrayal? Would they

believe him? His sister had always possessed a talent for charming the rabble. No, better to let them discover her treachery for themselves.

"Your mission is to find out what has become of Lady Lavinia and escort her back here to safety."

He then gave the newly promoted captain a small token that would lead the troops straight toward Lavinia, tracking her by the common blood bond. There hadn't been time to infuse his power into another set of individual talismans.

The necklaces took too much time to prepare, especially for so many at once. It was a risk sending his men out with their free will intact, but right now he had no choice. The longer he delayed seeking retribution, the weaker he would appear and the better chance that Lavinia and whoever was aiding her would find another hiding place.

Worse yet, they might join forces with others who would oppose him. That could prove disastrous if they attacked before he was ready for them. Once his power reached its full potential, no one would be able to stand against him.

Until then, though . . .

"Ride, warriors of Agathia! May the gods guide and protect you! Avenge your captain, avenge your friends, avenge the honor of your ruler and your land!"

The troops saluted him with drawn swords and shouts of victory to come as they rode out. He dutifully stood by and watched until the last one was out of sight. Appearances were everything, especially when he was surrounded by the members of his court. He'd already suffered two defeats and couldn't risk his people questioning his ability to rule Agathia.

Once they dragged Lavinia before him in chains, he would spill her bastard blood on his altar, supping richly on its power. Then everyone would know for all time that he was the strongest of the Keirthan lineage. Hoping that day would soon arrive, he led the procession back inside, the dim interior a relief after standing in the burn of the midday sun.

A gaggle of lesser nobles and merchants waited inside, all of them wanting to vie for his attention. His first instinct was to lash out, to order them from his sight. But common sense dictated that he continue to act the part of a duke who actually cared about his people.

He waved the first man forward. "Attend to me, Lord Vulan, and tell me how I can be of help."

Chapter 26

Josup had proven to be a master of organization. While Duncan saw to his own preparations for travel, the guard had set his men to loading the wagons with the basic necessities for their trip across the mountains to safety.

The plan was for the guards and sisters to depart at dawn. After burying one of their own, the guards had helped with the funeral pyre for the duke's men. With so many to send on their way to their final rest, there'd simply been too much to do to leave before the sun faded in the west. The switchback was tricky enough in daylight. To attempt it at night with wagons was asking for disaster.

Duncan added the last of his gear to the pile by the door, and then looked up and down the hall. Where had Lavinia disappeared to? Had she decided to do the sensible thing and ride with him and Sarra for Lady Merewen's keep? He truly hoped so. If she even hinted that she planned to stay here at the abbey alone or that she wanted to ride with the other sisters, he'd have to do something drastic.

He didn't want that to happen. Josup and men had been hired to protect the sisters and the abbey. Would they stand against him if they thought Duncan was a threat to Lavinia? Surely she wouldn't put them all at risk.

The guards were loading crates of books into the wagons, so she'd finished sorting the library. He was guessing that she had left her own packing for last, which meant most likely she was in her quarters. If they were going to argue about her plans, he'd prefer to do so in privacy. Once he had her convinced to come with him, they could present a united front to the other sisters.

If he could convince her.

He knocked softly on the office door. No answer. He slipped inside anyway. Her office looked as if it hadn't been touched. It seemed unlikely to him that she'd leave behind everything in the room.

The garden was empty, too, and her scrying bowl was exactly where they'd left it earlier. Now he knew for sure that something was wrong. Lavinia might not be able to pack the heavy metal stand, but she would never abandon the bowl itself, not when it was her connection to the gods. He crossed the garden to listen outside her bedroom door.

She was in there. He could hear her mumbling to herself as soon as he approached the door. Should he knock first? Even though she'd shared her bed with him, he wasn't sure of his welcome now.

A choked-off sob took the decision out of his hands. If she was that upset, if she needed a shoulder to cry on, he would offer his. He found her perched on the edge of her bed with her face buried in her hands.

Not wanting to startle her, he whispered her name. "Lavinia?"

At first, she didn't respond, but then she let her hands fall down to her lap. Her eyes were red and swollen, her cheeks stained with the tracks of tears. Clearly she'd been crying as if her heart had been broken. Maybe it was. Evil had reached right through the thick walls of the abbey not once, but twice, both times targeting Lavinia.

She had to be terrified. Any rational person would be. He stepped closer, finally sitting down beside her to put his arm around her shoulder. When she ducked back to avoid his embrace, he didn't try again.

"I'm so sorry, Lavinia."

She scrubbed at her face with the sleeve of her robe. "Why? You're not the one who sent those men after me."

"True, I didn't. However, I truly regret that your brother has chosen to follow such a twisted path, and that his actions are hurting you and those you care about."

She scooted farther away from him. That small distance left him feeling cold and alone. "Lavinia, I can't help if I don't know what you're thinking."

Rather than answer right away, she left the bed to pace the length of the room and back. On the second trip around, she finally spoke.

"Your goddess spoke of *your* honor, *your* duty."

By now, her tears had dried up, but they'd left their mark on her soft skin. There was nothing soft about the look she gave him now. "She also said that your concern for me has divided your loyalties. That I'm making you weak."

"But I've already told you—"

Without waiting for him to reply, she resumed walking. "I understand her concerns, but I must consider *my* own duty and honor. Certainly, the sisters look to me for leadership. No doubt they expect me to leave with them in the morning, even knowing that I took a solemn vow to protect this abbey and its library. How can I run at the first hint of danger?"

She rounded on him again, arguing with him even though he'd yet to say a word. "I know we're sending the most precious books with the sisters. And, yes, many of the books can be replaced if necessary, but that is beside the point. What does it say of my personal honor if I abandon not only my post but the very things I have sworn to protect?"

He wanted to shake some sense into her, to make her realize that she was infinitely more precious than even the rarest of the books in the abbey library.

"One woman cannot stand against Duke Keirthan alone, Lavinia. Not even you." Clearly, for all the attention she paid to him, he was pouring water on infertile soil. "Lavinia, you must—"

Big mistake. Her eyes flared wide as she glared at him. "Do not try to tell me what I must or must not do, Duncan. You don't have the right."

She wielded the sharp edge of her words with deadly accuracy, leaving his heart bleeding. True, he had no claim on her and was in no position to make one, not when his days numbered so few. But, by the gods, she mattered.

Rather than argue when she was obviously not ready to listen to him, he waved his hand, telling her without words to continue. She jerked her head in a sharp nod and began pacing again.

"We both know that Ifre is not going to give up. If I go with the sisters, his men will follow after us. I cannot be responsible for visiting his evil on another group of innocent sisters, especially in another country. Agathia has enough trouble without inciting a war with our neighbors."

"So what have you decided to do?"

"Isn't it obvious, Duncan? I have to leave with you. Even then, my brother's men will likely follow us right to Lady Merewen's gate. And I will be responsible for bringing harm to her door again. Yet what choice do I have? We must band together to fight Ifre's evil or most assuredly we will all perish at his hands."

She paused to pick up a small vase. To him, it looked

perfectly ordinary, but she cradled it as if it were most precious. Why?

"This belonged to my mother. It and my scrying bowl are the only two things of hers I was able to keep. Everything else was given to the maids or else burned."

Her next words came out on a choked sob. "Once again I am being forced out of my home, taking only what I can fit into saddlebags."

She moved as if to throw the vase against the wall, but Duncan caught her hand before she could.

"We will make room for this and the bowl. Bring what is most important to you. We can always take a second packhorse if necessary."

He pried the vase out of her fingers. "I well understand losing everything that holds meaning in your life. This vase might remind you of your mother, Lavinia, but she isn't in this vase. She lives on in your heart just as my mother lives in mine."

He set the vase aside and wrapped his arms around Lavinia, relieved that she didn't fight him this time. "I will do everything in my power to ensure that you will once again know peace in your life. But until that day, I need you to let me keep you safe."

"Who keeps you safe, Duncan? When will you know peace?"

A question that had no happy answer. "My friends and I stand together."

She settled against him. "I look forward to meeting them."

He smiled at the thought. "That will be interesting. For certain, you will like Lady Merewen. She's a strong woman just like you."

Finally, Lavinia sighed and stepped back. "I should start packing if I want to be ready to leave with you in the morning."

Good. One less battle for him to fight. "Good. Sarra will be happy to know that you'll be with her."

"There is that, but it's not as if I have a choice in the matter. But as I said, Ifre will follow. He's already proven his magic will allow him to seek me out wherever I go. Better that I ride to where there are warriors prepared to fight him. Any other choice would only put the sisters at risk."

Lying was of no value to either of them.

"That much is true, Lavinia, but always remember that none of this is your fault. Ifre set all of this in motion when he sent his men after you, but I am sorry that it has come to this for you."

He started to leave, but he had even harder news for her. "The three of us will leave tonight."

Her eyes widened. "But I've already told everyone to be ready to depart in the morning."

"That's safest for them. The trail up the hillside may have been compromised by the duke's attack. Josup will need clear vision to be able to safely maneuver the wagons down to the valley floor. My ability to see at night is far superior to a normal man's, so I can guide us safely down the hillside. Besides, their tracks will help hide ours. We'll cut cross-country for a while rather than follow the road. I'm hoping that will help throw the duke's men off our trail."

The defeat in her posture was painful to see. "Fine, then. As you wish. Packing will not take me long."

He looked around her room. "You can send much of this with the sisters. Once we've defeated Keirthan, you can either send for your things or rejoin the sisters here at the abbey. For now, take your vase and the scrying bowl. Add to that a change or two of clothing, personal items, and anything else that a horse can carry that you cannot bear to leave behind."

"The books—"

He stopped her. "I've already packed the few you said we'd need to take with us to Lady Merewen's keep. The others that we can't risk falling into the duke's hands are already in the wagon. I asked the sisters to move the rest of the library into the workroom.

"Before we leave, you can strengthen the wards. That's the most any of us can do right now. Meanwhile, Sister Margaret has put together food for us, and Sister Joetta has helped Sarra prepare for the journey."

For the first time since he'd walked in, Lavinia's eyes sparked with life. "You're making me feel like so much baggage. I'm surprised you didn't tie me on one of the packhorses."

Her comment startled a laugh out of him. "I probably shouldn't admit this, but I considered doing exactly that if you refused to ride with me."

From the shocked look on her face, she must have believed him. "I can't believe you would admit to such an outrage. How dare you!"

His smile faded. "I would do that and more to protect you, Lavinia."

Her anger faded as quickly as it had come. "I apologize, Duncan. I well know that you are not the enemy here."

Then she surprised him. "I'm not sure I could've watched you ride away without me. My first duty is to the sisters and the library I've sworn to protect, but everything that's happened has convinced me that my true path runs beside yours."

"We both understand what our gods expect of us."

Then she surprised him. "It's not my duty that has me riding with you, Duncan. It's my heart. I care about you too much to watch you disappear from my life one minute before you have to."

His own heart pounded in his chest as she said the

words he'd never hoped to hear. "And I care about you, as well, Lavinia. Your courage, your strength, everything about you."

He drew her closer once more. "And I will keep you safe or die trying. This I swear."

Then he kissed her long and hard to seal his promise. Lavinia responded with such sweetness, enticing him to deepen the kiss. Would that they had time to do more than simply taste each other, but the duke would've already unleashed more of his troops to avenge the deaths of his men.

As it was, Duncan and his two charges would pass perilously close to the road to the capital city on their way back to Lady Merewen's keep. If they timed it wrong, they could very well cross paths with their pursuers.

He broke off the kiss, wishing he could slam the door closed and carry her down onto the bed. But no, that way lay folly.

"Pack what you need, Lavinia, while I finish saddling the horses. As soon as you're done, we ride to join my friends."

"I'll be ready."

Lavinia walked beside Duncan, leading her horse and the pack animal while he led his own mount and the one Sarra rode. The little girl had quit complaining about having to leave the abbey as soon as she'd found out that Lavinia would be going with her. There'd been a few tears when Sister Joetta had hugged each of them goodbye, but Sarra hadn't hesitated to let Duncan boost her up into the saddle.

Lavinia understood why they had to take Sarra with them, but were they only leading the girl into the path of more danger? She prayed the gods would show mercy on Sarra; she'd already lost so much in her young life.

Duncan stopped suddenly and handed off the reins to her as he leaned in close to murmur, "Wait here."

He drew his sword and slipped off into the darkness, leaving her and Sarra on the trail alone. She bit back the urge to demand an explanation. Clearly he'd sensed something might be amiss ahead. Delaying him could only make the situation worse, but she hated feeling so vulnerable, especially with Sarra beside her.

Time dragged on. They'd left the abbey only a short time ago, but the distance traveled was far greater than the length of trail they'd walked. No matter what happened next, her heart told her that her life behind cloistered walls had come to an end. The horses stirred restlessly, no doubt as anxious as she was to be moving. Being caught here on the hillside, neither up nor down, was unsettling.

One of the shadows down the trail moved. Her breath caught in her throat until she recognized Duncan leading a horse behind him. He quickly stripped the saddle and bridle off the horse and dumped them behind a thick clump of brush. When Duncan was finished, he slapped the animal on the rump, but the horse stubbornly stayed right where it was.

"Fine. Stay or go. It matters not to me."

She hid a smile at the disgust in Duncan's voice as he started the march on down the hillside, picking up the pace as he led his own horse and Sarra's past the animal. Lavinia passed by next, trying not to laugh when the big gray fell in behind the packhorse.

Maybe the animal had the right of it. He'd lost his own herd, so welcome or not, he joined their small band. Wasn't that what both she and Sarra had done when they came to live with the sisters after losing their real families?

Now that family was gone, too, at least for now. She studied Duncan's broad shoulders as he led the way down the trail and realized that she didn't feel abandoned this time. Yes, her life was changing yet again, and the future was unpredictable.

But for right now, Duncan was with her, and that was enough. As long as he stood beside her, she could face whatever tomorrow would bring. At that reassuring thought, she trudged on down the hillside, cocooned in the shadows and chill of the night air.

Chapter 27

Sigil swung down off his weary mount's back, glad to be done riding for the day. Murdoch had been driving both men and beasts hard for two days, stopping only to rest the horses. There wasn't a single part of Sigil that didn't hurt, but soldiers didn't complain about such things.

Well, actually they did, but right now he was too tired to bother. He unsaddled his horse and then walked the exhausted animal until it cooled down. Afterward, they both drank their fill of cool, clear water from a small stream.

Murdoch had ridden on ahead to scout the trail for a short distance, but Sigil expected him back soon. Neither of them would stay awake much later than sundown, so he gathered up an armload of dried wood to start a fire.

They'd been surviving on cold rations ever since leaving the keep behind, but earlier Shadow had brought down a small deer and offered it to Murdoch. To keep up this pace and still have strength left to fight, they needed something more substantial than dried fruit and a few bites of cheese.

Sigil had never expected to be grateful to a mountain cat. But then, nothing had been normal since he'd awakened in Lady Merewen's keep with no memory of his past and an uncertain future.

The first tendrils of smoke were snaking skyward

when Murdoch finally reappeared, looking as tired as Sigil felt. He didn't bother trying to strike up a conversation, concentrating instead on feeding more kindling to the fire and slowly coaxing the flames to life.

About the time he had the deer on a makeshift spit and was turning it, Murdoch dropped down a log on the other side of the fire.

"See anything?"

The big man shook his head. "No sign of anyone in the area. No fresh tracks on the trail in either direction."

"I guess that's good."

A movement in the brush behind Murdoch had Sigil reaching for his weapon. Before he could draw it, Shadow stepped out of the bushes. It wasn't the first time she'd managed to startle him. She stared across at him, her mouth open in a cat grin that flaunted her fangs.

"Cursed animal!"

Her owner chuckled and gave her a good scratching under her chin. "Be nice. She's the reason we can both sleep tonight instead of standing guard."

That much was true, but it didn't mean Sigil trusted the beast. "Who's going to protect us from her?"

But even as he spoke, he tossed Shadow a large piece of raw meat he'd held back for her. After all, a hunter deserved to be rewarded for her labors. Shadow picked up her dinner with great delicacy and disappeared back into the bushes.

He'd also put tea on to steep. After handing a cup to Murdoch, he poured one for himself. The liquid was hot enough to scald, but it cleared the trail dust from his throat.

"How much farther, do you think?"

Murdoch sat staring into the fire, his big hands wrapped around his mug. "Less than another day if the map was accurate."

He glanced over his shoulder in the direction Shadow

had taken before murmuring, "It's at times like these that it would be nice to have one of the birds for my avatar. There's an advantage to being able to see through their eyes when you need to scout an area."

For the first time all day, Sigil laughed. "Are you afraid of hurting that cat's feelings?"

Murdoch looked embarrassed. "Not afraid exactly. But considering she provided dinner for us, I didn't want to sound ungrateful. Besides, we'll need her if we run into the duke's men out here."

There was that. Sigil shoved another few pieces of wood into the fire and turned the meat. When he looked up, Murdoch was watching him.

"What?"

"Does any of this area look familiar to you?"

"I wish it did, but it's all strange to me."

He rocked back on his heels to stare at the dark outlines of the surrounding hills. "You'd think I would recognize something if I served in this area."

"So nothing is coming back to you?"

"Not yet." Sigil hated the note of pity in Murdoch's voice. He picked up a rock and threw it as far as he could.

"How can I know some things and not others? I know I'm a soldier and how to defend myself. I can do everyday things like riding a horse or cooking dinner over an open fire. But no matter how hard I try to remember, there's still a gaping hole in my mind where *I* used to be. Everything there is simply gone as if it had been cut out with a knife."

"Mayhap you are trying too hard or—" Murdoch hesitated briefly as if searching for the right words. "Or maybe you don't want to remember."

Enough was enough. Sigil surged to his feet, glaring down at his companion. "That's not true! By the gods, do you think I fear facing judgment at the hands of your captain? That I'm a coward?"

Murdoch remained seated, his pale eyes glittering up at Sigil. "I may not know your real name, Sigil, or what drove you to serve a bastard like Duke Keirthan, but you are no coward. If I had to guess, I think your former master did something to your mind. From what Lady Alina and Lady Merewen remember of that night, there was a flash like lightning when the sword penetrated that talisman you wore. Something like that would be enough to jangle anyone's memories."

His calm assessment soothed Sigil's temper. "Perhaps you are right. Let's eat and get some sleep. According to the map, we're close to the main road to the capital city. If so, we could encounter one of the duke's patrols at any time now."

He carved up the meat and passed Murdoch his share. Shadow slipped back into camp, watching every move Sigil made. Finally, he broke off a chunk of his own dinner and tossed it to the cat. It wasn't that he liked her any better, but as Murdoch said, she was standing guard so they could sleep.

As he carried the food scraps some distance from their camp, a cloud drifted in front of the moon overhead, leaving him in total darkness. How appropriate.

He listened to the night: the whisper of the breeze, the scurry of small feet in the underbrush, and the call of a hawk. All normal, but there was something else out there.

Something that made his skin crawl, an itch that was almost familiar to him. A memory dancing back out of reach. Something to do with pain and death and power.

He knew that much to be true. The cloud moved on, and once again the world was bathed in the cold light of the moon. A shiver ran right up his spine, as if pure evil had cast its eye in his direction as it hunted for its prey.

If Murdoch's friend was out there somewhere, he was in grave danger, the kind that one man wouldn't stand a chance against. He would need help, maybe more than two men and a mountain cat could provide, but they were the only hope he had. If they didn't reach Duncan soon, he feared Murdoch would lose one of his own.

Sigil took off running back toward camp, yelling Murdoch's name. So much for a night's sleep.

Duncan hated to push his two charges so hard, but his instincts had been screaming at him all night and well into the day that it was imperative they keep going. Kiva had returned with a terse note from Gideon that he was sending Murdoch to meet them. Until then, the three of them were on their own.

Duncan slowed his horse to let Lavinia catch up. From the way she sat slumped in the saddle, a good breeze would knock her off her horse's back. He'd been riding with Sarra asleep in his arms for the past two hours or more.

"We'll stop when we reach the edge of those trees up ahead. If I remember correctly, there's a stream and good grazing for the horses."

Lavinia sat up straighter and looked around. "Good. I'm not worried about myself, but you have to be exhausted, too. It can't be easy riding with her like that."

No, it wasn't, and he'd worried about what would happen if they did run into trouble with him encumbered with the sleeping child. He said the only thing he could.

"It's not much farther."

But he felt every step the horse took, aching from the lack of sleep and hours upon hours of maintaining a constant vigil while his two charges dozed in the saddle.

Even when they did reach the campsite, his day wouldn't be over. There was wood to gather, a fire to start, a meal to prepare. The list was endless. He couldn't remember the last time he'd been this exhausted. Even though the Damned frequently fought long and hard, it usually didn't leave him in such bad shape.

"Duncan!"

The exasperated note in Lavinia's voice jerked him out of his reverie. "What's wrong?"

"Didn't you mean to stop at the water's edge?"

He looked behind him to find he'd ridden straight through the stream and kept right on going. Cursing himself for a fool, he wheeled his horse back around. Mistakes like that could get all of them killed.

"I'm sorry."

"No apologies necessary," Lavinia said as she dismounted. "I'm surprised either one of us is able to think at all. Let me fix a place for Sarra to sleep, and then I'll take her from you."

When she had the bedroll spread out, she held up her arms to take Sarra. The little girl barely stirred as Lavinia gently lowered her to the ground and tugged a blanket up over her.

Duncan hoped his legs would support him as he swung down out of the saddle. He'd lost feeling in them hours ago. "Loosen the cinches, but don't unsaddle the horses."

Lavinia didn't ask why, but her worried look made it clear that she understood. They both knew Keirthan wouldn't have taken another defeat without planning an immediate retaliation. He could only hope that Josup had gotten the other sisters away from the abbey without mishap.

"After I rest for a few minutes, I could try scrying if you think it would help."

It was tempting. He planned to send Kiva out scouting, but the owl could cover only so much territory. Duncan also needed the bird to watch over them while they slept.

"Let's wait until after we eat before deciding. I'll gather wood and draw water while you lay out the food. We can have a fire, but keep it small. Enough to heat water and our dinner. After that, we'll need to douse it."

Their safety depended on not drawing any unnecessary attention to themselves. The three of them would eat, sleep a little, and then leave once the moon was high enough to light the trail for them.

He headed into the woods to look for deadfall limbs. As he walked, he prayed to the goddess that he would be able to get Sarra and Lavinia to safety. Death was stalking them. He knew it in his warrior's soul.

After gathering an armload of wood, he returned to their campsite. Lavinia had been busy, too. Two more bedrolls were spread out on the ground, one on each side of Sarra's. He understood why, but he couldn't help but wish that he could hold Lavinia in his arms while they slept.

She looked up just as he stepped out of the trees. "If you'll set the wood down here, I'll get the fire started."

She'd already gathered some small twigs and dried grass into a pile. But rather than using a flint to spark a flame, she held her hands palm down over the kindling. As soon as she started murmuring under her breath, a small whiff of smoke rose slowly in the air. When she repeated the same words again, louder this time, flames appeared. She continued chanting as she began feeding larger pieces of wood to the flames. In half the time it would've taken him, she had the fire blazing. She smiled as she set two pots near the flames to heat. For the moment, there was nothing more to be done.

"I watered the horses, including your friend there."

He shot the stray horse a disgusted look. "I can't believe he is still tagging along with us."

Lavinia laughed. "I think he likes you."

Duncan didn't want to honor that remark with a response, but he couldn't resist Lavinia when she was in a teasing mood. "Then he'll have to earn his keep. No more light duty. I'll put your saddle on him before we leave."

"Why not ride him yourself?"

"Because he and Sarra's mount haven't been ridden as hard as my horse or yours. I want you both on the freshest mounts we have if we come under attack. If that happens, you take Sarra and run fast and hard. Don't look back."

"But what about you? Won't you be with us?"

He changed the subject rather than answer. "The food should be hot by now. Why don't you wake Sarra while I serve us? The sooner we eat, the sooner we can all get some sleep."

The darkness that settled over them as they ate had little to do with the sun going down.

"Duncan, wake up. It's Sarra."

He opened his eyes to find Lavinia hovering over him, her pretty face stark with worry.

"What about her?"

Then he realized the little girl's bed was empty. He jerked upright and looked around their camp.

"Where did she go?"

Lavinia pointed over toward where he'd picketed the horses. Sarra was standing nose to nose with the dappled gray. What was going on? Duncan left his bedroll behind and slowly made his way toward the horses, trying not to spook them. One wrong step was all it would take for Sarra to get seriously hurt.

As he drew closer, he could hear her talking. Actually, not her, but that same adult voice she used when speaking her prophecies. He paused to listen.

The deep voice carried well on the night air, making it even more disturbing than usual. "Thank you. I will warn Duncan and Lady Lavinia."

He pitched his voice to carry only a short distance. "Tell me what, Sarra?"

Both she and the gelding turned in Duncan's direction.

"They're coming."

He edged closer and then knelt down on one knee, to better converse at her level. "Who is coming?"

Sarra patted the horse on the neck. "Some of his old herd is moving in this direction." Then her voice deepened as the gods spoke through her again. "They aren't far, so you must ride now. Don't stop to gather anything but your weapons. With the gods' grace, your friends will reach you before the duke's men do."

Duncan believed her. He lurched back to his feet. "Lavinia! We ride!"

He immediately tightened the cinch on Sarra's mount and tossed the girl up in the saddle. By the time Lavinia joined them, he'd also secured her saddle on the big gray. He gave her a boost up.

"Go! Lady Merewen's keep lies to the southwest. Kiva can guide you if necessary, but I'll be right behind you."

He could already hear the faint creak and jingle of mounted riders on the far side of the stream, still far enough away that their normal human senses wouldn't pick up on the sound of Lavinia and Sarra riding away. On the other hand, if the troop was following their tracks from yesterday, there was little chance the duke's men would pass by without seeing the scattered remains of the camp.

Duncan handed the packhorse's reins to Lavinia. "Turn him loose as soon as you're out of sight. Don't slow yourself down by holding on to him. Most likely he'll follow you anyway."

Lavinia nodded and started after Sarra. Before Duncan mounted up, he paused to study their camp. There was no time to gather their things. Even if there was, he couldn't hide the charred remains of last night's fire.

Or maybe he could. He flexed his fingers and remembered the tingle of the magic Lavinia had taught him.

Her warding spell in the abbey library kept the secret collection hidden right in plain view. It was worth the risk of a few seconds to attempt the spell himself, especially if it bought Lavinia and Sarra more time to get away.

He stepped closer to the camp and planted his feet in a wide stance. At first the words refused to come, his mind spinning too hard with all the possibilities, none of them good. He slumped his shoulders, forcing himself to relax and find that inner circle of calm deep within. Without it, he might as well be spouting gibberish.

Finally, he pictured Lavinia's beautiful face, her smile, the scent of her skin, the way she fit in his arms. For her, he would do this or die trying.

Once again he chanted the spell, this time feeling the spark of magic rippling over his skin. At first, he put up a simple ward around the bedrolls and the cold ashes of the campfire. It wasn't enough. Hiding the camp wouldn't mean a thing if the duke's men could immediately pick up Lavinia's fresh tracks.

May the Lady of the River forgive him, but he had to do more. He stared at the trees on the far side of the clearing and then slowly turned, mentally stretching the faint shimmer of energy from point to point until it encompassed more than the camp itself. He infused the spell with more power, ripping it from the ground beneath his feet and the very air that surrounded him.

The rich spice of endless power tasted sweet in his mouth and heated his blood. If the enemy were to ride into sight right at that moment, he would throw enough power into the wards to burn them to ash.

"Yes!" he crowed, reveling in his newfound strength. Once the enemy was dead, he would ride straight for the capital city, find Ifre Keirthan, and rip the bastard's heart out of his chest. He deserved no less for threatening a gentlewoman like Lavinia. If Duncan could go back in time, he would teach his father the same lesson for his abuse of his wife and son.

No one would stand against him then. In his mind's eye, he saw himself riding forth with his friends at his side. Together they would rid the land of all evil, starting with Keirthan's blood magic. When it came time to face judgment, he would tell the goddess how they should—

No, what was he thinking? It was not his place to tell the Lady of the River anything.

"Duncan, what are you about?"

He knew that voice. It belonged to the Lady of the River, the one who owned his allegiance. Her image filled his mind and his soul with the soothing, cool ripple of her strength. He dropped to his knees as the burn of pure magic drained from his body. The woods were quiet except for the murmur of the nearby stream. If the duke's men were nearby, he couldn't sense them. His fear for Lavinia and Sarra coiled in his chest, stealing his breath.

He bowed his head and rested his hands on his thighs as he struggled to make his lungs work.

"I am sorry for my weakness, my lady. If you can't find it in your heart to forgive me, I pray you will not hold my foolishness against Gideon and the others. They are not at fault."

"Rise, Warrior. Time to defend those you have claimed as your own is running short."

The Lady's voice flowed gently through his mind. *"You are forgiven this time, but only because your intentions were not selfish ones. Now draw your sword and prepare to fight. They come."*

Chapter 28

*T*he low branches smacked against Lavinia as she tore through the woods, chasing after Sarra. Normally, she would have led the way, but right now it was more important that she stay between the girl and their enemy. The pounding of her heart mixed with the heavy thud of the horses' hooves on the hard ground made it impossible for her to hear much else.

With visibility so poor, she couldn't even risk a look back to see if Duncan had caught up with them yet. The trees gradually thinned, giving way to open grasslands. Riding became easier but offered little in the way of cover. When Lavinia caught up with her, Sarra had slowed her horse to a fast trot. She then stood up in her stirrups and seemed to be searching in the distance for something.

Before Lavinia could call out to ask, Sarra pointed ahead. Sure enough, two men were riding straight for them with swords drawn.

The little girl smiled back in Lavinia's direction. "Duncan's friends!"

Sarra spoke in her own voice this time, yet she sounded sure of herself. Even so, Lavinia wished Duncan were there to vouch for them. Sarra's guides had never proven false as far as Lavinia knew, but with their lives at stake, a little caution was in order.

It was impossible to tell if the men had spotted them

yet. But then Kiva swept past her, his huge wings carrying him directly toward the two warriors. When the bigger of the two men waved at Duncan's avatar, the owl banked around in a slow curve and came flying right toward Lavinia and Sarra. The men changed directions to ride straight at them.

Thank the gods, they had to be Duncan's friends. "Sarra, we'll wait here."

As she pulled back on the reins, she turned the gray in a wide circle, hoping to find Duncan riding behind them. Her heart plummeted when she realized he was nowhere in sight. That was bad enough, but it was the sound of battle cries in the distance that had her screaming his name.

"Stop!"

Murdoch rode up beside the woman and made a fast grab for her reins when she ignored his order and kept riding straight back to the woods.

Lady protect him from stubborn women!

He tried one more time to cut her off. "We can't fight and protect you at the same time! Stay with the girl!"

She was already shaking her head. "They've cornered Duncan in the woods! I can help!"

Before he could stop her, she spurred the gray forward, leaving him behind. He sent a mental shout to Shadow, asking her to guard the child.

Stay with her! If we don't return, you and Kiva lead her to the keep.

The growl inside his head made it clear that the cat would prefer to fight at his side, but she was already turning back toward the little girl.

Sigil hung back until Shadow reached the child before he came riding hard to catch up with Murdoch. They'd reached the edge of the woods, but it was difficult to see very far under the canopy of thick foliage. At least the pale color of the woman's horse made it easy to track her.

The trees forced them to slow down. Sigil glanced over toward Murdoch. "I'm guessing that's Lady Lavinia, the woman Duncan told Gideon about."

"Yes, no doubt," Murdoch grumbled. "Let's hope she can lead us to Duncan in time to keep the idiot from getting skewered. I didn't ride all this distance on no sleep just to bury him."

Sigil started to smile, but then he pointed into the trees off to the left. "Murdoch! There!"

A line of three riders was circling through the trees, probably trying to cut off any avenue of escape for Duncan and the woman. The leader abruptly pulled back on the reins and pointed his horse in their direction. He drew his sword as did his two companions.

"Attack!"

As the three men charged forward, Sigil accepted their challenge. "Go, Murdoch. I can handle these three."

Murdoch didn't hesitate; right now he needed to find Duncan and the woman, whom he could no longer see. But despite the darkness, he had no trouble tracking them. The sounds of fighting carried all too clearly through the night air.

When he reached the edge of a clearing, the situation was as bad as he feared. Duncan was surrounded by a dozen of the duke's men. Two others were on the ground, dead or dying. The woman had dismounted and now stood at Duncan's side.

Murdoch watched as Duncan shoved her behind him as he faced off against the enemy. Lavinia moved to the side as she raised her hands toward the enemy and started chanting. A small blue whirlwind appeared above her palms, spinning and spinning as it grew in size and strength. How was she doing that?

And like Murdoch, the guards froze as they stared at the whirling wind in stunned horror.

Duncan stood next to Lavinia, brandishing his sword at the guards. He didn't dare take his eyes off them or even reach out to touch her. She was chanting, the first tendrils of power sparkling in the air around them.

"Please don't do this, Lavinia. Our goddess forbids the abuse of magic. Let me handle this!"

Duncan tried desperately to distract her, to make her stop, but she shook her head.

"There are too many of them, and you're already hurt! They want to kill you and drag me and Sarra back to the capital city for Ifre to play with. I love you too much to let that happen!"

"And I love you too much to allow you to get killed in my place!" He wasn't hurt badly enough to slow him down. "Lavinia, stop! I can and will carry out my duty to protect you."

Clearly she wasn't going to release the spell until the guards were rendered harmless, unless she burned herself out first. Already the blue shimmer of energy was spreading, encompassing her hands and arms. Soon it would cover her completely. He had no idea what effect it would have if that were to happen.

Meanwhile, the guards were already backing away, looks of horrified terror replacing the aggression that had been there only seconds before. He didn't blame them. Lavinia would never hurt him, but the duke's men had no such protection from her magic.

They knew it, too. Any second now they would bolt and run, but the poor bastards didn't act quickly enough. The whirling mass of power lashed across the clearing to pick up the struggling guards and heave them against trees and boulders.

As soon as the last one slid to the ground, Lavinia shouted one last word and then dropped her hands. Duncan barely caught her as she collapsed, his heart in his throat as her eyes rolled up in her head. If he hadn't felt the pounding of her pulse, he would've been terrified.

He sank to the ground, holding her close and praying that she'd not done herself irreparable harm. At least the Lady of the River hadn't returned to smite them both. The thought no sooner crossed his mind than he heard the Lady's voice echoing inside his head.

"Unlike you, Warrior, your lady was born to bear the burden of her magic. She'll need support, not condemnation if she is to aid your cause."

"Thank you, my lady," he whispered.

As he spoke, the ache in his chest eased, and even the pain from the gash on his arm abated. Even better, Lavinia stirred in his arms, her eyes fluttering open to stare up at him in confusion.

"Did it work?"

He nodded. "Yes."

Her face paled as she twisted her head to stare at the bodies scattered across the clearing. "Did I kill them all?"

Murdoch, whose arrival had gone unnoticed, was the one to answer. "No, she knocked them out. They'll have a few bumps, bruises, and maybe a broken bone or two, but they'll all survive."

The huge warrior approached the two of them warily, his gaze firmly on Duncan as he avoided even glancing at Lavinia. His attitude infuriated Duncan, even though he wasn't all that comfortable about what had just occurred, either. The unconscious guards would wake up happier about the outcome of the battle than if they'd crossed swords with Duncan and Murdoch.

If his friend wouldn't acknowledge Lavinia on his own, Duncan would force the issue. "Sir Murdoch, may I present Lady Lavinia?"

The warrior barely glanced her way, not even a hint of softening in his stern expression. "Lady Lavinia."

The chill in his words caused her to flinch. Before Duncan could call him on it, Lavinia frowned. "Duncan, I'm sensing something. It has the same feel as the coins and the medallions we took off the guards who attacked the abbey."

He helped her up from the ground and trailed after her as she wandered closer to the guards. After a few seconds, her steps became more purposeful as she moved from body to body, never lingering until she reached the last one.

"This man is carrying something Ifre made."

Murdoch had joined them. "Who is Ifre?"

Duncan glanced at Lavinia before answering. This wasn't going to make Murdoch any more comfortable about having her with them. "Ifre is Duke Keirthan's first name."

His friend looked surprised. "You know him well enough for such informality?"

Her cheeks flushed pink. "He's my half brother, although I have not seen him in years. I was raised at court but was sent away after my mother died. She was his father's mistress."

Murdoch clearly wasn't happy with that bit of information. "So that explains the magic."

He spit out the last word as if it tasted foul. That was enough. Duncan might have felt the same way when he first encountered Lavinia's gift, but she was nothing like her sibling. He put his arm around her shoulders, making it clear to both her and his friend that he would stand with her in this matter.

Before he could defend her, Lavinia answered for

herself. "My gift also comes from my mother's side of the family and draws its power from the world around us. The dark magic Ifre uses requires the sacrifice of blood and life to replenish his power. I am an earth mage and control the magic I wield without any such sacrifice. Ifre's magic will eventually control him, if it doesn't already."

Murdoch looked no happier. "I will check on Sigil and the girl."

Lavinia stiffened. "Her name is Sarra. Is she safe?"

"She is fine. I left her with Shadow. I'll fetch her as soon as I see if Sigil needs any help."

Lavinia blinked up at Murdoch in confusion, so Duncan explained. "Shadow is a mountain cat. She serves Murdoch much as Kiva serves me. No one will get past that cat to harm the girl. Sigil is a warrior who has recently joined our cause."

Or at least it appeared that way. Else, why would Gideon have allowed him out of the keep?

"I'll return as soon as possible."

Lavinia stared down at the unconscious guardsman. "While you're gone, I will do what I can to destroy the link to Duke Keirthan."

Duncan shook his head. "The minute we do that, Keirthan will know that his men have failed again. We should wait until right before we leave."

"All right."

Lavinia walked away to start gathering up their scattered belongings. Both men studied the guards, who had yet to move or even make a sound.

"Do you trust her?"

Duncan didn't hesitate. "With my life."

"I hate magic. Give me a good sword any day, but the decision is not mine or even yours. Gideon has no fondness for magic, especially after the attacks on Scim and Lady Merewen's horses."

Murdoch wasn't saying anything Duncan hadn't thought a hundred times himself. "We'll be ready to ride when you return, but it's imperative that we destroy whatever it is that Lavinia is sensing."

"Fine." Murdoch swung up in the saddle. "I know we're all tired, but Gideon wants us back at the keep as soon as possible."

Then he spurred his mare and disappeared into the trees. Lavinia waited until he was gone to speak again. She wrapped her arms around her waist, her shoulders slumped in exhaustion and worry.

"I frighten your friend."

She'd frightened Duncan, too, but he schooled his features to make sure she did not discover the truth. "None of us has any experience with such power except that practiced by our gods. I think he was surprised more than frightened. He'll adjust."

They all would. They'd have to if they were going to defeat the enemy. With that in mind, they needed to keep moving. The guards wouldn't stay down for long. Even without their weapons they presented a danger. Once they located their horses, the guardsmen would be back on Lavinia's trail. They served an unforgiving master, one who wouldn't accept another defeat lightly.

"Why don't you have a seat? I'll pack up our gear."

Lavinia was already shaking her head. "First let me see to your wound."

She obviously needed something to focus on other than what had just happened. As he let her fuss over him, he wondered just how badly she'd frightened herself with her magic. After all, this was only a small skirmish. The battles that likely lay ahead carried the potential for far greater violence and bloodshed.

This time she'd only damaged her opponents. When it came time to kill, he could only hope that she found the strength to live with the consequences.

* * *

Riding into battle had felt right to him. Natural. The only thing Sigil had known about himself since awakening in Lady Merewen's keep was that he was a soldier. His function in life was all he knew.

He bellowed in challenge at an approaching noise, not sure of the meaning behind the words he shouted. He knew only that they felt right.

The deep shadows prevented him from seeing the face of his enemy, but that would change as soon as they crossed swords. Enemies shared an intimacy unlike any other, a dance filled with blood and fear and a fierce joy of triumph that came with victory.

Defeat didn't matter. An honorable death held its own blessing.

Two of the guards reached him at the same time. The first swing of Sigil's sword sent one catapulting off his horse right under the hooves of his partner's. His scream was choked off in the middle, his body trampled into the dirt.

The second guard managed to control his horse and attacked again. There was no time to wonder what had happened to the third guard. He could be approaching from behind, but Sigil couldn't risk a look until he dealt with his current opponent.

The fighting had taken them from the trees and out into the grasslands beyond. The silvery moonlight brought everything into sharp focus: faces flushed with effort; blood, liquid and black; the flash of blades cutting through the air. The second guard slipped from the saddle to hit the ground, silent and unmoving.

That left one.

Sigil yanked hard on the reins, spinning his horse around sharply. Sure enough, the third guard was charging right for him. As he closed in on Sigil, his eyes widened in shock. He fought to stop his horse, but it was too late. The animal carried the man forward and right onto Sigil's sword.

After Sigil yanked his sword free, his enemy stared down at the gaping wound in his stomach. He swayed in the saddle as he tried to staunch the flow of blood. Sigil dismounted and caught him as he slowly toppled out of the saddle. He lowered the dying man to the ground.

As the guardsman stared up into Sigil's eyes, his expression wasn't one of defeat but of confused betrayal.

"Captain Ter—"

The words came out on a pain-wracked sigh. What was he trying to say? Had they known each other when Sigil had served the duke? He stared down into the dying man's face, searching for even a hint of familiarity and finding none. He forced himself to ask the question he wasn't even sure he wanted answered.

"Do you know my name? Who am I?"

But it was too late. The last hint of life had faded away, any knowledge the man had about Sigil's past dying with him. He closed the guard's eyes and crossed his arms over his chest. He'd been a soldier and deserved Sigil's respect.

Did the man have family? How long would they wait before they knew he wasn't coming back home? He prayed for them as much as he did for the three fallen guards. He took no pride in their deaths. This wasn't a victory when he truly had no idea what he was fighting for. How could a man know his duty when he didn't even know his name?

A heavy hand came down on his shoulder. "If I'd been the enemy, you'd be dead."

Murdoch knelt beside him, looking puzzled. "Are you all right?"

No, he truly wasn't.

"I'm not wounded." Sigil stood up and wiped the

blood off his sword before sheathing it. "Did you find Duncan?"

"He's fine. He killed one of the guards and wounded another. Lady Lavinia took care of the rest."

The big man shuddered, clearly spooked by whatever had transpired. Before Sigil could ask for details, Murdoch continued. "They're packing up their camp. I came to check on you and to fetch the girl."

Sigil had forgotten all about her. They both looked out toward the grasslands. She was heading right for them with Shadow guiding the way.

"She doesn't need to see these bodies. I'll stay behind to bury them. I can follow your trail back to the keep."

He owed the dead that much, although Murdoch might not agree. The warrior was already shaking his head.

"Lady Lavinia used her magic to render the rest of the guards unconscious. They can take care of their own dead and wounded. We'll take these three back to Duncan's camp so their comrades will find them."

Even better. Their families would still know the pain of loss but not the endless uncertainty. It wasn't much of a comfort, but it was all he could offer them.

As they settled the dead soldiers across their horses' backs, Sigil said, "You'll have to tell me more about this magic that she used."

Murdoch stepped back and clenched his fists. "Maybe later. Right now we need to concentrate on getting back to the keep."

Interesting. It must have been an impressive display of power to rattle Murdoch. Now wasn't the time to press for details, not with the little girl rapidly approaching.

"Why don't you wait here with her until Lady Lavinia and Duncan arrive while I move the bodies?"

Murdoch nodded. "Don't linger. We need to put as much distance as possible between us and the surviving guards. I don't know if they'll come after us again or skulk back to the capital with their tails between their legs."

Sigil bit back the need to defend the guardsmen, the reaction as unexpected as it was powerful. Rather than say anything at all, he gathered the reins of the three horses and handed them off to Murdoch until he was mounted himself.

Regardless of how Murdoch and Duncan felt about the guards, Sigil knew on a gut level that these men had not truly been his enemies. Yes, he'd killed all three, but only because they would've killed him. At least that was true for the first two he'd faced. It was the third one's indecision that had cost him his life.

Sigil yet wondered at the cause for the man's hesitation. Most likely he'd never know the truth. Mayhap it had been Sigil's true name he'd been trying to say, but he could've also been calling for a friend.

As he made his way through the woods, Sigil admitted one last thing to himself. Just as he knew he was a soldier, he now knew that he was used to being called Captain. There was a sense of the familiar when the guard had called that out. He smiled; another small piece of his identity regained. He tucked that little bit of knowledge away to think about later when they were all safely back behind the palisade of Lady Merewen's keep.

Chapter 29

$\mathcal{D}$uncan's friends had been strangely quiet for hours. No doubt they were tired from riding for two days, stopping only when absolutely necessary. Lavinia felt every mile they'd ridden, too, but that wasn't the reason behind their silence. It also hadn't passed her notice that Duncan had made sure to stay between her and Murdoch.

Clearly the other man had been horrified by her use of powerful magic, but what had he expected her to do? Back in the woods, the guards had been attacking Duncan all at once, making it unlikely he would've survived the battle. When she'd seen Duncan cornered and outnumbered, she'd done the only thing she could. At least she could draw comfort from knowing she hadn't killed anyone.

Later, both Murdoch and Sigil stared at her in horrified fascination as she destroyed the medallion she'd found tucked in that guard's pocket. She'd carried it some distance away from everyone else, careful not to touch it directly. Using the same spell she'd used to destroy the coins and the medallions, she'd crushed it with her own magic.

There had been a brief but painful backlash that caused her to stumble a step or two. Sigil had also been affected by the blast of magic, wincing as if in pain. She found that odd, but some people were more sensitive to magic of all kinds. Right now she was too weary to make sense of much of anything.

Duncan guided his horse closer to hers. Once again he was carrying a sleeping Sarra. All three men had been trading off carrying her whenever the riding had become too much for the little girl. It also allowed them to rest one of the horses.

"We'll be stopping soon where Murdoch and Sigil abandoned their camp when they realized we would come under attack. After a few hours' rest, we'll make the final push to the keep."

It was testimony to how exhausted she was that she hadn't even questioned how Duncan's friends happened to arrive at exactly the right moment.

"If they were this far away from us, how did they know we were about to be attacked?"

It was Sigil who answered. "I sensed something dark and evil hunting for you."

"You have a gift for magic? I wondered when you reacted to the destruction of Duke Keirthan's medallion."

His face turned stony. "I wouldn't know."

She watched as he spurred his horse ahead, leaving a cloud of dust in his wake.

"Did I say something wrong?"

Duncan waited until Sigil was some distance away before answering. "He was one of the duke's men sent to take back control of Lady Merewen's keep on behalf of her uncle. At the end of the fighting, Lord Fagan tried to kill his own wife and Murdoch, but Sigil threw himself between Fagan and his intended targets. The blow Sigil took destroyed the medallion he wore around his neck, and with it any memory of who he is."

They both stared at the warrior for several seconds. Even with her mind clouded with exhaustion, it wasn't difficult to make the connections.

"It must have been one of the same talismans that the guards who attacked the abbey were wearing. That would've given Ifre a great deal of power over Sigil's actions."

It was another example of her half brother's abuse. "Interesting that Sigil could've broken free of that control long enough to protect the lady and Murdoch. It speaks well of the man's character and his inner strength."

Then she smiled at Duncan and once again lapsed into silence, concentrating on staying in the saddle long enough to reach the campsite.

Duncan agreed with Lavinia's assessment of Sigil. He'd already proven himself to be a worthy ally, another reminder that this calling was different. The Damned rarely allowed outsiders to get too close, but their list of allies was growing longer by the day: Lady Merewen, Lady Alina, Sigil, young Sarra, and Lavinia herself.

Duncan could only hope that when they reached the keep, Gideon would accept the necessity of Lavinia's mage craft to the success of their cause. Murdoch had already made his feelings on the subject all too clear. He'd come to terms with Lady Merewen's gifts. They all had. Breeding top-quality horses was something familiar, safe.

Lavinia's magic could be used as a weapon, both dangerous and powerful. So far, she hadn't used it to kill, but that day would come.

As Murdoch had said, it would be up to Gideon what role Lavinia would be allowed to play in their war against her half brother, if any. Duncan would tell him about how the Lady of the River had appeared before both him and Lavinia, and that she'd also spoken directly to him.

Once Gideon had made his decision, then Duncan

would have to make his. He prayed that it wouldn't come down to a choice between his duty to the Damned and his love for Lavinia. He'd yet to speak to her of his feelings, but he would. In all his long life, he'd never expected to find love, and here he had. She'd saved not only his life but his sanity, giving him a new purpose to fight for. He wouldn't leave this earth again without Lavinia knowing that although his soul belonged to the goddess, his heart belonged to Lavinia.

She deserved that truth, but not until they were both rested and someplace private. Soon, though. And that thought kept him moving forward, one weary hour at a time.

Sarra had been remarkably talkative once she'd gotten a good night's sleep. She divided her time between all three men pretty equally, making them smile with her constant questions and comments. Right now she was giggling over something Murdoch had said to her.

On the other hand, the farther they rode this morning, the more solemn Duncan became. Clearly he wasn't looking forward to reuniting with his captain. There could be only one reason for his concern, and that was Lavinia herself. Was he regretting his decision to bring her back with him? Hadn't he insisted they had no other choice?

Sigil slowed his horse to drop back even with her. "We should be able to see the keep when we clear that next rise."

"That's good. I'm looking forward to walking on my own two feet for a while. I've never spent this much time on horseback in my entire life."

"I would never have guessed that. You and Sarra have handled this brutal pace as well as any soldier would have."

The compliment surprised her. "Thank you."

It was the first time she'd really had a chance to study

the handsome soldier for any length of time. There was something familiar about his looks, although she was sure she'd never met him before. His dark blond hair and brown eyes were nothing distinctive, especially in Agathia. There was just something about his profile or perhaps in the way he moved that stood out to her.

Before she could follow that line of thought any farther, Sarra started screaming and holding her head. All four adults charged toward the distraught child. Murdoch dismounted and grabbed the reins of her horse to keep it under control.

"Sarra! What is it?"

The little girl's hands dropped away from her head, her eyes wide with horror. When her mouth opened, she wasn't the one speaking. Murdoch stumbled back a step or two, but then he held his ground while Sigil stared at Sarra as if he'd never seen her before.

She sought out Lavinia. "He's going to kill the horses again. We've got to stop him. They're so scared."

Duncan kept his voice calm, but then he'd had previous experience with Sarra's guides. "Where do we need to go?"

The little girl pointed straight ahead, toward the keep. "That way. The horses are in a pasture behind the keep."

Sigil was already riding hard while Murdoch remounted after handing the reins to Duncan. He spurred his mare off after Sigil.

"Hold on tight, Sarra."

She nodded and grabbed on to her horse's mane with both hands. As soon as she was settled, Duncan led the charge toward the keep.

They rode at a bone-jarring pace across the grassland and then through some rocky outcroppings. When they reached the keep, the gate was already opening. Looking for an enemy who was nowhere to be seen, men-at-arms charged out into the bailey, swords drawn.

Lavinia followed Duncan straight through the bailey, barely giving Lady Merewen's people a chance to get out of the way. When she reached the pasture, she dismounted to join the men at the fence. None of the horses appeared to have been hurt, but they were clearly agitated. A woman, who could only be Lady Merewen, stood with an old man as they tried to calm the restless animals.

Another man stood with his hands on Merewen's shoulders. Duncan and Murdoch immediately flanked him, marking him as Captain Gideon himself. Sigil picked up Sarra and carried her toward the group, leaving Lavinia to follow on her own.

But when she stepped into the pasture, the stench of Ifre's filthy magic clogged her throat and her mind. She brought all of her focus and energy to bear on clearing it out so that she could focus. Ifre's attack was approaching at speed from outside the palisade.

Lavinia ran to the center of the pasture and turned her back on the cluster of worried people to study the sky to the north. There! In the distance, she could pick out the glow of light that shouldn't be there.

Glancing back over her shoulder, she yelled, "Duncan, get everyone away from here! Now, before it's too late!"

Leaving it to him to make that happen, she returned her attention to the approaching light, by now much larger. It was now clear that what she was seeing were several balls of light clustered together.

It had to be the same weapon that Ifre had used against the abbey. The thick stone walls had held up against the assault, but the fragile flesh of horses and people wouldn't stand a chance of survival.

Raising her hands palm up, she called on the gods to aid her. Then she chanted the strongest words she knew, injecting into them every bit of power she could pull from the ground around her. Normally, she controlled the flow, keeping the channel open and providing a path for the power to follow as water did a riverbed.

This time she took no such precautions, opening herself up to the burning hot pain of her magic unleashed. Someone was hollering. Duncan? Yes, she heard his voice amidst the clamor of noise in her head.

She paused in her chanting to say, "Ward them. It's the only way."

The light was coming in fast and low, aiming right for where she stood. The world and her life narrowed down to this single moment where she would do battle with her brother. Whether she lived or died, Ifre would suffer for his wickedness. She'd make sure of it, her only regret being that she couldn't remind Duncan how much she loved him.

With her skin on fire and her throat raw from the burn of power, she ripped away the last bit of caution left in her and sent her first blast of power heading skyward.

Chapter 30

Gideon stepped in front of Lady Merewen, planting himself between her and Lavinia. "Duncan, what in the name of the gods is she doing?"

"She's trying to stop the attack. Now do as she said, and get out of the pasture."

Nobody moved one step closer to the fence. Merewen was fighting Gideon's efforts to get her out of harm's way, insisting she needed to calm the horses. Murdoch stared at Lavinia, his fear of her power all too clear. When he started toward her, Duncan blocked him.

His friend glared down at him. "The goddess forbids the use of dark magic. You might be willing to risk your soul for her, but I'm not."

Duncan went for his sword. "You will not touch her, Murdoch."

Gideon had joined them. "You would choose her over your duty? Over us?"

He laid the truth out for them. "Only if you threaten her in any way. She *is* my duty. The goddess said the magic was Lavinia's burden to bear, but that we need her."

She looked to him then. He couldn't hear her words, but her meaning was clear. He needed to ward his friends from the impact of her magic and Ifre's.

"Stand close together while I do what I can to shield all of you."

Gideon might not have liked Lavinia's magic, but he would do anything it took to keep his own lady safe. He wrapped Merewen up in his arms, ignoring her struggles to be free. Murdoch stepped close to the captain while Sigil took the other side, holding Sarra with her face buried in his shoulder. The old man who'd been helping with the horses huddled next to them.

Duncan met the gaze of each of his friends and then started chanting himself. He ignored Murdoch's curse when he saw the shimmering ward building around them. Once the circle was complete, Duncan strengthened it just as he had in the woods when the goddess had protested his actions.

This time, there was no warning or response from his goddess, perhaps because she knew she could lose three of her five warriors if Lavinia's efforts to block her brother's attacks failed. Once he had the ward grounded, he stepped through it and ran to where Lavinia faced off against a powerful enemy.

He wasn't sure his touch would help her, but he wouldn't let her stand alone. If this was to be the end of his life, he would face it at Lavinia's side.

The balls of light were almost upon them. He braced himself for their impact just as Lavinia shouted to the heavens above and launched her counterattack.

The world exploded in a crack of fire and thunder. Duncan was blind, deaf, and very possibly dead. But as the noise faded and the dust settled, he was still standing, his friends were safe, and the woman he loved was crumpled on the ground at his feet, her eyes wide and unseeing.

"Lavinia!"

Duncan dropped to his knees at her side and shook her shoulders. "Lavinia, don't you dare leave me! Not now."

No response. Desperately, he looked around for help, for someone who could do something. As soon as he dropped his ward, Lady Merewen came running. She joined him on the ground and put her hand on Lavinia's forehead.

Gideon followed, taking Merewen's other hand in his. Murdoch came next, then Sigil and Sarra. Even the old man added his gnarled hand to the chain, taking Sarra's small one and then reaching out to Duncan. Duncan completed the circle by taking Lavinia's cold hand in his.

Time stopped as they all prayed and offered up their pleas to the gods to bring Lavinia back to the living.

Then the Lady of the River whispered in Duncan's mind. *"Your woman is a warrior, Sir Duncan. She should be rewarded for her bravery."*

As her last word faded away, Lavinia stirred, her skin warming to the touch, her chest heaving as she drew in a shallow breath and then another. Then her beautiful eyes opened to stare right into Duncan's, full of love and wonder.

"Your Lady led me back to you."

Everyone else sighed in relief and moved back as Duncan gathered Lavinia into his arms and held on with everything he had.

"That's because we belong together, Lavinia, for all the days I have left, however few they may be. But know this: I will love you forever."

Tears trickled down her cheeks. "And I will love you with every breath I take."

Gently, not wanting to hurt her, he sealed their pledge with a kiss.

Chapter 31

*H*ours later, Duncan left the library, barely resisting the urge to slam the door. He longed to get back to Lavinia and check on her recovery, but first he needed to walk off some of his frustration. Rather than return directly to their room, he headed downstairs and straight out the door. Once he reached the bailey, he paused, trying to decide which way to go. It was unlikely anyone would be wandering out in the garden at this hour, making it the best choice.

As soon as he turned in that direction, Kiva called out in warning as he swooped down out of the trees. Duncan held out his arm, bracing himself for the impact. He carried the owl over to the bench and let the bird step off before sitting down beside him. Duncan connected with his avatar's thoughts and smiled.

"I'm glad you found the hunting good."

The owl turned his head to face Duncan and sent him an image of Duncan's hand and his own feathers. Taking the hint, Duncan began stroking his companion's feathers. The connection gradually calmed them both. He enjoyed the brief moment of solitude, knowing it wouldn't last long.

A few seconds later, Gideon stepped out of the shadows. "Thought I'd find you out here."

Kiva immediately took off, probably figuring he'd done as much as he could to soothe Duncan's own ruffled feathers. Gideon took the bird's place on the bench. They both sat in silence for several minutes. Something else that wouldn't last.

"Are you all right?"

"What do you think?" Duncan asked, but then answered his own question. "No, I'm not. Lavinia saved all of our lives at nearly the cost of her own. She deserves our gratitude, not our mistrust."

"That she does, Duncan. I think we're all feeling unsettled at the many changes in our lives."

Gideon leaned back to stare up at the starlit sky. "When have we ever had this many people we care so deeply about, starting with Lady Merewen? And anyone can see Murdoch and Lady Alina have strong feelings for each other."

Duncan let his frustration show. "Does he not understand that I feel the same way about Lavinia? I believe these new bonds are blessed by our goddess."

"He probably hasn't thought it through yet." Gideon paused before continuing. "If Murdoch doesn't figure that out for himself, I'll explain it to him myself, even if I have to use my fists. And it's not Lavinia he mistrusts, but the magic."

"I realize that, but his doubts only make it harder on her." Duncan shared another of his burdens. "I'm also concerned about what will become of Sarra when all of this is over. I can't sleep for worrying about what will happen when I'm not there to protect them."

As he spoke, a cloud passed in front of the rising moon, casting the garden in near-total darkness.

"Who knows, mayhap Sigil will be able to help with that. My instincts say he's an honorable man at heart, even if he's made poor decisions in the past."

That was something the two of them understood all too well. Duncan stood up. "I should return to Lavinia. She'll be wondering what was decided in the meeting."

His friend and leader fell into step with him as they returned to the keep. When they parted at the top of the stairs, Gideon clapped him on the shoulder. "I'm glad you are back. I missed you."

"I missed you as well. I hope Kane and Averel return quickly."

"Me, too." Gideon started to walk away, but he stopped and looked back. "And, Duncan, one more thing. Thank your lady for me and tell her we'll talk more tomorrow. Sleep well."

Hours later, Lavinia stood on the small balcony and watched the horses peacefully grazing in the moonlit pasture below. Everything looked so peaceful, so normal, as if the attack on the keep had never happened.

But it had. Between Lady Merewen and the Lady of the River, the damage to Lavinia's body had been mended. Her spirit was a different matter, although Duncan's kiss had greatly eased that pain as well.

He truly loved her. She hugged that thought close, drawing such comfort from it. Most men would've been terrified by her display of power. Certainly his friends had obvious misgivings about it. She understood that. After all, it was her half brother who'd tried to kill them with his own twisted magic.

The last thing she wanted to do was drive a wedge between Duncan and the men he'd served with for centuries. Right now, they were all in the library. Lady Merewen and Lady Alina had been invited to the meeting, but not Lavinia. No doubt, it would be awkward to discuss her fate with her in the room.

The door to her chambers opened. Since anyone else would've knocked, it had to be Duncan. She braced herself for the verdict as she turned to face him.

"Well? Do I need to saddle my horse again?"

His smile answered that for her. "No, although Gideon

wants to meet with you to discuss what happened out there. We need to figure out how best to deal with Keirthan, and you'll be playing a big part in that plan."

Then his smile faded a bit. "No one has ever seen anything like it, but they are all well aware of how many lives you saved. It may take some time for my friends to grow comfortable around your magic, but they'll come around. They know my heart belongs to you."

She ached for this man. "As mine belongs to you and always will." Even after the gods once again called him back to face their judgment.

Although she left that last part unspoken, Duncan understood where her thoughts had taken her. "None of us knows how the future will unfold, and we have time yet, Lavinia. Should we not enjoy the hours we have here and now?"

She wanted to say yes, but they still had unfinished business. "Is Captain Gideon waiting to see me now?"

Duncan cocked his head to the side and stared at her from top to toe. "He knows better. I told him we had plans for the remainder of the night, and that you will need your rest."

The heat in his pale eyes left little doubt as to what those plans might entail. For the first time since they'd left the pasture behind, she felt truly warm.

Suddenly even the distance of a few feet between them was far too much. "Perhaps you should tell me more about these plans we have."

Duncan met her halfway. "It would be better if I were to show you."

Then he proceeded to do exactly that.

Continue reading for a preview of

A Time for Home
by Alexis Morgan

Available in September 2013 from Signet Eclipse

"*We're* almost there, boy. Then you can stretch your legs."

Nick's canine companion was too busy sniffing the wind to care. Mooch had kept his nose stuck out the window since the minute they'd gotten in the truck. He reached over to pat the dog on the back, still carrying on the one-sided conversation.

"I bet it smells a whole lot different than the streets of Afghanistan. Doesn't it?"

Mooch thumped his tail in agreement. In truth, everything here was a whole lot different. Nick scanned the road ahead—there was so much green that it hurt his eyes. He had to tip his head back to see to the top of the firs and cedars that were crowded close to the two-lane highway. They made him claustrophobic. Too many hiding spots for snipers. Only one way through them, leaving him no avenue of escape.

Nick flexed his hands on the steering wheel and reminded himself that he'd left all that behind weeks ago.

No one here wanted him dead. Not yet, anyway.

"Think she'll forgive me?"

Nick hoped so, because he hadn't been able to forgive himself. Something in his voice finally had Mooch looking at him, the dog's dark eyes filled with sympathy. Of course, maybe Nick was only imagining that the mutt understood every word he said. There was no denying that the dog had known his own share of suffering back in his homeland.

Mooch's shaggy fur didn't quite hide the jagged scar where a bullet had caught him in the shoulder. He'd taken one for the team after he'd barked to warn them about an asshole lying in ambush. The bastard had shot the dog to shut him up, but too late to do himself any good. In retaliation, the squad had made damn sure it was the last time he ever pulled a trigger. Nick's buddy Spence had carried the wounded dog back to camp and conned one of the army vets into stitching him up. After a brief swearing-in ceremony, Mooch had become a full-fledged member of their unit.

In war, some heroes walked on four legs, not two.

Nick spotted a sign up ahead. He slowed to read it, hoping he was about to reach civilization. He'd left I-5 behind some time ago and hadn't expected it to take this long to reach Snowberry Creek. He had mixed feelings about what would happen once he reached the small town, but he and Mooch had been on the move long enough. Some downtime would feel pretty good.

But instead of announcing the city limits, the sign marked the entrance of a small cemetery. Nick started to drive on past, but a sick feeling in his gut had him slowing down and then backing up.

He put the truck in PARK and dropped his forehead down on the top of the steering wheel. In a town the size of Snowberry Creek, how many cemeteries could there be? He reached for the door handle and forced himself to get out of the truck. Sooner or later he was going to have to do this. Nick had never been a coward and wasn't about to become one now.

"Come on, Mooch. We've got a stop to make."

The dog crawled down out of the seat. Once on the ground, he gave himself a thorough shake from nose to tail before following Nick up the slope toward the rows of gravestones. Normally Mooch liked to explore new places on his own, but this time he walked alongside Nick, silently offering his support.

It didn't take long to find what they were looking for. There were several granite markers with the last name Lang. Nick hung a right and followed the row, finally reaching a longer than normal stone that held the names of a husband and wife, most likely Spence's parents. Nick had to force himself to take those last few steps past it to stand in front of the last headstone.

He dropped to his knees on the green grass and wrapped his arms around his stomach. God, it hurt so fucking much to see Spence's name etched there in block letters. His eyes burned with the need to cry, but the tears refused to come. Instead the pain stayed locked tight inside his chest and in his head, a burden he'd been carrying since he'd held Spence's bloody dog tags in his hand.

As the memories began playing out in Nick's head, Mooch whined and snuggled closer. But even the familiar touch of the dog's soft fur couldn't keep Nick grounded in the present. His guilt and his fear sucked him right back to the last place he wanted to be. Just that quickly, he was in the streets of Afghanistan, riding next to Spence on yet another patrol. Instead of breathing the cool, damp air of Washington, Nick was sucking in hot, dry air and feeling the sun burning down from above as he got caught up in the past, living through it all over again.

The fiery depths of hell had nothing on the heat in Afghanistan in July. Maybe if he could've stripped down to a pair of cargo shorts and a sleeveless T-shirt, it would've been bearable. But only a fool would go on patrol without all of his protective gear, and Nick was no fool.

The back of his neck itched. It had nothing to do with the ever-present dust and grit that grated against his skin like sandpaper. No, there were eyes on them. Had been since they'd entered the city. A couple of well-placed shots had cut them off from the rest of the patrol. They were trying to circle around to catch up with the others.

Nick scanned the surrounding area, constantly sweeping the buildings ahead, looking for some sign of who was watching them. In that neighborhood, it could be anyone from a mother worried about her kids to someone with his finger on the trigger.

Leif stirred restlessly. "You feeling it, too?"

"Yeah. Spence, do you see anything?"

Before his friend could answer, a burst of gunfire rained down on them from the roof of a building half a block down on the right. A second shooter opened fire from a doorway on the opposite side of the street, catching them in the cross fire.

Nick returned short bursts of fire while Spence drove like the maniac he was, trying to get them the hell out of Dodge. Leif hopped on the radio, yelling to make himself heard over the racket. After calling in, he'd joined Nick in trying to pick off the shooters.

"Hold on! This ride's about to get interesting."

If more than two wheels were on the ground when Spence took the corner, Nick would happily eat MREs for the rest of his natural life. Not that he was complaining. His friend's extreme driving style had saved their asses too often. The M-ATV lurched hard as it straightened coming out of the turn.

"Fuck yeah, that was fun!" Spence's grin was a mile wide as he laughed and flung their ride around another corner.

The crazy bastard was actually enjoying this. Nick shook his head. He loved the guy like a brother, but damn. They made it another two blocks before the shooting began again, this time from behind them.

Leif yelled over the racket, "Ever get the feeling we're being herded?"

Nick nodded. The thought had occurred to him, but what choice did they have but to keep going? The street was too narrow to hang a U-turn and stopping sure as hell wasn't an option. He continued to scan the area for more shooters and left the driving to Spence, who knew the streets in this area better than anyone. It was like the man had a built-in GPS system. He'd find a way out for them if anyone could.

The gunfire was sporadic now with longer periods of silence between shots. The streets remained empty, as if the locals had been warned to crawl into the deepest hole they could find and stay there.

"Think we're in the clear?" Leif asked, still studying the rooftops and doorways for new threats.

Before Nick could answer, the whole world exploded in fire and smoke. A sharp pain ripped up the length of his upper arm as their vehicle started rockin'-and-rollin' on them. It went airborne and finally bounced to a stop, lying on its side up against a building.

With considerable effort, Nick managed to climb out. He retrieved his weapon and shook his head to clear it. The blast had left him deaf and, thanks to the cloud of dust and smoke, damn near blind. Nick found Spence more by feel than sight. He was lying facedown in the dirt with blood trickling from his ears and nose.

Nick checked for a pulse. Thready and weak. Son of a bitch, this was a major clusterfuck. He spotted Leif writhing in pain a few feet away. He crawled over to him.

"Are you hit?"

"My ankle. It's busted up pretty bad."

If the bastards who'd been shooting at them weren't already closing in, they would be soon. Nick needed to get Leif and Spence somewhere safe—and fast.

He got down in Leif's face. "Give it to me straight up. Can you walk?"

After one look at the twisted mess that had been

Leif's ankle, Nick didn't wait for an answer. Neither of his friends could make it back to safety on their own, but which one should he help first? Spence was completely defenseless while Leif might be able to protect himself for a while.

On the other hand, Leif was bleeding; already his coloring was piss poor. Nick crawled back to the rubble that had been their vehicle and pulled out the first-aid kit. He bandaged Leif's damaged ankle as best he could, but he'd seen enough wounds to know Leif was going to need surgery and damn quick. His decision made, Nick crawled back to his unconscious buddy.

"Spence, I'm going for help. I'll be back for you ASAP."

Then he muscled Leif up off the ground and half carried, half dragged the poor bastard as fast as he could. The rest of their unit would be pouring into the area, looking for them. A minute later, he spotted them two blocks down and waved his rifle over his head to get their attention.

Their medic hit the ground running. "What do we have?"

"His ankle looks bad, but we've got to go back for Spence. I was afraid to move him."

They carried Leif the rest of the way back to one of the vehicles. Nick patted his friend on the shoulder. "They'll get you to the medics. Save a couple of the prettier nurses for Spence."

Leif managed a small smile. "Like hell. Tell him he's on his own."

"Get yourself patched up. We'll be along soon." He stepped back and checked his rifle for ammunition. "Let's move out."

The medic stopped him. "You're bleeding, too. We'll get Spence. You go with the corporal."

No, not happening. He'd return for Spence even if he had to crawl. "I'm all right. Besides, I promised I'd come back for him. Wouldn't want to piss him off. The man's got a temper."

The medic didn't much like it, but he nodded. "Lead the way."

Nick's ears were finally starting to function again, and he could hear gunfire in the distance. Son of a bitch! He picked up the pace, doing his best to watch for hostiles as he led the charge back to where he'd left Spence. When they were a block short of their destination, the deafening thunder of another explosion sent all of them diving for cover.

Before the echoes had died away, Nick was up and running, screaming Spence's name. He was dimly aware of the rest of his squad joining him in the mad race to save their friend. Nick's heart pounded loud enough to drown out the agonizing truth that he was too late, with too little. The building next to where he'd left Spence was nothing but a smoking pile of rubble.

He coasted to a stop at the corner. The horror of what had happened and what he'd done washed over him in waves. "Spence, where the hell are you? Come on, you dumb son of a bitch, this is no time for hide-and-seek."

Please, God, let him have regained consciousness and crawled to safety.

But he hadn't; Nick knew it in his gut just as he knew it was his fault. There was nothing left of their vehicle now except scrap metal. A huge hole had been ripped in the street right where Spence had been lying, and the building had caved in on itself, leaving the street strewn with rubble. While several of the men stood watch, Nick joined the rest digging in the dirt with their bare fingers, heaving aside rocks and jagged fragments of metal, looking and praying for some sign of Spence.

Finally the medic froze. He looked across at Nick and slowly lifted his hand. A set of bloody dog tags dangled from his fingers.

"Aw, damn, Spence."

Tears streamed down Nick's cheeks as he reached for the broken chain. He clamped his fingers around the small pieces of bloody metal and held on to the last piece of his friend with an iron grip.

The medic motioned to the rest of the men. When they had formed up, he took Nick by the arm and tugged him back down the street.

"Come on, Sarge, let's go get your arm looked at. We'll get you all fixed up."

Nick let himself be led away, but only because the longer they lingered in the area, the more likely it was that someone else would get hurt or worse. But they all knew there was no fixing this. Not today. Not ever.

Spence was—

A sharp pain dragged Nick back to the grassy slope of the graveyard. Mooch whined and licked the small mark where he'd just nipped Nick's arm. The poor dog looked worried. How long had Nick been gone this time? Long enough to be damp from the rain that had started falling since he'd knelt in the grass. The dog shoved his head under Nick's hand, demanding a good scratching that felt as good to Nick as it did to the dog.

"Sorry, Mooch. We'll get going here in a minute."

He pushed himself back up to his feet and dusted off his pants, focusing hard on the moment. It was too easy to get caught up in spinning his wheels in the past. He needed to keep moving forward, if for no other reason than he had to make sure Mooch reached his final destination.

Nick had something to say first. Standing at attention felt odd when he wasn't in uniform, but the moment called for a bit of formality. He cleared his throat and swallowed hard.

"Spence, I miss you so damn much. Wherever you are, I hope they have fast cars and faster women."

Then he sketched a half-assed salute and walked away.